PJ Grondin

Flash Drive

PD House Books

Copyright © 2021 by PJ Grondin

First Edition

The characters and events in this book are fictitious. Any similarity to real persons, living or dead is coincidental and not intended by the author.

PD House Holdings, LLC
910 S. Meadow Drive
Sandusky, Ohio 44870

Library of Congress Control Number: 2021907082

www.pjgrondin.com

pjgron@pjgrondin.com

ISBN: 978-0-9984644-9-7

Dedication

This book is dedicated to the men and women of the United States Customs and Border Protection and the United States Immigration and Customs Enforcement agencies. They have been maligned and disrespected by certain politicians and citizens of the United States while performing essential functions. The primary mission of Customs and Border Protection agency is "to detect and prevent the illegal entry of aliens into the United States (www.cbp.gov). Similarly, the primary mission of Immigration and Customs Enforcement is to protect America from the cross-border crime and illegal immigration that threaten national security and public safety (www.ice.gov). Recently, these missions have been challenging. There is certainly more than one reason for the surge of migrants at the southern border, but these men and women on the front lines of defense or our borders, like active-duty military and military veterans, deserve our respect and full support. God bless them.

Acknowledgements

My dear wife, Debbie, is a saint. Without her encouragement and patience, I might still be working on this story with no end date in sight. To my old neighbor, Nick Prutchick, who gave me the idea to use a drone as a key part of the main plot. This caused a significant, positive shift in key elements of the story. Thanks, Nick. To Lisa Galindo for allowing me to use the Galindo family name for one of the story's prominent characters. Thanks, Lisa. To Joanne Ruthsatz and Kimberly Stephens, co-authors of *The Prodigy's Cousin – The Family Link Between Autism and Extraordinary Talent*. Their non-fiction work inspired the characters Ian Tabler, a math and science prodigy, and his brother, Jonah Tabler, a savant with a brilliant mind but extremely limited social skills. The brothers are key characters in Flash Drive. To my editor, Elizabeth 'Bee' Love. Thank you so much for your attention to detail and feedback. Great job, as usual. Finally, to all of my readers who have told me how much you love my stories. It is your encouragement that keeps my creative juices flowing. I hope I have a few more yarns to spin before I run out of gas.

Flash Drive

Prologue

Tuesday, August 10, 1992, 7:25 PM

The scowl on his face conveying his displeasure, Colonel Alton Woodburn glared at the enlisted man casually standing in front of his desk. The brash, young sergeant had walked directly into Woodburn's office without knocking. He had no official business with the colonel because he would have requested the meeting through proper channels. During working hours, a staff member would have stopped the enlisted man, but all of the colonel's staff had left for the day. The interruption invaded the solitude he normally enjoyed, wrapping up his day's work and reviewing plans for the next.

His immediate gut-feeling at the intrusion was anger. Anyone with half a brain knew that you didn't violate the colonel's space without an appointment unless you were one of a handful of Woodburn's superiors. But those men, mostly generals, would summon him to their offices, not make the trip to his. This soldier, a sergeant, was much too low in the chain of command to stroll into the colonel's office unannounced. As a sergeant, he would know better. He would also know that he was in a world of trouble.

Woodburn's brain shifted gears with warning flags waving, turning his thoughts to incidents of enlisted men killing their superiors over some obscure grievance. He wondered if this young man – *Tate,* according to his uniform's nametag – had some beef with the Army or just had some bug up his ass. Maybe he wasn't playing with a full deck. Regardless, Woodburn leaned back in his overstuffed chair and folded his hands on his desk, outwardly relaxed, as he used his knee to open the desk's center drawer just enough to expose his

Beretta M9, the semi-automatic pistol that he kept within easy reach.

The man in green BDUs (battle dress uniform), the working uniform of the day, smiled, not moving his eyes away from the colonel's. He slowly, without permission, eased himself into one of the guest chairs in front of the colonel's desk.

The quiet office suddenly boomed with Colonel Woodburn's voice. "What the hell do you think you're doing," the colonel made it a point to look at the man's nametag, "Sergeant Tate?"

The colonel's visitor continued to smile and stare. He slowly reached into the front left shirt pocket of his uniform and extracted several papers and what appeared to be photographs. He held the small stack in his right hand and leaned back in the chair. The bright fluorescent lights of the office highlighted the features of his face, which made his smile appear menacing, even antagonistic, as if he was whacking a hornet's nest with a stick.

To the colonel, the soldier was no more than a kid, maybe nineteen or twenty years old, his face having slight Eastern European features. Being a sergeant meant that he had been in the Army for about four years, maybe more; therefore, he would have to be at least twenty-two. Regardless, he had work to do, and this intrusion would cost the kid dearly.

"Son, I don't have time for games here. Who's your company commander?"

The soldier's smile tightened as if the colonel was telling jokes that weren't funny, but he was obliged to play along. He sat forward on the chair, his back erect, and addressed the colonel. "Colonel Woodburn, sir, before you get all UCMJ (Uniform Code of Military Justice) on me, I have something that you should see."

Sergeant Tate tossed the stack of pictures, face-up, on the desk in front of Woodburn. The pictures spread out in a hap-hazard manner, exposing portions of each shot. The top picture was of the colonel's wife watching their two children as they played at a park. The colonel's brow furrowed, not understanding why this soldier had pictures of his family.

"What are you doing with ..."

"Keep looking, Colonel."

Woodburn looked back down at the pictures, slowing taking in each one, trying to find the purpose in his visit. There were ten pictures in all. Six were of his wife and children at different locations around the base or in town. The seventh was of an inexpensive casket sitting in a sterile-looking room with a lead seal on the latch. The lead seal was broken so that the casket could be opened. The eighth through tenth shots were pictures of the inside of the casket.

Colonel Woodburn recognized the room. He also knew the type of lead seal that was on the casket and the significance of the seal being broken. The room was used by Army Specialists who received the bodies of men killed in action or who met their demise through some other mishap while on active duty. The specialists groomed and prepared the bodies for burial prior to release of the deceased soldier's body to the next of kin.

Sometimes the physical work of making the soldier presentable to their family was easy, when little or no external trauma caused death. Other times, the work was nearly impossible, when death was the result of a roadside bomb or a large caliber round to the head. But the colonel knew that the men who performed these reconstructions were professionals. The most difficult part of the job was the actual presentation of the remains to the family. It was always a deeply emotional, gut-wrenching experience in the best of circumstances.

The photos before the colonel were not sickening in that way, but they caused the senior officer's stomach to tighten. His eyes flew up from the pictures to the man sitting confidently in his office. His brain worked overtime. *How did this kid get these pictures? Why were pictures of his family included?*

In a voice more controlled and less commanding, the colonel asked, "Where did you get these?"

The smile was still plastered on Sergeant Tate's smug face.

"My turn to talk." He took a deep breath. "I want in. Not only do I want in, I'm taking over, and you're going to do exactly what I say, at least when it comes to our business relationship."

"Son, we don't have a business relationship."

"We do now, and the first thing you're going to do is stop calling me 'son.' If you do as I say, not only will you keep your illustrious military career intact, you'll be rich beyond your wildest dreams, and you can move on to more important things, like a serious political career."

Woodburn gave the kid a sarcastic laugh. He thought the young man was out of his mind, thinking that he could simply walk into his office and make demands. But he did have some brass. And he had some leverage. Maybe he could be useful.

Recovered from his initial shock at seeing the pictures, the colonel, in a confident tone, said, "Maybe I can use you within our group. You've obviously stumbled onto something that you ..."

"Shut up and listen!"

The rebuke took the colonel by surprise. His anger spiked. He opened his mouth to speak but found himself looking into the business end of an AN1911 forty-five caliber pistol. Tate's face was beet red. "I said shut up!"

Woodburn did just that.

The sergeant calmed down but kept the gun pointed at Woodburn's face. "Now, slowly close that drawer. Don't even think about pulling out that pee-shooter."

With the drawer closed and the colonel's hands palms down on his desk, Tate continued. "The reason your family is in those pictures is for insurance. If you don't do exactly as I say, well, they will get hurt." He paused as a forced smile returned to his face. "But there's no reason for all this unpleasantness. We're just going to take this operation to the next level and beyond. Your organization is doing well, but it is small time and sloppy. You're going to get caught if you don't make some changes. If I had any scruples, you'd be on your way to Leavenworth right now. Lucky for you, I don't. Also lucky for you, I have a head for business." His smile widened. "Stick with me, Alton, and we'll be filthy rich ... and powerful."

Woodburn looked down at the pictures of his wife and children. His stomach churned as his mind raced. Then he looked at the three pictures of the open casket.

What have I done?

* * *

Two weeks prior to Sergeant Tate's surprise visit with Colonel Alton Woodburn, Tate had received an unexpected call to perform one of his more unpleasant duties. According to the Duty Officer who made the call, the body of Private First-Class Daniel Alderman was shipped to the mortuary at Fort Leavenworth, Kansas. The Casualty Officer's Assistant on call who was supposed to prepare the body for delivery to the Next of Kin, the NOK in military parlance, had called in sick. In reality, the young soldier was hungover from a night of hard drinking. Sergeant Tate, newly transferred in from Fort Bragg, North Carolina, was the next name on the duty roster and was called in to prepare the body for delivery to his parents.

Tate hated this part of his duty. Sometimes the job was easy, the soldier's cause of death being something that was outwardly difficult to detect. Other times, the bodies were mangled, burned, partially dismembered, or worse. It was Tate's job, and the job of his peers, to make their fellow soldiers as presentable as possible to their NOK. When the call came that day, he rolled his eyes and immediately tried to dodge his duty. Before he could think of an excuse, the Duty Officer told him that there was no one else available. He was it.

Without further discussion, he showered, dressed in his BDUs, and headed for the mortuary. Standing in front of the plain, basic casket, he bowed his head to gather his wits and to steel himself for the task at hand. After inhaling and holding a deep breath, he broke the lead seal on the casket and opened it.

His eyes widened in disbelief. It took a moment before he realized that he hadn't exhaled, unable to reconcile what he was seeing with what should have been in that casket. Taking several steps backwards, his butt hit against the metal desk where all the administrative forms were kept. He opened the lower left drawer and removed a Canon 35mm camera and took several pictures of the inside of the casket. He reclosed the casket and reassembled the lead seal on the casket's latch. With the exception of the lead seal, which he couldn't repair, he put the casket back in the condition that it was in when he entered the room. He could only hope that whoever came into the room next didn't realize the seal had already been broken.

He sat at the desk to think about his next move. His mind worked overtime. Where he should have seen a dead soldier's body parts, he saw dollar signs. He began to formulate a plan, one that would make him rich. He just had to figure out all of the players in the scheme. Most importantly, who was in charge? No matter. Tate had already decided that it was soon going to be his operation.

Chapter 1

Wednesday, August 11, 2020, 8:30 AM

The flash drive arrived by Express Courier with the usual receipt for a deposit to Ian Tabler's investment account in the amount of $30,000. It was the standard fee paid by FlashGamz LLC to beta testers of their new products long before the gaming systems ever hit the retail market. The package looked similar to other packages that Ian had received. Ian and his younger brother, Jonah, were two of a handful of testers regularly contracted by the company to help work out the bugs in the code for fast-moving, complex games that kept millions of kids – and adults – glued to their TV screens and computer monitors for hours on end, tracking down and killing imaginary enemies, or finding rewards after an arduous journey through a fictional kingdom. The initial payment was supplemented by a large bonus if the testers found flaws that smoothed the performance and improved the quality and playability of their video games.

Ian, age fifteen, and Jonah, a year younger, had already amassed savings and investments in excess of three-quarters of a million dollars each. A mathematics and physics prodigy, he sported an IQ that was nearly off the charts. In addition to his math and science skills, he was an economics wizard. He had religiously invested the proceeds from his testing services and more than quadrupled his and his brother's net worth. He split the earnings with Jonah fifty-fifty. Both boys were well on their way to becoming multi-millionaires.

Ian placed the deposit receipt in a flex folder in his desk drawer. Along with the receipt and the flash drive were testing instructions. He knew the drill. In order to identify bugs in the software, the testing protocol had to be followed precisely. Today's instructions required that the boys be ready to run the program at 10:30 AM so that all the testers were running the program at the same time. This stressed the system and gave everyone the opportunity to identify programming errors.

Ian handed the flash drive to Jonah, who took the device without a word and plugged it into the USB port of a computer that they didn't use for the game tests. A few seemingly effortless keystrokes and the computer went to work. While the computer whirred and the unit's fan kicked on, Jonah stared straight ahead. He didn't make a sound and didn't even acknowledge that his brother was in the room.

Ian read the instructions aloud so that his brother could hear. "It says that we have to be ready to start the test at 10:30 AM eastern standard time with all of our preliminary checks completed."

Jonah spoke for the first time all morning. He replied with a rapid series of numbers in a monotone, "One-zero-three-zero-one-one-three."

"That's right, 10:30 AM. Can we handle it?"

Again, Jonah spoke rapidly without any emotion, using only numbers. "Two-five-five-one-nine."

Ian smiled. It took him years to figure out that his severely autistic brother was communicating with him through numbers – kind of like a personal language code. It was even more challenging because his brother used only single-digit numbers, zero through nine, to spell out words by their number assignment. The letter 'A' was 'one,' 'B' equaled 'two.' That pattern worked through the letter 'I' – 'nine.' But after 'I,' the code changed. The letter 'J' to Jonah was 'one-zero,' which made following his spelling difficult. But Ian learned the subtle changes in Jonah's voice cadence, which eventually made it easier to decipher his brother's replies.

The only word, other than numbers, that Ian had ever heard his young brother speak was "Mom."

Ten years ago, the boys' mother had disappeared. No one knew where she went or why she left. None of her clothes were missing from her walk-in closet, but she left her car, her purse, and her medications. According to the boys' father, she was allergic to peanuts and bee stings. And she had high blood pressure. Ian wondered more than once why she hadn't taken her medications with her. But they most likely would never know the answer to any of the questions left in her wake.

Jonah, like his older brother, had a high IQ, but his social skills were non-existent. A savant who demonstrated no emotion except screams of apparent fear whenever anyone tried to approach him, he communicated using only numbers and spoke only to Ian. His life was restricted to the family compound, not by any rules or physical confinement. He just could not function around people. That included his father, Nicholas Tabler.

The computer beeped. Jonah removed the drive and handed it to Ian, who plugged it into their main gaming computer. After Ian made a few mouse clicks and some rapid keystrokes, four large forty-two-inch computer monitors came to life. Two of the monitors displayed the new game's introduction the other two displayed the computer code that generated the game's images. The boys had one of each type of display in front of them.

Jonah, expressionless, stared straight ahead at the bright colors of the game and the black and white numbers, letters, and special characters that seemed to flow rapidly down the screen.

Ian smiled as he watched his brother absorb the code. He turned back to his own screens and read the name of the game.

Assassin – Best in the Business.
* * *
Armand Vega, United States Senator from Georgia and the Chairman of the Senate Finance Committee, commanded the attention of the five men and one woman in the cramped conference room of the Savannah office of the Drug Enforcement Administration.

The three agents, their supervisor, and their director sat expressionless, tension etched on their faces. The sixth man was Michael Jess, Senator Vega's personal assistant. The air in the room, a mixture of fresh paint and industrial strength floor wax, made the atmosphere all the more uncomfortable. All five, the agents and their supervisors, were newly assigned to Savannah, coming from posts all around the country. They were hand-picked to replace the agents who used to be a part of the Savannah D.E.A. office, but were now facing charges ranging from corruption, extortion, and theft to attempted murder. The newly assigned agents expected the Senator to tell them that they would be under the watchful eye of their government, especially the committee headed by Vega.

Director Carl Erkskin called the meeting to order. "We all know the recent history of this office. You men, and you Ms. Ellis, were hand-picked to replace the agents who are no longer with the organization. We will have our meeting after this briefing by Senator Vega." He turned to Vega and motioned with his hand, indicating that he had the floor. "Senator?"

Armand Vega stood before the group of agents, exuding confidence, looking at each person in turn, making sure they were listening. He could see something in their eyes, as if challenging him to tie them to their predecessors' crimes. But he wasn't there to make that connection. He wanted this team of agents to know that they were starting with a clean slate, but they were also starting with a handicap. Their funding had been slashed significantly. There would be no more seed money for drug buys, and their every move would be documented. They were under the microscope, as was their supervision. In fact, the entire D.E.A. was going to feel the pain of the illegal actions of a handful of crooked agents.

Vega could have handed the task of delivering this message to a number of underlings, but he wanted to make a point – he wasn't going to shy away from the public and private outcry against his desire to cut funding for what he called "the failed War on Drugs." In fact, he was going to announce his efforts to every news outlet in the country.

He looked towards his aid, Michael Jess, whose eyes darted towards the clock on the wall, reminding the senator that they were on a tight schedule.

Vega's stern expression conveyed that his message was serious. Everyone in the room knew of the problems that plagued this office. There was a very public trial about to begin that would undoubtedly result in the conviction of three former agents and a Chatham County district attorney. A superior court judge who had been the ring leader of the group would not be tried because he was murdered outside the courthouse as he was led away in handcuffs.

Vega wasted no time. "You are here to restore the integrity of this office. You were handpicked for that reason. The expectations are high, and you *must* live up to them. It isn't going to be easy because funding has been drastically cut and oversight has been increased. You will feel the weight of that oversight daily. It will make your job more difficult, but in the end, if you play your cards right, this could enhance your futures within the D.E.A. or any other federal agency to which you might wish to move."

He paused for a moment, meeting the stares of those seated before him. When he spoke again, there was added weight to his words. "Not only will there be heightened oversight, but I will be watching you. I'll be getting reports from Director Erkskin." He turned and locked eyes with Erkskin momentarily. "My staff and members of the Finance Committee will be reviewing those reports and making decisions on future funding based on what we see and hear.

"Lastly, you all know that I personally believe that the 'War on Drugs' is a total waste of time and money. We've spent billions to battle this problem, and we've gotten nowhere. In fact, we're losing ground every year. We have to take a different approach, or we're going to pour billions more down the drain. This team was hand-picked to clean up a big mess. Maybe in the process of your cleanup, you can convince me that I'm wrong."

Vega looked at each pair of eyes seated before him, then turned and walked out the door of the conference room. It was 10:30 AM.

Michael Jess led the senator and two interns traveling with them towards the front door of the D.E.A. office building on Commerce Drive in Savannah, Georgia. As they walked out the door into the sunshine, Michael Jess said, "We have to be at the airport in twenty minutes. The jet is waiting, ready to go."

Vega stood on the steps in front of the office building. As they waited for the car to arrive, he recalled that this was the very spot where D.E.A. Agent Jarrod Deming had been shot and killed just months before as he was about to announce that he and his fellow agents had entrapped dozens of innocent young men and women while enriching themselves in a scheme that sent shockwaves throughout the Drug Enforcement Administration. He was deep in thought when he heard a buzzing sound, almost like a swarm of bees. He noticed that Jess was frowning and looking up in the sky. He turned his head as the buzzing grew louder. Then he spotted the drone rapidly approaching the group. The first pops were unmistakable. It was the sound of small arms fire.

* * *

Ian and Jonah Tabler maneuvered the attack drone with their game controllers as their computer monitors displayed a set of crosshairs on the horizon of an imaginary land. Their mission had just been relayed to them. They were to eliminate the leader of a foreign terror group. They were given the coordinates of the location where the leader was in a meeting with his top lieutenants and was set to emerge from that meeting at 7:00 PM. The program stated that the meeting was outside of Kabul, Afghanistan.

Ian said, "Man, these are some awesome graphics. It looks so real."

Jonah didn't respond to Ian's remark. He just kept guiding his drone towards his prospective target. Suddenly the crosshairs started flashing bright green on both of their screens. Jonah reacted first and hit a button on his controller. Bright flashes flew from the front of his drone as he unleashed his deadly attack. A split second after Jonah commenced his attack, Ian fired his rounds. His screen mimicked Jonah's, sending a deadly load of ordnance at their target.

    The four images on the screen fell to the ground. The attack was a complete success. Ian maneuvered his drone towards the target area to see if more targets were identified by the program. As he tapped the buttons and the mini-joystick on the controller, his two computer screens when black. Jonah's also went dark. Ian looked at his brother, who stared straight ahead at his darkened screen. He said, "What the ...?" As the words were leaving his lips, he smelled an acrid burning scent in the air. He looked around the room to see if they had an electrical failure. But the lights on their computers were still on. He was about to reach for the flash drive when a two-inch flame engulfed it. Ian jumped back. Jonah just stared. In less than two seconds, all that remained of the drive was a pile of ash.

Chapter 2

Peden Savage held the phone away from his ear, trying to protect his eardrum from the piercing voice of his ex-wife, Susan. She called demanding more money for their daughters' "school expenses," incurred while they both were away at two of the most expensive universities in the southeast. He hoped that she would calm down long enough for him to get a word in edgewise. That opportunity was unlikely to occur.

He wanted to tell her that his daughters had already blown past their established spending limit and were charging extravagant "field trips" to casinos, concerts, and bars, all under the guise of "school supplies." When Peden had agreed to pay for reasonable expenses associated with their classes, a dollar amount was set. Apparently, math wasn't either of their daughters' major.

The girls, Kaitlin, now twenty, and Kristi, eighteen, hated their father, even though they were the beneficiaries of his generosity. That animosity, Peden knew, had come mostly from their mother. Almost from the moment Susan announced that she wanted a divorce, their daughters began to avoid Peden. Susan had hired a great lawyer, who also happened to be her one-time lover. It was a short-lived fling, but rumor has it that it lasted long enough that she got a great deal on his billable hours – free.

Peden's friends, co-workers, and employees had practically begged him to get a lawyer right away when Susan threatened divorce, but he didn't. That had cost him then, and it continued to cost him real dollars for the past three years and likely well into the future. The bills would continue as long as the girls were in college, at least through attainment of their bachelor's degrees, or twenty-five years of age, whichever came first. He made another blunder by commenting loudly to his wife, in open court, that she was getting her legal services "pro-boner." The judge, a twice-divorced woman, didn't appreciate his comments, found him in contempt of court, and fined him $5000 for the derogatory comment. That slip-of-the-tongue had most likely swayed the judgment in his wife's favor. Not one of his finer moments.

Susan's affair was supposedly in retaliation for what she believed was Peden's workplace affair with his former partner at the FBI, Special Agent Megan Moore – an affair that never happened. Megan had made some harmless but flirtatious comments to Peden in front of his wife. She'd done it purposely to get under Susan's skin. It worked. Unfortunately for Peden, it worked too well and was now costing him big bucks. Megan told Peden that he was too good for her and he should have divorced her years ago.

But all that was history. Not hearing Susan's loud whining coming from the phone, he put it back up to his ear and waited for a few seconds, then asked, "Are you finished?"

"You haven't listened to a word I've said." There was a pause. "Peden, you're a real bastard. No wonder your girls hate you."

Peden let out a mocking laugh. "*Our* girls hate me because you've filled their heads full of lies. Listen, you tell them to stop treating their time at school like it's a four-year vacation with an unlimited money stream. I'm not paying for anything that isn't directly related to their classes and real, genuine living expenses. Understand? If they want to call me and talk about it, fine. They know where to reach me."

Susan started yelling something at him, and he again held the phone away from his ear. Just then, Megan Moore walked into his office. Peden held up a finger, letting her know that he would be finished in a minute.

Megan rolled her eyes, and she mouthed, "Susan?"

Peden nodded.

Megan walked slowly towards his desk and said in a loud voice, "Goodbye, Susan."

She reached out and snatched Peden's cell phone from him and disconnected the call. Peden's mouth dropped in disbelief. He stared at his former partner for several seconds.

"Close your mouth. We have a serious situation. Senator Vega was just shot in front of the Savannah D.E.A. office."

Peden immediately forgot about his wife and his daughters' money issues. "What the hell? How? You said shot, not killed."

"Grab your gun, I'll tell you on the way."

* * *

Megan Moore was the most serious, no-nonsense agent that Peden had ever met. He remembered her cracking a smile maybe twice during the entire ten years that they had worked together. The term "sense of humor" never crossed the lips of anyone that knew her. Her life was her job and vice versa. Peden had known her to make sarcastic comments from time to time, but she had the perfect poker face, which was wasted since she never played poker. But Peden believed that she was the best field agent in the FBI. She knew how to dig for facts and she was intimidating, even to those on her side. Odd since she was a very slender five feet, eight inches tall with short, strawberry blonde hair. But she had a persona that made you nervous as if you were being interrogated even without her asking a question.

The drive in Megan's 2013 green Honda Accord from Peden's office at 201 West Liberty Street to the D.E.A. office building was less than ten minutes. Megan rattled off as much detail as she knew and what she planned to do when they arrived at the crime scene.

"Vega was at the D.E.A. office for a come-to-Jesus meeting with the new staff. Pretty unusual for a Senator to talk with field agents from any agency. He, Michael Jess, and two staff interns were just leaving when a 'weaponized' drone flew up to within twenty-five to thirty feet of where they were standing on the front steps of the D.E.A. office building. It appears that the weapon was fully automatic and held thirty rounds based on what Jess could tell the first officers on the scene.

"Vega's in critical condition. Doctors aren't sure that he's going to make it. Jess was hit in the chest. One staff member was killed, a twenty-year-old male. The other, a twenty-three-year-old female, has just a flesh wound."

Peden was quiet for a few seconds as Megan turned right onto Park of Commerce Boulevard and approached a red brick building with white columns, the local office of United States Drug Enforcement Administration.

The building looked completely out of place among the private businesses in the commercial park. Peden frowned as he observed the crime scene tape surrounding the front of the building, a feeling of déjà-vu eliciting a shiver through his body. It looked eerily similar to the scene at this very spot back in June when Jarrod Deming was shot and killed on live television. He was set to deliver a news conference that would implicate himself, several fellow agents, a local district attorney, and a superior court judge in a scheme that embezzled millions of dollars from the federal government as well as imprisoned dozens of innocent people in the process. The arrest of those involved and the resulting fallout was the reason for the new agents at the Savannah office and the visit from Senator Vega.

Megan parked approximately one hundred and fifty feet from the building because it was the closest spot available. They approached a checkpoint where a Savannah Police officer prevented local reporters and curious bystanders from wandering into the crime scene. Megan flashed her FBI badge and, motioning to Peden, said, "He's with me." The officer let them pass.

At 11:20, the sun was bright and high overhead, with only light, wispy cirrus clouds visible against a vividly blue backdrop. A combination of high humidity and a temperature in the low nineties added to their discomfort. Peden hadn't exactly been friends with Senator Vega, but he had developed a comradery with his aid and bodyguard, Michael Jess. He was anxious to learn of their conditions and planned to push Megan to get to the hospital as soon as their work here was done.

When they reached the steps of the building, the spot where the four victims were struck, Peden saw several pools of blood on the steps. The scent of the blood baking in the sun was prominent. The amount of blood suggested that some of the wounds were severe. Peden noticed bits of plastic, metal, and charred electronics — remnants of the drone and weapon — scattered in the parking lot in front of the steps. Shell casings littered the area to the right of the bulk of the debris. Small numbered yellow plastic markers sat near the shell casings and larger pieces of the drone.

A big man in a white dress shirt that was a bit tight at the biceps was talking with one of the crime scene investigators, pointing at something in the debris field, directing the man to do something that Peden couldn't hear. He looked to be in his mid-to-late thirties, tanned leather skin from spending time outside, and short hair, receding on either side of an island of hair that refused to fade away. His demeanor seemed to imply that he was the man in charge. With Peden in tow, Megan walked up to him and stuck out her hand. "Megan Moore, FBI, Special Agent in Charge. This is Peden Savage, consultant to the FBI."

The young man stuck out his hand to Megan. In a deep, southern voice that seemed more suited for a radio announcer, he replied, "Daryl Shirley. I'm the lead investigator for Savannah and Chatham County." He turned and shook Peden's hand. When he turned back to Megan, he asked, "So, y'all takin' over?"

Megan's expression didn't change. "Yes. But don't take off, I can assure you that we need your assistance. Not sure how your brass will like it. I know mine won't be thrilled."

"Sounds good to me. Them fellas higher up don't have much of a sense of humor, but I think we can work somethin' out."

Megan didn't smile, but Peden could tell that she was pleased to get a rare, positive response from local law enforcement.

"What have you got so far?"

Detective Daryl Shirley pointed out the debris field that she and Peden had just viewed. He said that no one they'd spoken with heard the drone, except the victims.

"Before he was hauled off in the ambulance, the senator's aid, Mr. Jess, said that everyone in the group turned when they heard the drone approach, but they had no idea what it was until it was nearly on top of 'em. He wasn't able to tell the first officers on the scene too much. They rushed him off to Memorial." Memorial Health University Medical Center had the only level one trauma center in the region. "That's also where the senator was taken. The one intern that had only minor wounds was treated by some EMTs. She's at the station now. She was in shock and wasn't real helpful – she's an emotional wreck. We were planning to question her on what she saw, but they gave her a sedative, and she conked out."

Megan looked around at the debris field. "Have your crime scene investigators come up with anything beyond the obvious?"

"Not yet, but these kids are good. If there's anything to be found, they'll find it. That was Jimmy Lowell that I was chattin' with when y'all walked up. He said that the drone had an explosive charge on it that was sufficient to destroy the drone and the weapon. But there are some pieces that are big enough, there might be some serial numbers or DNA. They have to get this stuff back to the lab, so I told him I'd leave him be while he worked."

"We'll provide additional resources to the crime scene guys. I'll make the call when we're done talking." Megan wasn't asking permission.

Detective Shirley said, "Thank y'all, ma'am."

Peden jumped in. "I'll get Lee Sparks over here. He'll be able to assist with the electronics from the drone."

Detective Shirley nodded. "How soon can you get these resources here?"

Peden replied, "Lee will be here within minutes, if I can reach him." Peden turned to Megan. "If there's nothing else to discuss here, we should get up to Mercy."

Megan turned to the detective and asked, "Did you question the D.E.A. agents that were here?"

"Yes, ma'am, we did. We understand that they were all in the conference room with their director during the attack. They're going to the station to answer questions."

Megan handed him her card. She said, "Thank you, Detective. Call me on my cell if you find anything new. How can I contact you?"

Shirley produced a couple business cards. He handed one to Megan, the other to Peden. "I'll be in touch."

Chapter 3

Ian Tabler had opened the basement windows as soon as the flash drive stopped burning. Though it seemed to Ian that it was much longer, the drive burned for less than three seconds, filling the basement with smoke, soot, and the acrid odor of burning electronics. There was another scent that Ian couldn't immediately identify, but it seemed out of place, something chemical that caused irritation in his throat. He grabbed two bottles of cold water from their mini-refrigerator, opened both, and handed one to his brother, who took the bottle and drank from it without looking away from his computer monitor.

The boys had shut down their computers and were now performing diagnostic checks on all the functions and programs. So far, everything checked out fine, running without a hitch. All of their attached equipment − printers, a scanner, several external hard drives, and the modem worked fine. Only the flash drive was destroyed. Even the slot where the drive was inserted worked after a new flash drive was plugged in. Ian pulled up several files and checked them out. Again, it worked perfectly.

The flash drive that caught fire was little more than ash. The flame that had shot out of the device − no larger than a pack of gum − was indeed hot. Ian wondered what could have caused the malfunction. He was puzzled by the intensity of the flame. A tinkerer almost from birth, he'd taken any number of these types of storage devices apart, wanting to know what made them work. He frequently disassembled computers, printers, radios, CD players, even cell phones and then reassembled them. They always worked perfectly after he was through. The result was that he knew what was in most devices and, more importantly, what was not. And he knew that there should have been nothing inside the drive that would have caused such an intense flame. Had there been a lithium-ion battery present, maybe, but flash drives received their power from whatever computer or TV it was attached.

It had been a mere ten minutes since the flash drive failure when Ian heard footsteps coming down the basement steps. The door to their computer lab opened. Their father, Nicholas Tabler, stepped in. He quickly scanned the room, scrunching up his face as the acrid odor assaulted his eyes, nose, and throat.

In a calm, controlled voice, Ian's father asked, "What happened, son? I thought you were testing that new program?"

Ian pushed back his chair and stood, facing his father, his body stiff as if at military attention. Jonah still stared at his monitor and didn't move.

"We were, Dad. The flash drive from FlashGamz failed. It burst into flames." He pointed to the trash can where he deposited what little remained of the drive. "You should have seen it, it was like a blow torch for a few seconds, then it stopped. Never seen anything like it."

Ian looked directly at his father's eyes as he spoke. He was searching for any warning that Nicholas Tabler might lose his temper, but instead, he saw understanding. Ian slowly let out his breath, feeling confident that there would be no punishment for his brother and himself. Ian saw his father look past him at Jonah.

"Is your brother okay? I mean, neither of you is hurt, right?" He spoke to Ian as if Jonah wasn't in the room, or like his son was a piece of furniture. He always did that, and it bothered Ian. He knew it bothered Jonah as well.

"We're good. We weren't too close when it failed, and it only burned for a few seconds."

Their father looked back at Ian. "I'll send Jenkins down, have him air the place out." Jenkins was one of the staff members that kept the household running.

Nicholas Tabler employed three groups of people, "divisions" as he called them. There was a grounds maintenance team, a housekeeping team, and security. Grounds maintenance and housekeeping were on duty primarily during the day, but Jenkins was on call around the clock. Housekeeping cleaned, prepared meals, and did laundry. Security worked three shifts, seven days a week. They manned a guardhouse at the front gate of the estate on Tybee Island and walked the grounds, trying to blend in with nature, staying out of sight as much as possible. Ian heard his father tell the head of security, Victor Popov, that he needed the estate to appear welcoming, not like a fort or a prison. He didn't want his boys to feel confined. That was all well and good, but in reality, Ian and Jonah rarely left the compound.

"Okay, Dad. Sorry about this." Ian waved his hand towards the wastebasket.

"It wasn't your fault, Ian. Contact the company. We need to make sure this never happens again."

Nicholas Tabler turned and headed back upstairs. He never looked at Jonah before leaving.

Ian took a deep breath, then exhaled loudly. He hadn't realized how stressed he had been in his father's presence. He looked around the room at the posters on the wall: A sketch of Steven Hawking in his personally designed wheelchair with a picture of the universe at his back, Neil deGrasse Tyson pointing at the moon, and one with twenty-four of the leading astrophysicists of all time.

A smile crept across his face. It was relaxing to him being in the presence of some of the greatest minds in history. This room gave him comfort and solitude, a place he could think and solve problems and work with his brother. Unbeknownst to anyone else in the world, Jonah's mind was nearly computer-like when it came to mathematics. And he could translate any location on the map instantly to its longitude and latitude coordinates. But without the ability to relay this knowledge to others, he was doomed to a life of isolation, Ian his only conduit to the outside world. Being that Ian didn't much care for that world, Jonah's options for a normal life were slim.

Ian heard his brother rattle off a series of numbers. He never once looked away from the computer screen. He deciphered Jonah's message, and his smile melted away. Jonah's message was, "I wish I was more like you."

"Listen, little brother, you are brilliant. You are much smarter than Dad and everyone else here."

Ian knew what he said was true. His brother's IQ when it came to mathematics was off the charts, but something apparently wasn't wired right in his brain when it came to "normal" communications. His brain functioned more like a computer – all numbers.

Jonah rattled off another series of numbers. This series didn't spell out any words. Jonah repeated the numbers then pointed to the computer monitor. He said them again, this time a little faster.

"Slow down, brother. What is it?"

Jonah simply repeated the numbers. Ian rubbed his head in frustration, trying to understand what his little brother was trying to tell him. Then Jonah changed the numbers to four-five-one. He said the numbers again, then pointed at the screen and calmly repeated the original set of numbers.

Ian asked, "D.E.A.? What do you mean?"

Jonah pointed at the screen again. "Four-five-one-two-two-one-nine-one-two-four-nine-one-four-seven."

"D.E.A. building? What about it?"

Jonah didn't say anything else. With no emotion, he just stared straight ahead, pointing at the screen.

* * *

David Walsh checked the national news feed on his *NewsToYou* account on a sixty-inch flat panel smart TV, one of seven placed around his basement office that was set up like a sports bar. But his televisions were tuned to news feeds from the United States and around the world. His favorite sport was politics – in particular, U. S. politics and how world governments responded to the ever-changing power block in Washington, D.C. He kept abreast of current turmoil and schemed on how he could exploit each new situation. Someone at the highest levels of government always needed certain problems "fixed" without going through official channels. As

Country Joe said back in Woodstock, *There's plenty of good money to be made arming the Army with the tools of the trade.* That was true even if the armies weren't sanctioned by any recognized government.

He smiled at the breaking story out of Savannah, Georgia, on the assassination attempt on Senator Armand Vega. He was still alive, but according to the grim-faced anchor, his condition was critical. It was a shame that one of his young interns was killed. Shame as well that Michael Jess had survived the attack, though he wasn't the intended target. Jess might be a problem down the road. He had a reputation of being a fighter. If he felt that he'd failed Vega by not protecting him, he would make it his personal mission to find the shooter.

Bring it on, Mr. Jess. Of course, you'll never be able to tie me to this. I'm just that good! I'm guessing the FBI is literally piecing the drone and the weapon back together – at least what's left of it.

Walsh took a sip of sparkling water then clicked on the icon to his newly opened bank account in the Cayman Islands. A few keystrokes and he was looking at his balance. There it was – $2.5 million dollars for services rendered. A handful more keystrokes and he transferred the money to two additional accounts, then closed the trailing accounts out to slow down the money's traceability. It was nearly impossible to completely erase the links that could lead any investigator worth his credentials to the owner of an account, but this would cause issues that would buy the necessary time to get the money into gold coins. At that point, without serial numbers, the money was as clean as it could get.

He wasn't concerned that Vega had lived. The hit on the senator sent a message. The government must continue the War on Drugs. No doubt the talking heads behind closed doors in the nation's capital were wringing hands and wiping brows trying to determine the meaning of the attack. This had all the makings of political retaliation; some far-right-wing wacko ordering the hit because of Vega's desire to end the War on

Drugs, or change the mission to one of legalizing certain recreational and medical aspects of drug use. At least, that is what some in the left-wing national media would speculate.

His computer emitted a quiet '*ding*.' He looked at the center monitor, the second of the seven that were set up in his basement office. A small icon that looked like a hand waving an envelope flashed green. He smiled and hovered over the icon with his mouse. A small message box opened with the words '*Casket Keeper*.' He smiled again and clicked on the icon.

The message said, "I have more work for you. Will send itinerary soon."

He typed "K" in the reply box and hit send. He rubbed his hands together and smiled. "Time for a Macallan's."

Walsh stood, looking around at the other news feeds on the other screens, all muted with closed caption scrolling across the bottom. Several overseas channels were picking up the Vega storyline. He smiled, walked to the large bar at the end of the room, and poured himself two fingers of Macallan twelve-year-old scotch.

He raised his glass and smiled. "To unbridled power."

Chapter 4

Walking to Megan Moore's green Honda Accord with the traffic noise from Interstate 16 in the background, Peden barely heard his cell phone ring. He looked at the screen, but the glare made it impossible to read. He turned to Megan. "If it's important, they'll call back."

"You should answer it."

Her stern look made him feel as if he was in elementary school being scolded by his third-grade teacher, the one who made the Wicked Witch of the West look compassionate and caring, that he should sit down in his seat and remain quiet. He sheepishly swiped the phone's screen and answered, "Savage Investigative Consultants."

"Wow, took you long enough."

He immediately recognized the jovial voice of Marcus Cook.

Marcus Cook, D.E.A. squad leader and former Army Ranger who served in Iraq with distinction, was a close, personal friend of Peden's. A dark-skinned black man at six feet five inches and two hundred forty-five pounds, and built like an NFL linebacker, he was an imposing sight. He had played a key role in bringing down a group of crooked agents who embezzled money from the federal government and entrapped young kids for crimes they did not commit. For his work on that assignment, he was promoted and given a supervisory role in the D.E.A.'s regional office in Atlanta, Georgia.

"Marcus. How are you? How's the job going?"

"It was going just fine until your buddy Vega got himself shot. Director Erkskin called and said I should reach out to the SAIC (Special Agent in Charge). I figured that she was with you, so I called you instead. Sounds like you're standing in the middle of rush hour traffic."

Savage frowned at Marcus' comment about Senator Vega. "Megan and I are just leaving the D.E.A. office in Savannah, on our way to see him and Jess now. We hear Vega's in bad shape, and Jess isn't much better. I'll let you know the details after we talk with him."

"That's why I'm calling. We're going to investigate all the new agents at the Savannah office, see if there are any ties to Mercado and his buddies." Vincent Mercado was the lead agent in the Savannah office that was busted when Agent Jarrod Deming was assassinated on live television during a news conference. "Since they were already screened before being assigned there, I don't expect we'll find much, if anything, but the order came from Washington. Gonna be under the microscope for a while, like we weren't already. Also, we'd like to find out the details on that drone. We can't get directly involved in that part of the investigation, but could you keep me in the loop?"

Peden's phone buzzed in his ear, signaling another incoming call.

"Sure, Marcus. Can you hold on a sec. Got another call."

Peden hit a button. "Savage Investigative Consultants."

"Hey, Peden. Fosco."

Roland Fosco was Megan Moore's boss and Peden's former boss when he was with the Bureau. Roland Fosco was directly responsible for putting Peden in his current business while keeping him and the Bureau out of a very intense, negative spotlight. Several of Peden's fellow agents were planting evidence against major drug dealers to solidify the prospects of convictions. When Peden discovered the systematic frame-ups by his team, he threatened to go public. When he approached Fosco about what he knew, his boss convinced him to keep it to himself, that he and his director would address the issue internally. Fosco was good to his word and fired the offending agents. He also set up Peden in his current business, providing consulting services and specialized tools to all levels of law enforcement.

"Hey, Roland. What can I do for you?"

"First, you can help Megan find out who killed Armand Vega."

"Wait. What?"

"I just got the call. Vega died about fifteen minutes ago." There was a brief moment of silence on the call. "This is a murder investigation. I'm hiring you to help Megan. Your usual terms. Are you good with that?"

Peden was shaken. He should have known that there was a possibility the senator wasn't going to survive the attack, but the reality of it hit him hard.

"Peden, you there?"

In a voice that was subdued, he answered, "Yeah, I'm still here. Your answer is yes, I'll help. Usual terms. Send me a contract, and I'll get it back to you ASAP. Megan and I are on our way to the hospital now. We're going to question Michael Jess, then we're heading to the Savannah Police department to talk with the intern."

"Okay. Tell Megan to call me when you get done with Jess."

"You got it, boss."

"Oh, and Peden, it goes without saying, but keep the details of this close to the chest. We don't want any of this leaking to the press or others who might be involved. Got it?"

That last order was going to be a problem. Implied in his order was a ban on talking with members of other federal agencies, especially D.E.A. agents. That included Marcus Cook.

"Got it. I've got someone on the other line. I'll let Megan know to call you." He looked at Megan and nodded just as they got to her car.

The line disconnected and Peden was back talking with Marcus as he sat in the passenger seat. "That was Roland. He hired me ... with some stipulations. Can I call you later?"

There was a brief hesitation on the line. Marcus was apparently trying to imagine Fosco's stipulations. "Sure, Peden. Thanks. Later."

When Peden put his phone down, Megan glanced his way. Always the serious look, she said, "So how are you going to handle Marcus' request? Wait, maybe you shouldn't answer that. I don't want to know so I can't implicate you."

Peden's teeth clenched as the stress of his new assignment was already starting to build. The investigation was barely off the ground, and already there were edicts that would tie his hands, but there were always ways to get around the roadblocks. And Megan was right: the less she knew about certain conversations, the better. He would share all the information that he received from his sources with her … and whoever he believed needed to know. That list was short, but his new boss might not see things that way.

After the twenty-minute drive, Megan pulled into the hospital parking lot and picked the closest non-handicapped spot that she could find. There had to be thirty empty handicapped parking spots closer to the main entrance, but neither he nor Megan complained about the walk. It gave them time to talk about the morning's events.

Michael Jess' room was on the third floor at the northernmost end of the corridor with an armed, muscular, and serious-looking Savannah Policeman stationed outside his door. When Megan and Peden approached the room, the officer frowned and turned to face them.

Megan already had her FBI credentials in hand and raised them to eye level so the officer could easily match her picture with her face. He took a moment to read the information, then relaxed some and nodded. He waved his hand like a game-show host, directing them into the room, then resumed his position next to Jess' door.

Michael Jess was lying in a hospital bed with multiple IVs hanging on a rack near his head, the slow drip of saline and whatever antibiotic and other medical concoction that might be included running through tubes into Jess' left arm. Apparently, he heard their footsteps and turned to greet them.

Normally a picture of health, the light-skinned black man looked so pale that he almost looked Caucasian. His usually fit body folded into the bed like a stack of blankets. His eyes were bloodshot, either from medication or from the stress that goes along with getting shot, coupled with the death of two people who were close, both physically and emotionally.

Peden and Megan approached his bedside, Peden placing his hand on Jess' arm. The man's face tensed, and, for a moment, Peden thought he might cry.

Peden wasn't sure how to break the thick silence. "I guess you heard."

Jess took short, shallow breaths. "Yeah. The attending Doc came in after … said the damage was just too severe." He went quiet, deep in thought, then pain caused him to tense. "I figured as much before the paramedics arrived. I crawled over to him, but I was hurting. Nothing I could do."

Peden replied, "From what I saw, I agree."

They fell silent. He didn't want to push Jess yet. He figured that Megan would take the lead when she felt the time was right. They didn't have to wait. Jess knew what was coming and wanted to quickly give them as much information as possible.

Jess began, wincing in pain every few words, "The meeting was … over. Senator Vega spoke to the new agents … for less than ten minutes. We had another appointment in DC and … we had to get to the airport right after we finished at the D.E.A. office." He paused and took a series of short breaths. "We were just heading out … the front of the building. I was going to get the car … and that drone flew right up to us. I didn't have time … to draw my weapon." He paused again"

Peden said, "We can talk later, Michael."

"No time." He paused again. "I could see the thirty-round-mag hanging from the bottom of the drone and I knew … damn. There wasn't anything I could do."

Jess turned his head away towards the far wall. He cleared his throat several times as if trying to expel something foul. He turned back and reached for his water jug. Peden grabbed it and held it for him so he didn't have to lift his head too high. When he finished, he looked back at them and said, "I told Vega that he needed ... to be more serious about security. I had a bad feeling that ... somebody, some nut-job was going to take exception to his drug policy position." Jess was referring to Vega's public statement that the War on Drugs be scaled back and money diverted to prevention and treatment. The senator had received dozens of death threats, but, according to Jess, he didn't take any of them seriously.

Megan asked, "Who knew about the senator's schedule? That drone attack had to have some serious prep time. They, whoever they are, had to know his schedule down to the minute."

Jess looked at the ceiling, deep in thought. He knew Megan was right. There was a tiny window of opportunity for the attack.

"I can think of at least a dozen people who knew. He basically told ... the entire Finance Committee, at least those in his party." Jess winced in obvious pain. "Plus, he told ... his staff, the interns that came here with us. These kids probably told their parents. You know, flying in a Learjet with a senator." Another wave of pain took hold. After a moment he continued. "That's a big deal for these kids. Then, we were supposed to head back to Washington ... for a meeting with some of his top donors, so he told them about the meeting and that he might be late."

Peden and Megan were beginning to get the idea that they might have to question twenty to thirty people, and the pool of suspects would grow from there. That wasn't going to be easy.

Megan asked, "Was there any one or two people of those who knew that you might suspect would want Vega dead?"

"Off the top, no. I mean, there are a lot of people who don't like his politics – and I'm not just talking about people on the streets – I talking about Capitol Hill." Jess's whole body stiffened and his monitor showed that his blood pressure was creeping up. "But that's a real leap from not agreeing with a peer to murder, especially in such a public way. It's like the perp was trying to … send a message – *no more talk about defunding the War on Drugs.*"

Chapter 5

At 7:20 AM, Alton Woodburn, President of the United States, sat alone in the Oval Office after completing his review of the daily briefing papers. Not much had changed from the previous morning. The bad actors in the world were still acting bad, threatening their sworn enemies and chanting *Death to America*, and the supposed allies of the United States still paid lip service to their NATO commitments and were still behind on their financial obligations to the United Nations, which directly affected U.S. Taxpayers. The U.N. was years in arrears for several lease payments on properties and local hotel bills for their diplomats. But Uncle Sam paid those bills with taxpayer dollars and kept the local businesses in New York City happy, solvent, even prosperous.

The most disconcerting news of the week was the assassination of Senator Armand Vega at the D.E.A. office building in Savannah, Georgia, in broad daylight. The fact that a drone delivered the hardware to carry out the attack was even more alarming. *What if the target had been a busy federal building with hundreds of employees and the weapon had been a bomb?*

Director Herbert Massey gave Woodburn a personal update on the Federal Bureau of Investigation's efforts towards finding Vega's killer. Massey advised the president that the case was complex. Very few parts of the sophisticated drone or the weapon which it carried survived the explosion. Massey informed the president that the drone's destruction was most likely intentional to eliminate evidence that could be used to track down the identity of the manufacturer and the purchaser of the components of the weapons system.

Woodburn's jaw tightened as he pointed a large, fat finger at Massey and, in a stern, gravelly voice said, "Herb, sounds like you don't have squat. You put more assets on the ground and get the bastards who did this. We may not have agreed with Vega on the drug issue – hell, on a lot of issues – but he was a United States Senator. We can't have assassins running around with untraceable drones picking off our public servants. I want quick resolution on this. The American people demand it."

Massey nodded. "Yes, Mr. President. I've already given the order. This is not just our top priority: it is our only priority."

"That's a great sound bite, Herb, but nothing speaks louder than results. I want reports *at least* every four hours, around the clock. Is that clear?"

"Yes, Mr. President."

Woodburn nodded his dismissal to the FBI director, who rose from his chair and headed out the visitor's entrance of the oval office. When he was gone, the President leaned back in his overstuffed chair and rubbed his face. He thought, *A frickin' drone with a military assault rifle.* He shook his head, wondering if he might be next on the hit list.

His mind wandered back to when he was a colonel in the U.S. Army, sitting at his desk preparing for his next day's schedule when a young, enlisted man barged into his office. That visit had dramatically and irreversibly changed his life.

In some ways, his life was far better. He had more money than he would ever need, even with his wife's spending habits. There was so much cash coming in that he had to start a number of businesses to launder the money. That was before he entered public life. When he was coerced to run for public office, his campaigns, first for the U.S. House of Representatives, then for the U.S. Senate, were financed by drug profits. He was quickly identified as a potential Republican candidate for the presidency. His rise to stardom in politics was swift and relatively smooth. Being a decorated Army war veteran helped. He had the backing of the party and a host of big-money donors, as well as his own fortune. And his message resonated with conservatives. His public views leaned to the right but were close enough to the center of the political spectrum that he had a modest following from Democratic voters.

If only the masses knew the real story.

That fateful day back when President Alton Woodburn was a Colonel, he had no intention to enter public life, but the kid who had put Woodburn's scheme into overdrive had him in a figurative stranglehold. The kid had told him back then that he had choices, but there was only one right path. He was going to do whatever the kid directed, or he would be exposed and his military career would go down the toilet. He would spend the rest of his life in Leavenworth prison, his family disgraced. The flip side was a life of wealth and privilege.

The young sergeant had a great mind for business and several ideas to move the money from the black market to legitimacy. It was all brilliant. And frightening. But these days, sitting in the Oval Office, Alton Woodburn was insulated from the daily operation of the business.

He was deep in thought when an electronic chirp pulled him out of his trance. He opened his left-hand desk drawer and looked to see which cell phone was sounding off.

It was his personal phone. Only a dozen people knew that number, and he hoped the caller was his wife, but that wasn't to be. He read the number and visibly tensed. He didn't want to answer. As Nevin Tate said years ago, he had choices, but there was only one right decision.

He picked up the phone, swiped across the screen, and barked into the phone, "I told you to never call me on this phone when I'm here."

It took a moment for the caller to respond. In a voice more suited to a mother scolding her insolent child that he knew better than to talk back, he said, "Now Alton, I don't call unless it's important, right? Well, this is important. Besides, we haven't conversed in such a long time."

Woodburn rolled his eyes and took a deep breath. "Fine, Tate! What's so important that you couldn't wait until this evening?"

"I'm sure you've heard about the late Senator Armand

Vega. I'd like to suggest to you that we need a hard-liner to head up the Senate Finance Committee, and I have a suggestion."

Woodburn thought that the caller, Nevin Tate, the man who had instantly changed the direction of his life many years ago, had lost his mind. "You know I don't have any sway on decisions like that. That's a matter for the Senate. They make their own selection."

There was silence on the line for several seconds. "Alton, don't treat me like a second-grader. I'll come to your office and kick your ..."

"Enough already. Why do you think I can have any influence on the senate?"

"I don't. I just want to run a name past you and see what you think. Then maybe you can make a courtesy call to members of the Senate and, you know, suggest that the name I'm going to give you would be a good choice. By the way, I already have a write-up prepared for this person."

Woodburn rolled his eyes again. From the moment he met Nevin Tate in his office many years ago, he hated everything about him. He was smug, cocky, arrogant, and conceited. And those were his good traits. There was only one thing Woodburn liked about the guy. When he said he was going to do something, he did it quickly and effectively.

"Okay, okay. Give me the name and let's move on."

"Now that's the right attitude. See, we can work together just fine. Morgan Pickett."

"Morgan Pickett? You're insane. He might be in prison by next week."

"Alton." Tate spoke the president's name as if he was schooling an ignorant child. "My dear Alton, Morgan Pickett will be cleared of any connection to the assassination of Armand Vega, and he will win the election in a landslide. Haven't you learned to trust me on these matters?"

Woodburn found it hard to control his temper, but he knew that Tate had him under his thumb. He knew too much of Woodburn's past dealings, and he had physical evidence tying the president to certain crimes. He couldn't afford to anger the man. He took a sip of water then took a deep breath. "Even if he wins the election, what makes you think that he can assume the powerful position of Chairman of the Finance Committee? He'll be the most junior Senator on the floor and certainly the most junior on the committee."

"You shouldn't worry about such minor details, Alton. Don't you have a country to run? This is small potatoes. Just make the calls to your friends in the Senate and leave the rest to me. Got it?"

"Just one more question, Tate. How are we going to keep this out of the press? When those wolves see a rookie taking the reins of one of the most powerful committees in the Senate, they're going to ask all kinds of questions. We'll be under a microscope for an appointment like this. It'll be impossible to keep the heat off."

By the tone of Tate's response, it was becoming clear that he wasn't in the mood for a lot of discussion. In a sharp reprimand, Tate said, "Listen to me, Alton, and listen good. You don't need to concern yourself with this. Just make the calls. If you want to keep the press away from this, create something else for them to look at. You know, wag the dog. Start a war or something. I don't care what kind of red herring you throw out there, just do what I say and we'll be fine. Am I making myself clear?"

In a low huff, Woodburn responded, "Yeah. Crystal."

When the call disconnected, Alton Woodburn, President of the United States of America, supposedly one of the most powerful men in the world, put his face in his hands and wondered how he could get out from under Nevin Tate's control. As with every other time he had this thought, the answer was clear.

He couldn't.

He picked up the desk phone and started to dial the senator who had assumed temporary chair of the Senate Finance Committee since the assassination of Armand Vega. He stopped with the receiver midway to his ear, then placed it back in the cradle.

What the hell am I supposed to say? 'Hey, if this newbie wins the election, he should chair the Senate Finance Committee, what do you think? He seems like an okay guy.' Jeez.

Then he thought about how he might be able to get the press corps' primary focus on some other issue of importance. Nothing immediately came to mind.

His personal cell phone chirped, again interrupting his thoughts. This time it was his wife.

He answered. "Hello, sweetheart."

"Hi, Darling. Sorry to bother you at work."

"Honey, you know you can call anytime."

"Well, I'm just so upset. I needed to talk with you. I just got a call from my sister, Jean. She said her neighbor, an elderly woman, was killed when a piece of concrete broke loose from a bridge on Route 33 in Hocking County in Ohio and smashed through her windshield. The bridge was in such deplorable condition. She said some local residents have been warning the county commissioners that the bridge needed to be repaired, that something like this was going to happen, but they've been putting it off because they don't have enough money to fix it. They have higher priorities. Can't you do something to help these small, poor counties with some kind of funding for road and bridge repairs?"

"Dear, you know that the federal government is trillions in debt itself. I don't know ..."

Woodburn stopped in mid-sentence. He had to talk with his communications coordinator, but maybe he could make this his red herring and help local governments with some bread crumbs at the same time.

"I'll tell you what, dear, you call your sister and tell her we're going to do something about those bridges. And send our condolences to the family of that woman. No, wait. Get me the contact information for the family. I'll call them myself. Thank you for bringing this to my attention."

"Jean will be happy to hear about this."

"Tell her to watch the headlines. I'm not going to waste any time on this. I love you, dear."

After he tapped the red handset on his cell phone's screen, he smiled and rubbed his hands together. His red herring just fell into his lap.

Chapter 6

Peden Savage and Megan Moore interviewed the late Senator Armand Vega's surviving intern at the Savannah Police Station in a dull room with no windows, three chairs and a small round table. It was more suited for interviewing suspected murderers or rapists, which must have heightened the anxiety of the poor young woman. Still barely able to string together coherent thoughts, the twenty-one-year-old, third-year political science major was still traumatized by nearly being killed during the drone attack and watching her boss and fellow intern murdered right before her eyes. During the interview, they learned that she and the deceased intern were dating, the relationship getting serious, which made the episode all the more horrifying. In short, no new, relevant information was gained that they hadn't already heard from Michael Jess.

Agent Moore had so many incoming calls on her cell phone since the announcement just hours before that she was assigned as the Special Agent in Charge (SAIC) that she had to leave the interview room multiple times to answer calls that were mostly a waste of her time. During one of her exits, she called her boss, Roland Fosco, and relayed the news that there was no news. She brought him up to date on who they had interviewed and who was on their list next. Fosco had suggested that they look into Vega's political rivals, particularly Morgan Pickett, the Republican challenger for Vega's Senate seat. Fosco said that the Democratic Party planned to fill the seat with a young, popular Georgia State Senator whose ideals aligned with those of Vega. He was being pressured to file the necessary paperwork to run for the seat in the upcoming general election, but it was too soon to tell if he would try to make his appointment permanent.

Peden sat in his office on the ground floor of the nineteenth-century Bird-Baldwin House on Savannah's West

Liberty Street. Megan was in a chair next to him, pen and pad at the ready to take notes if needed. The fifty-five-inch flat panel television sat on a table to the left of Peden's desk. The TV could not be mounted on the wall due to some local regulations about defacing any building of historical significance. The Bird-Baldwin House, built prior to the Mexican-American war, was on that list. Showing on the screen was one of Morgan Pickett's political campaign commercials. It was more accurately described as an attack ad aimed at Armand Vega and his family.

The ad said nothing of what Pickett would do to make life better for Georgians, but it ripped Armand Vega and his purported political views on everything from United States involvement in foreign conflicts to infrastructure reform, and a host of other issues. But the most vicious attack was concerning Vega's stand against the War on Drugs. The ad implied that back-tracking the "progress" made by the federal government and cutting back on the financial assistance they provided to governments at all levels throughout the country would allow drugs to flood our streets, addicting everyone's children, destroying the American Dream for all future generations. In Morgan Pickett's view, it would decimate the youth of the country, including children in wealthy suburbs.

According to the narrator, "No one will completely escape the horrors of drug addiction." While the narrator explained the flaws in Vega's reasoning, the video displayed addicts lying in alleys, their filthy, emaciated bodies starved for food, track marks up and down their arms, used needles at their fingertips. The ad went on to state that the only reason Vega wanted to end the War on Drugs was to protect his drug-abusing son. It was a direct and very personal attack against Vega and his family.

The legal fine print stated, "Paid for by Restore America." Peden wondered whose names were behind the political action committee.

When the video ended and the legal small-print faded away, Peden's unblinking eyes just stared. He was astonished that a network would allow such a blatant attack on a candidate, not to mention the reference to Vega's son. He wondered if Vega had seen the ad before he was killed. They would have to circle back with Michael Jess and see if his boss had seen it and if they had planned to run ads to counteract the accusations.

Megan broke into his thoughts. "That was something. I'll get our guys working to find out who is behind the Restore America PAC. It should be simple enough. And we should talk to Pickett personally. It shouldn't be too hard to track him down if he's campaigning for the Senate."

Without a word, Peden cued up the next ad. They watched in silence as the next Vega-bashing TV commercial played. It was more of the same: a blatant attack against the late Senator. The same group was behind this ad as well. They used the same rhetoric and several of the same junkies, painting a horrific picture of life for those addicted to opiates. And Morgan Pickett stated that this is what ending the War on Drugs would look like in every city in the great state of Georgia and across the rest of America.

Megan said, "I guess we know where he stands on the issue."

Peden shook his head. "What other leads do we have, or do we have anything else?"

"Jess gave us Vega's laptop and his password book. We have techs going over his emails now to see if there are any with threats. And we have his cell phone. If they find anything, they're going to call me right away. Also, the new D.E.A. agents are on our list to interview, though I don't expect to find anyone in that group with an ax to grind. They were all screened recently and were brought in specifically to clean the place up. But we can't leave anything out. We have to check their files again, if nothing else, to satisfy Roland and his boss that they should be excluded as persons of interest. I'll call their director and get his people lined up. I'm sure he's going to want to cooperate. Marcus will want to sit in on the interviews. I'm sure he's conducting an internal investigation."

"Yeah. He is, not that I've shared any information."

Peden rubbed his face while he stared at the now blank TV screen, thinking about the possibility of a political foe assassinating his rival. It was one thing to spend hundreds of thousands of dollars attacking your opponent. It was an entirely different matter having that opponent assassinated, especially in such a public manner. Maybe that happened in other countries, but surely not the United States. But as Megan said, they needed to ask the tough questions of Morgan Pickett, if nothing else than to exclude him or get him on record stating he had nothing to do with it. If what they had just watched was justification to accuse someone of murder, then most every politician in the land was a suspect in some kind of crime. In these times, political ads were simply toxic.

Megan's phone rang for the umpteenth time. She didn't even pull it out of her small purse. Peden looked at her with a questioning expression. She said, "It's probably just another reporter."

"In the words of a pretty smart woman I know, 'Answer it. It could be important.'"

She rolled her eyes, retrieved her smart-phone and brushed her finger across the screen. "Moore."

It was the FBI crime lab.

Peden watched as Megan listened to the caller, her expression a stern frown. Then he saw her lips curl up just the slightest. It was almost a smile.

When she tapped her phone's screen to disconnect the call, she said, "That woman you know must be pretty smart. We have some new information that might be helpful. The hard drive on the drone wasn't completely destroyed. Our techs got some bits and pieces of data that point to an IP address, possibly the source of the signal directing the drone. They have the address of the computer where the commands came from. We have a tactical team getting ready to raid the place now."

Peden's face brightened. "Where?"

"Woodfin, North Carolina. It's a single-family home. The team should be hitting the place within the next two hours.

It's a wealthy suburb of Asheville. Pretty hilly and exclusive. We're gathering information about the owner now."

Peden's phone chirped. Megan gave him a look, which she did each time he had an incoming call, as if scolding him for such a wimpy ring tone. He made a mental note to change it. He answered. It was his contract IT specialist, Elijah "Lee" Sparks.

He answered. "Hey, Lee. What's up?"

"Hey, Peden. I know you haven't hired me yet, but I'm working on some theories about the drone attack on Vega."

Sparks contracted with Peden on approximately ninety percent of his cases, developing software to help with everything from operating miniature spy cameras to deciphering code from malware to tracking wire transfers. Some of Sparks' work was borderline-legal, but he never used the information for Peden's or his personal gain. Even if he was asked to perform a questionable search, he would tell Peden when he was approaching the line and the consequences of crossing that line.

"Let's hear it."

"Two things. This isn't some kid experimenting in his backyard with a hundred-dollar drone. Whoever put this thing together was a professional. He's done this before. Remember back a few years when a drone dropped right in front of the German Chancellor while she was giving a speech at a podium? I can't remember the occasion, but if that drone had had a bomb on board, a whole lot of people would have been smoked. I think whoever controlled that drone is the same person we're looking for now.

"Second, whoever they are, they're getting paid a boat load of money to carry out the assassination. They have some powerful equipment. Hundreds of thousands of dollars, just for the drone and computer equipment required to make that trip. You see, the operator has to remain in contact with the drone's navigation equipment for it to maneuver with enough precision to make a strike. Also, the optics on board have to provide video feedback in real-time. That takes a lot of power. Then, add to that controlling the weapon. That was one sophisticated piece of equipment. Whoever it is, dude knows his stuff."

"So, you think it's a dude? A guy, I mean?"

"Yeah, I do. Only woman I know mean enough to kill someone like that is your ex-wife." There was a pause. "Hey, man, I'm just kiddin' ... I think."

Peden's phone buzzed. He looked at the screen. The incoming call was from his ex-wife, Susan. He got a chill because of Lee Sparks' comment and the timing of her call and decided to ignore it.

"Hey, Lee, you're hired. Megan and I are heading out to do some interviews. When we're finished, I need to talk to you about how I can defend myself against my ex."

"Sorry, man. You can't pay me enough to get in the middle of that. You're on your own there. But call me about the drone. I'm ready to help with that."

The call disconnected. Peden looked at Megan, who was on her phone again. She rolled her eyes at him. This new call must be another waste of her time.

In a stern rebuke, she said, "When I have information that I can release to the public, I will hold a press conference. Everybody will get the same information at the same time."

Without waiting for a reply, she hit the phone's screen and disconnected the call.

She looked at Peden. "Let's go. We can talk in my car."

Chapter 7

Twelve FBI agents in tactical gear sat in a leased UPS step van at the staging area behind the UPS store on Merrimon Avenue in Woodfin, North Carolina, an upscale suburb on the northern outskirts of Asheville. Making a stealthy approach to the target, the home of Mr. and Mrs. Wilson Andrews would be nearly impossible. It was late in the day, and the entire neighborhood was covered with a continuous canopy of a variety of deciduous trees, providing some cover from the heat of the sun, but little cover for anyone driving into the cul de sac where the home was located. Worse, there were three other houses on the entire stretch of narrow roadway leading up to the Andrews house. Any vehicle on the road not belonging to one of the owners in the tight-knit community would be spotted right away. The FBI's team leader figured that the UPS truck obtained for use in the raid would only buy the team a few extra seconds. Once the team began streaming out of the van in full gear, nobody would be fooled.

The Andrews forty-two-hundred-square-foot home was just over one hundred fifty feet from the street up a driveway lined by mature trees. Only a small section of the building's tan siding was visible. A single window from a room over the garage could be seen, and at least one security camera faced their approach path.

The drive to the target home from the staging area was less than two minutes. If the green light was given, barring any glitches, the raid would be over in less than five minutes, making way for the search for evidence. A team of crime scene investigators was nearby and ready to move in on the team leader's signal.

Megan Moore was in direct communication with the leader, Alex Pinnetta. She had audio and video from multiple cameras perched atop the helmets of several team members.

Both audio and video were exceptionally clear. Peden was at the FBI building with her, listening to the team leader's instructions regarding team member assignments once they breached the doorways to the residence.

"Any questions?"

Silence. Megan could feel the tension in the UPS van from hundreds of miles away. She had worked with Pinnetta before. He was a professional, always serious during operations. He didn't tolerate anything less from his team while they were "on the clock." Pinnetta's question brought closure to the abbreviated planning and preparation phase of the meeting.

Over the communications line, Megan asked, "Agent Pinnetta, do you have the green light yet?"

"No, ma'am, we do not. We are expecting it at any moment."

As if on cue, his communications team member said, "Agent Pinnetta, we have a signed search warrant for 102 Brookwood Court, Woodfin, North Carolina. From Director Massey, we have a green light."

"Very well. Agent Moore, we are a go. Please maintain radio silence while we conduct this operation."

"Copy, Agent Pinnetta."

The agents immediately took their seats along each side of the back of the UPS van. Megan could see the various camera feeds where each of the men seemed to be bowing their heads. She saw at least two team members cross themselves and thought to herself, *Keep your heads down.*

The UPS van turned right out of the parking lot onto Merrimon Avenue, passing a number of fast-food restaurants and local businesses, then turned right onto Wembley Road. After a short stretch, Wembley began a steady rise into the hills bounding the exclusive Country Club of Asheville, it's fairways unnaturally bright green through the camera feed. Wembley turned into Windsor Road, which skirted the 18th fairway at the golf course. At a fork, the van veered right onto Robinhood Road, then right again at Brookwood Road. A rise in the terrain caused the men to brace themselves. The road took a steeper incline after the final left turn onto Brookwood Court. The UPS van's motor downshifted, the engine straining to make headway.

The van pulled up to the apron of the driveway at 102 Brookwood Court, the driver setting the parking brake and shutting down the engine. Pinnetta gave a visual sign for the men to rise, then with his left hand signaled down from three, two, one, fist. *Go.*

Megan and Peden watched as the back doors of the van burst open and the twelve members of the team poured out onto the street. Pinnetta and his communications man exited the front passenger side of the van. The team automatically bent their bodies low in a crouch as they formed two lines on either side of the driveway, trying without success to find some means of concealment. They could clearly see that the entire team was in full view of a second-floor window and a security camera.

Megan made sure that her microphone was off and commented to Peden, "If they're watching from the house, those guys are sitting ducks. Their best bet is to move fast and forget stealth. There's no place to hide."

The sound of a lawn mower could be heard over Megan and Peden's audio. Then the mower shut down. Now the only sound was heavy breathing and the faint sound of leaves rustling in the breeze. No one on the team said a word.

When they were within twenty-five feet of the closed garage door, Pinnetta made a motion both left and right. Immediately, six men went left and six went right. After a few more steps, the two groups of six split again into four groups of three. One of the men in the group that went to the front door carried a battering ram. There was a five-second pause to allow the sub-groups to get into place, then Pinnetta raised his hand again, holding up three fingers, then two, one …

The door opened and a beautiful, fit and trim, thirty-something woman in shorts and a tank top looked startled to see three men in full assault gear and military-grade weapons at her door. She just held the door as if in shock.

Pinnetta shouted, "Get on the ground, now!"

The woman threw up her hands and went to her knees. She looked as though she might wet herself, her eyes open wide, her mouth working as if trying to say something, but no words escaped.

Megan and Peden's attention shifted to the rear patio door, where three men slammed the sliding glass door open and rushed into what appeared to be a breakfast nook. They fanned out with their weapons shouldered, sweeping the room as they went. Two teen girls looked up from their cell phones in shock. The men shouted for them to lie down on the floor. Both girls did, but they held onto their phones. One man shouted, "Drop the phones!" The girls complied and began crying.

Quick, loud steps could be heard in the background. Two team members pointed their weapons down a hallway off of the kitchen. A middle-aged man with a receding salt-and-pepper hairline in blue jeans and a *ZZ Top* tee shirt stepped off the stairs from the second floor. He saw the men with their weapons pointed in his direction and shouted, "What the hell's going on? Who ..."

Before he could finish, the two men shouted for him to get down on the floor and keep his hands and arms spread. They asked who else was in the house.

He replied, "Just my son."

"Where is he?"

"In his room at the top of the steps, to the left. What the hell ..."

"Shut up. Don't say another word."

One team member moved in to cover the man on the floor and the two girls while the other two men moved to the steps and began their ascent. When they were half-way up the steps, a teenage boy with shoulder-length, sandy-blond hair, wearing shorts and a blank tee-shirt, opened a bedroom door and yelled, "Mom, Dad, what's going on?"

Then he saw the men on the steps. Even on the video

feed, Megan and Peden could see the boy's color drain from his face. He stopped dead in his tracks.

Megan saw it first. In his right hand, he held a black object that looked like it might be a hand gun. The boy moved his hand too quickly, obscuring the view of the object.

The two men in unison shouted, "Drop your weapon now!"

The boy's face was a sudden ball of confusion. He held his hands high and looked at whatever was in his hand. He looked back down at the men and their assault weapons and began to shake with fear.

In a barely audible, shaky voice that cracked, the boy said, "It's a game controller."

He let it drop to the floor, then fell to his knees. The men kept their weapons trained on the boy as they slowly walked to the top of the steps. One man covered him while the other placed pull-ties on the boy's wrists. They both looked at the object the boy had dropped. It was, in fact, a video game controller. They escorted him down the steps.

As they reached the bottom of the stairway, one man thought he had muted his microphone. Megan and Peden heard him say, "Jesus. I thought it was a gun. I almost shot him."

"Yeah." There was a pause. "Something doesn't add up here."

The boy was escorted downstairs with the rest of his family. They were all seated in the living room while Pinnetta took stock of the raid. It had taken less than two minutes to secure the residence. When they had the five occupants of the house seated in the living room, Pinnetta told them that they exercised the raid per a federal search warrant. He told Mr. Andrews that he could view the warrant when they were back at the local FBI office in downtown Asheville.

Wilson Andrews bellowed, "Federal search warrant?! For what?!"

Pinnetta, his face stone-cold serious, replied, "Evidence in the murder of Senator Armand Vega."

The statement drew gasps from members of the family.

One of the girls began hysterically crying anew and blurted out, "Can I call my parents? I don't even live here."

Wilson Andrews' expression was, at first, one of shock. Then his demeanor changed as he thought about something. "This was the senator killed by the drone attack down in Georgia, right?"

"Yes, sir, that's right. Please don't say anything else. You'll be questioned at length when you get downtown. You have the right to have an attorney present, you ..."

"You bet your ass I want an attorney present ... and an accountant to calculate how much we're going to sue for. You guys screwed up big time."

Pinnetta felt good about how the raid had gone. His team hadn't done anything wrong, but this family just didn't fit the profile of professional assassins. He was getting the feeling that this wasn't going to turn out well for the FBI.

* * *

Back in the FBI's Savannah office
, Megan and Peden were feeling the same doubt and concern. The raid went well on paper, extremely well, in fact. But Wilson Andrews looked like anything but an assassin.

"Pedee, how would you like to sit in on the interviews of the Andrews family?"

He hated it when she called him *Pedee*. "Love to. When do we leave?"

"I think we're going to do it by video conference. I'll talk with Pinnetta once he gets the family to the office in Asheville. Should be about half an hour."

* * *

Nothing at the federal level of government takes half an hour, Peden thought, and he was right. The plan was that the Andrews family would be brought in to the interrogation room one at a time in front of the camera to be questioned, with their lawyer present. They were being kept in separate rooms to prevent them from making up a collaborated cover story. Two hours later, Mr. Andrews went first.

* * *

By the end of the first three interviews, it was clear that Mr. and Mrs. Andrews and their daughter knew nothing of the Vega assassination except what was covered on television news casts. When their son, Simon Andrews, sat in front of the camera, things changed in a hurry.

With the family lawyer at his side, Simon Andrews appeared to sink into his chair, hoping to disappear. After recording the date, time, and the reason for the interview, Pinnetta got right to the point, asking Simon where he was on Wednesday, August 19, at 10:00 AM.

"I was in my room testing a new video game."

"What do you mean, testing? Don't you mean, playing?"

The kid gave his lawyer a nervous look. The lawyer nodded.

"No. I do beta testing for new video games. I mean, I get paid to test games, to, uh, you know, like, help work out the bugs so that when they get sold, they work the way they're supposed to."

As he listened in to the kid's answers, Peden said to Megan, "Tell Pinnetta to ask the kid more about the video game he was testing."

Before she could relay Peden's request to Pinnetta, Simon Andrews said, "I'm probably not gonna get paid for this game, though. The flash drive from the company that had the test program on it burned up."

It was Pinnetta's turn to look confused. "Burned up? What do you mean?"

"I mean, it smoked, flamed out. The thing burned to nothing but ashes."

"Has this ever happened to you before?"

"Nope. First and only time. I didn't know those things were flammable. Anyway, like, I just finished the attack and the drive went up in smoke. Mom was pissed. So was Dad. But it wasn't my fault. How was I supposed to know the thing would burn up? I tried calling my contact at the company, but there's no answer."

Megan said into her microphone, "Ask the kid about the game he was testing."

He acknowledged Megan's order then asked Simon, "Tell me about the game you were testing."

Simon asked, "You mean, what's the game about or …"

"Yeah. Exactly. What type of a game is it?"

"Well, it isn't really officially named, but FlashGamz calls it *Assassin – Best in the Business*."

Megan immediately spoke, "Alex, send me that company name and all the contact information the kid can give you. And give the kid a break, then we'd like to ask him some questions directly."

"You got it, Megan."

Chapter 8

Megan Moore's office was as plain as sugarless vanilla ice cream with no toppings. The air had the slight aroma of industrial cleaners. There were no flowers to add a natural fragrance to the room. The walls had only stock pictures: one of the American Flag and another with some motivational slogan under a picture of a marathon runner near collapse. Peden had known Megan for nearly ten years, and the pictures hadn't changed. They hung on walls painted off-white. Her metal, government-issue desk was devoid of pictures of any kind: no family, no boyfriend, no pets. The only objects on her desktop were a lamp, a pen, a pencil, and a thin manila folder with a label on the front. The folder was new: no twisted corners, coffee stains, or smudge marks. Peden figured it must be the Vega murder file which was destined to grow quickly in volume.

He couldn't tell if Megan was in a good mood or a bad mood. She didn't wear her emotions on her sleeve. As usual, she was all business. She tapped her smartphone screen, disconnecting the call that she'd been on for just a few minutes.

"We're meeting Morgan Pickett's tour bus by the convention center. He's holding a rally there at 4:30, so we have about an hour before he takes the stage. His campaign manager said we could have ten minutes before the rally starts."

Peden raised his eyebrows at this limitation.

"I didn't tell him that we'd take whatever time we needed."

This brought a smile to Peden's face. He knew how convincing Megan could be when she was pushed. It usually didn't turn out well for the pusher.

"What's the plan of attack?"

"Well, Pedee, I think that you should just observe. I'll

ask the questions. I'm going to start with the attack ads and move on to personal correspondence. We found that Pickett sent Vega a number of tersely worded emails that attacked his stance on the 'War on Drugs.'" Megan put finger quotes in the air around the popular description associated with the expenditure of billions of dollars to combat illicit drug sales and abuse. "They appear to go beyond the generally accepted boundaries of personal correspondence."

Peden raised his eyebrows at that. He wondered where those lines were drawn or if they had been erased altogether. Certainly, paid political advertisements had no moral or ethical restrictions.

"I can do that. If you need me to jump in, just send me some kind of signal."

"Very covert, Peden. Like spy stuff. Good cop, bad cop." She paused, making the point that she wouldn't need much support. "You being there, that's all I need."

They arrived at the convention center ten minutes before the campaign bus. As the bus door opened, Megan, in her usual aggressive manner, stepped up into the bus, making two staff members back up the steps. Peden followed.

In a voice heard over the idling engine, she called out, "Morgan Pickett."

"Agent Moore. Back here."

Megan turned to Peden. "That was Pickett's campaign manager."

They moved down the narrow aisle towards the rear of the bus, passing half a dozen people dressed in pantsuits and sports coats, scrambling for folders, briefcases, and stacks of campaign signs. It reminded Peden of a passenger jet as it completed taxiing to the gate, with people hustling to get their stuff out of the overhead bins and jockeying for position in the aisle. The campaign workers on the bus clearly had marching orders.

The temperature inside the bus was quite cool, near 68 degrees. The campaign workers were in for a shock when they exited. The outdoor temperature was close to 90 degrees with an oppressively high humidity level. The air had the aroma of diesel fumes that migrated in from the open bus door, plus cologne, perfume, and tension sweat.

The interior looked like a normal tour bus until you noticed the back ten feet. A room had been built into the rear section. A narrow door segregated the room from the rest of the bus. The door was open, and a tall, slender man, Peden guessed in his late thirties, stood in the doorway, wearing a gray, pricey-looking, tailored suit. His unnaturally black hair was slicked back. Peden thought he could use a haircut.

They made their way down the aisle, past the campaign workers, to the room.

"Come right in, Agent Moore." The man smiled and extended his hand. Megan shook it with her firm grip. "Grady Carlson, Senator Pickett's campaign manager." He looked at Peden with a questioning glance.

"This is Peden Savage. He's a consultant to the FBI."

Peden smiled and shook Carlson's hand without saying a word. He could barely see past the campaign manager's frame, but he caught a glimpse of Morgan Pickett at a small desk on a cell phone. Pickett looked polished, like he'd just stepped off a camera shoot for *Gentlemen's Quarterly* magazine. His loud, thick southern accent filled the office and bellowed out into the bus's interior. He was giving his opinion on some political matter that Peden couldn't determine. It didn't matter. They weren't here to talk politics.

Carlson gestured to two seats in front of the desk. Surprisingly, there was a good amount of space in the office, and the seats were quite comfortable. Pickett smiled at his guests and raised his finger, indicating that he would be finished on the phone in just a moment.

Pickett's southern accent was thick with drawl. "Yessa, yessa, that was such a tragedy and an act of cowardice. I think every candidate for higher office in the country is going to have to rethink their security measures." There was a pause on Pickett's end of the line, then he replied to his caller. "I'm sure the FBI will track down the killa in short order. As a matter of fact, I must go. I have a meeting with a couple of their agents now."

After a bit more chatter, Pickett ended the call. He stood and extended his hand to both Megan and Peden. "Sorry for the delay. Call me Mort."

After brief introductions, Megan started by ignoring his request to call him 'Mort' and saying, "The reason we're here, Mr. Pickett, is we have to question anyone with a motive to kill Armand Vega."

The senator didn't waste a second before a booming retort. "Motive to kill? What motive do I have to kill Vega? He was a political rival, nothing more. If that is motive, then we'd have thousands of politically motivated killings every election cycle."

He let out a short laugh, and his face took on an exaggerated look of disdain for the very idea. His cell phone rang, and he reached out and silenced it. Peden thought, *At least he's taking this seriously.*

Megan moved right in. "We just viewed your ads, literally right before this meeting, and the level of rhetoric is at such a personal level, I know a lot of district attorneys who would introduce them as evidence in a murder trial."

The look on Pickett's face went from disdain to incredulous. He made a dismissive wave of his hand. "Ms. Moore, that's ..."

"Special Agent Moore."

"Yes, ma'am." He rolled his eyes slightly and continued. "Excuse me. Special Agent Moore." His tone was mocking Megan's rebuke. "I don't have any *direct* input to the content of those ads. We give the company our talking points, and they run with it. That's how people get elected these days. The nastier the ads, the better the poll numbers. That's just the way it is."

"So that part about you 'approving this message,' that's not really true?"

"Let me put it to y'all this way: my staff takes care of all of that and I approve of their actions. Their job is to get me elected. If the numbers go in our favor, then they're earning their money, and I approve of that. They know if the numbers don't go our way, then there're a dozen other people waiting to take their place. Same with the ad company. Get results or get replaced."

Peden thought he might have seen Megan's lip curl up, but it was so slight that it could have been his imagination. He could tell that she was ready to jump.

"So, I guess the several emails that you sent to Senator Vega were from some lower-level staff member? You know, the ones that had the same personal attacks in them as the television ads?"

Pickett turned his smile back on and looked directly at Megan. He hesitated just a beat before he answered. "As a matter of fact, Special Agent Moore, my email account is monitored and controlled by a staff member. There are actually two people who are assigned the job of responding to any emails that require a response. Of the hundreds of emails that I receive daily, I understand that my people respond to fewer than ten percent. I do not direct any of those replies. They have a small folder that has my position outlined for most issues, and they keep their replies within the bounds of those points. But, in the case of the emails sent to the late Senator Vega, I did write up several points that I wanted included in them. I wanted it to be clear that I was opposed to his ludicrous position on drugs. His plan would flood the streets of this country with dope, and I wanted him to know that I would be very vocal in my opposition."

"You are admitting that you threatened him? Those emails contained very personal attacks, specifically against his son." Megan took out a sheet of paper from her small purse and unfolded it. She looked it over before continuing. "You said, and I quote, 'Your very liberal, nearly criminal policy would not only flood our streets with drugs and create countless future addicts, you are condemning future generations to a lifetime of misery. Worse, you are doing this to protect your drug-addicted son. For that, you should be prosecuted. In fact, thousands of deaths have been associated with heroin addiction just in the last year. You should be held responsible for those deaths.'"

"What did you mean when you said that Senator Vega 'should be held responsible for those deaths?'"

Pickett's smile remained, but his jaw tightened. He paused for the briefest of moments. "What I meant, Special Agent Moore, was that he should be held politically responsible by being removed from office. In no way did that statement imply that I thought that he should be killed."

Pickett looked at his watch. He wanted the interview to end, and he was hoping to use his ten-minute time limit as a means to escape Megan's questions.

"Just a few more questions, Senator. I know you're on a tight schedule, and something as inconvenient as the murder of your opponent can't interfere with the wheels of the campaign."

Pickett's smile disappeared. This last comment ticked him off. He opened his mouth to speak, but Megan cut him off.

"Senator, we know that you didn't pull the trigger on the gun that killed Senator Vega. But we must look into every possible person of interest. By your actions, you have placed yourself on the list of persons of interest. So, if you would like to help this investigation move forward, answer this question as honestly and directly as you can. Do you know of anyone who would want Senator Vega dead?"

"Yes. Several million conservative voters in the great state of Georgia. Senator Vega wanted this country to abandon the efforts of law enforcement to stop ..."

Megan held up a hand. "I'm not looking for one of your political ads as a response. I really want to know if you know of a person, or persons, by name, who would want Vega dead."

Pickett sat back for the first time since they entered the office. He was actually taking Megan's question seriously, or at least he was putting on a good act. Finally, he leaned forward again and asked, "Can I get back to you on that?"

Megan was direct. "No. We don't have time for political games. It is possible that the killer may have another target already in his sights. If you know anything, you'd better tell us now. Who knows? You might be the next target. We don't know this person's motive."

That seemed to surprise Pickett. He quickly recovered and returned to the sly politician.

"Special Agent Moore, I wish I could help you with anything besides the fact that I'm not your man. So at least you can stop wasting your time on me." He paused. "Is there anything further?"

"We'll be in touch."

As Megan and Peden walked away from the bus in the intense sun and midday heat, Peden leaned over and said, "He's not our killer."

"Yeah, I know. He was too surprised by the idea that he might be next."

As they approached Peden's car, he asked, "Where did you get that information anyway?"

"I made it up."

Chapter 9

Ian Tabler sat at his work station in the basement level of his father's house at the end of Horsepen Point Drive, Tybee Island, Georgia, running his hands through his thick, shoulder-length, sandy-brown hair. He could still smell the faint scent of burnt electronics in the room. In his mind, he had poured over the events of the previous day so many times that he could recall every detail as it unfolded. He was troubled because he knew that he and Jonah had performed every step of the game's beta test by the manufacturer's specifications. They had tested hundreds of programs for a half-dozen companies over the past three years − so many programs that they knew each company's procedures by heart − and they had never had such a colossal failure. Even though they tested video games frequently, they reviewed the manufacturer's specific test procedures every time they contracted for a new job. *How could something so simple go so abysmally wrong?*

Some of the programs didn't work well on their first, second, and even third round of tests. Eventually, the company's programmers fixed the lion's share of issues, and the testing would proceed. But a few tests were never completed because those highly skilled, highly paid programmers were unable to make the games work as intended. But never had a piece of hardware physically failed in such a dramatic and catastrophic manner.

That was another fact that bothered Ian. He knew flash drives inside and out, and nothing in that drive should have caused it to ignite. In his opinion, what happened to the flash drive, under any conditions, was impossible. He had retrieved the remnants of the device from the trash in hopes of performing some chemical analysis of the ashes, but he would have to study his chemistry programs to figure out how to test what remained of the device.

The fact that they couldn't reach their contact at FlashGamz was also disconcerting. Previously, when they had an issue with a program, their contact was just a phone call or an instant message away. Sometimes they had even contacted their handler during testing and described the issues to him so that he might be able to replicate it and work on the problem in real-time.

FlashGamz wasn't a new company to the brothers. Their father had even checked them out. Nicholas Tabler told Ian that they were a solid, reputable company.

Then there were Jonah's repeated attempts to tell him something about the D.E.A. He tried his best to understand what his brother was telling him. He kept repeating some numbers that didn't add up to anything. He even spelled out "D.E.A. building." What was bugging him? What had he seen, or what did he figure out that he just couldn't convey?

It wasn't in Ian's nature to simply forget about an issue such as this. He couldn't just sit back and relax and act as if nothing significant had occurred. His mind raced every minute of every hour of every day. He couldn't turn it off. His psychologist said it was part of his nature, part of being a 'prodigy,' as he had called it. Ian slept little, just over four hours each night, unless he had a major project in the works, then he sometimes slept as little as an hour. Even with this lack of sleep, he maintained a high energy level, working at his computer, studying textbooks, and looking for solutions to problems that many scholars found elusive. He had already graduated from college with advanced degrees in chemistry and mechanical engineering. Now he was studying telecommunications. He wasn't seeking another degree. The whole idea of electronic communications captured his interest. Part of that interest came from his desire to help Jonah learn to integrate with society in some meaningful way. Maybe he could come up with some device that could assist his younger brother in translating his number code to real words so regular people could hear what he was saying.

But there was something else. Ian, himself felt cut off

from the world at large. He never had the opportunity to interact with other kids his own age, normal kids with normal interests and normal IQs: in other words, kids with normal lives. As he grew and matured, it was an isolation that was becoming more difficult to bear. He often wondered if he would ever meet a girl and go on a date or, someday, get married and have children of his own. At fifteen, girls definitely interested him, but he was so isolated at the compound that he believed he might never have an opportunity to meet any woman, much less the woman of his dreams.

He vowed to himself that he would never leave his brother's side. Jonah needed protection from just about everything. His reactions to outside stimulus were automatic and extreme: usually a loud, harsh scream or squeal while pulling away from the harmless touch of a stranger's hand. His reactions were easily misunderstood and usually drew an equally defensive reaction by the unintentional offender. People who experienced Jonah's outbursts assumed that he was an imbecile, or at least mentally unstable.

While his anti-social condition might be considered a mental illness, he was certainly no idiot. His skills and knowledge of mathematics and physics were comparable to college-level professors. He had been one of several young people who were the subjects of a study of savants, people with high levels of skills in certain fields, but limited-to-no ability to function in what is considered by most a normal social environment.

Ian believed that his brother felt trapped, unable to escape the anti-social barriers in his brain. He also believed that Jonah was lonely, hungry for at least some minimal recognition, particularly from his father. But Ian was all too aware that the recognition his brother sought would never come. Ian felt trapped into being his brother's only window to the outside world and his only potential connection to their father. Knowing this made him want to concentrate all the more on projects that would help keep his mind off of his own problems and the slim hopes that his life would change for the better.

    As he sat concentrating on the timeline of events, he could hear murmurs from beyond the block wall that separated his and Jonah's workroom from their father's office, a room he had only seen once in his life. The room looked much like his and Jonah's workroom: several television screens and computer monitors, comfortable chairs, and earth-tone painted walls. He wished he could hear those conversations between his dad and whoever was on the other end of his phone. It might be fun to learn just what his father did for a living. Certainly, he must be making tons of money, buying and selling stocks, bonds, real estate, gold, and other financial vehicles. Ian knew a lot about finances, tracking markets, and identifying up-and-coming companies with great growth potential. He also was good at studying the character and capabilities of corporate executive officers and other board members. He seemed to know when a company was about to make big moves, either up or down. Ian believed that he could help his father by giving him advice on what to buy, what to hold, and what to sell, and, more importantly, when to do each, but it was apparent that his father didn't need his help. They lived on a compound that was worth millions, and he had hired help on the grounds to take care of their every need.

    Ian had a plan that he was about to execute when the FlashGamz fiasco happened. Through his telecommunications studies, he was learning about how to monitor phone lines, whether physical, hardwired lines, or whether they were nothing more than signals flying through the air. It didn't matter. Ian was going to tap into his father's lines, one way or another.

    As he sat in silence, alternately thinking about the flash drive fiasco and how to proceed to bug his father's line, Jonah walked into the room, a sandwich in one hand and a bottled water in the other. He walked straight to his workstation and sat. Without a word or any emotion, he used a remote to turn on one of the televisions in the room and flip the channel. The news at noon was just starting on Channel 8.

The lead story was coverage on the assassination of Senator Armand Vega. Jonah, with an emotionless stare, raised his hand and pointed a finger at the screen.

"One-two-one-five-one-five-one-one." Jonah's code came out in a quiet monotone, but Ian heard his brother and saw him point. He looked at the screen as the news anchor, an attractive blonde with a flawless TV voice, described the crime scene and updated the television audience on the latest developments. She then deferred to a reporter, Derek Manson, who was at the crime scene. Manson was a trim, light-skinned black man whose head filled the TV screen as he described the current lack of any police activity. He went on to say that it was a stark contrast to the multitude of law enforcement and crime scene technicians who dominated the scene the day before. The report changed to a film of that activity taken yesterday afternoon. It was indeed a vision of a beehive with dozens of people in motion. The camera view panned the scene. That is when Ian noticed the familiar surroundings: the trees, the expanse of parking, the red brick of the building's plain facade. It was the exact same building as the one in their video game. The Drug Enforcement Administration building in Savannah, Georgia. It was what Jonah was trying to tell him yesterday.

It was then that the realization hit him. His heart rate spiked, he began to sweat, and he involuntarily sucked in a deep breath. Could it be that he and Jonah killed the senator?

He looked at Jonah, who was taking a bite of his sandwich while he stood expressionless, staring at the television. He wondered if Jonah had the same fear, hidden behind his emotionless face.

Chapter 10

Three hours had passed since the initial interviews with the Andrews family. Each family member sat alone in different rooms at the FBI satellite office in Asheville. The father had called the family lawyer, who was allowed to speak with each family member separately. He was warned to not share information that would allow the family to coordinate their stories. Howard E. Spawn, who specialized in finance and real estate law, agreed, but he planned to bring another attorney from his firm whose specialty more closely aligned with the circumstances for which the Andrews family home was raided. He spent less than ten minutes with the father, then asked for clarification on why they were being held. Agent Pinetta deferred questions to Special Agent in Charge Megan Moore.

Megan spoke to Mr. Spawn in her usual manner and tone, which didn't appear to faze the attorney. She said that the FBI had evidence that directed them to the Andrews home. That evidence could be reviewed by him at the proper time if his clients were charged with a crime. She said that they were not under arrest but that she would expect their full cooperation with the FBI's investigation because it was in their best interest to do so.

When Spawn asked about the nature of the evidence, Megan only replied that it was electronic evidence retrieved from the crime scene in Savannah. Megan then told Spawn that they intended to question the son, Simon Andrews, and that he or his counterpart from his firm could be with Simon during that questioning. Spawn had only two requests. First, that both he and his partner be present during questioning. Second, after questioning, unless arrested, the family was free to go. Moore agreed.

* * *

Megan Moore passed the contact information for FlashGamz to

Peden, who made numerous attempts to contact anyone at the company. He quickly realized that the contact information was useless. Peden performed internet searches on the company and had multiple pages of hits, but when he called the contact numbers available on the websites, which were different from the number provided by Simon Andrews, the phone was not answered. It wasn't disconnected, it just rang until the caller received a message that the recipient had not set up their voice mail so they should try again later. Peden suspected that the "company phones" were burner phones and were most likely destroyed and discarded by now.

Peden put Lee Sparks on a flight to the FBI crime lab at Quantico, Virginia, where the remnants of the drone and its cargo were sent. He was directed to participate in the analysis of Simon Andrews' computer and game testing system. He had just arrived at Quantico and was en route to the FBI lab. Peden hoped that Sparks could extract something useful from the code in the kid's computer. But just like the information that led the FBI to the Andrews' house, he was concerned that the killer was ahead of them, purposely leaving red herrings, sending them on wild goose chases. He warned Sparks that he and the FBI technicians should do a deep dive and not jump to conclusions. Sparks replied that the FBI techs weren't going to be thrilled that they had a babysitter telling them how to do their jobs. Peden told him to man-up and not be intimidated, that he was to take the lead during the testing, and any reluctance by the FBI techs should be referred to Megan.

Peden and Megan agreed that, clearly, no one in the Andrews family had an ax to grind with Vega. On the contrary, Mr. and Mrs. Andrews agreed with Vega's position that it was time to reevaluate the War on Drugs, even though they were registered Republicans. The daughter didn't care about politics one way or another. She was scared to death and just wanted to go home. Her friend was released to the custody of her parents.

Initial reports from the crime lab technicians at the Andrews home were that they found absolutely nothing that would lead them to suspect that anyone in the Andrews family was a skilled assassin who could carry out a plan such as the Vega killing. The family, for all appearances, was a typical, hard-working, upper-middle-class family who enjoyed their lives. They had nice clothes, cars, electronic entertainment systems, closets filled with nice, relatively expensive clothing, and jet skis in the garage. They had a safe in the master bedroom that contained important papers and a modest amount of cash, appearing to be an emergency fund. Mr. Andrews did have a gun safe with multiple firearms, but they were hunting rifles, all unloaded. He had two pistols, a forty caliber Smith and Wesson and a Walther nine-millimeter. He volunteered that the forty was his and the nine was his wife's. The Smith and Wesson was loaded with the safety on. He stated that it was for home protection, though crime in the area was nearly non-existent.

The FBI's telecommunications team set up a two-way video conference between the FBI offices in Asheville and Savannah so that Megan and Peden could interview Simon Andrews directly without travelling to North Carolina. Megan asked Peden to conduct the interview so that the poor kid didn't get scared with Megan's all-too-serious attitude. Peden agreed that it was the best course.

Peden noticed that the Andrews' two lawyers, Spawn and the criminal lawyer Spawn had brought in, sat on either side of Simon: Spawn on his right, the other man on his left. There were no microphones visible to Peden in the massive video monitor. The camera was centered on Simon, his hair looking a bit unkempt. He looked tired and just a little nervous. Both lawyers wore expensive suits and ties, but each had loosened his tie, maybe hoping that their client would feel relaxed.

Peden spoke. "Simon, I'd like to start by saying that we appreciate you talking with us. I know this whole thing is unsettling, but we're looking for a killer, and time is of the essence, and we haven't been able to reach your representative at FlashGamz. When was the last time you spoke with Mr. David Watts?"

Simon looked at Spawn. The lawyer said, "Answer the questions unless one of us puts our hands on your arm, then we'll help to clarify for you what the agent is asking or direct you to not answer. Are you clear about that?"

Spawn looked back at the screen and said in a rather loud voice, "Agent Savage, you may proceed."

"Thank you, Mr. Spawn, but please call me Peden, or if you must, Mr. Savage. I'm not an agent. I'm a contracted private investigator."

"Very well, Mr. Savage."

Simon replied, "His name is David Walsh, not Watts. And I spoke to him exactly five minutes prior to the start of the test. It was 9:55 AM two days ago. He said that everyone was ready to start."

"When you say 'everyone,' were there other testers?"

Simon looked at Spawn, who nodded. "Yes. I'm pretty sure that there are about half a dozen testers for each beta test."

This surprised Peden. He made a note to talk with Lee Sparks about how beta testing is performed.

Peden. "During testing, prior to the flash drive catching fire, was there anything unusual, anything at all, with how the testing was proceeding?"

This time, Simon didn't look to Spawn before answering. He appeared to relax just a bit. "No, nothing. The test started, and I directed the drone to the point of attack." Simon looked down at the table and was holding his hands as if he were operating a game controller, possibly trying to recall the moments right after the start of the test. "When I hit the button to fire the weapon, at first, it didn't shoot, but then I noticed that the red light was still on."

"Red light?"

He looked up at the screen momentarily. "Yeah. In the instructions, it tells you that your drone is out of range until the light changes to green, so, like, your weapon isn't activated until the light is green." He looked back down at his hands, this time pressing imaginary buttons. "As soon as I saw the green light, I hit the button to take the shot and it worked. So, to answer your question, it worked just like it was supposed to work. As soon as the target went down, my monitor went blank, then the flash drive lit up like a little torch. Within seconds, it was over, except that my room was filled with smoke."

"When you say, 'It was over'; what do you mean?"

Simon looked at the screen like the answer was obvious, then said, "I mean, like, like I said, the screen went blank, and the drive lit up. I jumped up and shouted something, I don't remember what, and before I knew it, the drive was nothing but ashes and a few strands of wire hanging out of my computer. Dad was in my room within a few seconds. He knew something was wrong."

"What did you do with the burned-up flash drive?"

Simon shrugged his shoulders. "I guess Mom tossed it out. Either Mom or Dad."

Peden looked at Megan, who stood and left the room. He knew she was calling Alex Pinetta to see if they retrieved the remnants of the drive. If not, they needed to question the parents and see if that was possible.

"Okay, Simon. Have you ever contacted any of the other testers?"

Simon looked at Spawn, who nodded.

"I haven't actually talked with them. It's really against the rules to communicate with the other testers. I guess the company is worried that we might steal the program and start our own company with their gaming system, but that's kinda stupid. We're just kids, plus they have copyright protection. We'd get our asses sued." He looked at Spawn and said, "Sorry."

Spawn smiled. "No problem."

Peden asked, "How did you communicate with the others?"

"We texted back and forth mostly. I know that there were at least five others at four different locations. One kid, a girl, is from Ohio, near Sandusky, I think. Another's from Saratoga Springs, New York. One from Wytheville, Virginia.

Then there's two brothers, from near Savannah, Georgia."

"Besides cell phone numbers, do you have any other contact information for these kids?"

Peden realized that Simon might be concerned about being labeled a snitch if he gave up any information on the other testers. Their families might be subjected to the same treatment to which he and his family had been through. He looked down at the table again, hesitating. Peden waited him out, the silence making the young man nervous.

Finally, Simon said, "I have home and email addresses for all of the testers except the two brothers. All I know about them is that they're from somewhere near Savannah."

At that moment, Megan sat back down next to Peden. She whispered in Peden's ear that they would most likely be able to retrieve what was left of the drive. Simon's mom swept the ashes into a small trash bag along with the metal pieces pulled from the USB drive slot.

Peden asked, "Was there any damage to your computer?"

"No. It works like a champ. Even the printer, scanner, and everything else linked to the computer works great."

"Simon, Agent Pinetta is going to ask you for the information for the other testers. Please give it to him. Okay?"

With apparent reluctance, Simon nodded.

"Mr. Spawn, once we receive that information from Simon, the family is free to go." Peden looked at Megan, who nodded in approval. "Please advise them that we would appreciate it if they remained available for further questioning, if necessary."

"Mr. Savage, are my clients suspects?"

Peden looked at Megan, then used his hand to indicate that she should answer Spawn's question.

"Mr. Spawn, your clients are not suspects, but Simon is, at least, a witness to the assassination of a U.S. Senator. So please make sure your clients are available as Mr. Savage requested. And Simon?" The young man looked up. "Do not contact the other testers, at all. Is that understood?"

In a sheepish voice that was more tired than worried, Simon Andrews answered, "Yes, ma'am."

Chapter 11

The walls and ceiling were painted bright white. The stainless-steel workbenches and tables reflected the high lumen fluorescent lights. He guessed the temperature in the lab at around sixty-five degrees. The only thing cooler than the air temperature was the attitude of the nerds at the FBI Lab at the Marine Corps base at Quantico, Virginia. If Lee Sparks thought he might be trampling on some large FBI technicians' egos, he was right. They immediately turned colder when he introduced himself and told the two men, Liam and Parker, and two women, Sharda and Peta, that he was instructed to not only assist, but was to direct all the testing and analysis of the remnants of the drone and the weapon from the crime scene. They literally turned their backs on him after a brief stare of disbelief that quickly descended into outright dismissal.

Sparks immediately pulled out his cell phone and called Peden. He knew Megan Moore well and could have called her directly, but he worked for Peden and wanted to make sure that the appropriate lines of communication were not crossed. He had sarcastically warned Peden before he boarded the jet to Virginia that he might get a less-than-enthusiastic reception. It was exactly as he had anticipated.

Five minutes after his call to Peden, the lab's phone rang. The technician who answered the phone turned and called across the lab. "Liam, it's for you."

Liam was the lead technician, and he didn't look happy. He had to hold the phone away from his ear a few times even though the conversation was short and obviously to-the-point. Sparks recognized Megan's voice from twenty-five feet away as she read Liam the riot act. Megan had no problem crossing the chain of command, cutting out Liam's boss and giving him direct orders that mirrored what Lee had told them during his introduction. When the call ended, Liam turned to Sparks with a forced smile on his face.

"Mr. Sparks, it looks like you're part of the team." He turned to his lab-mates and said, "Everyone, please welcome Lee Sparks. He is a computer coder and investigator for Savage Investigative Consultants and is contracted by our bosses to assist in the Vega murder investigation."

He turned back to Lee with his tense smile still plastered on his face. Lee knew this must have been a blow to his ego and his sense of importance, but it wasn't his job to stroke Liam's pride and he wasn't about to let the opportunity pass to establish some ground rules. He didn't have a commanding voice and was more comfortable in front of a keyboard than he was talking to a group of people, regardless the size. But he was a gifted technician and analyst and he knew how people liked to be treated.

He looked at the four techies, then said, "Everyone, gather around. Let's talk."

The four stone-faced crime scene technicians stood in a semi-circle around Sparks, disdain emanating from every cell in their bodies.

He continued. "I understand that this is your lab and Liam is your lead. I'm not here to question his authority, your abilities, your techniques, or anything else. I'm here at the request of the Special Agent in Charge of this investigation because she knows my skill set. It isn't going to detract from what you do. But we are going to work together during the time I'm assigned here. And I mean *together*, not against each other. So, if you feel like I'm here to babysit, you're wrong. I'm here to work with you and hopefully add something positive to this case. If you think I'm going to question your work, you're right, as I expect you review each other's work. We have to get this right as fast as we can with no mistakes. If you think we can't work together, let me know now and I'll get you reassigned. But we don't have time for petty jealousy and office games here. We need to catch a killer, and we're the agency's best team to point the field agents in the right direction to accomplish that. If you have a beef with that, tell me now."

He looked from Liam to the others, one by one, then continued. "Good. Now, I need a brief from each of you, what you are working on and what you've found to date. Liam, you first."

Liam, a pale-looking guy, about thirty years old with short hair slicked back with some kind of hair gel, took just a second longer than necessary, once again trying to assert that he was the top dog in this lab, then he began. "Mr. Sparks, I …"

"Wait, call me Lee. We can talk about personal histories while we're working, but first names, please."

He motioned for Liam to continue.

"Lee, I am taking the lead on analysis of the drone body. We know it wasn't some cheap model purchased at a box store. The shell was made of a high-end, durable plastic of the type used in some military applications. It isn't like the bomb delivery vehicles used overseas, but it is similar to those used for covert surveillance. That might give us a break because there aren't too many models on the market with this level of sophistication. And there aren't too many people with the knowledge of drones of the level used by the military and how to purchase one."

Sparks' eyebrows rose. "How many commercial sources are there for hardware like this?"

"We're not done looking but probably less than a dozen."

Sparks nodded. "Excellent. Who's next?"

Liam nodded to Sharda, a slightly plump black woman who looked to Lee like she was still in high school and stood just under five feet tall. Sharda had dark skin, dark eyes, and soft lips. She wore dark, shiny lip gloss. Her hair was braided, frosted golden, and pulled back into a long pony tail.

"I'm the computer techie in the group. I'm working on the software and hardware related to the computer program used on the drone. The hard drive was badly damaged. The drone was equipped with an explosive charge designed to make the drone self-destruct. The explosives were enough to cause severe damage to the computer components, the drone body, and the weapon, but not enough for total destruction. We've recovered some information from the hard drive, some of which was used to identify the house that was raided earlier today. I think we'll be able to identify other IP addresses from the drive. It won't be easy with the amount of damage."

"I can help with that. What else?"

"The signal that was used to control the drone and the weapon, I think it had to be from a satellite link. Either that or the person at the controls had to be very close to the crime scene, and that doesn't seem likely. I mean, there's a lot of open space around the D.E.A. building. They could have been in a vehicle at the car dealership nearby, something like that, but that's a stretch."

"Can you figure out for certain if the source was routed through a satellite link? Wouldn't that have to be authorized by some government agency?"

Sharda shook her head. "Not really. There are tons of commercial satellites that a skilled hacker could get into. The satellite owner might not even know their equipment was hacked unless they have really good techs on the payroll. Even then, there might not be anything out of the ordinary that they would catch it."

"What about recovery of other IP addresses? Does that seem likely at this point?"

"Yes, I was just reviewing some of the retrieved code when you came in. I think I'm in an area of code that deciphered incoming signals and chose which signals to use for various functions on the drone. That includes navigation and weaponry."

"Great. When we finish here, you can show me exactly what it is you've found."

Lee looked back to Liam. "Who's next?"

The remaining two technicians gave their update, and Lee nodded to Liam for him to get his people back to work. Lee followed Sharda to her workstation. It looked like the control room for a nuclear power plant, except that there were multiple large monitors in a loose semi-circle facing her chair. She had some of the fluorescent lights turned off above her workstation. Lee knew that was so the glare from the lights didn't reflect off of her monitors.

She hit a few keys, and the monitors quickly came to life, displaying a string of code that was in plain white letters on the black screen. She used an electronic screen pointer to highlight a section of code. Lee immediately recognized the code as a point in the program where incoming signals were directed to other code within the program.

As Sharda continued to work through the code, Sparks counted four input signals. He asked, "Have you identified the source of the four signals?"

"Just two. The other two are going to take more work. The complete code couldn't be retrieved from the hard drive yet, because of the amount of damage, but we're still working on it. Peta is tasked with finding and cleaning up the code that isn't too far gone. I don't envy her that task. But she's good. If anyone can do it, she can. And there might actually be five input signals, but, again, the damage to the drive on the drone was severe. She said she might have something within the hour."

Sparks nodded his head. These folks were good, no doubt about it.

Sharda's face lit up as she looked over the code again. She shifted her attention to a second screen to her left and highlighted two sets of numbers separated by periods. Sparks immediately recognized the numbers as IP addresses. With this information, they could now track down the computers that were used to send signals to the drone. They had already used the initial IP address to identify the Andrews home. In a matter of minutes, they would have two more locations. Sharda turned to a third screen and pointed to two addresses, complete with the names of the owners of the homes and all the family members who were identified as residents.

Sparks said, "I need a printout of that, and can you

capture those in a .pdf and send it to my cell? Also, send a copy to Megan Moore."

Sharda nodded and went to work, her fingers flying over her keyboard.

He pulled out his cell phone and hit the speed dial number for Peden. Before Peden answered, he leaned over and said to Sharda, "Good work. Let me know when you have the other addresses."

Sharda nodded, her fingers still a blur as they did their magic.

"Peden, we've got something for you and Megan. We're sending you two more addresses that may have been involved in the drone attack. You should have the information in a few minutes."

"Great, Lee. How did you do it?"

"Wasn't me. They have some really skilled folks here."

"Are any of the addresses in Sandusky, Ohio; Saratoga Springs, New York; Wytheville, Virginia; or Savannah, Georgia?"

Sparks was shocked. How had Peden figured that out? After a moment's hesitation, he said, "One from Sandusky and one from Wytheville. We're still trying to find the other two."

"Good man, Lee. Simon Andrews said he and the other beta testers used text messages and e-mail to communicate, so that's how we got the physical locations. If you can find addresses for New York and Georgia, let me know right away. Give the lab folks kudos and encouragement. I'll let you know what we find on this end."

As Sparks turned back towards Sharda, Liam walked up and said, "We have the list of possible suppliers. It's pretty short, but they're spread all across the country. Some of them are big-time defense contractors. Others are relatively small."

"Great. Let's take a look."

He turned to Sharda. "Do you want me to update Liam on what you found, or do you want to do it?"

"You can. No office games, right?"

Lee smiled. "Right."

Chapter 12

After playing the video of Armand Vega's assassination over and over on his large forty-two-inch monitor, Ian Tabler had all but convinced himself that he or Jonah had fired the fatal shots from the drone that killed the senator and his intern. He paced back and forth in his bedroom, staring at the posters on the light blue walls, looking to his scientist heroes for answers. All they did was stare back with all-knowing, accusing eyes, as if shaming him for his actions.

He had solved many complex problems over the years. By nine, he had unraveled scientific riddles that intelligent men with advanced degrees couldn't solve. Rarely was he faced with an issue so daunting that he didn't know where to start or what logical steps to take to break down the problem into manageable segments and get to the root cause.

He stopped in his tracks and looked up at the classic poster of Albert Einstein, throwing his arms out to his side as he asked, "So, Mr. Einstein, what am I supposed to do now?" He looked around the room, seeing if some imaginary spy was listening in on his conversation with arguably the greatest physicists of all time. "I'm not sure I did anything wrong. I mean, there were at least four other testers besides Jonah and me. What are the odds that one of us ..." His voice trailed off, and his eyes fell to the floor. He put his hands in his back pants pockets and shook his head.

The image played in his head again. He saw the animated image of the group of people on the screen rapidly getting larger as the drone closed the distance. The red light was still lit on the screen's control console. The light turned green. His concentration was so intense that he hadn't heard or seen Jonah's actions. That wasn't unusual during beta tests. They worked side-by-side but independently, neither knowing how successful the other was until the testing was complete.

Normally, they received a report from their contact at FlashGamz, but this time, with the failure of the drive and the ensuing chaos, the complete lack of contact was worrisome. It wasn't like they lost money on the test. That payment had been deposited, but any future payouts from the test's success were in jeopardy.

He wondered, could people at FlashGamz be responsible for the senator's death? Had they planned the whole thing, using Ian, Jonah, and the other testers as their paid assassins? Was the idea that crazy? He didn't have much contact with the world beyond the walls of their father's property. Since their mother's disappearance ten years before, their father and members of the support staff were the only human contact either boy had, aside from the covert text messages between the testers. High-paid professors were brought in to tutor the boys, continuing their formal education, but that was becoming laughable. Most tutors left telling their father that there was no more that they could teach the boys. They were beyond traditional "learning" and were now fully engaged in real-life scientific analysis.

One of the professors told Nicholas Tabler, "You need to get Ian to a university, not just for his benefit, but for the benefit of others. He has gifts that must be utilized for the development of whatever field he decides is his greatest interest." Ian heard the exchange between his father and the professor and immediately thought of Jonah. They hadn't even considered that Jonah, despite his social skills deficit that made others overlook his talents, was also brilliant beyond his years.

Ian's limited human contact wasn't very stimulating to a boy with an IQ higher than many scientists. But he did get the local, national, and world news on his computer. It was astounding what pain and agony humans inflicted on each other every day. Was it possible that someone at FlashGamz was the killer and the beta testers were their executioners? Ian was convinced that, however remote, yes, it was possible.

He stepped backwards and fell onto his bed, landing with his feet hanging over the edge. Now staring at the ceiling instead of the floor, his mind took off on another involuntary replay of the game. It was like the slow drip of a leaky faucet, and nothing would stop the constant, annoying sound.

As he rested on the bed, he thought of the only human contact that he enjoyed. The rules for beta testing specific games included that testers could not communicate with other beta testers associated with that game. But Ian received an instant message from another tester. It was a young girl from Sandusky, Ohio. She said her name was Carlita. She wouldn't give Ian her last name, but they struck up a dialogue of sorts. At first, it was all about game testing and their experience with various companies. Then they moved on to more personal topics. Ian liked texting back and forth with Carlita and hoped that they wouldn't end because of the problems with this last test. He hadn't heard from her in two days. Maybe she had moved on.

He noticed that his heart was pounding in his chest as he thought about the girl. His face broke into a nervous smile just with the thought of her. He'd never even seen a picture of her, but he knew he liked her. Maybe she was waiting for him to make the next move. He closed his eyes and swore to himself that he would … soon.

Ian heard the slow, methodical footsteps of his younger brother coming down the hall. It was common for Jonah to walk into Ian's room without knocking. Since he had done it all his life, it never before bothered Ian. Everything he had was also Jonah's. Only recently had Ian felt a need for at least some privacy and showed reluctance to allow Jonah the freedom to come right into his room. Now, Ian was having a personal tug-of-war about whether to ask Jonah to knock before entering. He was also uncertain regarding what to tell his father of the assassination. Jonah being in his room was a distraction. He didn't believe that he could have this conversation with his brother, thinking that Jonah wasn't emotionally equipped to handle the real possibility of what they might have done.

Surprisingly, there was a quiet knock on the door. That had never happened before. He was so shocked at the knock that it took him a few seconds to react.

"Come on in."

The door opened slowly, just a few inches. Ian, still lying on the bed, rolled his head towards the door and said again, "Hey, brother, come in."

Jonah moved the door so slowly that it creaked. He finally stepped into Ian's room and closed the door behind him. Ian looked at his sibling from his prone position as Jonah moved deeper into Ian's bedroom. As always, Jonah wore no emotion, walking towards Ian's television. He picked up the remote and turned it on, staring at the blank screen until Channel 8 appeared. Breaking news was in progress as a young female reporter, standing at the foot of a street that sloped upward into a neighborhood, described the scene that occurred the previous afternoon. As she spoke, the image on the screen showed armed men in SWAT gear with the letters FBI across their backs and chests, standing at the foot of a driveway to a home that couldn't be seen from the camera's vantage point. In a monotone, Jonah rattled off a series of numbers so fast that Ian had to sit up and pay attention.

"What did you say, brother?"

"199131514."

It took Ian a few seconds to realize that Jonah had spelled out "Simon." His puzzled look triggered Jonah to say the numbers again. This time Ian realized that he was talking about one of the other testers: Simon Anderson.

"The FBI raided Simon's house? Oh no. We have to tell Dad."

"1415!"

Jonah's code for 'No' came out with force and emotion. Ian stared at his brother. He'd never seen or heard anything like it from Jonah before in his entire life. He was so startled that he, at first, didn't know what to say.

"Why not? Simon might be charged with a crime that we committed."

In code, Jonah repeated 'No' multiple times, again with emotion, but the outburst was subsiding. Finally, he added, in code, "Dad is dangerous."

Ian looked at Jonah in disbelief. "Dangerous? What do you mean?"

The next numbers spelled out, "Trust me."

* * *

Ian was puzzled by Jonah's obvious fear of their father. He knew Nicholas Tabler could be strict and had a short temper with his staff at times, but he felt no reason to be afraid to tell his father anything. At least, anything that a normal fifteen-year-old would tell his parents. But, as Ian knew, he and Jonah were anything but normal teens.

Half an hour after Jonah left his room and he watched more of the coverage of the raid on Simon Andrews' house, he struggled mightily with the need to get a handle on what had happened with the beta test. He went down to the basement lab, a room next to their computer test office, and prepared to analyze the burnt remnants of the FlashGamz flash drive. His lab was equipped with some elaborate equipment and chemicals on par with many professional labs, and he had some computer research that he'd performed earlier. He went to work.

He separated the burned ashes into five separate samples. Using a razor, he scooped four of the samples into small test tubes, then stored the samples in a lockable cabinet. He further divided the remaining remnants with a razor into six. The samples were so small that he could barely see them. Placing one sample between a set of microscope slides, he placed the sample into a spectrometer. On a monitor attached to the spectrometer, he viewed the colorful display of the light spectrum. A computer program ran in the background and determined the elements present in the sample. He compared the sample to one that he had run earlier in the day of a new, identical flash drive that he purposely crushed and burned. The samples were identical, except for two small slivers of light on the screen from the FlashGamz drive. Carbon disulfide. It was barely visible on the screen, but Ian had read that it was a common fire accelerant used by arsonists. In this case, only a small amount would be needed to completely destroy the flash drive. The only other requirement was an ignition source. That was the easy part. A signal from a program at a predetermined point could set off a tiny spark in the drive and poof.

Now all he had to do was determine why.

He was still tempted to talk with his father and explain what he had found, but Jonah's reaction to his plan was enough to hold him back. He had to know why Jonah was adamant about keeping this between the two of them. Jonah was so fearful that he had an unprecedented emotional response to just the suggestion of going to their father. That was a good enough reason for him to at least wait.

The other question was, were they next to be raided by the FBI? If Simon Andrews had been raided, the odds were pretty good that they were in the FBI's sights.

Chapter 13

President Alton Woodburn paced across the rug bearing the presidential seal in the open space of the oval office, jaw clenched, wringing his hands together, his thoughts colliding with one another. His personal doctor had visited earlier, monitoring his vital signs. When his blood pressure registered an exceptionally high reading, Doctor Prescott's eyebrows shot up in alarm. He tried to recover so as to not worry his patient and add to his already frazzled state, but Woodburn had caught the change in the doctor's face.

"That bad, huh?"

Prescott kept his voice as calm and even as possible. "Well, Mr. President, it is elevated. We'll monitor it more closely over the next few days so that it doesn't get out of hand."

Woodburn saw right through the doctor's attempts to remain calm. He knew he had to get his anxiety under control – and fast.

Now alone, Woodburn rubbed his hands over his face as he moved in deliberate steps from one side of the office to the other, occasionally stopping in front of the massive, bullet-proof window looking out over the White House lawn. *I can't continue to live like this. What the hell is that psycho going to do next? Who else is he going kill?*

But who could he talk to about ending his personal nightmare? He believed that many of the original members of their "import/export business" felt the same as he did, but they were all in the same boat; they loathed Tate but feared him even more. And for good reason. He was certifiably insane, and, from time to time, he made sure that the others knew it.

Soon after he took control of their business, one of their former associates decided he didn't want to play by Tate's rules. That was a big mistake. He happened to be the soldier who had been on call the night Sergeant Tate was called in on his off-duty time to prepare the body of a fellow soldier, supposedly an Army Ranger, for burial. Suffering from a major hangover, he had skipped out on his responsibility, so Tate was next on the call list. Instead of the remains of a fellow soldier, the casket contained a large shipment of Afghan heroin. After watching the operation for a few weeks, Tate made his move to take over.

Soon after the takeover, he made demands on the six original members of the operation. The downside was more work, longer hours spent after normal military duties. The upside was more money. Lots more money. All six men went along with the plan, not that they had much choice. Tate had threatened to go to Colonel Woodburn's boss with evidence of the illegal business. And Tate had a mountain of evidence, including pictures and tape recordings of all the men actively participating in the procurement and delivery of the illegal drugs. That meant a lot of time in Fort Leavenworth military prison for everyone involved. There was no way out, and if everyone continued to play by Tate's rules, everyone continued to stockpile cash.

But the one guy who had blown his assignment that had let Tate in the door decided he wasn't going to play along. He told Tate he didn't have the balls to go over Woodburn's head.

On one hand, he was right. Tate didn't report the operation. On the other hand, he was dead wrong. Instead of going over Woodburn's head, he killed the reluctant soldier in a painful, heinous way. Then he cut off and mailed the soldier's fingers, one to each of the other members of the team, with a note reminding them who was in charge. He admonished them to never discuss leaving the group again, not with him and not with each other. From that moment on, their silence had been absolute.

Woodburn, still burning a path across the presidential seal, fretting over the recent murder of Senator Vega, wondered if he was next. He'd kept quiet all these years. At best, he was liable for a lifetime in prison. Or worse, he could be killed, just like Vega. And he believed Tate would go after his family.

Was Tate so insane that he believed he could assassinate a sitting president? Woodburn believed he was. He couldn't live with the pressure any longer. He had to do something.

He walked to the massive presidential desk, opened the center desk drawer, pulled out his personal cell phone, and prepared to call the CIA's Deputy Director for Afghan Affairs, Ernest Porter. He stopped before he hit the first digit. Had Tate been able to bug his personal cell phone? Had he bugged the oval office? He shook his head. That's not possible. The office was regularly swept for listening devices by the Secret Service using the best equipment available.

But Tate seemed to have a sixth sense and called him at the most inopportune times, usually with information that only a handful of people knew, or should have known.

He placed the phone back in the drawer and closed it. That was it. He had to schedule a clandestine meeting with Porter, but who could he use to make the arrangements? He smiled when the idea came to him.

He scribbled out a short note on a plain sheet of paper and placed his initials at the bottom of the page, folded the paper then tucked it into a business-sized envelope and sealed it. He left the exterior of the envelope blank, choosing to give verbal instructions for delivery.

He sent for one of the many interns working in the White House and gave the twenty-something man instructions to deliver the envelope to Ernest Porter, Deputy Director of the CIA for Afghan Affairs, at Langley. He told the kid that he was not to talk to anyone about where he was going or his instructions, except security personnel at CIA headquarters. He stressed that secrecy was of the utmost importance and that violating that directive could result in, at a minimum, his dismissal from his duties at the White House.

The poor kid turned white as a sheet, nodded that he understood, then left for his most important errand. He probably believed that he had top-secret information on some clandestine operation.

Woodburn took a deep breath and plopped down into the cushy seat behind his desk. His mind wouldn't stop churning out thoughts of doom. What if Tate found out? What if he knows that poor kid has the note and intercepts him before he can deliver it? Would he kill an unsuspecting college kid just for being the randomly selected messenger? Tate had already proven the answer to that question was "yes."

The trip from the White House to Langley this time of day should take the intern less than half an hour. The pressure cooker of angst waiting for Porter's response was massive. All the more reason to get this job done sooner rather than later.

* * *

Ernest Porter was in his office alone when he received the plain white envelope. He had received a call from security that a "kid" had delivered it and claimed that the envelope was from the President of the United States. He said the poor kid looked scared to death.

Porter laid the envelope on his desk and stared at it for several moments, leaning back in his chair, afraid of what the note might say. Would Woodburn be so stupid to put anything incriminating in writing? They'd known each other for nearly thirty years, stretching back to their Army years when they started a small side business to make some extra money. Their relationship had been close until that fateful day when a man named Nevin Tate strode into their lives.

Porter rubbed his hand over his face, stopping at his chin, feeling the grayish stubble already evident before lunchtime. *This used to be fun. All the money in the world isn't worth the stress.*

He looked back down at the envelope. It was still there, plain and white, daring him to open it. And it wasn't going away. He couldn't ignore it any longer, even though he knew it didn't have anything to do with his job at Langley. He picked it up and held it up towards the fluorescent lights that bathed his office in bright light, trying to read its contents. *What the hell.*

Might as well get it over with.

He opened his desk drawer and took out the gold-plated letter opener, slicing the top of the envelope. He removed the single sheet of paper and unfolded it, reading the short, handwritten note.

He realized that he'd been holding his breath as he exhaled, long and slow. The note was short and to the point.

Meet me for dinner tonight at the White House. Just you and me. No others. Do not call to confirm. We'll meet in a safe room. See you then.

* * *

Porter was whisked through the White House's security checkpoint. The guard was instructed by the president to leave the visit off of the official log, and he did as he was told. The CIA man met Woodburn in the west wing, and they proceeded to a small room with a table that would accommodate only four people, or in this case, two people and dinner. As he approached the tiny meeting room, he caught the aroma of steak, cooked to perfection. When he turned the corner, he saw the spread of food. It was enough for six, but there were only two place settings.

The room was one of many inside the west wing of the White House used for private meetings. It had minimal creature comforts. The walls were adorned with pictures of military men from the Revolutionary War. The paint on the walls was a very light yellow. The trim a high gloss gold.

The men shook hands. "Ed, thanks for coming and thanks for keeping this under wraps. I hope I got your drink right."

Ed Porter looked at his old friend, who seemed to have aged ten years since the last time they'd spoken, with eyes that were sunken and bags that bulged. He looked at the president and decided that they better get right to the point of the meeting.

"Good to see you, Al, but why the secrecy?"

The president's eyes widened, and he moved quickly to close the door. Porter was surprised by the move, and he immediately knew the reason for the clandestine nature of their meeting. Edward Porter was a smart man and tough as they come. He held one of the highest offices in the CIA, and he had to deal with some nearly impossible issues of national security, but this topic scared him more than any other.

When Woodburn didn't immediately respond, Porter said, "Please tell me this doesn't have to do with Tate."

Woodburn looked up and nodded his head ever so slightly. Then he motioned for Porter to take a seat.

"Ed, you know that Tate is behind Vega's murder. I don't know if he did it or he just ordered it, but ..."

"How can you be sure?"

"He called me." He paused, then said, "Listen, let's grab some of this great steak and a drink, then we can talk."

Porter didn't want to admit that he'd lost his appetite, so he sat, took a long drink of an expensive whisky on the rocks, and filled his plate. He forced himself to take a few bites, then urged Woodburn to start talking.

Woodburn had taken just a few bites himself when he looked up at Porter. "I know he did it. Without saying it, he pretty much told me that he did, and that he wanted me to get the senate to select his replacement on the Senate Finance Committee. He wants that guy from Georgia, Pickett, to take the chair. Hell, he hasn't even been elected yet. How the hell am I going to convince the senate to put a nub at the chair." Holding his knife and fork so tight that his knuckles were turning white, he spoke like a defeated boxer, "I can't take it anymore, Ed. We've got to do something. He was nuts years ago; now, he's gone completely over the edge."

Porter looked around the room as if he might find listening devices in plain sight recording their meeting. He took a deep breath and asked, "Al, what are you saying?"

"Do you know anyone who can take care of our problem?"

Porter's eyes widened in shock. Was the president of the United States asking him if he knew an assassin who could take out Tate? The thought had crossed his mind as well, but actually talking about it was another matter. The fact that they were even discussing it placed them both in extreme danger. The man they were talking about had already killed one of their partners and threatened to kill them if they did the very thing that they were now doing.

Porter took a deep breath. Since they'd come this far, there was no turning back.

"Yeah, I know a guy."

"Should we tell the others?"

Again, Porter had a shock of fear course through his body.

"Absolutely not." He paused for a moment, then said, "They can thank us afterwards."

Chapter 14

Peden Savage received information on the two known locations from Lee Sparks just after dinner. Between the information from Simon Andrews and the FBI technicians at Quantico, they located the two remaining beta test locations used by FlashGamz and did a data dump of personal information on all members of the families. Sparks warned his boss in advance that there was nothing of particular interest in the data, but he encouraged Peden to take a closer, more detailed look.

Peden did exactly what his technical guru recommended and poured over the paper version of the lives of the families living in Sandusky, Ohio, and Wytheville, Virginia. In line with what Lee Sparks had told him in advance, what he found was unremarkable, except that the kids testing these video games were brilliant.

The Galindo family from Sandusky, was second- and third-generation natural-born citizens of Mexican descent. The youngest members of the family were in grade school; the eldest, the matriarch herself a naturalized citizen, was in her early eighties. All working-age members of the relatively large family were employed and had stable employment histories. None of the Galindo clan appeared to have any axes to grind with anyone, much less a senator from Georgia.

The one family member who stuck out from the rest was a fourteen-year-old girl who was financially ahead of the game. She had amassed nearly one hundred thousand dollars in savings and investments. The deposits were in ten-thousand-dollar increments. The source of the income – FlashGamz and other video game companies.

Carlita Galindo, a young prodigy with exceptional talents – a member of the debate team, chess club, math club, and toastmasters club – was identified by school counselors as a candidate for early college classes and accelerated degree programs. She had been featured in several local newspapers, including the *Sandusky Register*, the *Toledo Blade*, and the *Cleveland Plain Dealer*. The highlight of the articles? Her ability to conquer video games.

Peden read the most recent article in the *Sandusky Register* featuring Miss Galindo, where numerous companies sought to employ her exclusively to test video games and other electronic devices. But she wanted to keep her options open and, with the help of her guidance counselor, hired an agent so that she could contract with different companies on a short-term basis. According to the article, that led her to FlashGamz, a relatively new company with a handful of new, action-adventure games. She was credited with testing several games that were rising in popularity among gamers across the country and were starting to make inroads into markets around the globe.

Peden made a note of her family's address and phone number and her parents' names. He also made several notes about the article, including the journalist credited with the story, her e-mail address, and the *Register's* main phone number.

Peden moved on to Ricky Lee Lyle, a sixteen-year-old from Wytheville, Virginia. An internet search of the Lyle family revealed that they were long-time residents of Wytheville. The first member of the Lyle family to settle in Wytheville was Jeb Lyle, back in June of 1839. Jeb was a tradesman and helped rebuild the town after a disastrous fire that destroyed much of the town earlier that year. He loved the location and bought land on what was then the outskirts of town. He met and married Isabella Wythe, a descendent of the town's namesake, George Wythe.

While Ricky Lee Lyle had a great story to tell about his ancestry, he didn't receive any wealth from his ancestors. The Lyle family of present were all hard-working folks. Ricky had two brothers, both of whom were tradesmen like their many greats-grandfather Jeb. They made a good living at a young age, but neither was wealthy.

Ricky Lee did have a substantial savings and investment account, but, like his brothers, he helped support their mother. Ricky's father had passed away from lung cancer a decade ago.

Ricky had been testing for FlashGamz for a short time but had accumulated just over twenty-five thousand dollars. He was helping his mother pay off some of the debt from his father's battle with cancer. If the family continued their current rate of payments, that debt would be paid off within a year.

Ricky did have a social media account and posted regularly, responding to comments by his friends and posting about the success, or failure, of his game testing. He recently had a post about the new game testing that went terribly wrong. He described the game and how he thought it was going to be a hit if the company would fix the program. He noted the failure of the flash drive that he'd received from the company and the fact that he couldn't reach his representative. But he assured his friends that once contact was reestablished, the testing would be completed, and he guaranteed that people were going to love the game.

The contact information for the other testers, one from Saratoga Springs, New York, the others from Savannah, Georgia, was waiting for him in his e-mail inbox. He opened his email account and signed in. Among the twenty-five unopened emails, he found the one from Lee Sparks and double-clicked. Two attachments, one for each location, were to the right of the email. He double-clicked the one titled SaratogaSprings.pdf, and an eight-page file opened.

He was reading the first lines of the report when his cell phone chirped. The display showed a picture of his eldest daughter, Kaitlin. He smiled, but it was a smile not of joy but of expectation that his daughter was calling at the behest of her mother. He knew that she wouldn't call on her own because she hated her father. This was only the second time that she'd called him in nearly a year. The first call was not pleasant, and Peden expected this call to be more of the same.

He swiped across the screen. "Hello, sweetie. How are

you?"

"Not good, Dad. Mom says that you won't cover my charges for school. How am I supposed to live on campus without money?"

"I didn't know that there was a casino on campus. And I didn't realize that attending two-hundred-dollar-per-ticket concerts was part of your studies. Or ..."

"Dad, what am I supposed to do, stay locked away in my dorm room while I'm not in class?"

"No, sweetie. You're supposed to use the money for reasonable expenses related to your studies, and not blow your budget. I agreed to pay ..."

"Dad. This is stressful. I have to relax somehow."

"How about getting a part-time job. That way you can relieve stress and help pay for your concerts and gambling and credit card ..."

"Can't you just pay off my credit card so I can pay for some of my expenses? I have stuff coming due, and I don't have the money to pay for them."

"Kaitlin, you put yourself in this situation. You figure out how to get back on track. When you do that, then call me back. Right now, you're out of control. I don't have ..."

"God, Dad. Mom said you would be a jerk, and she was right. Just go to hell."

"Sweetie ..."

Silence. His daughter had disconnected the call. After a few moments of reflection, Peden decided that he'd done and said the right things. Both of his daughters were out of control, spending money as if the supply was unlimited. His wife, Susan, wasn't helping. In fact, she was encouraging their daughters to ignore their father's warnings and do what they pleased. Peden was going to put a stop to it. At some point, Kaitlin and Kristi would come around and see how destructive their mother's advice was. At least, that was his hope.

But now, he had bigger priorities: find Armand Vega's murderer. He looked back to the computer screen and read through the data on a family from Saratoga Springs. The Pirelli family had moved just north of the capitol region of New York State just eighteen months earlier. They had been living in Groton, Connecticut, where Anthony Pirelli had worked in the Naval Shipyard building submarines. He worked on the engine compartment section of the ship. Knolls Atomic Power Laboratory offered him a job at a little-known site in West Milton, New York, near Saratoga Springs. He jumped at the offer, hoping to get his prodigy son a better opportunity at honing his mathematics and physics skills. The son, Anthony Pirelli, Jr., had few friends and, based on the data in the file from Lee, had a number of issues with bullies at his school. The thirteen-year-old boy was now home-schooled and had a game-by-game contract with FlashGamz and two other companies.

Peden was just getting to the part about the failed test when his cell phone chirped. At first, he ignored it, and the ring tone went silent. Maybe the caller would get the message that he was busy. But moments later, the phone chirped again. He looked at the screen: his ex-wife Susan.

Geez! Here we go.

He swiped the screen and held the phone to his ear. "Yes, Susan."

"I just got a call from your daughter, and ..."

"*Our* daughter. And it's funny because, if you mean Kaitlin, I just got off the phone with her."

Susan's tone was already at an angry pitch. "Don't cut me off, Peden. Your daughter called you for help, hoping that you would listen to reason. She said she tried to explain why she needed more money, but you wouldn't let her finish. Why would you do that to your daughter?"

"Again, Susan: she is *our* daughter. I already explained to you and to her and her sister that the money I provide is for school expenses. We set a limit. Both girls have far exceeded ..."

"They need the money, Peden." Her voice was reaching a level that made it uncomfortable to hold the phone to his ear. "They each have credit cards that are maxed out because you don't send them enough money to survive while at school. What are they supposed to do?"

"They could start by getting jobs and stop partying every night."

"Get jobs? They can hardly keep up with their school work. How can they get jobs? Any job they get wouldn't pay peanuts, so how is that supposed to help?"

"For starters, they wouldn't have time to go out partying all the time." Peden paused to calm himself and try to tone down the rhetoric. When he spoke again, it was in a quiet tone. "Look, we've been over this at least a dozen times. I'm not paying anything beyond genuine school expenses. When they, and you, get that concept, then we can have a discussion about their expenses. Until then, they need to figure out how they're paying for this full-time party that they've been having."

There was silence on the line. Peden hoped that he was finally getting through to his ex-wife. But he was being overly optimistic.

When she spoke, it was short and filled with venom.

"Peden, you're an ass."

The phone disconnected.

"That went well."

"What went well?"

Megan Moore's voice startled him. Sometime during the call with his ex-wife, she had walked into his office.

"Nothing." He rubbed his hands through his hair. "We have information on the kids from Sandusky, Wytheville, and Saratoga Springs. We have the names of the kids from Savannah, but we haven't got any data on them yet. So far, it looks similar to our boy from North Carolina: exceptionally smart kids, all hired by FlashGamz, all with a particular skill in testing and playing video games. But none of them, or their families, seem to have a particular beef with the government. On the contrary, they seem pretty darn normal, apart from being brilliant."

Megan took a seat in front of Peden's desk. She said,

"Let's review the data together. Maybe something will pop. By the way, when do we expect to get the data on the two kids from Savannah? They're local. Maybe we could just pay them a visit."

"We should be getting something from Lee anytime now. That's a good idea about a visit. It'll break up the monotony."

"How much money are you sending your girls, Pedee?"

Peden just shook his head.

Chapter 15

Harold H. Herald, a dayshift Georgia Ports Authority superintendent, checked the manifest as semi-truck-sized containers were latched and lifted from the container ship *CMA CGM J. Adams* and placed in the staging area where super-duty lift-trucks and gantry cranes moved them to their designated locations. Everyone had their protective gear on, including hardhats, work gloves, and sunglasses that were rated for UVA/UVB sunlight protection as well as high-velocity impact protection. As usual, the late morning sun caused reflective glare off objects around the shipyard. The team of longshoremen didn't complain. They were paid exceptionally well and the work, for the most part, was not physically taxing, with specialized machines doing most of the heavy work.

The *J. Adams* was registered to Malta, but that hardly mattered to anyone besides the ship's owners. The tiny island country in the Mediterranean Sea just south of the Italian island of Sicily registered many cargo ships at lower rates than most countries in the world. But that fact was unknown to Harold H. Herald and his crew. He had other more pressing issues on his mind.

With a radio in one hand and paperwork on the desk in front of him, he stood in one of the control rooms at the Port of Savannah's Miles and Taylor Plantation site, giving orders to three crane operators, one in the fore of the ship, one amidships, and one aft, as they quickly and efficiently removed the cargo containers from the ship. They had a deadline to meet. Trucks were already lined up, ready to have their assigned container strapped and bolted to the flatbed trailer and shipped to areas around the southeast. The evening crew of Longshoreman expected that all would be ready when they came in to reload the ship with partially filled containers headed for customers overseas. It was unfortunate, Herald, or

HC, short for H-cubed, as his friends and crew called him, that the containers coming in were pack to capacity with foreign goods, while those going out were at a fraction of their available load capacity. But that was the reality of today's global economy.

A voice came in over his radio. "Hey, HC, I'm moving container 879824525 to staging block Gibbons 221W."

"Roger that, Jimmy."

Herald smiled at the report. Of the nearly two hundred containers on the ship, that was the one of most interest to him and his partner, Nevin Tate. The Gibbons Drive staging area was in the center of the Miles and Taylor Plantation site, so having this particular container in that location meant that it would blend in with the other red, green, white, blue, and yellow containers: inconspicuous to anyone.

The official cargo was listed as Hot Wheels cars, tracks, Play-Doh, and other toys made in China. The United States imported tons of toys headed for big box stores. Federal inspectors rarely gave containers such as this a second glance. HC was counting on that. He was busy making notations in his manifest for the next communication from one of his crane operators when his cell phone chirped. He finished the notation and looked at his phone.

Nevin Tate.

Herald rolled his eyes. The guy called at the most inopportune times. He hesitated, thinking that maybe he would let the call go to voicemail, but a chill went down his spine as his thoughts traveled back in time to when he'd received the finger of a former Army comrade and business partner in the mail, convincing him that he should answer.

"Hey, Tate, this isn't a good time. I'm right in the middle ..."

"Make the time, Herald. Has our package arrived?"

"Yeah, and it is right on schedule for pickup. No need to worry, but I'm busy as ..."

"It's my job to worry. Without me, you clowns would all be breaking big rocks into little ones. You just do your job and call me immediately if you run into any bumps along the way."

"Got it. I've really got to go."

"Hold on, Herald. I have a change in plans that you need to account for. We ..."

HC's radio crackled with one of his crew relaying information on the next box coming off the ship. Herald responded that he received the message. That exchange was quickly followed by one of the other crane operators on the radio.

Herald barked into his cell, "Tate, I can't talk right now. Gotta go." He disconnected the call and turned his full attention back to the ship's unloading. He couldn't afford to lose track of the cargo. All hell would break loose if containers were misplaced. He figured that Tate wouldn't appreciate being cut off, but he didn't have time to worry about that right now. He had a job to do. Later that evening, when the majority of the crew was gone, he had more work to do on container 879824525. Several customers would be there to deliver their cash payments and take their products for distribution on the streets across the United States.

This one shipment of Afghan heroin was worth more than ten million dollars. HC smiled because his cut was well over a million.

Not bad for a few hours work.

* * *

Nevin Tate heard the phone go silent before he had the chance to tell HC that there was a small change of plans. Tate had a new customer lined up and planned to bring him to the terminal later that evening after all the regular customers were gone. He was going to direct HC to hold back several kilos of product to demonstrate its purity and assure him that they could deal in whatever quantities the new man needed. He would wait another hour and call HC back and explain the change. He also planned to remind the superintendent of who called the shots and to never hang up on him again.

Nevin Tate had concerns about his organization. He had

just four main players, all of them from the early days before Tate took over. Three of the four were key players in the operation, but Alton Woodburn was useless, except for maintaining the façade of a strong stance on the War on Drugs. He knew that Woodburn had to keep the pressure on Congress to supply funding for the various law enforcement agencies and prison systems to let the American people know that fighting the opioid crisis was paramount. It was the best way to keep the price of their product high. Once the namby-pamby liberals got their way to legalize and decriminalize street drugs, the black market would crash, right along with any prospects of making millions in the heroin trade in the future.

His key man was Harold H. Herald. He was the main man in the shipyard. He kept the product moving from the ship to the market in the least amount of time possible. And he was smooth under pressure.

The third man was the CIA Deputy Director for Afghan Affairs, Ernest Porter. His role was to keep the CIA out of their business and run interference for the group if suspicions of their operation surfaced within the walls at Langley. So far, Porter had proven his worth when an agent in Afghanistan stumbled upon a group loading the heroin into boxes headed for the shipping port. Porter was able to redirect his focus to another issue. By the time the agent reported what he'd found to his agent in charge, the method and route for loading the ship were changed, leading the agent to believe it was a one-time deal.

The fourth member of the team was a man named Kardaar Nawabi. He had been an American Army soldier who changed his name and life in order to take control of the procurement end of the operation. Nawabi had been a field agent fifteen years prior, but it became clear to Tate that they needed a man on the ground in Afghanistan to coordinate purchases and shipment details. He claimed to be a Muslim. In reality, he wasn't affiliated with any organized religion. He was HC's counterpart in Afghanistan and the two communicated frequently on shipping details.

A ringtone sounded from Tate's middle desk drawer. He opened the drawer and eyed four different phones before picking up the one with a lighted screen. He viewed the incoming number and smiled, then swiped across the screen. "Mr. Delgato. How are you this morning?"

"Mr. Tate. Just checking to make sure that we're still on for this evening."

"Yes, sir. I will meet you just as we planned and take you to the location. As discussed, we'll meet with one of my men, and you can test the product right from the package. If you like what you see, we'll work out the details for future business."

"Sounds good, Mr. Tate. I and one of my men will meet you as previously discussed. As I'm sure you feel the same way I do, I don't like surprises, so if anything changes between now and our meeting time, please call me in advance."

"I assure you, Mr. Delgato, that you and I are of the same opinion regarding surprises. There will be none. You should plan to increase your business reach with this new arrangement. It will be mutually beneficial, I guarantee it."

Tate could hear the man on the other end of the phone exhale slowly, trying to hide the fact that he was anxious about their meeting. Tate loved these meetings. His adrenaline spiked with each transaction. He loved counting the money made on each deal, which continued to ramp up and up, without expanding the organization. Life was good.

Tate had to make one more call. He hadn't touched base with Ernest Porter in a few weeks. He liked to call his team out of the blue, mainly to keep them off guard and to remind them of who ran the show. Porter was easy. He kept up his end of the bargain and did whatever Tate wanted him to do: a good soldier even with his rise to upper management at the CIA. Tate also knew that Porter and President Woodburn were good friends, so he got the double satisfaction of knowing that Porter would tell Woodburn about his call. Even with a Secret Service detail, Woodburn was scared to death that Tate was going to kill him. That made him smile.

When he hit the speed dial number for Porter, he sat back and waited. It took only two electronic rings for the Deputy Director for Afghan Affairs to answer.

"Tate, I'm kinda busy, but what's up?"

"You know, HC just said the same thing. I think all of you should remember who you're talking with."

"Yeah, okay, no problem, Tate. What can I do for you?"

"Just keeping you in the loop about today's arrival. HC says everything's good to go. You should check your account around midnight. If you don't see it by 2:00 AM, then call me, but I'm not expecting anything out of the ordinary."

"Good. Did you want me to inform anyone else?"

"Sure. You can give Alton the good news. Oh, and remind him that I'm waiting on his distraction. He'll know what I mean."

"Okay, Tate. Will do."

With that, the line went silent.

Chapter 16

The news conference had been arranged at lightning speed, even for the White House. Reporters from every news agency packed the press briefing room, the major networks staking their claim to the chairs in the middle front, while lesser news outlet reporters were seated on chairs a relative distant semi-circle away from the podium, while still others stood elbow to elbow around the room's perimeter. Bright lights from video cameras illuminated the room at odd angles, causing shadows against walls, chairs, and the presidential seal on the podium. A low hum emanated from the crowd as many of the reporters briefed their audiences on the expectations from the president when he finally arrived, only moments away, assuming he kept to his schedule.

They had been given a summary of the purpose of what was expected to be a major announcement on a spending shift for the president's upcoming budget proposal as well as an emergency measure to address the United States' failing transportation infrastructure. For the uninitiated, this didn't appear to be a big deal, but to those who knew this president and his policy stance on increased spending, any move to bolster funding for roads and bridges was an abrupt change.

On the small stage behind the podium, three chairs were promptly set up, causing a stir among the news crews who now scrambled to wrap up their introductions and get to their seats before the president's arrival. The camera crews retreated to the perimeter of the room, jostling for any open space so that they could get the best possible angle on the president and his guests, whoever they were. The signal was given, indicating that the news conference was just one minute away. The murmur in the crowd continued until the door to the left of the stage opened, and a middle-aged man and woman and a young girl, who appeared to be no more than six years old, were escorted to the seats on stage. The crowd remained standing until President Alton Woodburn strode into the room and indicated that everyone should be seated. He turned to the man, woman and young girl first, took their hands and, in a solemn exchange, said something that wasn't loud enough for the reporters to hear. He nodded to the group then turned to the podium. Once the room quieted down and all that could be heard were stifled coughs, the rustling of paper, and the clicking of cameras, the president grabbed each side of the podium and looked around the room. There were no smiles. His mood conveyed a heavy sadness as if he were set to deliver a eulogy.

"Thank you all for being here this morning. Today I am announcing a major change in spending priorities for the federal government, but before I do, I would like to introduce the Parker family from Logan, Ohio, to the country. Logan is a small town in southeast Ohio on Highway 33 in Hocking County, some of the most beautiful scenery in the great state of Ohio. Andrew, Cynthia, and little Kayla Parker here, suffered a great loss this past week. Cynthia's mother, Kayla's grandmother, Andrew's mother-in-law, was killed while driving along Highway 33 on her way to church to help with a food drive for the local food bank. She wasn't the victim of foul play or a personal medical emergency. No, she lost her life when a piece of concrete and metal dislodged and fell from the bottom of an aging, dilapidated bridge that was in desperate need of repairs, and had, in fact, been scheduled for repairs many times for at least the past eighteen years. Those projects were scrapped because the state of Ohio and the local county didn't have the funding for the repair. There were 'other priorities' that took precedence over infrastructure."

The president went on to describe the grief that seized the family on hearing of their matriarch's death and the manner in which she died. Sometime during his description, Cynthia and Kayla Parker broke down. Cameras zoomed in to catch the full effect of their grief. One of the president's staff rushed over and provided tissues to each.

The president then made his pitch to the country and to Congress. He rattled off statistics illustrating that this was not an isolated incident. Infrastructure failures were happening throughout the country. The Parker's were not the only family suffering through death and serious injury from failing infrastructure. He cited the losses felt by three other families by name and location around the country to emphasize that this wasn't an issue specific to southeast Ohio. The entire country's highway system was aging and in need of triage, immediate action that can only be accomplished by an infusion of a large amount of money.

Then the president noted that the shift in priorities could not come at the cost of robbing other national priorities, such as health care and the War on Drugs. And with that, the president requested immediate action by Congress to pass an emergency spending bill specifically for highway bridge and related infrastructure repair "to prevent future tragedies such as the Parker family and others were now suffering."

He turned to the family and made some solemn remarks, summoned his aide to provide more tissues to the grieving women, then turned back to the podium. He fielded a few questions from the press, most of which were softballs, then thanked the press for their participation. He turned to the Parker family and directed them to the door to the left of the podium.

When they were gone and the door was closed, the reporters and their cameramen quickly set up to make closing remarks to their anchors at various newsrooms around the country while other reporters simply closed their notepads and headed for the press corps exit. And just like that, the president requested that hundreds of billions of dollars be shifted from programs that were deemed previously to be of the utmost importance to a new, concerted effort to get the nation's infrastructure fixed.

Once back at the oval office, Alton Woodburn sat in his overstuffed presidential chair and wiped his face. He felt guilty, even dirty, for having used the Parker family as pawns in the scheme to redirect the attention of the American people away from the Armand Vega assassination and the movement to end the War on Drugs to an issue that wasn't even on the radar of most senators and house members. The issue was certainly authentic and urgent, one that had been discussed at all levels of government around the country, but it was also one that would cause a shift in budgets that would have a ripple effect through many government agencies. No one had the guts to tell taxpayers that they needed to ante up to fix their roads, bridges, water and sewer systems, and other key infrastructure.

But for Alton Woodburn, Nevin Tate, and the rest of the crew, it would have immediate and tangible benefits. First, it would keep Congress busy for a period of time answering questions from the press and their constituents back home. Many local mayors, county commissioners, and state congressional members would be calling their representatives, demanding that they support the president's bold proposal. Second, it would keep the money flowing for the War on Drugs while removing the majority of the focus that had been consuming the nation for the last few days, a focus driven by the national news media. Now the media had a new bone to chew on, and they would divert the attention of the American people to this new shiny object.

Woodburn was busy wrestling with his conscience when a phone chirped from his desk's center drawer. He looked at the phones and saw that it was his personal cell. His wife was calling.

"Hello, Darling."

His wife had apparently been crying. When she spoke, it was between sniffles. "Alton, dear, thank you. I watched your news conference, and you were very convincing. I just hope those do-nothings in Congress get off their collective duffs and get something done."

Woodburn smiled. That was about as fierce as his wife ever got. He was proud of her for her tenacity in this issue, but his thoughts immediately went back to his own personal, selfish motives.

"Sweetheart, we're going to keep up the pressure and make sure they do the right thing. That isn't easy in this town, but I think this time it will work."

He wanted to change the subject in the worst way and asked, "Would you like me to meet you for lunch?"

"I'd love that dear, but I'm meeting Sylvia. I can cancel."

"No, no. You go ahead. We'll meet for dinner then."

Just then, his cell phone chirped. Without looking, Woodburn knew it was Nevin Tate. He looked up at the ceiling, then back down at his desk and rubbed his forehead.

"Sweetheart, I've got to go. I have another call."

"Okay, dear. Goodbye."

Woodburn tapped the red hang-up icon then tapped the green icon.

In a tone that showed he didn't want to hear from his partner, he said, "Yeah Tate, what do you want?"

Tate's reply was laced with false praise, "Bravo, Alton. Bravo. I knew you could do it. And it isn't even a phony issue. I actually shed a tear for that couple and their child, what was her name, Kayla? I think you hit that one out of the park."

"Yeah. Okay. Anything else? I'm busy."

"I'm so glad you asked. I'm going to be busy this evening with HC. Seems like business is great and getting better."

"I can't talk about this now. You know that."

"Alton, you worry too much. You're covered. You're the frickin' President of the United States. You're untouchable. Haven't you learned that by now? Jeez. Listen. We need …"

Woodburn heard a chirping sound over the phone. He assumed that Tate was receiving a call. He hoped so. He didn't want to hear anything else about their business while he was in the oval office. He could feel his heart pounding harder in his chest the longer he was on the phone with this lunatic.

Tate spoke. "Alton, I have another call. I'll talk with you later."

The phone disconnected. Woodburn dropped the phone

in his center desk drawer and took a deep breath. He hoped Ernest Porter would get their plan moving. Eliminating Tate was paramount to his health. His blood pressure was through the roof, right along with his anxiety. Even his wife noticed that he was always tense. The duties of POTUS – President of the United States – were demanding and tended to negatively impact the commander in chief's health. The added strain of dealing with a complete psychopath like Tate raised that health risk exponentially. Added to that was the Republican party's assumption that Woodburn was going to run for a second term: something that he had yet to decide. Unless he could eliminate some of the stress in his life, he wondered if he would live to seek a second term.

There were lots of reasons to not run. He had more money than he could spend in several lifetimes. He had a wonderful wife, two great kids, and a handful of grandkids whom he adored but never saw because of his job. Maybe one term was enough.

That wasn't possible unless Tate was out of the picture. He was depending on Ernest Porter to make that happen. Then the stress level would drop, at least to something a little more manageable.

Chapter 17

As the private, chartered jet touched-down at the Erie-Ottawa International Airport in Ottawa County in north-central Ohio, Peden and Megan finished packing up their notes on Ricky Lee Lyle. They had stopped their review in time to see the shoreline of Lake Erie. As they descended from east to west, they got a bird's eye view of the Cedar Point amusement park, touted as the greatest amusement park in the world, and they could see why. Well over a dozen major roller coasters dominated the skyline above the park. Further out over the lake stood Perry's Victory and International Peace Memorial standing over three hundred and fifty feet into the sky from near Put-In-Bay on South Bass Island. What they didn't see were the thousands of partiers in numerous bars on the island. They also saw the massive cooling tower for the Davis-Besse Nuclear Power Station emitting a large plum of water vapor.

The name "Erie-Ottawa International Airport" set their expectations much higher than the actual facilities. The airport consisted of two runways, one east-west, which could accommodate small jets, such as the one in which they were seated, and large prop planes. The other runway, oriented north-south was for smaller, personal planes. The terminal was a one-room building approximately forty feet wide and thirty feet deep. They had arranged ahead for the local Sandusky FBI office to provide a rental car. The front desk at the terminal had the keys ready for them. The staff was very helpful, making sure that they knew how to operate the GPS as well as providing directions to Route 2. They also provided pamphlets to the many local tourist attractions, "just in case their business finished early and allowed them some time to explore the many fine establishments in northern Ohio."

Their interview of Ricky Lee Lyle back in Wytheville, Virginia, had taken just over an hour. It would have taken less time, but Ricky Lee's mother insisted that he have their family lawyer present. The lawyer, whose specialty was real estate law, ever concerned that the FBI was out to frame his client for a very high-profile crime, kept interrupting, asking for clarification on numerous questions. Megan tried to make it as clear as possible that, although his client was a person of interest, Ricky Lee wasn't a suspect and that they just wanted to get collaboration on information that they had received from others who had worked for FlashGamz. They wrapped up the interview with Megan wishing that they could arrest the lawyer for something, anything, for wasting their time, but that wasn't to be.

All in all, Ricky Lee appeared to be a good, brilliant, well-mannered kid who just wanted to help his mother and family. He made money testing video games, but he also worked with his older brothers in their family business. Because of his father's healthcare bills and the financial pit that the family found themselves in, he did express some bitterness towards the Affordable Care Act and the state of healthcare in the country in general, but he had no strong opinion on the War on Drugs.

When they asked him about what he remembered of the actual test of the video game, his story mirrored that of Simon Andrews. He spoke quietly but clearly, his eyes closed as he recounted the approach of the attack drone. He mentioned the red lights and how he watched closely for the lights to turn green. When he finally received the green lights, he pressed the controller buttons to fire the weapon. He said that there was a slight hesitation in the firing of the weapon, but it was a fraction of a second in actual time. Then the screen went blank and the thumb drive "smoked." A short "tongue of flame" turned the drive to ash.

Then he opened his eyes and said, "That's it."

They asked if the burned thumb drive caused any damage to his computer, to which he replied in the negative. In fact, he was surprised that no other damage occurred. It was such an intense flame that he thought for certain his computer would be damaged, but, as with the Andrews' kid's computer, everything checked out fine.

They had thanked Ricky Lee for his time, that he should not contact the other testers, and that he should contact them if he thought of anything additional, no matter how small of a detail, that might help them. When he took Megan's card, he politely thanked them and said that he would.

Now in a Chevy Equinox headed east on Route 2, they road on the causeway near the Edison Bridge over the Sandusky Bay and enjoyed the view of the expanse of water. The late afternoon sun angled in from the west, causing a beautiful bright red line on the surface of the water.

On the route to the Galindo family residence, there was a combination of small businesses and mixed-use commercial space. A few larger factories were apparently running at full capacity, the parking lots nearly full with workers' cars. Other industrial sites were idle, with weeds working hard to reclaim the gravel parking lots, inch at a time. Many new warehouse-style buildings with tin siding were in evidence, indicating a renaissance at some level for the local job market. At first impression, the city appeared to Peden to be making a comeback after some economic setbacks.

They had both been quiet, thinking of the information that they had so far, trying to make sense of the attack on a prominent senator in a most unconventional method. From what they had learned from Simon Andrews and Ricky Lee Lyle, it was likely that the video game testers had no idea that they were pawns in a very dangerous game, far more sinister than a pretend game of spies and evildoers.

The GPS signal directed them to the west end of Sandusky to the fourteen hundred block of Pearl Street. The Galindo home was on the east side of the street. A two-story home that appeared to have been built in the early twentieth century, the family had recently remodeled the home with a new roof, siding, trim and a new, two-car-wide driveway that was shared with a next-door neighbor. It was early evening, after 6:30 PM. Peden hoped that Carlita Galindo and her parents were home so that they didn't have to make an appointment for another day.

They were in luck as a middle-aged woman answered the door.

With a questioning look at the two official-looking people on her front porch, she asked, "Can I help you?"

Per their plan, Megan took the lead. "I'm Special Agent Megan Moore with the FBI. This is Peden Savage, a consultant with my office. We'd like to speak with Carlita Galindo."

With a look that radiated fear, concern, and reeked with anxiety, she asked, "Can I ask what this is about?"

"Certainly. Are you Carlita's mother, Rosa?"

A slow, drawn-out, "Yes."

Peden was concerned that Megan, with her no-nonsense approach and perpetual frown, might scare Rosa Galindo. He jumped in and said, "If we could take a minute of your time and explain to you why we're here, then if you feel comfortable, you could ask Carlita to join us. Would that work?"

Rosa Galindo reluctantly stepped aside and indicated that they should take a seat in the living room. Peden noted that the interior of the old house complimented the upgraded exterior with new carpet and freshly painted walls and ceilings. Family pictures adorned the walls, as well as a handful of paintings with a southwest theme. The furniture was dated but clean.

Megan and Peden took a seat on the couch. Rosa sat in a matching chair to their left. All the chairs in the room faced a large flat-panel TV.

Peden began. "Mrs. Galindo, first, let me start by telling you that Carlita isn't in any trouble. We're investigating a company called FlashGamz, and we understand that your daughter performs testing for the company?"

The concerned mother hesitated before she spoke. She asked, "Does my daughter need a lawyer?"

Peden and Megan did a sideways glance at each other, then Megan spoke. "That is always your option, and we can't advise you on that one way or another. If you wish to have an attorney present, we can wait until they get here. But your daughter is not a suspect in our investigation. It is just that she may have information about the company that could be helpful to us."

A tense silence followed. Peden was reluctant to fill the void, hoping that Rosa Galindo would feel the need to speak first. He knew that Megan would wait as long as necessary. It turned out that they didn't have to wait. A teenaged girl walked into the room and asked her mother if she needed help with dinner dishes. Rosa Galindo looked up and smiled at her daughter, but the smile was apparently not natural enough to fool her young, brilliant daughter.

She turned to her daughter. "Sweety, come sit." She indicated the chair closest to her. Carlita Galindo looked at the two agents and nervously nodded.

Her mother continued. "Honey, this is Special Agent Megan ..."

She forgot Megan's last name, and Megan jumped in, speaking in an unusually calm voice. Peden looked over at her to make sure she hadn't morphed into another person. He had never heard her speak with such an easy, soft tone.

"Carlita, I'm Special Agent Megan Moore. This is my partner, Peden Savage. He is not an FBI agent, but is working with us on a very important case. We need to ask you some questions about your video game testing and your relationship with a company called FlashGamz."

She nodded. "You're here about the smoked flash drive."

Megan nodded. "What can you tell us about the testing and, please, be very specific. Don't leave out any details, regardless of how small."

While her mother looked on, her face etched with concern, Carlita Galindo recalled the testing for the day Senator Armand Vega was assassinated. Her memory of the events was remarkably similar to Simon Andrews and Ricky Lee Lyle's story, including the destruction of the flash drive and that nothing on her computer was damaged. She also said that she lost contact with her representative at FlashGamz. She originally figured that maybe the company was so stunned by the failure that they wanted to cut contact with their testers while they worked out the issues that caused the drives to fail.

When she said "drives to fail," Peden jumped in. "You said drives. How do you know that there were other drives that failed?"

Carlita looked down at the carpet, then looked over at her mother. She turned back to Peden and said, "We're not supposed to have any contact with the other testers, but we don't exactly follow that particular rule, not completely anyway."

Peden asked, "So do you know the other testers?"

"Well, yeah."

"By name?"

"Yeah."

Peden looked at Carlita with a look that said, *We're listening.*

"Well, there's Ricky Lee in Virginia, Simon in North Carolina, Anthony in Saratoga Springs, New York, and the brothers in Georgia."

"What are the brothers' names, please."

"Ian and Jonah. Ian is really nice. He's helped me understand some of the coding issues that were keeping other FlashGamz programs from working. He's a genius. His brother is, too, but he can't communicate with other people too well. Ian says Jonah is a savant. But Ian, he's special."

She smiled, and her face flushed when she mentioned Ian's name for the second time. Mrs. Galindo put her hand on her daughter's arm and gave her a stern look. Carlita's gaze fell to the floor again.

Peden asked, "Can you tell us anything more about the brothers in Georgia?"

"Not really, except that they live in this huge house. Ian said it's more like a compound than a house. It's on Tybee Island at the end of a long private road. I looked it up on my map program."

Peden asked, "Can you show us?" Peden looked at Rosa Galindo and added, "With your permission, of course."

After a moment, Rosa Galindo nodded her approval.

Chapter 18

The banter on the teleconference line was light, almost jovial. To most normal people, this would seem odd, even bazaar, considering the topic of conversation was the assassination of a U.S. Senator. The participants weren't speaking about Senator Armand Vega; they were discussing the new target: the very liberal Democrat from New York State, Senator Lancaster Corrigan.

Corrigan and Vega hadn't been friends or allies during their time together in the United States Senate. They hardly spoke unless it was on matters of legislation that were near and dear to each of their hearts. But they did have one area in particular that they were both passionate about: the War on Drugs was a wasted effort and a huge money pit for American tax-payers.

They came from very different backgrounds. Vega was the descendent of Mexican immigrants. His great-grandfather had immigrated to the United States after the Civil War and settled near Savannah, Georgia. He started a successful Mexican restaurant where many members of the Vega family worked. Armand was the first in his family to go to college. He finished with a graduate degree in political science and went on to work for a law firm that did extensive lobbying in Washington for immigration reform. He ran for a House seat and won easily, backed by a number of big-spending liberals. After just three terms in the House, he won a Senate seat, displacing a relatively junior republican incumbent opponent.

Corrigan's lineage traced back to old money from the gun industry. He was the recipient of wealth from the Colt gun manufacturing company through his great-grandfather, a fact he preferred to keep private. Even though the majority of his net worth was derived from the manufacture and sale of small arms, he was an avid anti-gun democrat and extremely liberal on civil rights, including the right to use drugs, any kind of drugs, so long as you don't trample on others' rights in the process. Corrigan's path to the Senate was also paved in liberal donors' money. He was in his third term in the Senate and looked to be there as long as he wished, so long as he didn't change any of his core ideals.

Nevin Tate had initiated the call to three other extremely wealthy individuals around the globe. They were his peers in the heroin trade for their respective countries. Anything they could do to make sure that their wealth and power continued to grow unimpeded was a positive for them. If a few pawns had to be sacrificed along the way, so be it. Eliminating one, or even two, token senators was of no consequence as long as their product's price remained high and sales remained strong.

"So, gentlemen, if we are all in agreement, I'll take the lead on this next project. Wire your payments to the account. After everyone's payment is registered, I'll make the call. This should wrap up within the next three to four days, and we'll send a strong message to our governments that they must not let up on their War on Drugs."

The replies were all in favor of Tate's next move. Unbeknownst to the senator from the great state of New York, his days were numbered. They sealed the move with a long-distance toast, made a few more off-topic, politically incorrect jokes, and wished each other and their families well. Just another day at the office.

Nevin Tate tapped his phone screen and disconnected the call. He put the phone down, smiled, and rubbed his hands together as if warming them up, preparing to count more money. Of course, with the method used to transfer this amount of money, it was all done electronically. But it was all good.

Tate pulled up a spreadsheet with the schedules of several U.S. Senators that he had paid for in cash. He scrolled down the list until he got to Senator Lancaster Corrigan. He skipped ahead three days, which was the time he needed to code the next phase of his operation, get the new flash drives loaded with the code, get them mailed out to his testers, and prepare them for this next "test." He knew that he'd have to apologize for the lack of contact after the last failed test, which in his eyes, was actually a stellar success. The kids would be curious and confused about why he hadn't answered their calls. But kids were easy to manipulate. And the $20,000 payment for the new test, which was an extra $5000 each, would help make up for the lack of contact and calm their frustrations. As long as their parents didn't get involved, there shouldn't be a problem.

He scrolled through the senator's itinerary, looking for the right date, time, and location. "Let's see. Breakfast with other senators, a meeting of the Sub-Committee on Foreign Affairs. Nothing good Thursday. Friday morning. Breakfast with staff. Another meeting. Then a drive out to Dulles for a flight to Albany International Airport. A late dinner with the wife at Angelo's 677 Prime. Let's see if that'll work."

He typed the name of the restaurant into his browser and waited just seconds for information to pop up. *Superb food and top-shelf beverages. It's not just dinner, it's a dining experience.*

Using a map program, he viewed the building from directly above and used street-level views to get an idea of the logistics involved in catching the senator alone on the street. After studying the site for nearly half an hour and reviewing the senator's schedule, he was satisfied that the location was an excellent choice for the project.

Getting the coordinates for the front of the restaurant was easy. His program had that information with just a few keystrokes. Now all he had to do was type the code into the gaming program. For the average computer user, this task would have been impossible, but for him, it was child's play. In another thirty minutes, the initial programming would be complete. After a few test-runs with a new drone, he would be ready for the flight to a private airfield in upstate New York. The flight would take a few hours, plus he'd need a rental pickup truck and car. The biggest issue was making sure that his house staff took good care of his boys while he was gone. He didn't like leaving them in other people's care, but he couldn't turn this part of his business over to anyone.

He looked around his home office and smiled. Here he was, a billionaire, and he spent most of his time in a basement office surrounded by computer screens spitting out news broadcasts from around the world: his own little reality show. But that was okay because he controlled much of what happened in Washington, D. C., and in other countries around the world. If only the masses knew.

He thought back to his meeting at the Savannah Miles and Taylor Plantation Shipyard with Javier Delgato. It went very well. His new buyer liked what he saw. The product tested well for purity. He was ready to go as soon as a new shipment could be arranged. The weight that he needed was within his crew's capability to supply. He had thanked Delgato and said that he would receive a call within the next two days. Both men walked away pleased at the new partnership.

Once Delgato was out of sight, Nevin Tate had turned to Harold H. Herald. His bright smile disappeared.

He had asked, "Who do you think you're screwing with HC?"

Herald appeared to be taken by surprise, though Tate thought he should have seen it coming. "Nobody, and I mean, nobody hangs up on me." He stared daggers through his key man at the port. When he spoke again, HC turned pale.

"If you think you can't be replaced, just let me know. There're a thousand guys who can do your job. All I've got to do is say the word and you're gone. And I don't mean fired. I mean gone – for good! You got it?"

Tate had moved closer, his finger pointed directly into the chest of the much bigger man. He made HC take small steps backwards until the man nearly tripped over a cable at the edge of the road used by giant fork trucks. Herald had looked down to make sure nothing else was behind him that he might trip over. When he looked back, Tate had an AN1911 45 caliber pistol pointed at his head.

"You see the size of that hole, HC? Look at it! I said look at it! No more disrespect! When I call, you listen. If you have to stop operations while I'm talking to you. You do just that. Am I making myself clear?"

HC's mouth moved, trying to get the words out, but nothing coherent came out for several seconds. Then he managed to spit out a choked-off, "Yeah, Nev. I got it."

Thinking back on the moment, Tate smiled. He thought HC was going to wet himself right then and there. But his smile quickly disappeared. Their business was expanding again, and he needed each of the team to step up, not choke. He'd told HC that he could easily replace him, but they both knew it was a lie. He had to keep the team in line, thinking about the job and the rewards. There was still a lot of money to be made.

But these days, Tate was less interested in the money. He loved the power, the fact that he could make demands of the President of the United States and knew that his orders would be followed. He controlled the man who was arguably the most powerful man in the world.

His smile returned. He stood and walked into his private restroom. He relieved himself, washed his hands, looked in the mirror, and smiled at the image staring back at him. "Okay, Nevin, time to play David Walsh, representative for FlashGamz."

And just like that, Neven Tate became David Walsh.

* * *

Peden and Megan were in the air on their way to Saratoga Springs from the Erie-Ottawa International Airport. Their destination was the Albany International Airport, where they planned to pick up another rental car and head north on Interstate 87 Northway. Peden believed that they were wasting time questioning another tester and that they would get the same story that they got from Simon Andrews and Carlita Galindo. The best new information that they received from the Galindo girl was the names of the beta testers in Savannah. He thought that they should head home and head out to Tybee

Island first thing in the morning.

Megan had other ideas. She wanted to make sure that they spoke with all the testers that were out of the Savannah area first. Then they could head home and not have to worry about taking another trip north. Peden didn't argue. Her boss was writing his checks, so he went along. Besides, she was a brilliant agent with spot-on instincts, so it was always a safe bet following her lead.

Their next tester was a seventeen-year-old kid by the name of Anthony Pirelli, Jr. His dad was an engineer at Knolls Atomic Power Laboratory in West Milton, New York. His mother was a professor at Skidmore College.

Anthony was a kid with a high IQ and a drive to do nothing but sit around and play video games. He was so good that he was elected unanimously by his peers to be the president of the local gamers club. Peden hoped that the Pirelli kid had something of value to offer. Otherwise, it was going to be a waste of a lot of time and jet fuel.

Chapter 19

David Walsh, *aka* Nevin Tate, had everything he needed to set the next part of the plan into motion. The new attack program was written, tested, and downloaded to six flash drives: five for distribution to his testers and one – the one that really controlled the drone – that he would keep for his own use.

He had his storyline set for the inevitable questions from his young, impressionable testers, but they were just kids. He would explain the facts of being in the creation and marketing of video games and how other companies would spy on them and even sabotage their testing. To protect them, the game program, and the company, he had to cut all contact with them and determine if they were being targeted by major players in the video gaming industry.

These were smart kids, and he knew there would be tough questions. He would convince them, and they would be ready to "test" *Assassin – Best in the Business*.

When he got confirmation that the kids were set to resume testing, he would send the flash drives out by overnight delivery. They should have them, along with the instructions, by two in the afternoon Friday. He would call each tester beginning at 3:00 PM tomorrow. The toughest call would be to Ian. He was by far the brightest and most talented of the testers, and Walsh was certain that he would have the hardest questions.

He sat back in his chair, monitoring the world news on the many monitors hanging on the walls around his workstation. Nothing of significance was happening, though there was always some tension in the Middle East. Early this morning, Hamas had launched numerous missiles into Israeli neighborhoods, and Israel had retaliated by bombing the suspected launch sights with precision missiles fired from American-made F-18 fighter jets. There was nothing fair about the fight, but when you know you are outmanned and outgunned, you probably shouldn't throw the first punch.

A phone chirped from his desk drawer. He reached in and picked up the one with the lighted screen. It was Porter, the CIA Deputy Director for Afghan affairs. Walsh smiled, turned on a device that disguised his voice, and answered.

"Walsh."

"Mr. Walsh, this is Ernest ..."

"I know, Ernie. What do you want?"

"I have a job for you. In the continental U.S. Usual terms?"

"I need more information before I agree. Where and who?"

There was a pause before Porter answered. "I'll send the details within the next ten minutes. If you agree, send your reply."

"All right, Ernie."

Walsh disconnected the call. He didn't like getting details over the phone, but the truth was, if the government wanted to hear your calls, there wasn't much you could do about it. The only way around it was to change phones and phone companies often, encrypt the messages, or a combination of the two. David Walsh was too busy to constantly change phones and phone numbers.

He sat back and smiled and wondered who had to die next so he could make over a million bucks. His email account on his computer beeped long before the full ten minutes was up. A smile swept across his face as adrenaline pumped through his body.

He saved the encrypted attachment to a flash drive and ran the decryption program. He rubbed his hands together, the excitement growing as the program created the new file. Finally, the file reached one hundred percent and opened.

Two million dollars. Job must be completed by the end of the coming week. Evidence must be provided by photograph of the target after the job is completed. The target is ...

"What the hell? Those sons-a-bitches!"

Nevin Tate.

Nevin Tate was David Walsh's next target. He was being hired to kill himself.

The assassin felt his blood pressure rise as his muscles tightened. He grabbed a gold-plated paper-weight and hurled it across the room. It hit a concrete wall and bounced off, falling harmlessly to the floor. He clenched his fists, his face turning bright red. He grabbed his phone, his rage building. He swiped across his phone's screen and was about to call Porter on speed dial when he caught himself.

Out loud to himself, he said, "Cool down. Get control of yourself. They don't know, and I can't let them know. There's plenty of time to deal with Porter and that nitwit, Woodburn."

David Walsh, one of the most successful assassins used covertly by the CIA, was Nevin Tate, though no one in the world knew that fact. He sat back in his chair and took a long drink of ice-cold water. He needed to cool down and think through his next move. The Corrigan hit was already in motion. That was the first order of business, then he'd tackle the tricky issue of dealing with Woodburn and Porter.

"They literally don't know who they're dealing with, but that's going to change ... soon and in a dramatic way."

* * *

Ian Tabler finished the latest chapter in the lesson on digital communications. This particular chapter dealt with the reception of digital messages. As the lesson progressed, he was rebuilding a device that would capture and decipher digital signals. To him, it appeared relatively simple. The concept was not difficult, at least, not to him. But to actually build and place a device in service? Now that was another story.

Ian had to engineer the entire project from ground zero. He had to order about twenty different electronic components, hardware, and specialty tools to complete the job. This was his second attempt, as he'd already built one but came up short on function and portability. Jonah had recommended a few electronic design changes that resolved one of the major function issues, which was the ability to decipher and tune into specific digital signals.

Making the changes that Jonah suggested took some time since Jonah had to spell out every word using his number code. Ian had a difficult time with some of the complex electronic component descriptions, but they worked through that together. They were solid recommendations, and after listening to the most recent lesson, he understood why the previous attempts had failed. It wasn't just a matter of swapping a few wires. He had to completely disassemble the electronics and start over. That took nearly a full day, but he believed he could have it ready by tomorrow, mid-morning.

Ian was just heating the soldering iron in his home lab when his cell phone dinged, indicating he had a new text message. His heart fluttered because he hoped it was Carlita Galindo, one of the few contacts that he had with the outside world. Carlita was a few years younger than him, but she was one of the only hopes that he had of meeting a person of the opposite sex.

He picked up his phone and hit the text message icon. *Yes!*

Hi Ian. How are you? I'm very nervous about telling you this but there were two people, FBI agents, at my house yesterday asking questions about our beta testing for FlashGamz. They asked me if I've had any contact with Mr. Walsh since the testing failed. I told him that I hadn't. But they also asked me if I knew any other testers. I'm sorry, but I told them about you and Jonah ... and the others. I was super nervous. Anyway, I hope you're not mad. Stay in touch, please.

Ian's heart skipped a beat. He read the entire message through several times, smiling to himself. That FBI agents had questioned her wasn't surprising, given that Simon Andrews' house was raided, and what he and his brother suspected about their test and how it appeared to have been somehow used to kill Senator Vega. He wasn't sure if the agents had let Carlita know about the possible link. She didn't mention that in her text, and he wasn't about to tell her and have her worried sick about it. He was just glad that she texted him, even if it was related to their testing. He answered right away.

> *Hi Carlita. Great to hear from you. Don't worry. I'm not going anywhere. And don't worry about answering honestly. If you lie to the FBI, that's serious stuff so I'm glad you told the truth. I haven't heard anything from Mr. Walsh either. I expect that we won't. But there are other companies. I'm sure we'll all stay busy for a long time. I think we're all going to be rich someday.*

Ian hit send, then thought for a minute. He decided to stop talking shop and ask more about Carlita the person.

He typed:

> *I don't mean to be nosey and personal, but tell me about life in Sandusky. Do you ever get to that amusement park with all the roller coasters?*

* * *

Carlita Galindo was lying on her bed playing a rather violent war game when she heard her cell phone chime. She put down her controller and looked at her text messages. She blushed then giggled when she read Ian's second text, asking her about something besides video game testing. She and a few her of friends went to Cedar Point amusement park at least five times each summer. She had personally ridden every roller coaster at the park at least three times, most many more. *How should I answer?*

> *Life here is good. I love going to Cedar Point. I go with a few friends during the season. The park doesn't open until May and sometimes it's too cold to go then. If you can make it up here sometime, I'd be happy to take you and spend the day there.*

She hesitated, smiled to herself, giggled, then hit send.

Her mother had talked to her at length after the FBI left. Even though Rosa Galindo and her family had been U.S.

citizens for decades, she was nervous that the federal authorities might find something in their past that would cause them to send her and her family to Mexico, a country that was as foreign to them as Russia. She asked Carlita if, maybe, she should stop testing video games for a while, to which her daughter replied with an emphatic "no." Why should she be concerned? She hadn't heard from David Walsh since the big test failure. She believed that she and the other testers wouldn't be working for FlashGamz again, contract or not.

Then Rosa Galindo asked her daughter about her relationship with that boy from Georgia. She saw the look on her daughter's face when the agents asked her if she had any contact with other testers. It was obvious that she was smitten with Ian.

Carlita had smiled and tried to brush it off, but she knew her mother wasn't fooled. Carlita had told her mother it was harmless, that Ian lived a world away and that it couldn't go anywhere. Besides, she had a plan that she had to attend to, and that plan didn't include boys. She needed to make money for her future so that she could take care of herself despite what might happen in her love life.

Rosa Galindo had given her daughter a skeptical look. She gave her one last word of advice. "You be careful what you get yourself into, young lady. You know you can talk to me about anything."

"Yes, Momma, I know. I love you."

Rosa's smile had been pure but clearly anxious.

Carlita's phone dinged again. She smiled in anticipation of Ian's next text message.

Chapter 20

With Megan Moore driving the rental car on the Interstate 87 Northway just north of Albany, New York, Peden had time to think. As the night wore on, he couldn't see much along the interstate except lighted strip malls and streetlights from subdivisions. Megan had the air conditioner on at a comfortable level. The GPS said that they were five minutes from Anthony Pirelli's home. They hadn't discussed the plan for questioning the kid, but they had called ahead, and the Pirellis were aware that the FBI was on their way to question their son. Anthony senior assured Megan that they would be there.

Peden believed they were wasting time questioning the kid. They already had a pattern established. Each of the three testers that they had questioned had literally the same experience. The descriptions were so close that Peden wondered if any of the kids actually controlled the attack drone. They may have been set up as red herrings to keep the FBI chasing their tails, as he believed they were doing now. The actual murder took place in Savannah, Georgia, so why were they running around in upstate New York? They were a long way from the murder scene, and time was of the essence.

But Megan was in charge, and she apparently believed that there was value in questioning the final tester, other than those who lived in Georgia. She was right about one thing: the kids at the house on Tybee Island would be close to home and easy to get to, so they should be last on their list. Also, it was interesting that Carlita Galindo knew the names of the boys in Georgia. She appeared to have a crush on the older boy, Ian. That was cute the way she blushed when she spoke about the young man. It was obvious that she didn't have much experience with the opposite sex. Her mother didn't seem pleased that she had those feelings, especially for a boy nearly a thousand miles way.

"Pedee, I want you to take the lead on asking questions when we get to the Pirelli's. If the kid's a typical New Yorker, he might have an attitude. If his dad stays during questioning, he will likely also have an attitude, and I'm a little short-fused right now."

"Sure, Megan, I can do that. Can you keep your cool?"

"I guess we'll find out soon."

Megan veered right at exit 12, State Route 67, and slowly approached the roundabout at the top of the rise. Peden looked scared as she asked, "What the hell is this?"

She slowed and did her best to follow the directions on the signs while avoiding what little traffic shared the road with her. She made her way around the first roundabout and headed west on 67. She had to navigate two more roundabouts in the road before making the additional quarter-mile stretch to Raymond Road, where she turned right. The Pirelli family lived on Timber Trace, which was the first road to the left off of Raymond. They found the house on the right side of the road. It wasn't hard to spot. Every home on Timber Trace looked to have over three thousand square feet. Each had a unique design and, based on real estate prices in the area that Peden had researched before they left Georgia, had to be worth just north of half a million dollars. The best feature of the homes was the land. Each home occupied at least an acre.

They parked in the driveway, Megan verifying the name and address on the mailbox. Lights on either side of the garage door and on the porch, along with an illuminated lamppost, made for a welcoming feel. "This is it."

As they approached the house, the screen door opened. A short man with thinning salt-and-pepper hair stood in the entry, a nervous smile on his face. In a strong New York accent, he said to Megan, "You must be Agent Moore. I'm Tony."

He stuck out his hand to Megan. They shook. He turned to Peden and asked, "And you are ..."

"Peden Savage. I'm a consultant working with Agent

Moore."

"Okay, please come in." Extending his hand to point the way, he said, "Take a seat."

Megan had her credentials out and showed them to the senior Pirelli, even though he hadn't asked to see them. He just nodded. Antony Pirelli, Jr. was standing in front of a chair in the living room. He looked nervous, even a bit pale. The elder Pirelli introduced his son, then asked if they wanted anything to drink, to which they replied no.

Anthony Pirelli, Sr. asked, "Does Tony need a lawyer?"

Megan, just as she had at the Galindo household, said, "I can't make that decision for you. Understand that your son isn't a suspect. But, if at any point you feel the need to have your attorney present, just say the word, and we'll stop the interview."

Pirelli nodded. He seemed satisfied that they could continue without a lawyer present. After everyone was seated, per Megan's directive, Peden began the questions.

"Anthony, can you tell us everything that you know about the company FlashGamz? Don't leave anything out, no matter how small a detail or how unimportant you might think it is."

Everyone, including his father, looked at Tony, Jr. He swallowed and had a hard time getting started. Megan jumped in, and for the second time that day, Peden wondered what possessed her. She was calm, nearly compassionate. He had a hard time keeping from asking her who she was and what had she done to Agent Moore, but he maintained his poker face as best he could.

She said, "Anthony, you're not in any trouble, you can relax. We're just gathering as much information as we can. Just take a deep breath and tell us like you're talking to your friends."

Young Tony Pirelli did just as Megan instructed. He took a deep breath and went through his relationship with FlashGamz, how he began testing for the company, the name of his contact, which was the same name the others mentioned.

Then he went through the actual test. Like the other testers, he described a slight hesitation before the weapon fired on the target. He said it was the only issue that he planned to report, but he couldn't since he lost contact with his company representative.

When he was finished with the attack, he said, "That's it."

Peden then asked, "Is that when the flash drive burned up?"

Tony looked at Peden, then to Megan, his face blank in a confused expression. He asked, "What do you mean, burned up?"

Peden said, "You know, the flash drive flamed out, burned to ashes, smoked."

Tony Pirelli shrugged his shoulders. "It didn't. I mean, I don't think it did. It wouldn't work after the attack, but it's still sitting on my desk."

Peden's jaw dropped in surprise. "You mean the flash drive is intact, no burns, no obvious damage?"

"Yeah. I mean, it looks fine, but I can't access it on my computer."

"Is your computer damaged in any way?"

Young Tony looked at Peden, confused at the question, then replied, "No. Not at all."

Megan stood as did Peden, followed by the Pirelli's. Megan jumped in before Peden could say anything. "Can you please show us the drive?"

"Sure, follow me."

They followed Tony and his father to the basement where a high-tech office was set up. The young beta tester had a number of computers and oversized monitors that would rival some Wall Street stock traders.

When they were all in the room, he picked up a thumb drive and extended his hand to give it to Peden, but Megan said, "Wait." She reached into her purse and pulled out a plastic bag with a zip lock top. She indicated that he should drop the drive in the bag, which he did. Megan asked about the packaging in which the drive had been delivered. Tony said that it had been thrown in the trash and was now at the local landfill.

Megan turned to Peden. "Do you have any more questions for Mr. Pirelli?"

"Nope, not now."

Megan told the Pirelli's to keep this visit to themselves, gave them her card, and asked them to call her if anything else came to mind.

Young Tony then said, "We're not supposed to communicate with the other testers, but I know them."

Megan replied, "Yeah, we heard about that. What's on your mind?"

"Well, all of us testers are really good, that's why these companies hire us. I mean, I'm good at what I do."

"We heard that you're the president of your local gamer's club."

"Yeah, that's true. But the brothers in Georgia, they're really good. I mean, head and shoulders above the rest of us. I'm thinking that they might know more about the folks at FlashGamz."

Megan nodded. "Thanks, Tony. You've been a great help. Oh, and don't contact any of the other testers about our visit."

* * *

On the drive back to Albany International Airport, Megan said, "Call Lee and let him know we have this drive, intact, and make sure he's ready to dissect it when we deliver it to him. When we get to the airport, we'll change the flight plan and head to Quantico. We'll get the drive to Lee, then head to Savannah and set up a meeting with the kids out on Tybee Island. Maybe we'll learn more there."

"I like the way you're thinking." He paused, then said, "I really thought we were wasting our time up here. You proved me wrong."

"You forgot something."

"What?"

" ... 'proved me wrong *again*.'"

Peden rolled his eyes, then hit the speed dial number for Lee Sparks. Lee answered on the second ring.

He sounded a bit groggy when he said, "Hey, Peden, what's up?"

Peden asked, "Have you been sleeping on the job?"

"Yeah, that's real funny. You work in a lab looking at data all day and see how peppy you are at 10:00. We just got finished running tests on the ashes that we got from the Andrews kid. There was an accelerant present. We're thinking that the drive was set up to self-destruct at a predetermined point, probably right after the weapon was emptied."

Peden jumped in, "We've got something else for you to test. The kid from Saratoga Springs, his drive didn't burn up. In fact, we have it in our possession and we're bringing it to you. You'll have it in a couple hours."

"Wait, you mean the thing's intact?"

"Yep. So, think about what you're going to do with it first. The Pirelli kid said he couldn't get it to work again after the attack, but maybe you could do a little voodoo on it and get it up and running, see what's on it. Then see if it was set to burn up but failed."

"Hey, Peden, leave the details to us experts. We'll let you know what we find."

"Okay, Mr. Bigshot. One other thing. What have you found out about the family out on Tybee?"

"Not too much. The property is owned by a corporation. We're digging into the names attached to the company now, but it's been tough. I tried to drill down into the company, but it isn't publicly traded. We're going to do a little more digging tomorrow and see if we can get better info."

"Okay, my man. How are the other lab rats treating you?"

"Good. We came to an understanding early. We're working well together. They're all very talented. Very open. Tell Megan that she's got a good team here."

"Okay, Lee. Thanks. See you in a few hours."

"Hey, Peden, wait up. You still there?"

"Yeah."

"We've narrowed down the search for the manufacturer and dealer for the drone. The manufacturer is a company out of Omaha, Nebraska. Pinnacle Aeronautics. Small company. They do some work for the Pentagon, but they also sell to private companies. They have separate divisions for government contracts and private sales, and no classified technology is supposed to cross company firewalls. But the drone used to kill Vega didn't have any real secret spook technology. It's pretty easy, relatively speaking, to attach a weapon to a drone. It's illegal but easy."

Peden was quiet for a moment, then he said, "Do you have a contact name and number for Pinnacle?"

"Yeah. I'll text it to you."

"Great. Thanks, Lee."

Peden hit the red phone receiver on his screen. He turned to Megan. "I've got good news. We're getting closer to our killer. I think we need to be very careful from here on out."

"You mean you haven't been up to now?"

Peden just rolled his eyes.

Chapter 21

Ian Tabler was feeling pretty good despite learning that at least one of his fellow beta testers had been questioned by the FBI. Texting back and forth with Carlita Galindo had his heart and mind soaring. He set his completed digital communications project aside and lay back on his bed, wondering what it would be like to ride the roller coasters at Cedar Point with a young woman at his side. He had used his virtual reality game to ride simulated roller coasters, and it was exciting, but he knew that being on a real coaster with the wind blowing his hair and the screams of other riders in his ears would be far more exhilarating, especially sharing the experience with Carlita. He didn't even know what she looked like and had never heard the sound of her voice, but that just added to the mystery and the twinge of excitement. He had asked her to send him a picture of her, hoping that he wasn't being too forward. She had said okay, but it would take a little while because she wanted to send him the best picture of her that she could find.

He smiled at the ceiling, thinking about her. Was she slim, dark-haired, olive-skinned, tall, like a model? Or was she a geek like himself? He really didn't care. She was sweet and thoughtful and concerned about him. It took guts to warn him of the visit from the FBI because he was certain that they told her to not warn her fellow testers. He took a deep breath and closed his eyes.

A quiet knock on his door broke into his thoughts. Still laying on his bed, he propped himself up on one elbow just as Jonah eased the door open and walked in without looking at him. He smiled as Jonah walked over to the seat in front of his television and sat down. Jonah's long, brown, curly hair was a mess, partially covering his expressionless face, but he didn't seem to care. He just sat without a word or any indication why he was here in Ian's room.

Ian asked, "What's on your mind, brother?"

Jonah rambled off a series of numbers in Jonah-code. Ian listened as the numbers rolled across his lips. When he finished, Ian smiled at the question.

"Am I sweet on Carlita? Is it that obvious?"

"25519." Yes.

"I don't know. Maybe. Well, yeah, I guess I am. But she's the only girl I know, and she's a thousand miles away." Ian paused. "Why do you ask?"

Jonah hesitated before saying anything. Then he replied. As Ian's mind translated the number string, he was taken aback. Jonah asked if he was going to leave him alone here, at the compound, with their dad.

He stared at Jonah, his heartbeat ramping up, pounding hard in his chest. It was a question he had asked himself many times before, but not in the context of leaving home for a girl. But he was fifteen and craving any outside human contact. He had often pondered what it would be like for his little brother to have to fend for himself, living here alone without him to translate his thoughts and dreams. He struggled with his own needs and desires versus those of his younger, socially inept little brother. But he had long ago come to the conclusion that there would never be a time that he wouldn't have the room, or the time in his life, for his closest friend and brother.

Ian stood. "Jonah, there is no way I'd ever leave you here alone." He held his hands to his chest. "We're in this together."

He thought he saw his brother's lips curl up in the slightest show of a smile, but he knew that such a gesture was unlikely. He just smiled back at Jonah, hoping that his brother believed that his words were true.

Without hesitation, Jonah stood and headed towards the door. As he reached Ian, he stopped and held out his arms. Ian's smile broadened. His brother, who was petrified of human touch, was soliciting a hug. Did he dare? Would it elicit an ugly response? It was worth a try.

Ian slowly put his arms around his brother, trying to

keep his touch light, making sure that Jonah didn't feel threatened or confined. He was even more surprised when he felt Jonah's arms around his. It brought tears to his eyes. They stayed like that for nearly ten seconds before Jonah slowly pulled away, turned towards the door, and closed it behind him.

Stunned, Ian sat back on his bed, tears streaming down his cheeks. His brother was changing. He hoped the changes were for the better, but time would tell if this was just a temporary state or if Jonah's mind was maturing along with his body.

After a few minutes of reflection, Ian's thoughts shifted to the failed test and its possible relation to the Vega murder. He was still torn about not telling his father of his and Jonah's belief that they might have actually been the killers. There had been many moments over the past few days where he felt compelled to tell his dad everything, but Jonah's emphatic "no" immediately popped into his thoughts. That image, another first for Jonah, kept Ian from telling their father his suspicions.

Why had the idea of talking with their father sparked Jonah's emotional response? It was a first. Ian wondered if that episode had tapped into an area of his brother's brain that had not previously been stimulated. Was that the kick-start that his emotions needed to begin expressing himself outwardly instead of keeping his feelings bottled up?

Ian's cell phone chirped, indicating a new text coming in. He looked at the date and time: 9:30 Wednesday, August 19. Someone was breaking the spell that had been cast first by Carlita Galindo and then by his brother. For the third time this evening, he was shocked. The text was from their FlashGamz representative, David Walsh.

Hi Ian. I know you and your brother are upset that we had to break off all communications during the last test. We had some issues that had to be addressed and we couldn't risk contacting you. But we're ready to restart the testing. I'm sending out a flash drive to all of our testers with the new program. I'd like for you and Jonah to be ready to begin testing Friday evening at 6:00 PM. Let me know if that's a problem.

Ian stared at the text. He sat in the chair where Jonah had just sat, his mind racing, wondering how he should respond. Before he decided if he and Jonah would continue with testing, he needed answers, but what questions could he ask without tipping his hand that they thought this game was somehow linked to the murder of Senator Vega. He decided to wait for a few minutes before he answered. He could always claim that he didn't have his phone with him to explain the delay.

This communication was too important to text back and forth, but he wanted a record of the call for his own protection. His communications project included a recording device that wirelessly tapped into incoming and outgoing signals on his cell phone and other electronic devices in close range. The unit took the signals, sent them to different channels, sorted them by signal strength, and recorded each separately. He had just completed the program and finished testing when he received his first text from Carlita. His pleasure at completing that part of the project was hijacked by the joy of hearing from Miss Galindo. Now, with the communication from David Walsh, his concentration again shifted back to the Vega murder and his potential role.

He didn't have enough run-time with the recording device to fine-tune the capture zone, so he set the unit up to harness only signals that were within fifty feet. The ten minutes spent preparing the unit gave him time to think back on his day, with so many issues tugging at his emotions. For a normal fifteen-year-old, the stress would have been difficult, but with Ian's extremely high IQ, his mind raced from one thought to another, never losing concentration on the highly technical task at hand.

He took a deep breath and smiled. The device, intended to capture his dad's conversations so he could help with financial matters, was now set up for an entirely different purpose. Another deep breath and he was ready to make the call to the FlashGamz representative, David Walsh. Before he dialed, he wondered if Walsh had contacted any of the other testers. This would be a great excuse to call Carlita.

Just then his phone chirped. A new text had arrived. What now? He tensed, reaching for his cell phone. He exhaled and smiled at the same time. It was Carlita, and her text had an attachment. His excitement grew.

He opened the attachment and smiled. The picture, a shot from her shoulders up, was professionally done. Dark hair framed a thin face as perfect as he'd ever seen. Her dark eyes and smile lifted his spirits. A small mole on the left side of her chin was slightly darker than her olive complexion.

Another chirp from his phone shattered his trance. His emotions were again shoved off a cliff. It was David Walsh again, asking if he had read his text yet. Decision time.

He texted back.

Let me call you tomorrow around lunchtime. I have to talk with Jonah first.

Walsh replied immediately.

Okay.

Ian took a deep breath then texted Carlita.

I hope I'm not being too forward, but you are beautiful. Thank you for the picture. I don't mean to switch to business, but I just heard from David Walsh. Did he contact you?

Ian waited for her reply. He didn't have to wait long.

No. Did he tell you what's going on, why no contact after the test failure?

Ian wanted to text back. He decided to call her instead. His nerves were in overdrive as he hit the green phone icon. His heart pounded in his chest as the ring tones sounded in his ear.

In a quiet, tentative voice, the beautiful sound of Carlita Galindo came over his phone. "Hello?"

It took Ian a second to clear his throat, but he finally choked out, "Hi, Carlita. It's Ian."

She giggled quietly, then said, "I know, Ian. Your name

popped up on my phone. I hope you liked the picture."

"It is beautiful." He hesitated, his nerves on overdrive. "I mean, you're beautiful. Thank you. And thank you for telling me about your visitors. Like I said, don't worry about telling them about Jonah and me. It was the right thing to do."

"I still feel kinda weird about it. So, tell me about Mr. Walsh. What's going on?"

Ian took a deep breath. He really didn't want to talk about David Walsh, or FlashGamz, or the continuation of testing. He really just wanted to get to know this young lady. But the text from Walsh was the primary reason for the call.

"I haven't texted him back yet except to let him know that I got his text. I'll call him tomorrow. I think we need to let the others know that he wants us to keep testing, but I need to figure out the real reason for the delay."

Carlita said, "Ian, be careful what you say. This whole thing frightens me. I'm still not sure why the FBI was here asking about our testing. I haven't heard from anyone else since the day after the test failed. Simon Andrews hasn't texted me at all. Neither have Tony or Ricky Lee. Have you heard from them?"

"No, just you. How about you text Simon and Ricky Lee, I'll text Tony, and I'll talk with Jonah. Tell them to text you the minute they get the word that testing is starting up again. Tell them to not let Mr. Walsh know that they already heard about it. Stress that point with them, please."

"Ian, I'm scared. Have we done something illegal?"

"No. No, we haven't. I'll let you know what Walsh says tomorrow."

"Okay." There was a pause. "Ian, it's nice to finally hear your voice. Now you have to send me your picture so I can put a face to your voice."

Ian thought for a minute. He didn't really have any pictures of himself, but he could take a selfie and send it to her. "I'll send you one right away. It won't be as nice as yours, I guarantee that."

Carlita laughed. "That's okay. Bye."

Within seconds after hanging up, Ian took the selfie and sent it to Carlita. After he hit send, he smiled. It felt good to talk with someone other than Jonah, not that their conversations weren't interesting and fun. Talking with Carlita was different: new and exciting.

He took a deep breath as a smile grew.

Chapter 22

The call with Carlita last evening had Ian walking on air. He was overwhelmed with emotions that he'd never, in his entire life, experienced before. Was he in a real relationship with a girl? It was all new to him, and he wondered where this might go. Was it love? If yes, he liked it and hoped it would never end.

But it was interrupted. After returning to his bedroom just after lunch, dread befell him. Sitting in front of his television, he eyed his cell phone for as long as he dared. If he delayed much longer, he would avoid the call completely, which wasn't an option. He rubbed his eyes as he took a deep breath, picked up the phone, and tapped in the number for David Walsh.

Ian listened as the phone rang once, then twice. His hopes jumped that Walsh would be gone forever, but those hopes were dashed when the familiar voice of his FlashGamz contact answered.

"Ian, I was just getting ready to call you."

He had a plan, but the intensity of the moment caught his tongue. As usual, his mind raced at the speed of light until a thought hit him – *calm down, remember the plan.* He took a deep breath. It was time to talk about testing.

David Walsh again said, "Hello, Ian. Are you there?"

In a calm voice and with as much confidence as he could muster, Ian replied, "Mr. Walsh, I've been trying to reach you. What happened?" *Good job. Keep it simple and to the point.* "Jonah and I figured that we might never hear from you again."

"No, son, we just ran into some issues." There was a brief pause, then Walsh continued. "We think that another company hacked our system and stole the code for the new game, but we determined that they couldn't have. But we did run some tests and made some changes to our security, just to be sure that there won't be another opportunity for those pirates to steal from us in the future. We also made some programming changes to the app, and we'd like to get our testing team back in the game."

Ian relaxed more as Walsh spoke. His voice was smooth as silk. Ian thought it was odd that Walsh called him son, but for all he knew, the guy might be old enough to be his dad, so he brushed it off.

Ian said, "You know, we had some real problems with the last test, not just with the code either."

Walsh asked, "What do you mean?"

"The flash drive burned up."

There was a moment of silence before Walsh spoke, as if he was trying to figure out what Ian had said. "When you say, 'burned up,' what do you mean, exactly?"

"Burned up, flamed out, physically burnt to a crisp. All that was left was ashes and the metal USB plug."

"Damn. I'm sorry about that. Was anything damaged? Your equipment or the house?"

Ian replied, "No, nothing. I was actually surprised that it didn't destroy anything, but the only damage was to the flash drive. That was totally destroyed."

"Wow. I bet your old man was pissed."

"Actually, he wasn't as mad about it as I thought he would be. He took it in stride. We got everything cleaned up. The smell lingered, but that was it."

"Did it freak you and your brother out? I mean, that had to be pretty, uh, exciting isn't the right word. How about terrifying?"

"No, more like surprised. It was quick."

Walsh waited for a moment, then got to the point of his call. "I hope you guys can support this new round of testing. It'll be tomorrow at 6:00 PM. I know this is rushed and it's around dinner time, but we have some time constraints that require us to test at that time. And we're offering a five-thousand-dollar bonus on top of our normal fifteen-thousand-dollar payment each for you and your brother. And if you find any issues or things that can improve the game's performance, there's the usual bonuses after the game hits the market. We'll wire the money to your account after I get your verbal confirmation that you'll both participate. Are you in?"

Ian paused just a moment, brushed back his hair with his free hand, then answered, "Yeah, we're in."

Obviously pleased, Walsh answered, "Excellent. I'll overnight the flash drive to you. I hope to get the other testers on board in the next hour. No real changes to the test procedure. You guys probably know it by heart. But please look it over anyways. Just to be sure."

"We will, Mr. Walsh."

"Excellent."

The call, which lasted all of four minutes, disconnected. Ian took a deep breath and sat down on the edge of his bed. He had pulled it off, kept his cool, and didn't lead on that he suspected that FlashGamz might be involved in killing Senator Vega.

After several minutes passed, he heard the familiar sound of feet bounding up the steps to his bedroom and knew his dad was on his way. He placed his recording device on the floor behind his bed. He didn't want to spoil the surprise until he fine-tuned his invention. There was a knock on the door, then it opened a crack. Nicholas Tabler leaned his head in and looked around the room.

"Hey, son. Is your brother here?"

"No, sir. I think he's in his room."

"Excellent. Have you heard from that Walsh guy from FlashGamz yet?"

Ian was taken aback. His father hadn't asked about the testing or the FlashGamz representative since the morning of the drive failure. Was this just a coincidence? Was his dad somehow monitoring his calls? If he was, he had better tell him the truth.

"Yes, sir. I just got off the phone with him. I mean, just a few minutes ago."

"Wow. Took him long enough. What did he say?"

Ian told his father about Walsh's explanation of an attempted hack into their computers and that they were giving the testers a bonus because of the inconvenience. He thought about telling his dad that he was skeptical of the reasons, but something told him to skip his feelings and stick to the facts.

Ian finished by saying, "So, testing is on for tomorrow night at 6:00 . I haven't told Jonah yet, but I know he'll be ready."

Nichols Tabler seemed pleased. He nodded, "Excellent, son. Sounds like this might be back on track."

"Yes, sir."

Without another word, Ian's father turned and closed the door behind him.

Ian heard the footsteps as they made their way down the staircase. He took another deep breath. Something was bothering him. He couldn't put his finger on it, but thoughts were bouncing around his head related to the call from David Walsh and his father's showing up immediately after. He couldn't dwell on it. He had a recording device to fine-tune. He'd use the recently recorded conversation with Walsh to do it.

Maybe he would call Carlita Galindo later and see how her conversation went with David Walsh. She seemed genuinely concerned when they spoke earlier. He wanted her to know that everything went fine with the FlashGamz representative. Thinking about her caused him to momentarily forget about his recording project. He smiled.

There were more footsteps just outside his door, and he knew from the slow, quiet cadence that it was Jonah. After a quiet knock on his door, Jonah opened it slowly and walked in.

"Hey, brother. I have news. I just got a call from David Walsh."

The news caused Jonah to stop in his tracks. He turned and faced Ian. Was there fear in those dark, normally emotionless eyes?

"What's the matter?"

Jonah was silent. He continued to stare, but his focus wasn't on Ian. His eyes appeared distant, as if deep in thought. Ian was becoming unnerved. His younger brother, with whom he spent nearly every waking hour since his birth, was changing before his eyes. Ian again wondered if the changes in Jonah's body and mind were awakening in him feelings that had previously been suppressed, buried somewhere in the complexity of a computer-like mind.

After a minute, Jonah's eyes locked on Ian. He spoke in code, rattling off a series of numbers. Ian tried to follow the message but was stunned. Prior to this moment, Jonah had never had a strong opinion about much of anything. Now, he was refusing to participate in the next round of beta testing. Ian's jaw dropped, and his eyes widened in surprise.

"What do you mean you won't test? I already told Mr. Walsh that we would both be testing. He's getting the others lined up. The test is tomorrow at 6:00 PM."

Jonah replied, "1415." No.

"Why?"

Jonah's next string of numbers translated to the question, *Do you want to help him kill again?*

Ian took a deep breath and turned away from Jonah's stare. He knew that the FBI was already looking into FlashGamz but wasn't sure how close they were to figuring out who was responsible for the murder. He turned back to Jonah and said, "No. Of course not. But I think we can come up with a plan to prove that none of the testers had anything to do with the last murder. Maybe this test is really just to test the game this time."

Jonah said nothing. Instead, he headed towards the door and motioned for Ian to follow him. Ian picked up his phone and followed his brother down the steps, across the house, then down another set of steps to their computer lab. Jonah walked over to his computer, hit hundreds of keys at lightning speed, and stepped back. The massive flat panel monitor was filled with computer code. After just a brief glance, Ian knew that they were looking at the original code for the game *Assassin-*

Best in the Business.

"Where did you get this?"

Jonah rattled off a long monologue using his code. Ian listened as his younger brother explained that he copied the code from the flash drive before the last test. He explained that he always did that just so he could look for ways to improve the code, sometimes even before they ran the official beta tests.

Jonah stared straight at the monitor and pointed to a spot on the screen. Ian read the code at the tip of Jonah's finger.

There it was. The evidence that clearly and purposely triggered the flash drive to self-destruct. There was no doubt about it, David Walsh, or someone within FlashGamz, wanted the evidence destroyed.

The brothers heard footsteps. Their father was headed their way. Ian thought it might be time to tell their dad what they knew. He turned to talk with Jonah about confiding in their father, but his brother was busy closing the program and putting a different video game up on the monitor. When finished, he turned to Ian and vigorously shook his head – *No!*

Ian was still trying to figure out why Jonah wanted their dad out of the loop when the lab door opened. Nicholas Tabler walked in, a puzzled look on his face.

"Are you guys all set for testing tomorrow?"

Ian had gathered his wits and replied, "Yes, sir, except that we don't have the new flash drive with the code yet. Once we get that, we'll be all set."

"As soon as it arrives, I'll get it to you."

"Thank you, sir."

An awkward silence ensued. No one said a word for nearly a full minute when Ian's phone chirped. He hoped that it was Carlita Galindo, not David Walsh.

Ian noticed that Jonah stared straight ahead at the computer monitor. He hadn't made a sound.

Nicholas Tabler nodded. "Alright then." He left and closed the door behind him.

Ian took a deep breath and turned to his brother.

Jonah's shoulders were slumped down, and he was no longer looking at the large computer screen. He was looking at the floor. Once again, Ian's mind raced, individual thoughts competing for his attention. Which topic had priority? He walked over to his brother and lightly, slowly put a hand on his shoulder. Jonah didn't flinch, didn't jerk back, didn't show any response.

"You okay, little brother?"

Jonah took a deep breath and said, "9239121225." *I will be.* After a pause, he said, "920891411." *I think.*

Ian looked at his phone. He smiled when he saw that the text was from Carlita. When he looked up, Jonah was staring at him. He didn't know exactly why, but he felt guilty.

Jonah took a deep breath, headed out the door, and closed it behind him.

Ian waited for a moment before reading Carlita's text.

Received call from Walsh. He said you and Jonah have signed on to continue testing. I agreed to test as well. Call me when you can.

Ian looked at the time on his cell phone. 9:53 PM. The question bouncing around in his mind was how much should he tell Carlita. Another chirp on his phone. It was her wondering if he had read her text. He hit the phone icon near her name. After just one ring, she answered.

"Hi, Ian."

Ian smiled. He tucked his troubles away, far in the back of his mind.

Chapter 23

Sitting in a dining room down the hall from the oval office, Alton Woodburn closed his eyes for the thousandth time, hoping that when he opened them, the world would be a different, safer place for him and his family: an odd thought for a man with arguably the most extensive personal security on the planet.

He wasn't concerned about world events, even though the Middle East was a tinderbox, ready to explode at the first provocation by any number of extremist groups. To the east, the friction between Pakistan and India held potential nuclear disaster. Russia and Ukraine were always on the brink of war over some obscure stretch of land along their common border, whether real or fabricated by the Russian President, and China was constantly probing for an opportunity to "welcome" Taiwan, "their rebellious province," back into the fold. There was enough tension in the world that any one of those conflicts, or a dozen more in different parts of the world, some much closer to home, could drive any person crazy.

But that wasn't what troubled the President of the United States this day. Alton Woodburn was concerned about one event in particular, and he was awaiting word on its status. He knew that he could have no direct ties to the demise of Nevin Tate, hence his request that his friend and business partner, Ernest Porter, handle the job. Porter's hands already had blood on them: actions that were sanctioned by his country, though approved at a level that placed them into the classification of "dark ops." Porter knew the right people to get the job done in a way that left no path back to the source of those requests. That's what Woodburn needed now. He needed Tate gone, and without a trace.

Today of all days, Woodburn's wife decided to have a late lunch with her husband. He tried, without success, to hide the edginess in his manner. He was physically in the room with her, but his attention and his blank stare were somewhere else. She had asked what was wrong. He had said that the job was just a little tough right now, that he couldn't talk about it, but that the issue would soon be resolved and the world would be a better, safer place when the job was finished.

She just smiled and finished her Cobb salad with iced tea, then left the room. Before she left, she kissed his forehead and told him to not let the job get him down.

He forced a smile and watched her leave. He had barely touched his lunch and drank only water. When he got back to the oval office, he'd have a couple fingers of scotch to calm his nerves. He stood and closed the door to the small, private dining room and sat back down, pushing his plate away. With his elbows on the table, he closed his eyes, pushed his hair back, and held his head down, trying to imagine Nevin Tate lying on a stainless-steel gurney in the cold, dark basement of some medical examiner's domain. He envisioned Tate's pale-white body with a single bullet wound to the chest, his eyes closed, his body pale, cold, and still in the chilled environment.

Suddenly, Tate's eyes popped open. Woodburn jerked with a start. He opened his own eyes and muttered, "Oh God."

A cell phone rang in his coat pocket, which hung on a gold-plated coat rack by the door. Nearly knocking his chair over in his haste to get to the phone, he searched through the pockets in near panic. Was it good news? Was the beast dead? Could he get back to living his life in relative peace?

He finally located the right cell phone, yanked it out, and looked at the screen. He let out an audible, "Oh God."

It was Tate.

Woodburn thought about ignoring the call, but Tate would keep calling back until he answered, getting more agitated, and more dangerous each time Woodburn failed to answer. The man who was supposedly the most powerful man on the planet swiped across the screen and answered the call. He took a deep breath.

"What do you want, Tate?"

In his usual condescending, sing-song voice, Nevin Tate answered, "Alton. Is that any way to answer a call from your best friend in the world? I want to commend you again for the great job creating our distraction. Nobody from either party expected you to become a high-spending liberal. The press is focused on you now. That's good. And I have some great news."

Woodburn didn't speak. His nerves caused the hair on the back of his neck to grow prickly. The silence on the phone grew. When Tate didn't speak, Woodburn finally said, "What news?"

"We have a new client, one with deep pockets. We'll be expanding our business. And we're going to ensure that the War on Drugs continues. You'll read about it during your Saturday morning briefing, but it will be all over the news in a special report tomorrow evening. Isn't that great?"

Tate's proclamation meant only one thing. Someone else was set to die. Someone prominent, someone who was making noise about the cost of the ongoing War on Drugs. Only a handful of senators or house members were as vocal about the failed federal government program as Armand Vega, but the small chorus of voices had been growing over the last year. With the movement to legalize marijuana and decriminalize other drugs, the number of officials calling for scaling back the financial support for the program was spreading. But who was Tate's target? Would Porter be able to take him out before anyone else had to die?

Woodburn's stomach started to roil. He was glad that he hadn't eaten much of his lunch. He heard Tate's voice over his cell.

"Alton, are you still with me?"

"Yeah, Tate. I'm here. Who is it?"

"Sorry, Alton, you'll just have to be surprised. You can hear it on the news, just like the little people."

Woodburn realized that he had been staring at the table in front of him. When he looked up at the picture on the wall behind where his wife had sat, the room began to spin. His skin felt clammy and his mouth went dry. The next thing he knew, a secret service agent was helping him sit up on the floor next to the chair where he sat just a moment before. He had passed out.

The agent was on his radio requesting assistance. Within seconds, the room was filled with people, from secret service agents to White House staffers and medical personnel. One staff paramedic strapped a blood pressure cuff on his left arm while another shined a penlight in his eyes. After shaking his head to clear his thoughts, he asked, "Where's my cell phone?"

One of the agents said, "Right here, Mr. President."

Woodburn took the phone and looked at the screen. The call was disconnected. After a sigh of relief, the president, in a loud, commanding voice, said, "I'm fine. I just tripped when I stood." He ripped the blood pressure cuff from his arm and looked around the room. "You will not speak of this incident to anyone. Is that clear?"

When heads nodded slightly, he said louder, "I said is that clear?"

The men and women attending to him all replied, "Yes, Mr. President."

When the room cleared, Woodburn sat back down, rubbed his face and eyes, and shook his head again. He couldn't take this pressure much longer. He knew he shouldn't call, but he needed an update from Porter. He had to know when this nightmare would end.

The walk back to the oval office was a short one, but it seemed like the length of a football field, and he was on the twenty-yard line with the entire stadium staring down at him. He wasn't sure if the looks from White House staffers were of concern for his health or if they even knew that he had fallen. But he felt the weight of the stares on him, each one like a tractor beam, sucking the life out of him, draining the energy that he needed for other, important issues.

Issues? In his mind, there were no other issues – just one. If Tate were out of the picture, everything else would seem like child's play.

Woodburn strode through the door to the reception room next to the oval office and was surprised to see his personal physician waiting for him. He didn't know who, but someone had alerted the doctor of his episode. He forced a half-smile and cursed. "Christ, you can't keep a secret in this place. Come on in, Doc. Let's get this over with."

With a serious, rather grim look, Doctor Prescott followed the president into the oval office with his briefcase. Once Woodburn was seated, the doctor placed the briefcase on a table and pulled out a blood pressure unit and a stethoscope. He turned to Woodburn, who had already rolled his sleeve back, and placed the cuff over his left bicep. His expression conveyed a grim prognosis even before he began to take the most basic of vital readings.

"You know, Mr. President, that we've already discussed the seriousness of your hypertension and high cholesterol." He began to pump up the sleeve. When he finished pumping, he placed the buds of the stethoscope into his ears, then began releasing the air pressure. Within seconds, his brow furrowed even more than before. He released the pressure fully, then pulled the buds from his ear. "Mr. President, I'm not going to sugar-coat it. We need to do a full physical exam within the next few days. And we must take some immediate actions to relieve your stress. You are at extremely high risk for a stroke, even a heart attack."

Woodburn, with a smirk, said, "Tell me something I don't know, Doc. If I do the physical, I need this completed in secrecy. I can't have the country thinking that I'm ill."

"But, Mr. President, you are ill. And you're not getting better. I'm putting you on a very precise dietary regiment and an exercise routine that you must do daily." His face still conveying the gravity of his words, he continued, "I'll give strict instructions to the appropriate staffers and your wife."

Trying to laugh off the doctor's last comments, he said, "You wouldn't. Not my wife!" When Doctor Prescott's expression didn't change, he sighed. "Okay, Doctor, you win. I know you're right. Do what you have to, and I'll go along."

"It is for your own good, and the good of the country. Trust me, you'll thank me later."

Right.

When the doctor finally left him alone, Woodburn pulled out his private cell phone and hit the speed-dial number for Ernest Porter, who answered on the second ring.

"Alton, what's up?"

In a gruff voice that bordered on anger, Woodburn growled, "When is our problem going away?"

There was silence on the line. Porter was apparently weighing how much to say on a call that was most likely being monitored by several federal agencies. When he spoke, it was cryptic at best.

"I expect to hear back very soon."

The pitch of Woodburn's response grew in both volume and intensity. "Very soon, huh. That sounds like bullshit to me. Porter, you get that son of a bitch out ..."

In an abrupt, loud voice, Porter cut him off. "Alton! Alton! Stop! Not over the phone. Good God, man. Calm down."

Woodburn stopped, then said in a quieter tone filled with tension, "Just get it done."

Woodburn disconnected the call before Porter could reply.

Chapter 24

The jet made a smooth landing at Marine Corps Airstrip at Quantico, Virginia. A young FBI agent was there with an official-looking car to shuttle Megan and Peden away to the FBI lab just off of J. Edgar Hoover Road. The trip took less than ten minutes. They cleared security and walked into the lab just after midnight.

Lee Sparks and his FBI counterparts were at individual stations, researching FlashGamz, the beta testers, all their known associates, and any business dealings carried on by any of the subjects. They all looked groggy, burned out, and in need of sleep.

Megan reached into her purse as she approached Lee Sparks, pulled out a plastic bag and handed it to him. Lee held up the bag and saw the flash drive, looking as good as new. He attempted a smile but fell short. Peden could see that he was beyond fatigued and in drastic need of rest.

Peden suggested, "Hey, Lee, why don't you guys knock off and get some sleep. You're all just about nodding off at your desks as it is."

"We were waiting to get our hands on this drive." He held up the device that Megan had just handed over.

"Okay, you have it, now lock it up in a safe place and get some shut-eye. You won't be any good to us if you can't concentrate."

Megan spoke up. "Same goes for you guys. Liam, get everybody out of here and get some rest. If you fight me on this, I'll call Randall and have him give the order. He probably won't appreciate a call at this hour." Randall Fry was their direct supervisor.

Liam said, "No argument here, Agent Moore." He turned to his lab partners. "Let's wrap it up for tonight. We'll pick it back up in the morning."

One-by-one, the techies closed up their workstations and headed out the lab's door. Lee stayed behind and turned to Megan and Peden. "We can't find any good information on the property on Tybee Island. It's like the owners are ghosts. There are names listed on the company's website, but there's no way to contact them."

Peden replied, "Don't worry about it tonight. You just get some shut-eye and look at everything with fresh eyes tomorrow."

"All right, my man. They have a bed for me downstairs with a private bath and everything." He yawned loudly then waved to them as he made his way out the same door as his peers.

Megan turned to Peden. "We can't stay here tonight. I'll get us set up at the hotel off I-95, then we can fly out in the morning. Hope you brought some clean underwear."

Peden gave her the palms-up look as if to ask, *Where would I be hiding any clean clothes?*

She almost smiled, but not quite.

* * *

It was an interesting night at the hotel. According to Megan, they had only one available room with a queen-sized bed, which they shared. Peden felt like he was sleeping with his sister, trying to maintain some distance between them without falling out of bed. It was nearly impossible to get comfortable because the bed was worn and had a slope in the mattress that caused Peden and Megan to both roll to the center. Megan, stripped down to her bra and panties, fell asleep almost as soon as her head hit the stack of pillows. Peden, sleeping in his briefs, tossed and turned for what seemed like an eternity before getting a few hours of restless sleep.

It was very early Thursday morning. Megan was showering and Peden was thinking about the timeline of events. He picked up his cell phone and hit speed dial for Marcus Cook.

Marcus was an early riser. Peden figured that he'd be finished with his workout and heading to his office at the Drug

Enforcement Administration in Atlanta.

"My gosh, Peden. You're up early." Marcus sounded chipper, even energetic.

Peden answered in little more than a whisper, "Yeah, well, I didn't get much sleep. We're in a dive hotel outside Quantico. The bed's mattress should have been replaced years ago."

Marcus' voice had the unmistakable sound of disbelief. "And by 'we,' you mean you ... and Megan?"

Peden thought before he answered. The way he described it to Marcus, combined with him speaking in a hushed voice, made it sound like he had something to hide, or that he was implying that he and Megan slept together. He quickly tried to recover. "No, no, Marcus, we slept in the same bed but that was because there was only one room available. It was all innocent, trust me. You know Megan. All business."

"You don't have to convince me, my man. Just watch yourself. She is one tough broad."

Marcus helped Peden's discomfort regarding the situation by changing the subject. "Why the early call?"

Peden took a deep breath and looked towards the bathroom door. The shower was still running, so he was sure Megan was still occupied. "Lee is making progress working with the folks at the FBI lab. They have a line on the drone manufacturer and dealer. It's an outfit out of Omaha, Nebraska – Pinnacle Aeronautics. They do some business with the Pentagon, some law enforcement agencies, mostly at the state level and above, and some work for private aviation companies. Also, there's a company called FlashGamz that produces video games. They created a game called *Assassin – Best in the Business* that appears to be at the center of this. They hired teenage kids to do their beta testing on this game. The testers may have been controlling the drone and the weapon used to kill Vega."

"That's cold, man. Using kids to do your dirty work? I hope we catch the bastard."

The water in the shower turned off. Peden said to

Marcus, "I've gotta cut this short. Megan's finishing up, and I don't want her to know that I'm talking about the case with you."

"Gotcha. Call me again when you can. By the way, we finished our checks on all the new guys at the Savannah office. They're all clean. No worries there."

"Okay, Marcus, talk with you soon."

The call was disconnected. Peden put his phone on the nightstand and stood to stretch. After a few minutes, Megan came out with a towel wrapped around her body. She said, "Did Marcus have anything for us?"

Peden's jaw dropped.

* * *

Within the hour, Peden and Megan were on their way to the Marine Corps Air Strip at Quantico. Peden was thinking about their interview with Tony Pirelli and that his flash drive was intact. Why did one drive survive and the rest burnt to a crisp? All the other testers described identical failures: drives destroyed by a small flame that didn't cause any other damage to any computer equipment or anything else in the vicinity of the drive. Lee Sparks confirmed that an accelerant was used to produce the flame and that it must have had a signal of some kind to initiate the destruction of the drive. The flame was intense but sized perfectly to destroy only the drive. If a person can use that much precision to destroy four drives, it seemed odd to Peden that one drive would have a 'self-destruct' malfunction.

Megan broke into his thoughts. "I don't think it was a mistake that Pirelli's flash drive didn't smoke."

Peden looked at her, amazed that she read his thoughts. "I was just thinking the same thing. So, why leave one drive intact and destroy the other four?"

"To throw us off the trail, occupy our resources, to point us in the wrong direction. We have to question the folks at Pinnacle Aeronautics, see if we can get them to play ball. I'll have the Omaha office get a warrant for their sales records. It might take some convincing to get a judge to sign off on it, but

I think they may be the key to identify the purchaser."

Peden was again deep in thought. He worried that they were missing something in their interviews with the kids. They were geniuses, prodigies. Wouldn't they know if they were being played? Peden had read somewhere that some prodigies were super intelligent when it came to "book smarts" but had some challenges with common sense. Peden wondered if these kids would recognize the evil in someone trying to take advantage of their skills, which were laser-like focused.

He said, "Can you think of anything that we didn't ask these kids?"

Megan gave him a sideways glance then turned her head to look out the window. Their driver stopped forty feet from the steps leading into the Learjet. The engines were already warmed. The pilot met them as Megan ascended the four steps to the fuselage with Peden right behind her. The pilot told them to get buckled in because they had the all-clear to taxi into position for take-off. He said they would be in the air in just a few minutes.

Once seated, Megan said, "We never asked them about any of the games that they had previously tested for FlashGamz. What if this isn't the first time, maybe someone not as well known, or maybe a test run where the drone didn't get destroyed."

"We need to look at any data that was gathered from that drone that approached the German Chancellor a few years back. What if that was a test run?"

"Only problem with that is these kids weren't old enough to be testers back then."

Peden nodded. "But what if these kids weren't the original testers? Maybe these are the upgrades. The old testers weren't good enough, so they picked up these new, higher-performing kids to make sure they got the job done right."

The Lear rolled into place at the head of the runway. It barely hesitated as the engines roared to life, and the jet lurched forward, picking up speed. The nose lifted then the sound of the tires on the runway fell silent, and they were air-born, headed for Savannah/Hilton Head International Airport.

As the jet angled up and banked east over the Potomac River, the Chesapeake Bay came into view. Then after a few seconds, the Atlantic Ocean was visible in the distance. A thin, red line ran across the ocean's surface as the sun continued its rise above the horizon.

Megan turned to Peden and said, "Let's call Lee and get the team looking into the details of the German drone. Also, see if there were other, less well-known attacks or scares. Once we land, I'll call our office in Omaha and get them moving. You call Lee."

The rest of the flight was quiet because Peden fell asleep. He had some catching up to do after the disaster at the hotel.

* * *

Even though the pilot made a smooth landing, Peden awoke with a start. He had to clear his head while the Lear decelerated and headed for the private jet terminal. As soon as Peden turned on his cell phone, it rang. He looked at the screen but didn't recognize the number except that it had a Savannah area code.

He swiped across his screen and spoke, "Savage Investigative Consultants."

"This is Dr. Emerson Stram at Memorial Health University Medical Center. I was Mr. Michael Jess's surgeon. I'm sorry, but Mr. Jess passed away overnight."

Peden was shocked. He thought that Jess was on the road to recovery. It took a moment to think straight.

He asked, "How ... I mean, what changed?"

"Mr. Jess developed a blood clot that went to his heart, called a cardiogenic embolism. Basically, it stopped his heart from functioning. I'm sorry, we did everything we could."

Peden couldn't think of anything else to say, except, "Thank you, Doctor."

Chapter 25

As was usual for Ian Tabler, he slept for only three hours, a stretch of sleep that was far from restful; his dreams vivid almost from the moment his eyes closed. They ranged from calm, sweet images of Carlita Galindo to the hectic wartime scenarios in a variety of video games. In the final dream, before he woke with a start, he and Jonah were in the woods defending a Princess, whose face looked remarkably like Carlita, from an onslaught of cyber weapons. They fought valiantly to save the princess, but the enemies just kept coming. He awoke with a start, bathed in sweat.

He stumbled to his bathroom, relieved himself, stripped and jumped into the shower. So far, everything followed his normal routine, except that the dreams were more intense than usual. As he showered, he thought about Carlita and her beautiful picture, and her sweet, silky voice. Although the usual dozen topics competed for his attention, he focused on his – what, girlfriend? Or were they just friends, two people doing the same work, testing computer programs? *What if that is all we have in common? Maybe she has a boyfriend already?*

Ian made up his mind that he was going to call her later in the morning. He would talk about business, but he really just wanted to hear her voice, find out more about her, her interests, her family. *She's obviously intelligent, a high achiever. She already said she likes amusement parks. I wonder if she listens to music, or plays an instrument, or enjoys cooking?*

He dressed, picked up his digital recorder, and headed down to the basement computer room. He hoped that the device had recorded his conversation with David Walsh since the changes that he'd made just yesterday hadn't been tested. His and Jonah's powerful computers sat silent, waiting to be powered-up. At 4:30 AM, Ian didn't expect to hear from his little brother for at least another two hours. Jonah was also a habitual early riser, but he slept nearly eight full hours. He usually went to his room about 8:30 PM and was asleep by 10:00. Ian often wondered why their sleep patterns were so different. They both had high IQs with an elevated level of brain activity, but for some reason, Jonah was able to turn it off, or at least dial it back enough to achieve a deep sleep.

When they were much younger, they had shared a single bedroom. Their father explained to Ian that he felt better if he remained close to Jonah as much as possible. It was during this time that Ian had learned to communicate with Jonah and understand his little brother's code. Their father never spent enough time with his sons to catch on to the fact that Jonah was as brilliant as Ian in many ways.

When Jonah turned ten, he had told Ian that he wanted his own bedroom, his own space, that he didn't need a babysitter. Ian understood those feelings, but when he spoke with their father, he asked for his own room under the guise that it was at his request and for his benefit, not Jonah's. Nicholas had agreed that it was the proper time, and the change was made. Ian moved into his own room, and Jonah remained in their former joint bedroom.

Now that Ian was thinking about girls, he was grateful for the privacy, though Jonah could, and did, walk in unannounced. Only in the last few days had Jonah started knocking on the door before entering. It had never crossed Ian's mind that he might someday need even more privacy, until now.

Ian's thoughts took an abrupt turn to beta testing. He believed that tomorrow evening's test might be another real-to-life assassination. He wondered if there might be a way to prove that neither he nor his fellow testers were responsible for Senator Vega's murder. He certainly didn't want any part of another killing. But if they participated in the testing, how could they know that one of them wasn't in control of a killer drone? He needed to talk with the other testers. Between the six of them, they had some of the greatest young minds in the country. Certainly, they could come up with a plan to determine which one of them controlled the weapon and abort the attack – if the test was an actual assassination attempt.

Ian thought about the call to David Walsh that he had recorded. He placed the device on the desk in front of one of the large forty-two-inch monitors. As the unit powered up, he went back over the conversation in his mind. There was something about the way Walsh spoke to him. It wasn't what he said, but the way he said it. He shook it off, donned a set of earbuds, and pressed the volume down button to make sure he didn't blow out his eardrums. The time indicator, a bright red LED display, sat at sixty minutes. He frowned. He must have forgotten to turn the unit off after his call to Walsh ended. He hit the full-back button, and the timer reset to zero. He hit play and slowly raised the volume until he heard his own voice speaking to David Walsh on yesterday's call. A minor adjustment and the sound from the recorder came across as clear as the actual call.

Ian listened to the entire call, all four minutes of it. He was just about to reset the recording to zero when he heard a series of clicks, then several tones, as if someone was making another call. Curious, he waited as a ringtone sounded. Seconds later, a voice that he recognized came on. It was Carlita Galindo.

"*Hello.*"

"*Miss Galindo, this is David Walsh.*"

Ian heard Carlita take a deep breath.

"*Hello, Mr. Walsh. I wasn't sure that I would hear from you again.*"

"*Yes, well, we ran into some problems with the last test.*"

Ian was shellshocked. David Walsh's call to Carlita had to have originated in close proximity to the compound, unless the recorder had a longer range than he had anticipated. He turned his attention back to the call. The conversation was very similar to his exchange with Walsh.

Throughout the brief call, Carlita remained composed with not a hint of anxiety. He smiled to himself, knowing that her nerves must have been in overdrive. He wondered if Walsh would call the other testers, one after another, so he kept the recorder playing after the call disconnected. Within seconds of disconnecting the call with Carlita, Walsh called Tony Pirelli. He then called the remaining two testers, Ricky Lee Lyle and Simon Andrews. They all had agreed to participate in the next test, which was set to begin in a little over thirty-six hours. Ian's mind began to formulate a plan, but he had to communicate with the other testers, and soon.

During the calls, Ricky Lee Lyle appeared calm, his voice a smooth, southern drawl. There wasn't a hint of shock or concern. Both Tony Pirelli and Simon Andrews sounded hesitant, their voices laced in anxiety. Somehow, David Walsh calmed them down, not appearing overly concerned about their hesitation and unaware that the FBI had contacted each of the testers with questions about a connection to the very public murder of a prominent Senator. In the end, all four of the other testers were on board.

Ian looked at the recording device. He had stopped the playback after Walsh's final call, the one to Simon Andrews. He looked at the time display and noticed that all the recorded calls took slightly over twenty-eight minutes. He wondered what other calls David Walsh might have made. He hit the play button and listened as the sounds of tones indicated a call being made, then was answered in a gravelly, terse manner.

"What do you want, Tate?"

"Alton. Is that any way to answer a call from your best friend in the world? I want to commend you again for the great job creating our distraction. Nobody from either party expected you to become a high-spending liberal. The press is focused on you now. That's good. And I have some great news."

After a brief silence, *"What news?"*

"We have a new client, one with deep pockets. We'll be expanding our business. And we're going to ensure that the War on Drugs continues. You'll read about it during your Saturday morning briefing, but it will be all over the news in a special report Friday evening. Isn't that great?"

After a long pause, the man named Tate asked, *"Alton, are you still with me?"*

"Yeah, Tate. I'm here. Who is it?"

"Sorry, Alton, you'll just have to be surprised. You can hear it on the news, just like the little people."

Ian listened for several minutes. Abruptly, the call ended with the man named Tate saying, *"Alton? Alton, answer me."*

Then there was silence. Ian let the device play for another ten minutes, but there was nothing new.

Ian's mind was a whirlwind of thoughts. *Who is Tate? And who is Alton?* Ian replayed the conversation in his head, trying to make sense of the entire series of calls. *What distraction? The War on Drugs, the press, high-spending liberal? Saturday morning briefing? A new client with deep pockets?* It all sounded surreal, like a scene from a spy movie. *Who was concerned with the War on Drugs? Who constantly talked about liberals and conservatives?* That was almost exclusively officials at the federal government. *Alton. Alton Woodburn? The President of the United States?* Had he just heard a conversation involving the President? *No. No way.*

Ian looked at his invention. Could this contraption that he threw together in a few days capture signals from hundreds of miles away? But that didn't make any sense. Why would the program hone in on that particular call? No, this call, and the previous calls to the other beta testers had to have come from a phone in close proximity to the compound. *Or maybe from within the compound?*

The sound of the computer room door opening startled him. Jonah stood in the opening looking in. He didn't enter, he just stared at Ian without expression, but something in his eyes was different. The normally unfocused look and expressionless face were different. Was it worry that Ian saw? Maybe his own angst caused him to see things that were not there.

He took a deep breath. "What are you waiting for? Come on in."

Jonah just stood there for several seconds, then, as if he

wore lead shoes, walked over to his computer station and slowly sat in his chair. Ian could sense that he was troubled, that something was weighing heavily on Jonah's mind. Up until these past few weeks, Ian could not sense any emotion in his brother. Even now, most people seeing Jonah would assume that he couldn't have an emotional bone in his body. But Ian saw it as plain as the pictures on the wall. It was a significant transformation in Jonah's personality.

"Jonah, talk to me. What's on your mind?"

Jonah stared at his blank computer screen. After nearly a full minute of silence, he turned and faced Ian. Something akin to dread emanated from his face. He rattled off a series of numbers that shocked Ian.

"4141191212541315 13." Dad killed Mom.

Ian didn't say a word, thinking about the code his brother had just recited. He tried to rerun the numbers to make them mean something different, but there was no logical translation. He looked at his brother, who began to shake all over as if he was freezing.

"That can't be. Mom ran away. Dad said so."

Jonah took a deep breath, then repeated the code – Dad killed Mom.

Why do you think that?"

"9191238913415920." I saw him do it.

Ian's jaw dropped in disbelief.

Chapter 26

J. Christofer's was an easy walk east down Liberty Street from Peden's office. He ate breakfast there often, typically once each week. He sat at a table a few feet from a large roll-up door that was all glass, providing a nice view of the street and its shady treed boulevard. The aroma of freshly fried bacon, breakfast sausage and ham, fresh-brewed coffee, and toast filled the air. Peden had just finished a ham and cheese omelet and washed the last bite down with a gulp of now warm coffee. It still tasted better than the swill that he brewed at his office. He signaled for the waitress to refill his mug.

Michael Jess was on his mind. The strong, fit image of Jess the first time he had stood at Peden's office door contrasted sharply with the weak, pale soul who laid helpless in the hospital bed. A dark mood gripped Peden, knowing that Jess had died so senselessly.

As Peden was about to hale his waitress and ask for his check, his cell phone rang. He looked at the display. Lee Sparks.

He swiped the phone's screen and said, "Lee, what have you got?"

"Good morning to you, too, Peden."

"You sound chipper this morning. Must have slept well last night, or should I say, earlier this morning."

"Yes, yes, I did. And we've made some progress this morning, thanks to being rested and ready. So, get ready to take some notes."

Peden smiled as he pulled a notepad and pen from his pants pocket. "Go."

Lee told Peden that they were able to save the files from the flash drive that the Pirelli kid gave them. They moved the files to a hard drive so they could work on them separately from the analysis of the flash drive. One of the FBI techs was dissecting the files, trying to open each one. So far, none of the files contained code that would control the drone or the weapon. The remaining files were protected and would be a challenge to access.

As they spoke, the waitress refilled Peden's coffee.

Lee continued, "There wasn't even a trace of accelerant in or on the drive. There's no chance that the killer intended to destroy this one unless it was an oversight. But somebody who goes to the level of detail with a computer program that controls the flight path of a drone and the remote targeting of a mounted weapon doesn't seem likely that they would be sloppy and miss setting up one of several drives for self-destruction."

"I'm with you, Lee. The more I think about this, the more I'm thinking this was done with a purpose. Maybe they wanted to point us toward the Pirelli kid. But why him? Why not one of the others?"

"Maybe it was random, a red herring. Maybe he was selected because he's the furthest from the crime scene. Could the real killer be that smart, that calculating? Or are we overthinking this?"

Peden was silent for several seconds, thinking about how this twist fit into the puzzle. He took a long sip of fresh, hot coffee. Maybe Lee was right. The extra flight and drive to Tony Pirelli's house did add nearly a full day of travel to the investigation. The amount of time and energy that they were expending thinking about how this anomaly fit was a big drain on resources. Maybe they should just ignore the intact flash drive and treat it as if it had been destroyed. They did the analysis, now let it be. If necessary, they could always step back and take another look at it. Maybe it would make more sense after they had more information.

Peden asked, "Anything else?"

"Nope, but I'll call if we get anything new. We're doing mostly database searches and comparisons now. Oh, one other thing. The drone that fell at the feet of the German Chancellor? Same company produced it. That one wasn't weaponized, but it may have been a test run for future attacks. And there were other attacks, but none of them were widely publicized. The victims were lesser-known political types."

Peden's eyebrows shot up. "Do you have news articles or something? Maybe you could send me the links to the stories. And call Megan. She's at her office. Tell her what you just told me and send those links to both our emails."

"Will do. Later."

"Thanks, Lee."

* * *

The ride out to Tybee Island would have been relaxing on any other occasion. With the sun high overhead, the temperature moderating to the mid-eighties, and the humidity lower than normal, it would have been a great day to take the family to the beach. But the business at hand was far too serious for a leisurely trip to a tourist-rich island.

Traffic was a bit heavy on Highway 80 as they passed Fort Pulaski on the left, just across the South Channel of the Savannah River. From the passenger seat, Peden could see the top of Tybee Island Lighthouse ahead on the left. A few minutes later, Megan turned right onto South Campbell Avenue. After a quarter of a mile, South Campbell changed names to Horsepen Point Drive. The road dead-ended into a cul de sac, but there was only one driveway off of the circle. A fence nearly ten feet high ran in both directions for the length of a football field, with the gated driveway at about the halfway point. The driveway was isolated from the outside world by a massive iron gate. Peden took a look at the gate and the security system and whistled.

Megan pulled her Honda onto the Driveway's apron next to a keypad that was mounted in a metal stand and opened the driver's side window. A light scent of fish and rotting vegetation filled the car, the result of the salt marsh that surrounded the property. At least three cameras were mounted on either side of the gate, and a small camera was integrated with the keypad. Whatever the reason, Nicholas Tabler took security very seriously.

Megan was about to hit the call button when a smooth,

baritone voice came over a hidden speaker. "Agent Moore, I presume?"

"Yes. I'm Agent Moore, and I have …"

"That's fine. Please pull up the guardhouse, and Glen will greet you."

The two sections of the massive gate slowly but smoothly swung inward. Peden whispered, "Like the gates of heaven."

Megan didn't smile.

She followed the driveway about fifty yards to a brick building that was the size of a two-car garage. A door near the front corner was already open, and a man in a light-weight, pale gray suit stood on the drive. As Megan approached, the man raised his hand, indicating that she should stop, which she did.

The man leaned low to look inside the driver's side window. He looked at Megan and Peden then said, "Special Agent Megan Moore. I'm Glen." He smiled pleasantly. "May I please have both of your driver's licenses?"

Megan was not pleasant. She stated firmly, "No, Glen, you may not. You already know who I am. This is Peden Savage. He works for me. I'm sure that you've already got our pictures from the cameras mounted all around here, so we'll just head up to the house."

Glen tried his best to maintain his smile, but it was more like he was gritting his teeth. His full attention was now on Megan. He attempted to puff out his chest, but he saw that it wasn't going to work on her.

Megan said, "You're keeping your boss waiting."

Glen let out his breath. "Just follow the drive to the front door. Mr. Tabler will meet you there."

Without a word or change in her stern expression, Megan closed the car window and headed towards the house.

The front door to the massive home was open, and a trim, fit man in blue jeans and a pale green polo shirt stood at the top of the wide brick and concrete steps. He also wore a smile that Peden could see from a mile away.

When they exited the car, the man approached. He went straight to Megan and, still wearing the bright smile, extended his hand. His teeth were a little too perfect and a little too white. He sported a full head of hair that looked like it should be on the cover of *Barber's Quarterly*, if there was such a publication.

Megan shook his hand as he said, "Special Agent Moore. I'm Nicholas Tabler. Glen wasn't too pleased that you showed him up. But he'll get over it. He's good at his job. I hope you didn't find him overly pushy."

"Not at all. I expect people to do their jobs, Mr. Tabler."

"Please, call me Nick."

Megan only nodded. Tabler turned to Peden, extending his hand, introducing himself. He motioned for the duo to follow him into his home.

Peden took stock of their host. He held his nose a bit high, in what Peden construed as arrogance. He looked around as they approached the steps. The grounds were perfect. The shrubs that lined the front of the house were trimmed with precision, each plant a mirror image of the others. The grass was bright green, meticulously edged along the driveway. Whoever worked the grounds was a perfectionist.

They entered a large foyer with light gray marble floors. Light cream-colored walls were accented by ornate ceiling molding and baseboards. Beautiful arched passages connected a living room to the left, a library to the right, and what must have been a ballroom straight ahead. Impressive paintings hung on walls everywhere he looked.

Tabler motioned towards the living room. "Make yourselves comfortable. Can I get you anything to drink?"

Megan asked for ice-water and took a seat in a comfortable chair. Peden waived off the offer.

"I'll get that, and I'll have Ian join us."

Megan spoke. "Isn't your son, Jonah, also supposed to join us?"

"I can ask Jonah to sit in, but he can't answer any of

your questions. He has ..." Tabler paused to think of the right answer, "communications difficulties. He's a savant. He has a brilliant mind, but he has limited – well – no social skills."

Megan said, "I'd still like to have him sit in anyway. If it becomes a problem, then he can leave."

When Tabler nodded and left the room, Peden raised his eyebrows at Megan. This was an interesting twist. He wondered what Megan hoped to learn from a young boy with no communications skills, but didn't ask about her intentions. She noticed his expression but didn't say a word.

Moments later, Nicholas Tabler returned, followed by his two sons. He motioned for the boys to take seats across from their guests. Peden immediately noticed that Ian was nervous. His hair was long and wavy, parted on the left side, and hung down, nearly blocking his eyes. He wasn't sure what to do with his hands, so he held his left elbow with his right hand. He looked down at the area rug and didn't make eye contact with anyone, including his father.

Jonah was completely unreadable. He also had long hair that was unkempt. His expression was a blank stare. His eyes were straight ahead, unfocused. His face wore no emotion at all. When he sat, he moved as a blind man would, except that he didn't use his hands to find his seat. He lowered himself perfectly in the chair without feeling for the arms. He kept his back rigid. It was mechanical, almost robotic.

When everyone was seated, Megan jumped right in. Shifting her glance from Jonah to Ian, she asked, "Tell me about how you came to be testers for FlashGamz?"

Ian finally looked up. He cleared his throat and began describing how he and his brother were approached by the company. The FlashGamz representative had heard from other on-line gamers that he and Jonah were good, and he offered them money to test new games.

After several more questions, Megan said, "Take me through the test that failed."

Peden noticed it first. Jonah's eyes widened slightly, then went back to their unfocused state. Did the boy know something that he couldn't communicate or was it a fluke?

The remainder of Ian's description was remarkably similar to the other testers. After Ian described the flash drive's flameout, Megan asked what Ian did with the drive. Ian said that he threw it in the trash. She asked if he still had the ashes and Ian said no, that it was already gone.

Again, Peden noticed Jonah's eyes at Ian's reply. He wouldn't have thought anything of it, but those two eye movements were the only changes to Jonah's state.

Satisfied, Megan thanked the boys and their father. After handing business cards to Nicholas and Ian, and trying unsuccessfully to hand one to Jonah, she asked them to call her if they thought of anything else, whether they thought it important or not.

Once on Horsepen Point Drive, Megan asked, "Did you see Jonah's tell?"

Peden replied, "Yeah. I think there's more going on in that house than meets the eye. I wonder what has those boys so scared?"

Chapter 27

Peden Savage had a feeling of déjà vu standing in a remote section of the Toyota car dealership on Park of Commerce Way in Savannah, Georgia. The dealership's lot adjoined the property where the Savannah Drug Enforcement Administration building stood. The layout of dealership and the surrounding land was familiar to Peden. He had scouted this area, including the car dealership's lot and buildings, shortly after the Jarod Deming murder, which took place just months earlier. Deming, a D.E.A. agent, was gunned down on live television as he stepped up to a makeshift podium in the same location where Senator Armand Vega was killed. Deming had planned to implicate himself, his fellow agents, and other public officials in an extortion scheme involving millions of dollars in tax-payer money and the false imprisonment of numerous young men.

  The humidity was high as the morning sun beat down on the three men from a bright blue sky. Peden, Detective Daryl Shirley of the Savannah Police Department, and Steve Harman, the dealership's manager, stood next to a gray Ford F150 that was in need of bodywork. No one at the dealership took notice of the truck for several days. It sat in the south-westernmost point of the property: an area used for staging cars that were awaiting work in the dealership's body shop. It had been parked on the very edge of the property next to a row of mature arborvitae trees that offered a visual shield, hiding the wrecked vehicles from the surrounding businesses. Peden believed that it also provided good cover for someone staging a launch pad for a drone with deadly capabilities.

  From where Peden stood, he could not see the D.E.A. building due to the density of the privacy trees, but he knew that the front of the D.E.A. building was less than two hundred yards away. It would be child's play to launch a drone from the bed of the pickup truck and quickly move it into position to attack anyone on the front steps of the office building.

Peden listened as Detective Shirley asked Harman if he knew how long the truck had been on their property, but the manager shrugged his shoulders, raised his eyebrows, then said with a deep southern drawl, "It coulda been a couple weeks, maybe more. The last time a different wreck sat in this spot was the end of July. We had a Camry that had got popped in the rear a week or so before. We put it there" – he pointed to the spot where the truck sat – "because we knew that the parts was going to be held up for a week or two. We got the parts the last week in July, then we moved it into the shop."

Peden asked Harman, "It's been over three weeks since the Camry was moved. What made you think to call the police?"

"Our body shop manager, Jimmy Ray, said he was pullin' a car into the shop when he heard the pops from the gun the day the senator was killed. He recalled hearin' a buzzin' sound right before the shots. He didn't put two-and-two together 'til he seen the report on TV. This morning he noticed this truck. He knew he hadn't done any receipt paperwork on it, so he asked around. Nobody in his crew did either, so he came out here to check it out. That's when he saw the rig there."

The men looked into the truck bed where a number of two-by-fours were put together to construct a crude stand. Peden tried to imagine a drone with an automatic weapon supported underneath. Without the stand, a drone would have had to have long legs so that the weapon wouldn't drag on the ground, or it would require a stand with an open center able to support the short legs of the drone and the hanging weapon. The wood base was unsophisticated but perfectly constructed for that purpose.

Peden looked at the manager and asked, "Is your body shop manager on duty?"

"Yep, he's here."

"I think we're going to need to talk with him. In the

meantime, we need to rope off the area and get a crime scene crew out here."

Harman nodded. "He'll be right out."

The manager turned, heading for the bay door to the body shop.

Detective Shirley turned to Peden. "The Feds havin' any luck with findin' Vega's killer?"

"It doesn't feel like we're any closer. Seems like this guy, or gal, covers their tracks pretty well." Peden's phone buzzed in his pocket. He looked at the screen. "I have to take this."

It was Megan Moore. He took a few steps away from Shirley and answered, "Yeah, Megan."

"Hey. I just spoke with Lee and Liam at the lab. They contacted the drone manufacturer and sales rep. The guy who bought the drone has purchased several over a four-year period. They said the drones are custom-built, that the buyer has some pretty strict specifications for cameras, weight, battery life, maneuverability, and computer memory. But the big thing he requires is a high data transfer rate."

Peden thought for a second, then asked, "Did he give any reasons for these specs?"

"The buyer told the sales rep that he was part of a group that races drones over obstacle courses, and they bet large sums of money on the races. They also have other folks who bet on the outcome. The rep said it sounded like a bunch of grown-ups playing kids video games in real life."

"Did Lee tell them that their drone was involved in the Vega murder?"

"No, he didn't. We'll do that when we call them back. Are you still at the dealership?"

"Yeah. We're going to question the body shop guy. He apparently heard the drone and the gunfire but didn't figure out what it was until he found this pick-up truck on the lot. Nobody knows how it got here. No paperwork, nothing. We're getting a crime scene crew here to process the truck and surrounding area."

Megan asked, "Any cameras that monitor the dealership?"

"Yeah, but it'll take a lot of time to review all the video. They have a real wide date range when the truck could have been placed here."

There was silence on the line. Megan must have been thinking about the timeline. She finally said, "Get copies of the security footage. We'll concentrate on hours when the dealership was closed."

Peden chimed in, "We'll start at the end of July. That's when that space was opened up. It'll at least narrow down the screen time."

"One other thing that I got from Lee. When they spoke with the guy at Pinnacle Aeronautics, he said they shipped three drones in early August to the buyer. They were delivered to a place called Low Country Open Storage in Walterboro, South Carolina. They were delivered by a charter airline to Low Country Regional Airport. The drones were received by a guy named Olin Walters. We're doing database searches on the guy's name. So far, we can't find any Olin Walters living in the southeast. Probably a fake."

Peden looked towards the dealership. Steve Harman was walking towards the pickup truck with a tall, lanky kid in tow. He said into the phone, "Gotta go. The body shop guy is here. I'll let you know what he says."

The call was disconnected. He walked back to where Daryl Shirley waited for Harman and his body shop manager.

"Gentlemen, this here's Jimmy Ray Duncan. He's our body shop manager."

Jimmy Ray Duncan looked to be sixteen with greasy hair over his ears and down on the back of his neck, a very slim body, and a tanned face pockmarked with acne. He leaned to his left and looked around at the three men. He kept his hands in his back pockets.

Steve Harman prompted his employee, "Jimmy Ray, why don't you tell these gentlemen what you know."

In a syrupy southern drawl, he said, "Alright. That there

truck wadn't there at the end of July. I noticed it a few weeks ago cause I ain't checked it in. When I asked the guys in the shop, they all said they din't know where it come from. Then I saw that rig in the back of the truck and kinda wondered if it had somethin' ta do with that senator gettin' shot. So, I told Steve here 'bout it, and he said ta call the cops. And here we are."

When he finished, he shifted his body and leaned to the right. Peden asked, "Can you remember when you first noticed the truck sitting here?"

Jimmy Ray seemed to be deep in thought, scratching his left cheek, then he glanced at his boss. He used the back of his right hand to rub under his nose, then said, "Steve ain't gonna like this, but the first time I really noticed it was here was that Monday, a couple days before the shootin'. I was havin' a bad day. I was a little hungover. Me'n my old lady argued all weekend. I came out here Monday morning to have a smoke and get my head together. I was leaning against the truck. That's why I remember, but it might have been here a few weeks before that." He was quiet again and seemed to be contemplating something. Before Peden could ask another question, Jimmy Ray said, "Naw. Couldn't've been that long. I remember that we hauled that Jeep Cherokee outta the spot right here the week before. The truck weren't here then. That woulda been the Thursday before."

Peden ran through the dates in his mind. That narrowed down the timeframe significantly. That Thursday was August 6. Their search of the video footage would start after closing that evening.

Peden turned to Steve. "When can I get those copies of your security files?"

"I've got our folks making copies now. I figure within the hour."

"Great. Jimmy Ray, you've been very helpful. Thanks. If you think of anything else, please call me or Detective Shirley. Before we leave, I'll swing by your office, Steve, and pick up the files." Peden handed both men his card. Detective

Shirley did the same.

The men nodded and turned towards the dealership's maintenance building. Peden turned to Detective Shirley. "When I get back to my office, I'm going to search the videotape for this pickup truck. We need to see if we can identify the person who put it here."

"Peden, If I can lend a hand or two on this video search, let me know. We've got a couple interns that might be able to help."

"Great. Have them call me, and we'll put them to work."

As they shook hands, the crime scene crew approached. Peden spoke with the team lead and told him to send their report to Special Agent Megan Moore and to send copies of the report to his office.

The crew got right to work.

Chapter 28

Two interns from the Savannah Police Department, compliments of Detective Daryl Shirley, sat in Peden Savage's office in the historic Bird-Baldwin House on West Liberty Street. They sat at a make-shift desk – little more than a white, heavy plastic table of the type used at craft shows and yard sales – staring at the seemingly endless security footage from the car dealership where the beat-up gray pickup truck was found. Even at sixteen times normal speed, the images dragged on, with cars changing positions as the body shop workers moved wrecked cars into the garage and drove new-looking cars out. The two interns talked continuously through the process, which drove Peden crazy. Randy, a pudgy nineteen-year-old boy with natty-looking, dark hair and a nose ring, sat to his left. Sheryl, a too-skinny twenty-year-old girl with stringy blonde hair, was to his right.

Peden rubbed his eyes and stretched. He nearly missed the sudden appearance of the gray pickup truck in the back corner of the lot. Grabbing the computer's mouse, he clicked in the middle of the screen and paused the video. He clicked on the time bar at the bottom of the screen and backed the still video until the truck disappeared. He inched the line forward until the truck appeared again. Changing the settings to double speed, he narrowed the time where the truck pulled into the lot.

"Got him."

Randy and Sheryl stopped talking and looked at Peden, then stepped in behind him to look over his shoulder. The young man said, "You did it!" The two youngsters high-fived each other and smiled, a triumphant look on their faces, even though Peden made the discovery.

He set the timeline to just prior to the truck entering the lot. The display indicated that the vehicle was parked on the lot on Sunday, August 9 at 8:28 AM. He set the play time to normal speed, and the three watched as the pick-up slowly pulled to the back of the parking lot and eased into the spot where it was later discovered. The driver's side door opened. A figure exited the truck and walked casually along the fence towards the dealership's entrance and Park of Commerce Way.

Peden frowned. The person, a man, based on his build and manner, did nothing to the truck. He hadn't locked it or checked the truck bed, nothing. The timing of the placement of the truck was three days prior to the attack on Senator Vega. *How could he have known Vega's schedule that far in advance?*

Sheryl asked, "What's the matter?"

He took a deep breath and pointed at the image on the monitor, then said, "This is three days prior to attack. He put the truck in place, but the drone isn't in the truck."

She asked, "How do you know?"

"I don't know for certain, but he probably wouldn't leave the drone there in plain sight for anyone to see. It had an assault rifle attached to the bottom of it, so if anyone would have seen it, they would have reported it to the police."

The two interns nodded as they understood. Peden continued, "My guess is that he placed the drone in the back of the truck early in the morning on Wednesday, right before the attack."

Randy stepped back to his computer and manipulated his mouse several times. He said, "So you're thinking that he set the drone up just prior to the attack, but at a time when there was no one at the dealership?"

"Yeah, exactly."

Randy said, "I have the videos for that period of time. Give me a few minutes."

It didn't take that long before Randy's smile beamed. "Got it."

Peden got out of his chair and got behind Randy. He watched the intern run the video in real time.

Randy narrated the scene, "Wednesday, August 12 at 4:20 AM. He used a minivan that he backed up to the truck and unloaded a box into the truck bed. It looks like he's doing a couple checks on something. Now he's leaving. It took less than two minutes."

Peden looked at the screen as the minivan pulled away. He rubbed a hand over his face, took a deep breath, then up at the tiled ceiling. Now they knew for certain that the pick-up truck was used as the launchpad for the attack. But how was the drone controlled, and from where? Peden needed to call Megan, but he wanted to finish the surveillance of the truck. He said, "Randy, forward the security video to just before 10:00 AM."

The three watched as the screen went to fast forward, then slowed to normal speed at 9:59 AM. They watched as the drone slowly rose from the truck's bed just high enough to clear the fence and the line of arborvitae trees, then disappear off camera. Moments later, they heard the reports from the weapon suspended from the drone. Upon hearing the shots, Peden and the interns jumped, realizing that three people were murdered and another person's life was forever altered. The reports were followed by a muffled explosion as the drone self-destructed.

"I have to make a call. While I'm gone, see if you can freeze the frame on the guy in the minivan. Get the best picture you can and save it to a file and send copies to me and Special Agent Megan Moore. Also, print out a copy of each photo." He turned towards the door, then turned back and said, "Good job. Thanks for your help."

He left the office and stepped outside into the heat of the morning. He took a deep breath and sighed, feeling the sorrow of losing a friend in such a horrific way. He hadn't known Michael Jess for long, but they had developed a bond of mutual respect. Peden figured that the best way to honor him was to find his killer.

He hit the speed-dial number for Megan. She answered on the first ring. Peden could hear her talking with someone as she raised her phone to answer. "Hey, Pedee. How's the search going?"

"We've got something for you. We're going to send you some images and video clips. The truck was parked at the dealership Sunday morning at 8:28. Three days before the attack, so someone had to know Vega's schedule."

There was silence on the line. Peden figured that Megan was going over the timeline in her mind.

She said, "That's a pretty long time for the truck and the weapon to sit in the open. Was the drone in the open all that time?"

Peden said, "No. The drone wasn't put in the truck until the morning of the attack, 4:20. We have some stills of the driver and some video of the minivan used to deliver the drone. We're sending them to you now. Maybe Lee can do some facial recognition magic on them."

"He's good, but how clear are the images?"

"Not real clear. I'm sure it'll be a challenge for him. We're also sending shots of the minivan. Probably won't help much, but it's all we've got."

Peden heard a tone over the line. Megan must have an incoming text message.

She said, "I have several incoming instant messages. I guess I've got the digitals. You're sending these on to Lee and the gang at Quantico, right?"

"Yeah. They're on the way already."

Megan said, "Let me pick you up in, say, ten minutes, and you can ride with me back to the dealership. The crime scene team is there now. Maybe you can give them some help based on what you saw on the security footage."

"Yeah. I'll be here." There was a pause. "Megan, three days in advance. That's how long that truck was parked on that lot before the murder. That means that someone had to know the details about Vega's visit to the D.E.A. office in advance – well in advance, and with confidence that his schedule was solid. They couldn't have put together an attack like that on a moment's notice."

Megan said, "Jess said he was pretty loose with announcing his schedule. Are you suggesting that we start questioning people close to him?"

Peden thought for a second, then said, "I don't think it would buy us anything. Too many people in that pool. But it wouldn't hurt to start compiling a list of folks who might have known."

Megan replied, "Already working on it."

After the call disconnected, Peden brought up the first video and watched it all the way through without stopping. There was nothing remarkable about the parking of the truck or the man as he walked away. He watched the second video and frowned. The man handled the box with ease. Peden noticed that the box was about three feet square and one foot high. Once the man moved the box to the pick-up truck's bed, he made some moves around the bed, but the angle of the camera didn't allow Peden to see what he was doing. He didn't remove any cardboard or anything else from the back of the truck. He just hopped off the truck bed, entered the driver's side of the mini-van, and drove away.

He looked to see if there was a third video, but the remaining attachments were all still shots of the man. All the stills were of poor quality from a distance, with limited light. Lee Sparks would be challenged to glean anything from the photos other than they were of a man. But if anyone could pull something off the pictures, it was Lee.

He closed the prints just as Megan walked in. "Find anything new in the last ten minutes?"

"Nope. The pictures and videos may not help much, but it gives us specific times for when the truck and then the drone were put in place."

Megan raised her eyebrows. "Did you send copies to Lee?"

"Yeah."

"When we finish at the car dealership, maybe we can download them to my computer. We can use the monitor in my office to get a better look at them."

She was talking about the fifty-five-inch monitor that she used for video conferences. It was a high-density resolution screen with zoom capabilities.

* * *

On the way to the dealership, Peden called Lee Sparks at the lab in Quantico, Virginia, to ensure that he received the photos and videos. Lee answered that, yes, he received them and that he'd already started analyzing the photos.

While at the Toyota Dealership, they didn't provide much in the way of assistance, so they left and headed for Megan's office. By the time he got himself a cup of coffee, Megan had the first still photo on the screen. She had zoomed in on the man's face, but the image was distorted so much that they couldn't see much of anything. Peden watched as Megan slowly reduced the zoom. The image became clearer, but not enough to see facial details.

Megan's eyes were glued to the screen. She tilted her head slightly but remained silent. She quickly replaced the first still shot with the second. The lack of clarity on the second photo was similar to the first; not much useful detail. After a moment, she brought up the first video and clicked on the play arrow on the screen. The man in the video wore blue jeans, a light-colored tee-shirt, sneakers, and a ball cap. At first glance, the image was grainy, but as the video played, the sharpness of the image varied from fairly clear to blurry.

Megan said, "There's something familiar about that guy. I can't put my finger on it, but let's see what Lee comes up with."

Peden said, "If he can glean anything from this, I need to give him a raise."

"Good idea. And I want you to contact Low Country Storage and find out more about the delivery of those drones."

"Yes, ma'am. I'm on it."

Chapter 29

It was Thursday morning, August 20 and Nicholas Tabler had a bag packed with clothes adequate for three days' travel. He expected that he would be back late Friday night, but unexpected events might lead to a longer stay. He had been away from the compound regularly, mostly on day trips to visit various business partners. Most of his business was performed over the phone or by dispatching one of his staff to see to things. This particular task required his presence. It couldn't be avoided. In business like this, the less people knew, the better.

He summoned his sons to the living room where the meeting with Special Agent Megan Moore and Peden Savage had taken place. There was nothing special about the location. It was a neutral area of their home where he hoped the boys would feel at ease. Recently, he noticed tension in Ian's manner whenever he went to his son's room or the computer lab to talk with him. That was unusual because his eldest son always had something on his mind: some problem to solve, or an adjustment to a commercial product that made using the device easier or faster. Ian was maturing before his eyes and being confined to the compound wasn't healthy for a young man with growing physical needs, even if those needs were still foreign to him.

Jonah, well ... he just didn't know what to think about his youngest son. He wasn't sure if Jonah was even aware of the world around him, his blank stares unnerving to his father. The boy's manner was like the *Pinball Wizard* from that rock opera. He knew that Jonah wasn't deaf, dumb, or blind, but he seemed oblivious to the world around him. Ian believed his little brother to be some kind of genius. He was a wizard at video games. That was the one thing that he could do, and he did it as if he was part of the game – *part of the machine* – as the song goes.

Nicholas Tabler just shook his head at the thought of his two boys. He looked at his watch – 9:28 AM. They should arrive at any moment; they were always prompt. It was one of the habits that he pounded into them. They must be on time, regardless of the importance or lack of importance of the meeting. People judged you by your attention to detail, and the most important detail was being where you were supposed to be when you were required to be there. People respected punctuality in others. You could be trusted if you respected their time.

As if on cue, the boys walked into the room and stood just inside the archway.

"Hi, boys, take a seat. I need to talk with you."

Nicholas noticed that Ian tensed slightly as he moved towards the couch. Jonah followed his brother with his unfocused eyes. Both boys sat in unison, their backs straight. Ian's eyes lowered towards the expensive rug on the floor between the boys and their father. Jonah's unfocused eyes stared straight ahead towards the large window that opened to the front circular drive of the compound.

There was silence for several uncomfortable seconds. Nicholas cleared his throat then he spoke. "Something has come up, and I'm going away on business for a day or two. If you need anything, like any special food or drinks, anything like that, let Jenkins know. Anything else, tell Victor. They'll take care of it."

Jenkins was the head of household services. Victor was head of security. Nicholas knew that Ian didn't care for either of them. The two hired hands tried their best to be nice to the boys, but Nicholas could tell that Ian believed them to be little more than high-priced babysitters. There was plenty of food in the kitchen and walk-in pantry, and they had everything else that they needed, so Nicholas didn't expect that the boys would bother the staff as they went about maintaining and securing the compound.

Ian asked, "Do you know when you'll be back?"

"I expect to be back late tomorrow evening, but that

could change." There was a pause. "Any other questions?"

Ian answered, "No, sir."

That was it. A long, awkward silence followed before Nicholas Tabler stood and walked out of the room without a backward glance.

* * *

The late morning sun beat down on the brothers as Ian followed Jonah towards a remote area of the grounds near the southeast wall. To get there, they had to cross a vast open area between the house and the edge of the property. Sweat poured from his pores due to the heat and humidity, combined with Ian's over-charged nerves. The lawn around the house was meticulously maintained, mowed more often than most greens on the highest-rated country clubs. The beautiful, bright green grass yielded to a heavily wooded area, which covered most of the southern portion of the land near the privacy wall. A four-foot-wide gravel path was maintained along the inside of the eight-foot-high stone wall and extended along the entire permitter of the property. The air, thick with the scent of rotting vegetation and marine life from the salt marsh that surrounded the compound on three sides, assailed their nasal passages.

Jonah plodded along at a leisurely pace, his eyes straight ahead, unblinking, seemingly unfocused. He didn't appear to have a care in the world, though he had just hours ago told his brother that their father, a man Ian looked up to with tremendous respect – almost reverence – had murdered their mother. Ian hoped that Nicholas Tabler didn't notice his sheer terror when facing him less than an hour before when he announced that he was going away on business. After that meeting, Ian went down to the computer lab and broke out in a cold sweat. He wanted to ask Jonah what he remembered about their mother's death, but Jonah had told him *not inside the house*. In his code, he said that Ian should wait until they were outside.

Their father left the compound immediately after telling the boys about his trip, though they had no idea where he planned to travel, or what was the nature of his business. He never alluded to the sources of his income. It had to be substantial, given the size of the compound and number of support staff needed to maintain the grounds. Up until recently, Ian believed that he was a stock trader since he rarely left his office. Typically, when he ventured out, he had two people with him: Victor and one of Victor's subordinates to act as driver. For his current trip, Victor stayed at the compound.

Ian wasn't sure to what part of the grounds Jonah was headed, but he followed just off his younger brother's right elbow. As they walked, Ian looked over his shoulder with every other step, his nerves on overdrive, scared that they would be seen walking around the property.

Jonah said, "19201516." Stop.

Ian was puzzled. "Stop what?"

"121515119225118152l144." Looking around.

"I'm not looking around. What are you talking about?"

In code, Jonah replied, "You look guilty. We're just taking a walk. Don't act guilty. Relax."

Ian continued to follow his brother and put his mind to work, concentrating on the types of trees ahead of them. The boys rarely left the house as most of their activities revolved around computers. Today's venture was unusual. Ian was nervous that their trek might draw the attention of the security watch.

"What if Victor sees us out here?"

In numbers, "We live here. We're not doing anything wrong."

Ian took a deep breath, trying to relieve the tension that racked his body and mind. Jonah hadn't explained why he wanted Ian to follow him, but he thought Jonah might want to talk about their mother's murder away from the house.

As the boys entered the wooded area, Ian noted the complete change in scenery of the grounds. Tall southern pines mixed with palm trees and camphor trees, loaded with Spanish moss hanging from thick branches, swayed from the breeze coming off the Atlantic Ocean, giving off a spooky vibe.

Fifty feet into the tree line and thirty feet from the privacy wall, Jonah suddenly stopped. He looked up towards a large branch that arched overhead, loaded down with gray Spanish moss. He looked back down to the ground where they stood.

Jonah said, "85185." Here.

"What's here?"

"131513." Mom.

Ian's jaw dropped. He shook his head, a cold chill gripped him.

"You mean that Mom is buried here, or she was killed here?"

"25519. 215208." Yes. Both.

The boys were silent for nearly a full minute. Ian, looking down at the ground covered with pine needles and an assortment of leaves, was trying to comprehend the magnitude of his brother's accusation. For nearly ten years, he believed that their mother had simply left them and their father. At five years old, he had no concept of what would make a mother leave her children and her husband. He had just accepted their father's explanation that their mom had left and wasn't coming back. He had no reason to question his word. He thought back to the day Nicholas Tabler brought the boys into the living room – the same room where they had just met less than an hour ago – and explained to them that their mother had left very early in the morning. That she had left a note that she wasn't coming back. He never let either boy see any note, but they were only five and four years old. At that age, neither of them dared challenge him on any subject. Even with their lofty IQs, they weren't mature enough to ask the basic question of why she left. They could barely comprehend the magnitude of their mother's departure. Ian remembered that he cried, but Jonah's face remained emotionless.

Ian must have been in deep thought because he didn't hear Jonah approach him and touch his shoulder. Startled, he jumped. Jonah moved in closer again, this time using his finger to coax Ian closer. He leaned in close to Ian's ear, cupped his hands into a make-shift megaphone, and spoke in a whisper, so quiet that Ian had a difficult time hearing. But this time, he spoke without his code, using actual words. "Dad shot Mom. The gun had a silencer."

Astonished, Ian turned to face his little brother. It was the first time he ever heard Jonah speak using anything other than numbers.

Jonah again curled his finger and urged Ian to come closer. He again whispered, "I think Dad saw me that day. I've been terrified of him ever since. That's why I figured out how to communicate with you using numbers. I want Dad to think I'm … an imbecile. If he knew that I could tell anyone what I saw, I think he'd kill me and bury my body here with Mom's."

Ian said in a quiet voice, "Dad wouldn't do that. We're his flesh and blood."

Jonah looked around, fear in his eyes, and keeping his voice so low Ian had a difficult time making out the words, "Not so loud." He paused and looked around again. "Victor was with him when he did it."

This last revelation freaked Ian out. He immediately looked around to see if anyone was watching them. Again, Jonah whispered, "Stop. You can't act like that. Dad's gonna figure out that we know." He paused and looked down. "I'm scared. I don't know if I can keep acting like this. Dad's smart. He's going to figure it out."

"Figure what out?"

Jonah was frustrated that he couldn't get through to his older brother. "That I'm not as stupid as I act. It takes a lot to …"

Jonah stopped suddenly and looked straight ahead. Ian heard the sound of slow footsteps snapping twigs and rustling leaves. He turned and saw Victor approaching on the path along the wall. Thinking quickly, he grabbed Jonah's hand and said, "Come on, little brother, let's head back to the house."

When Victor was within forty feet of the boys, he called to them in a loud voice, "Hey, boys, what are you doing out here? I almost mistook you for someone trying to trespass."

Ian replied, "Sorry. I read something on palm trees that didn't make sense. It has to do with the way leaves form and the markings that are left when …"

Victor rolled his eyes. "I don't care. Just head back to the house. You shouldn't be out here."

"But we live here. It's our property. We can …"

"Just go. Your dad wouldn't like it."

Ian thought that he needed to make sure Victor didn't mention this trip to their father. He said to Victor, "I'll talk to Dad when he gets back. Tell him that you said we couldn't leave the house."

"Look, Ian, just go. No need to tick off your dad. Understand?"

Without another word, Ian led Jonah by the hand back towards the house. Neither boy glanced over their shoulders. Ian could feel his brother's sweaty palm. He knew that Jonah was as petrified as him.

Chapter 30

It was well past noon as Peden Savage took exit 53 off of Interstate 95 for Walterboro, South Carolina, headed to Low Country Outdoor Storage, just northeast of the city. He hadn't had lunch, but he wanted to get to the storage company as soon as possible. The manager of Pinnacle Aeronautics told Lee Sparks that the drones were delivered to Olin Walters, the sole proprietor of the storage company. Peden had tried, unsuccessfully, to reach Mr. Walters by phone. Since Walterboro was an hour's drive from Savannah, he decided to pay the business a visit.

Route 17 turned right in downtown Walterboro. After several minutes, Peden slowed, then turned left onto a narrow, two-lane road. Peden drove slowly along Phillips Road, looking for signs for Low Country Outdoor Storage. After a minute, he noticed a worn, wooden sign with peeling paint next to a gravel driveway that disappeared into a stand of overgrown trees. He had to stop to read the sun-bleached wording.

Peden thought to himself, *This is it?*

In his best fake southern accent, Peden said aloud to himself, "I reckon so."

He pulled his Dark Blue Chevy Tahoe off the road into the driveway and continued slowly onto the property. After passing under the trees, a house appeared on the left. Like the business sign, the house was wooden-sided and in serious need of a paint job. Peden noted that the front porch, which extended across the front of the house, sagged on the left side. The block supports under the post for that corner had deteriorated to the point of near collapse from age and neglect.

There was a gravel turn-off from the drive where an old pickup truck sat. At one time, it had been a mint green. Now it was sun-bleached pea-soup with rust. The rear tires needed replacement, and the tailgate was missing.

Peden pulled the Tahoe in next to the truck and turned the ignition off. He exited the Tahoe and stretched, trying to get his blood circulating again. As he stepped to the front of his vehicle, the side door to the house opened just ten feet from where he stood. A pretty, young lady stepped out onto the stoop. Peden guessed her age at twenty, maybe twenty-five.

She asked, "Can I help y'all?"

Peden smiled and said, "I'm looking for the owner, Olin Walters."

"Y'all from the government or something? We don't get many folks all dressed up out here."

"No, no. I'm Peden Savage, a private investigator. I'm doing some contract work for the FBI. Mr. Walters is not in any trouble. I just need to talk with him about one of his customers."

"Well, he's out back inspectin' the grounds. Y'all can wait inside. He'll be back soon. I got some cold iced tea in the fridge. My name's Maggie. I'm Olin's daughter."

Maggie flashed a smile in Peden's direction. He did his best to keep a straight face.

"A cold glass of iced tea sounds pretty good."

Maggie turned and ushered him into the house. They passed through a dark mudroom. Several pairs of men's shoes and work boots sat on a large rubber mat. About half the footwear was covered in red clay. A pair of blue jean coveralls hung from one of four hooks on the wall. The other three hooks were empty. The mudroom opened to a kitchen that was in need of a serious upgrade. There was little counter space. The sink once had been white porcelain but was now covered in grime and a hard-water rust stain that ran from a dripping spigot down to the drain.

The refrigerator stood out among the appliances. It was bright white and appeared to have been recently delivered. It was a large, energy-efficient side-by-side. Peden knew that because the Energy Star sticker was still on the freezer door.

Maggie went about preparing a tall glass with ice. She pulled a glass, gallon-sized pitcher filled with dark brown tea from the refrigerator and filled the glass. As she set the glass on the table in front of her guest, she again smiled at Peden, making him feel just a bit uncomfortable. He raised his glass in a toast of thanks and took a tentative sip. Peden's eyebrows raised as he tasted the tea. To his surprise, it was excellent. He'd expected it to be over-sweetened, but it was exactly how he liked his tea.

He set his glass on the kitchen table and remarked, "Maggie, that is excellent."

His attention was drawn to the back door opening and banging shut. A large man with a larger gut, probably in his mid-forties, walked in. He looked displeased to see Peden sitting in his kitchen.

He turned to his daughter. "Maggie, what'd I tell ya about lettin' strangers in the house? 'Specially when they's from the law?"

"Daddy, this man needs to talk with you. I figured he didn't need to stand out in the heat."

The old man raised an eyebrow and said, "Right."

Peden stood and extended his hand. "Mr. Walters, I'm Peden Savage, I'm a private investigator. I'm looking into the murder of Senator Armand Vega."

This revelation didn't seem to ring a bell for Olin Walters. He asked, "So what does that have to do with me or my daughter?"

Peden thought for a second, not understanding the question. He kept a straight face and said, "Mr. Walters, Armand Vega was the Senator from Georgia ..."

Walters cut him off. "Hold on a second, son. First off, call me Olin. Mr. Walters was my daddy. Second, y'all's here to talk about that dead politician?"

Peden answered, "Yes, sir."

"Y'all call me 'sir' one more time and you an' me's gonna mix it up. Understand?"

It took Peden a moment to figure out what Olin Walters was saying, but he needed to move on. He asked, "Olin, I understand that you store RVs, trailers, trucks, cars, and large machinery on your property, but do you also store smaller items, or provide self-storage for your customers?"

"Whatdya mean self-storage?"

"Do you have buildings where people can store household goods, like boxes of clothes, dishes, furniture? Things like that."

"Nah, everything we do is outdoor storage: RV's, boats, trucks, and the like."

Olin's daughter spoke up. "Daddy, we do have that one guy, David Walsh, who pays you to keep them boxes until he can pick them up." Maggie turned to Peden and smiled. "He was just here this morning. Picked up two boxes and left. Couldn't have been no more'n an two hours ago."

Peden asked, "How big were these boxes, Maggie?"

Her smile grew, "They was maybe three feet by three feet by a foot tall. Not real heavy cause Mr. Walsh handled 'em by his self."

Olin jumped in, "I offered to help him but he said no. Anyway, he paid me in cash, like always, and loaded them in his mini-van, and he was off."

Peden said, "Mr. Walters ... I mean, Olin, did he say where he was headed?"

"Nah, I don't pry into folks lives like that. It ain't none'a my bidniz. I wouldn't want people pryin' into my bidniz, so I figured I should stay outta theirs."

Peden thought that was prudent. His phone buzzed before he could ask his next question. It was Lee Sparks. He apologized to Olin Walters and his daughter, saying that he had to take the call, and stepped into the mudroom.

He answered, "Hi, Lee. What's up?"

"Hey, Peden. The photos you sent, I couldn't do too much with them, but I sent you the one we cleaned up that shows the most detail. I sent the video, too. I hope that ragged old phone of yours can handle it. I sent them to Megan, too."

"Hey, man, lay off my phone. It works just fine."

Lee chuckled, "Right. Anyway, we zoomed in on the subject in the video and sharpened that up a bit, too. Take a look. Let me know if there's anything else we can do."

"Alright, Lee. Thanks."

Peden went back into the kitchen just as his phone vibrated. The pictures or the video just landed on his phone. He swiped across the screen and opened the text message from Lee Sparks. It was the photo. The face in the picture was still quite blurry but much clearer than the original. Something looked vaguely familiar, but he couldn't put a name to the man in the picture.

Turning his attention back to Olin Walters and his daughter, Peden asked, "Can you describe David Walsh to me?"

Maggie jumped in before her dad could stop her. "Why yeah. He was about six feet or a little taller. Kind of handsome for a middle-age guy."

A wry smile spread over her face. Peden noticed her dad's frown. Peden thought that she had her dad wrapped around her little finger.

Maggie continued, "He was pretty fit, looked like he works out some, but he wasn't like a bodybuilder."

Peden's phone screen had gone blank, but he tapped the button on the side, and the picture from Lee Sparks popped back up. He turned the phone and showed it to the Walters. He said, "Does this look like David Walsh?"

They both took a long look at the blurry picture. Olin scratched his chin, then ran his hand over his mouth. He moved in closer, then said, "It might be, but that's a terrible picture."

Maggie moved in and took one look. She said, "Yeah, I think that's him. Like Daddy said, it's a little blurry, but that looks like David."

"Does Mr. Walsh bring the packages to you to store?"

"Nope. When he has a package to store, it gets transported here from the airport. One of the employees of my brother's company brings them."

Peden's eyebrows shot up. "Your brother's company?"

"Yeah. He runs the Low Country Airport. You probably passed it on the way in."

Maggie added, "Yeah, Uncle Virgil is rich. David Walsh pays him to transport the boxes here."

Peden couldn't miss the anger on Olin Walter's face. He said, "Girl, you need to control that mouth of yours."

"Well, it's true, Daddy. Didn't you tell me to always tell the truth?"

"Yeah, when asked a question, but don't go blabbin' your mouth all the time."

"Olin, do you know if Virgil is at the airport now?"

"Last I checked, he was, yeah."

Peden thanked Olin and Maggie. He headed to the car and the short trip to the Low Country regional Airport.

Chapter 31

Nicholas Tabler relaxed in the comfort of the Gulfstream G350. The pilot announced earlier that they were cruising at an altitude of forty-one thousand feet, high above the typical altitudes for commercial aircraft, and that they would be landing in approximately one hour. The smooth air aloft provided a comfortable ride, free of turbulence. Tabler appreciated that as he contemplated the urgent business that awaited him in Albany, New York. He had a dinner date, of sorts, with United States Senator Lancaster Corrigan. Corrigan wasn't expecting Tabler, but the senator would be briefly surprised by what Tabler had in store for him.

The only passenger on the flight – the pilot and co-pilot were the only other persons on board – Tabler had requested that he be left alone during the trip. He could get his own refreshments if needed. After all, it was his aircraft, and they were his employees. They were paid well to fly him where he wanted to go and to not ask questions. The flight crew went through a rigorous background check to make sure that they were single, flexible, very light drinkers such that they were able to fly on short notice. When they were hired, they were told in rather terse terms that their new boss did not like social interaction with the crew. They were to do their jobs, not ask questions, not speculate on the reasons for his many trips, and get him to his destinations and back on time. One other requirement, they were not to take on any other part-time or contract jobs, no matter how large or small. They were to be on call twenty-four-seven, no excuses. Their compensation reflected that contractual restriction, and the two men in the cockpit appeared pleased with the arrangement.

The flight plan would take them into Saratoga County Airport just west of Saratoga Springs, New York: the college and horse-racing town. For all the crew knew, he was there to bet on the ponies.

Tabler had pre-arranged delivery of a pickup truck with a full tank of gas. The drive to downtown Albany was less than an hour regardless of the route taken, but he wanted plenty of gas if his plans changed and he needed the truck for longer than one day. He could have flown into Albany International Airport, but decided that a drive on the back roads between Saratoga Springs and the capital city would be relaxing and allow him time to think through the operation.

He thought back to his chat with Virgil Walters at the Low Country airport east of Walterboro. He and his brother were a bit too inquisitive when he picked up his packages. It was time to end their arrangement. The brothers had been very cooperative in the past, handling his shipments and not questioning the reason for his receiving several identical boxes a few times each year. The verbal contract required that Olin store the packages in a climate-controlled storage unit that was independent of the few other buildings on his property. He was told that he was not to store the packages at other commercial self-storage companies, of which there were many in the vicinity of Walterboro. They were paid handsomely for a relatively easy task. Why they would now question his motives, he wasn't sure. They might be getting nervous, thinking that what they were doing was illegal and that they would get arrested for some crime or another. But whatever their reasons, it was time to move on from the half-wits and that sex-crazed daughter of Olin's. Every time he visited the storage business to pick up his packages, she practically undressed him with her eyes.

Tabler sat up and pulled out a map of the capital region, with Gansevoort to the north and Selkirk to the south. The map had sufficient detail that most backroads were easily identifiable. He had previously traced out a route that took him south and west from the little airport in Saratoga County, but he changed his mind, deciding to head east on State Route 67 to south U.S. Route 4. That would take him parallel to the Hudson River for a period of time before getting close to downtown Albany. The fastest route would be Interstate 87, the Adirondack Northway, but speed wasn't his goal on the way to the city. He had plenty of time to get to his destination, make all the preparations, and execute the plan. The tricky part of the operation was to get out of Albany unseen, or at least as just another face in the crowd.

Tabler closed his eyes and leaned back in his overstuffed chair. He conjured up an image of Senator Lancaster Corrigan in his head, watching him in a recorded speech from earlier in the year. He had been in attendance at the fundraiser, a five-hundred-dollar-per-plate dinner that served up inferior prime rib and cheap liquor. He purchased a table that seated twelve people and donated an additional twenty-five thousand dollars.

During the senator's speech, he pointed to his softening stance on the War on Drugs, that those addicted to opiates needed compassion, not judgement and incarceration. He went on to say that when users were weaned off of those drugs, that dealers would simply stop selling because they would run out of customers. Tabler nearly laughed out loud when he heard Corrigan spit out that theory. It was at best pie in the sky, and at least pure rubbish. But Tabler's point of view had no regard for the wellbeing or recovery of addicts. Those hooked on drugs were weak and headed for a premature death or a life of anguish. He couldn't care less for their lives. He just needed them alive long enough for them to fuel his enterprise. They were customers for as long as they could survive.

The drug trade was pure gold for Nicholas Tabler, and the only way for his business to thrive was for the price to remain high. If America softened its stance on drugs, then the price would inevitably drop and have a direct impact on the bottom line. These namby-pamby lawmakers needed a strong message; they must remain steadfast and vocal in support of the War on Drugs. Vega was the first high-profile target for delivery of that message. Corrigan was the next. That speech had sealed his fate.

* * *

Two hours had passed since the jet made a velvety soft landing at Saratoga County Airport. Tabler released the pilots for the evening, telling them to make sure their phones were charged and on in case his meetings were shorter than anticipated. They knew this, of course, but he always wanted to ensure that they understood who signed their paychecks. Both men had paid close attention to his instructions. They had already made reservations at the Brentwood Hotel near the Saratoga Harness Track and were set to have an early dinner and catch the races.

Nicholas Tabler had completed the trip to Albany in just over an hour. During the drive, he made the change to his persona. He was now David Walsh, the FlashGamz representative, preparing to run a beta test on a new game – *Assassin – Best in the Business*. The parking garage was a multi-deck structure next to the entry ramp to Interstate 787, an auxiliary highway connecting Interstate 87 to the south, State Route 7 at Troy to the north, and Interstate 90 just north of downtown Albany. This complex web of highways and backroads made the options for getaway attractive.

He picked a spot on the top floor of the parking deck next to the 677 Broadway building just west of the Hudson River. There were no other cars on the entire deck. The view from the parking deck across the river was surprisingly beautiful, with green trees as far as he could see, interrupted here and there by a bridge or an office building. The air was clear, the sky a vivid, clear blue, with a slight breeze. Tabler, now David Walsh, inhaled deeply, feeling that life was grand, at least for him. Within the next ninety minutes, it would change dramatically for Senator Corrigan.

It was still early, just 4:30 PM. He had well over an hour to make the final preparations and connect to the internet via satellite link. He knew that his team of testers was ready to continue their testing. It was thrilling having these kids as decoys for the Feds. Every one of them was intellectually brilliant, especially his son, Ian. He wasn't too sure about Jonah, who walked around like a zombie. It was unnerving at times, the way his son stared straight ahead, looking at nothing.

It happened around the time Tabler had killed his wife and made up a story about her running away from her family. He often wondered if the disappearance of his mother somehow triggered the boy's condition. He was surprised that Ian hadn't been more inquisitive now that he was older. Maybe the day would come when his curiosity pushed him for more answers. He hoped the day would never come, but if he did ask questions, Nicholas had an explanation ready.

Tabler kept the box with the drone in the back of the pickup truck, covered with a tarp, and held down with straps. When the time was right, he would take a box cutter and remove the straps and the top of the box, giving the drone and its payload room to rise above the truck bed and be on its way.

While planning this event, Tabler worried about the wind and that it might be too strong for control of the drone, but the restaurant was on the ground floor surrounded by other buildings that provided a windbreak. As long as he could maneuver the drone over the edge of the parking garage and down along the interstate entrance ramp, the rest of the trip would be child's play.

Tabler took another deep breath, looked out over the vastness of Eastern New York State, then got into the cab of the truck. He powered up his gaming computer and began the task of verifying the program that would link to the drone and control its movements and the payload. He smiled to himself until he heard an approaching vehicle. An Albany Police cruiser crested the deck on the up ramp. He tensed slightly, then relaxed. Nothing to worry about. Just smile and wave.

The cruiser slowly made a tour of the deck, the officer looking his way as he drove past. Tabler smiled and raised his hand in an easy-does-it wave. The officer tilted his head in acknowledgement and drove on, heading to the exit ramp. Within seconds, the cruiser was out of sight. His smile growing, Tabler thought that the cop didn't even take the time to phone in the truck's license plate. It wouldn't matter. The truck was in the name of an alias who couldn't be traced back to him. And his getaway car was parked on the ground floor below, registered to a different alias. He started to hum a Reggae song to himself. *Cause every little ting, is gonna be alright.*

Chapter 32

Harold H. Herald stood in the control center at the Port of Savannah's Miles and Taylor Plantation site reviewing the shipment manifest of the load of containers that had just been placed dockside. It seemed to Herald that everything that could go wrong did go wrong. Earlier in the shift, one of the massive cranes lost power with a container suspended halfway between the ship's deck and the landing spot. It took nearly three hours for the maintenance crew to get the crane moving again. Then a couple of Longshoremen got into an argument that nearly came to blows. Three other men intervened until, finally, everyone calmed down. The entire situation was a safety nightmare with the potential for significant injuries, not to mention damage to vital equipment and goods.

He couldn't concentrate on completing the paperwork because he had something on his mind, or more accurately, someone. The incident with Nevin Tate putting a forty-five-caliber pistol to his head on Monday had him wound tight. He knew Tate was a psychopath, but he didn't expect that the guy would pull a gun on him with such little provocation. All Herald did was tell Tate that he couldn't talk on the phone right then. He was in the middle of directing the unloading of dozens of shipping containers from a massive ship. It was not something that you could stop to take a phone call, no matter how important the call. And in Nevin Tate's case, the call was only important to him because his ego was the size of one of the container ships. How was he to know that Tate would go off the rails like that?

Herald tried to get back to the task at hand. Completing the paperwork was essential before he turned over the controls to the oncoming superintendent. He put the manifest on the table in front of him and got back to his review when the room shook at the sound of a loud bang. Startled, he dropped his pen and swung around towards the source of the noise.

"Sorry about that," the oncoming superintendent said with a smile. "You look like you just crapped your pants."

"Man, that isn't funny, not at all. What the hell did you do that for? This has been one hell of a shift."

Sammy Williams, Herald's counterpart and relief for the next shift, said, "I said I'm sorry, man. I got my hands full here, and the door just got away from me."

The entrance to the control room had a heavy metal door, and the wall where a doorstop had been destroyed and not replaced was also made of steel. It was common for the door to slam against the wall with a loud bang, so Williams was surprised to see Herald's reaction.

He asked, "Hey, HC, why so tense? You're wound pretty tight."

Herald didn't need for anyone at the shipyard to know his business, so he said, "It's just been a long shift and I didn't sleep well last night."

The last part was true. Not only hadn't he slept well last night, but the two previous nights as well, ever since his last encounter with Tate. His nerves were shot. He had dreams of Tate pointing that forty-five at his head and pulling the trigger. The worst part of the dream was that Herald saw flames shoot out of the barrel of the gun, then the bullet would appear headed for a spot right between his eyes. Each of the last three nights, he had the same nightmare multiple times. He awoke with a start, wringing wet with sweat. It was time to get out from under that psycho's thumb. He had to make a call that he was warned to never make.

After completing his shift, he sat in his car in the shipyard's parking lot, thinking about what he would say to the one guy he believed that he could trust: Ernest Porter. The more he thought about it, the more he was convinced that he had to make the call. Though he and Porter hadn't spoken in nearly a year and very infrequently previous to that, he had Porter's number on speed dial. He took a deep breath and made the call.

After three rings, Porter answered, reluctance in his voice, "HC."

"Porter, we need to talk."

"HC, we can't talk on the phone, you know that, and it isn't a real good idea for us to meet, and you know why."

Herald's shout back at Porter clearly showed the strain he was feeling, "Yeah, I know why! Tate's a nut-job! Do you know what that bastard did the other night?"

Porter hesitated as long as he could before saying again, this time with more force, "HC, we can't talk on the phone. If we absolutely have to meet, then we can do that, but this is a bad time."

Ignoring Porter's warnings, Herald angrily said, "Bad time, my ass. Tate's got to go. And you know what I mean. I haven't slept for days. Do you know what he did? He pointed a gun to …"

Porter shouted, "HC, stop!" There was a silence for several seconds, then Porter said in a calm, almost too quiet voice, "It's already in the works. It may have already happened. I'm waiting for a report."

"You mean you ordered a hit on …"

"Christ, man! Shut up! Just wait for me to call you!" There was silence on the line, then, in a calm, calculated voice, Porter said, "It should be over pretty soon."

Herald took a deep breath, then another. If Porter was taking Tate out, then he could wait for another day or two, but not much longer. If Tate found out that his business partners were plotting against him – were plotting to kill him – then none of them was safe, and Herald was the most vulnerable. He didn't have a government job with a protection detail. He would look over his shoulder everywhere he went until he knew Tate was dead. And he'd only believe it when he saw the body.

His breath coming in short, staccato bursts, he said to Porter, "Alright … Okay." A long, deep breath. "You let me know when it's over. And send pictures! I won't believe it unless I see it with my own eyes! You got that?"

"Yeah, HC. I got it. Try to calm down already. You're gonna get somebody killed."

HC wanted to tell Porter to screw himself, but he just disconnected the call. He started his car and headed for the employee parking lot exit. He wondered if he should get a hotel room for a couple nights, just for the added safety. But Herald knew that Tate had connections everywhere. He couldn't hide from the guy. He just had to hope that the crazy bastard wasn't on to the fact that his business partners were plotting to take him out.

* * *

Ernest Porter was a busy guy. As the Central Intelligence Agency's Deputy Director for Afghan Affairs, his plate was usually pretty full, having to deal with threat assessments, briefings to his boss, and communicating with the Pentagon at a moment's notice on troop movements, among a plethora of other issues that crossed his desk daily, even hourly. The call he had just received from Harold H. Herald put all of his official duties on the back burner, and he had to act fast.

He was awaiting word from his covert contact, David Walsh, on the assassination of Nevin Tate. Porter dealt with many dangerous, deranged people in his duties at the CIA, but none scared him as much as his business partner, Neven Tate. The guy was unpredictable, shrewd, fearless, ruthless, and had absolutely no regard for the law. Tate believed that he was invincible, and from what Porter saw over the years, he was starting to believe it himself.

Porter looked around his office. He wasn't married, so he had no family pictures on his desk. What he did have was an impressive collection of historical paintings from various wars and conflicts throughout U.S. military history. Many brave men were sent into battle to fight for grandiose principles, believing in a greater good, first dreaming of a better country, a way to limit government while unleashing the brilliance of mankind. He wondered how many of those men, now revered as our forefathers and soldiers of the great experiment – a democratic republic – actually held more personal goals, such as great wealth and power. He felt a twinge of guilt at his participation in the business venture he and his partners now ran from the shadows. Many years ago, he had joined the U. S. Army with hopes to get a good education, practical experience, and eventually land a good-paying job. When he first met Alton Woodburn, he thought that this was a man who could teach him about the workings of the military and how to move up the ranks in his unit. Then, quite by accident, he discovered that Woodburn wasn't as honorable as he first appeared. But Woodburn was making money by the casket-load, literally. Porter managed to work his way into the little organization that Woodburn had established. It was working out great.

Then Nevin Tate muscled his way into the picture and took over. Financially, it was unbelievable. Tate took control, and the group started making money faster than they could count it. But there was a cost. Tate was ruthless and didn't tolerate disloyalty. He made sure the others understood that. His latest stunt with HC was but one example.

Another of Tate's abilities was to take members of his group and move them into very powerful positions. How he peddled his influence, none of the men knew, but Porter suspected that he threw his money around to key decision-makers. Tate also sprinkled his monetary influence with not-so-subtle threats. The classic carrot and the stick approach, but with frightening consequences. He always said, "Do your job, don't dare question my methods or decisions, and you'll be rich beyond your wildest dreams."

He got results. Of that, there was no question.

Porter's thoughts returned to the practical matter of eliminating the immediate threat to his and the other partners' life and health. *I'm a senior official in the CIA. I have the greatest resources in the world at my disposal. I shouldn't be afraid of one man. He is just a man. All men bleed, and we all die someday. I just need to help Tate along.*

He picked up the cell-phone that he used for very private conversations, took a deep breath, and dialed the number for David Walsh.

Walsh picked up on the third ring. "Porter, why are you calling me?"

Porter heard the sound of traffic in the background, like Walsh might be outside next to a busy road. He said, "Just calling to check on the status of ..."

Walsh cut him off. "I told you to wait for my call. Don't call me again. I'll call you." He paused then said, "Expect it within twenty-four hours."

"Thank ..."

The traffic noise stopped. Walsh had hung up on Porter before he could finish.

Porter mumbled under his breath, "Asshole."

* * *

David Walsh, also known as Nicholas Tabler and Nevin Tate, stuck the phone back in his pocket as he jumped into the bed of the Ford F150 truck parked on the top floor of the parking garage. He used a boxcutter with a new blade to liberate the drone from the cardboard package where it had been since before leaving the warehouse at Pinnacle Aeronautics. He stuffed the waste cardboard into the cab of the truck. Flipping on the master control switch, he watched as the onboard computer powered up and went through a short sequence of tests. After just a few seconds, the screen on the drone's computer flashed "ready."

Walsh smiled to himself and looked at his watch; 5:30 PM. Plenty of time to take the computer from the truck's cab, walk down to the car on the main floor of the parking garage, and set up communications with his testers. Senator Corrigan would be arriving within the next half-hour. It also gave him time to think about where to stage the death of Nevin Tate, his other alter-ego. It appeared that his team was plotting against him. That was a serious mistake on their part. They would have to pay a big price.

Chapter 33

Peden walked into the office at the Low Country Airport outside of Walterboro, South Carolina. The airport was typical of small, regional airports, with several small hangars, numerous small, single-engine planes tethered to the ground near a taxiway just off of the main runway. The office was newly painted, clean, and organized, with florescent lights hanging from a relatively new drop ceiling. The office had a separate conference room off to the left of the main office area. Peden could hear a man with a deep southern drawl talking. He must have been on the phone because he heard the man pause then answer an unheard question. He made his way towards the door to the conference room and knocked lightly on the opened door.

A tall, lanky man of about fifty with the phone to his ear turned and acknowledged his visitor with a smile and a finger indicating that he would be with him in a moment. He put his hand over the phone and said, "Take a seat by my desk. I'll be with y'all in a second." He turned his attention back to the phone conversation and said, "No, I was talkin' to a guy who just walked in. Can I call y'all back in a few minutes?"

Peden was just seated when the man from the conference room came out, extended his hand, smiled and said, "Virgil Walters. How y'all doin'?"

Peden hopped up quickly. "I'm doing just fine. Peden Savage." Peden shook Virgil's hand.

Virgil asked, "So, what can I do fer y'all?"

Peden said, "Mr. Walters, I just …"

The man interrupted. "Virgil, please. Mr. Walters was my daddy."

"Okay, Virgil. I work for FBI Agent Megan Moore. She's the Special Agent in Charge of the investigation into the murder of Senator Armand Vega."

At that news, Virgil Walter's smile all but disappeared. His expression stiffened, his brow furrowed. "What does this have to do with me?"

Peden said, "I just spoke with your brother, Olin. He stores packages for a man that we're trying to contact. The packages come from a company called Pinnacle Aeronautics."

Virgil put his hand to his chin in a thinker's stance. "Yeah. We receive them packages via air transport directly from Pinnacle. They's addressed to Air Racers LLC, care of my brother, Olin. He stores 'em until the guy picks 'em up. We get paid pretty good for doin' not a whole lotta work." He paused for a moment, then said, "Olin an' me was startin' to think that the money was a little too good for what we did for the guy, so we asked him, kinda jokin', what he did fer a livin'. He seemed a bit displeased that we was askin'. I'm afraid that he might end our arrangement." He paused again. "Are y'all thinkin' that this guy might'a killed that senator?"

Peden replied, "I'm not really sure, but for now, I just want to talk with him. I understand that he just picked up two boxes from Olin today."

Virgil Walters was thinking. It looked like he was contemplating just how much he wanted to say when Peden said, "Look, Virgil, you're not in any trouble. We just need to find this guy. Do you know his name?"

"Yeah. Walsh. He never did tell us his first name. Just said to call him Walsh."

Peden reached into his shirt pocket and pulled out the grainy photo from the car dealership's parking lot. "Does this look like Mr. Walsh?"

Virgil rubbed the stubble on his chin while scrutinizing the photo. He tilted his head to one side and said, "Could be. Ain't much detail there, but it kinda looks like Walsh."

"Did Mr. Walsh say where he was going?"

"Nope. The pilot or co-pilot didn't file no flight plan. Just fueled up and took off. They took off on the main runway heading northeast, but they coulda headed any-which-way once they was air-born. He owns a nice jet, I'll tell ya that."

Peden then asked, "Do you have the make, model, and registration number?"

"Sure do." Walters hit a few keys on the computer using a slow hunt and peck, then read the information off the screen. "Gulfstream G350." He turned the screen so that the men could read the tail number for themselves. "It's a real beauty, that's for sure. They ain't cheap neither."

Peden asked, "Do you have security cameras on-site?"

"We do, but we mostly rely on Mr. Smith and Mr. Wesson." Virgil grinned at his own joke.

"Can I take a look at your security footage for the time Mr. Walsh was here?"

"Sure. Y'all can watch it from the monitor over there." He pointed to a desk about fifteen feet from where Peden stood. "There's four cameras around the office here. Y'all can look at all four angles at the same time. The screen shows 'em in like a four-square arrangement."

Walters went to the other desk, followed by his guest. He again hit several keys on an old keyboard. After several seconds, the screen showed four still shots of the office from different angles. Virgil pointed to each of the cameras that were bolted to the ceiling. He said, "Let me think. He was here around 11:15, so I can skip right to just before then." More slow keystrokes. "There y'all go. If ya want to drive, all ya have to do is hit the arrow buttons down here. Hit the space bar to pause the screen. All four views will work together."

He stepped aside, motioning for Peden to take control, which he did. He hit the right arrow button, and the screens came to life. Virgil mentioned that you could hit the arrow button again to speed up the time. Within a minute, they were watching as a thin man with a head full of hair and a bright smile strolled into the office. Peden hit the space bar to freeze the images. Peden said under his breath, "Tabler."

Virgil asked, "What was that?"

"Nothing. I just recognized the man. Now we have a face to go with the name."

The men watched for several more minutes looking for

any clue as to where he might be headed, but there was nothing more to be learned from the videos. Peden requested a copy of the footage that showed Nicholas Tabler walk into the office until the time he went out of camera range. Walters agreed and put the copies on a flash drive.

Peden thanked Virgil Walters and gave the man his card and requested that he not mention their visit to anyone, especially Mr. Walsh. "When Mr. Walsh returns, you call me, day or night. It doesn't matter what time. But do it when he is no longer around. If you happen to see which direction he heads, let me know that, but don't put yourself in danger."

Virgil said, "I understand."

The men shook hands. When Peden was back in his Tahoe, he thought, *Can we track this guy down by his tail numbers? I'm not sure. I'll have to give Megan a call.*

Peden looked at his watch. It was 3:45 PM. His stomach was growling. He hadn't eaten a thing since early morning. He decided to grab a bite and call Megan while he waited for his food.

Ten minutes later, Peden sat in the booth furthest from the door at Sunday's Soul Food on Jeffries Boulevard in Walterboro. Peden made the call to Megan and recapped his trip to Walterboro, including the use of Low Country Storage for storing the drones and Low Country Regional Airport for receipt of the drones from Pinnacle Aeronautics. Then Peden told her that he had video of Nicholas Tabler in the airport office and Virgil Walters' description of the arrangement that he and his brother had with Tabler. He included that Virgil Walters thought they may have asked too many questions of him and may have jeopardized their current deal.

As he chatted with Megan, his waitress delivered a catfish dinner with coleslaw, potato wedges, and green beans cooked with bacon and zucchini.

After inhaling the aroma of the meal, Peden said, "I hope that didn't spook him."

Megan asked, "So where is Tabler now?"

Peden replied, "He took off just before noon. He had a

pilot, co-pilot, and him flying a Gulfstream G350. They didn't file a flight plan. I don't know if you can track civilian flights."

Megan said, "Sure you can, as long as you got the tail number. You did get the tail number, right?"

Peden paused just long enough to tease his former partner. "Of course, I did."

"So, here's what you do. Contact Lee with the tail number. There's a computer website, FlightAware.com, that tracks all civilian flights by tail number. Don't ask me how, they just do. If the flight is still in the air, it'll show up."

Peden asked, "What if the plane already landed and shut down?"

"I'm not sure. You'll have to ask Lee. I suggest you get moving though. If he took off before noon, he's probably already at his destination, where ever that is."

Peden asked, "Is there anything else you need me to do before I hit the road again?"

"No, just come right to my office when you get back in town. We'll put all our info together and see where we go from here."

Peden replied, "Okay, Megan. I'm on it. See you in a couple hours, maybe less."

As soon as the call was disconnected, Peden hit the button to call Lee Sparks. Lee answered before the second ring. "Peden. What can I do for you?"

"Hey, Lee. I've got a lot of information for you, but I need to make this short. We've got a priority task for you. Megan tells me that you can track civilian flights, you know, private planes or small jets."

"Yeah, as long as they're powered up and we have a registration. I think the website is called flight aware. I used it a year ago or so."

"We need you to track this jet. It's a Gulfstream G350." Peden read off the tail number. "The jet left Low Country Regional Airport before noon today."

"Let's see what we can see."

Peden listened to the rapid-fire keystrokes over the

phone while Sparks hummed some tune. The humming stopped.

Sparks said, "There's nothing on that tail number right now, but I might be able to look back at the data. I'll have to look into it. I might have to do a little data mining that's real close to the line, if you know what I mean."

Sparks was letting Peden know that what he was about to do was borderline legal, maybe stretching the bounds of ethical behavior. Sparks was willing to do it because there were no financial interests at stake. But if any information was obtained by what was essentially a hack into the system, they wouldn't be able to use that information in court.

"Lee, do what you need to do. The guy's name is Nicholas Tabler, and he took two drones with him on this flight. He may be setting up another hit."

"I'm on it, boss. I'll let you know."

Chapter 34

Ian Tabler's head was spinning, stunned by his brother's revelation that their father killed their mother, that he had witnessed the killing, and that their mother's body was buried on the grounds of the compound. After they were discovered on the grounds by Victor this morning, it was all he could do to keep from running across the lush lawn to the house. He and Jonah nearly collided with the groundskeeper. When he got to his room, his thoughts were on overdrive, completely out of control. He didn't look up at his heroes, who were looking down on him from their posters on the walls of his room. He spent most of the afternoon trying to come up with a plan to stop the next test, but everything he thought of had holes in it.

There were other issues on his mind as well. His brother, whom Ian hadn't heard speak a word his entire life with the exception of numbers, spoke to him in full, coherent sentences. What was the first message that Jonah chose to deliver? That their father was a murderer; that he murdered their mother – in cold blood – and buried her body in clear line of sight from their bedroom windows!

He wondered how Jonah had kept this secret his entire life. He marveled at his brother's ability to act like an imbecile in the presence of their father and develop a code that only he and Jonah understood. The fear that Jonah must have experienced each and every day of his life, knowing that their father was capable of murder, and knowing that Nicholas Tabler could turn on him and Ian, must have been all-consuming.

He recalled times when he and Jonah were in the computer lab together working on computer games and their father would walk in. Jonah would keep his eyes glued to the monitor as if nothing else in the world existed. To find out now that it was all an act to protect them both was simply astonishing.

Now the brothers had to do something about their father's deeds while not letting on that they both knew what he had done over ten years ago. Jonah knocked on the door and slowly walked in. Ian looked up, and their eyes met for the first time since they left the location of their mother's unmarked grave.

Ian quietly asked, "How did you do it?"

Jonah looked at his brother, then looked around as if someone might be hiding behind Ian's bed or in the closet, then in a near whisper said. "Fear. I was so scared – I'm still scared – that Dad was going to kill me, too. I just shut down. I mean, I didn't leave my room for days. I acted like I was sick. You probably don't remember much about that time because you were so busy learning everything that you could back then, but I didn't sleep, maybe for weeks. Since he hadn't come for me, I figured as long as I acted like a zombie, he would leave me be."

"It worked." Ian thought for a moment, then, still whispering, said, "We have to do something about it. I think Dad is David Walsh and somebody named Nevin Tate."

Ian pulled up his recorder and explained how he recorded the call from David Walsh. Then he told Jonah how the recorder picked up calls from David Walsh to the other testers.

Jonah said, "That's impossible unless the calls originated close by. But wouldn't you be able to identify Dad's voice?"

"I thought about that. I think he uses some kind of distortion tool so that it alters his voice. One thing it can't alter is the way he uses certain words. Listen."

Ian turned the recorder on and played the call from David Walsh where he asked Ian if he and Jonah would be willing to continue testing. He started the call at the beginning and then hit pause. He said to his brother, "Listen to this next line; not the tone, but what he says." Ian hit play. David Walsh's recorded voice said, *No, son, we just ran into some issues.* Ian hit pause again.

"That sounds like something Dad would say, calling me 'son.' Nobody else calls me son."

Jonah looked skeptical.

Ian said, "That's not all. Listen to all the calls. He doesn't say son to Tony, Andrew, or Ricky Lee. Only to me."

Ian hit play, and the boys listened to each call to their testing peers. Ian could tell Jonah wasn't convinced, though he understood that the device Ian had created couldn't have a significant range, or it would pick up all kinds of random digital signals.

Then they got to the last call where some guy named Tate was talking with another guy named Alton. Jonah listened as Tate hinted at a big-money transaction and another event that would keep the War on Drugs funded.

Jonah's eyes widened, then he said, "They're going to kill somebody else." He paused. "He's going to make us help him do it. Tate is Walsh."

"Yeah. And Walsh is Dad. But I don't think we actually have control of the drone. There can only be one person controlling the drone that has the weapon, and I don't think a killer would leave it up to kids our age to carry out the killing. He would want positive control." The two boys sat in silence, overwhelmed by their realization.

Ian said, "I think we can prove it, but we have to talk with the others. Here's what we'll do. When the drone is armed and ready and on its final approach, we'll tell everyone that they have to veer off to the right or left. If the drone stays on course, then we know we aren't in control."

Jonah looked down. He said, "But that won't stop Dad from killing whoever he has set up to die."

Ian thought for a minute. "We need to call that agent, Megan Moore. We'll let her know what we've figured out." Ian looked at the clock. It was already 5:25 PM. They didn't have much time. They had to make the calls to their peers and the call to Agent Moore, and they had to be convincing.

Ian fished in his pocket for the agent's card but couldn't

find it. He asked Jonah if he had one, but Jonah shook his head no. Ian said, "Let's head to the lab. We can do this from there."

When they made their way down the two flights of stairs, they passed one of the housekeepers who asked if they'd like something to eat. Ian said no as they continued on. Jonah had to consciously remember that no one else but Ian knew he could talk. He had to stay in character and act like his old zombie self, which meant that he had to move slower than Ian. It was tough, knowing the consequence of taking too much time.

Once in the computer lab, Ian locked the door behind them. He said, "Let's get the computers up, and you can look up the numbers for the local FBI office. I'll look up that dude, Peden Savage. Then I'll text the other testers and have them get on a conference call."

* * *

Jonah got right to work, searching for the Savannah FBI office number. He found it within seconds. From his computer, he put on a headset with a microphone and speakers and dialed the number.

A soft, smooth female voice asked, "Federal Bureau of Investigation, Savannah office. I'm Shanique King. How may I be of service?"

Jonah took a deep breath. He was nervous and had a difficult time keeping his thoughts straight. He stammered, "Um ... my brother and I ... um ... we have information ... um ... for ... um ... Agent Moore."

In a calming voice, the woman asked, "To what does this information pertain?"

"Um ... a murder that is about to take place."

Without further discussion, Jonah heard a clicking sound over the line. A few seconds passed then another female answered. He recognized the voice of Megan Moore. "This is Special Agent Megan Moore. Who am I speaking with?"

"Jonah Tabler."

"Well, this is certainly a surprise. When we met, you supposedly couldn't talk. Shanique said you have information about a murder that hasn't happened yet. Tell me about this murder, Jonah."

"Um ... well ..."

"Jonah, please take a deep breath and calm down. Are you safe, and is your brother with you?"

"Yes. Do you want to talk with him?"

"Not yet. Let's just see how this goes. When is this murder supposed to take place?"

Jonah looked at the time on his computer. "In, like, thirty minutes."

"Jonah, tell me what you know about this murder. I already know when. I need to know the who, where, and why."

Jonah started by saying, "I don't know where. But it will be by drone, just like Senator Vega. The killer is my dad. The why is very complicated. I really don't know how to explain it. But I know my dad has already killed before. He killed our mom."

There was silence on the line for a second. Megan said, "We can talk about that later. Right now, do you know where your dad is?"

"No. He left this morning for a business trip, but we have some recordings of him planning to kill someone else. We don't know who."

"These recordings, they haven't been deleted, have they?"

"No ma'am. Ian's got them on his digital recording device that he made. It's pretty cool." Jonah stopped talking for a moment, then said, "Agent Moore, I'm really scared."

"Jonah, you're doing fine. We're going to help you and Ian. Do you trust me?"

"Yes, ma'am."

"Alright. We're going to get some agents over to your place as soon as possible. In the mean-time, you and Ian stay safe. Call my cell phone if your dad shows back up."

Jonah wrote down the number, and the call was disconnected.

Jonah looked over at Ian, who was texting like mad. He

paused and waited for replies. Within seconds he heard tones indicating that Ian was getting answers. He saw Ian take a deep breath. He turned to Jonah and said, "They're all ready. At least we'll know that we're not the killers. I'm ninety-nine percent sure."

Jonah didn't like those odds. He would have felt better if Ian had said one hundred percent. But there was no time for that level of certainty.

* * *

As Special Agent Megan Moore hung up the phone, Peden walked into her office. The clock on the wall read 5:33 PM.

Megan said, "Don't sit down. We have to get warrants and get over to the Tabler compound. The boys have evidence that their dad killed Vega. Tabler's got another hit lined up at six o'clock. We don't know where." She took a deep breath. "Have you heard anything new from Lee?"

"Not yet. He was going to dig deeper into the tracking website. He thinks ..."

Megan cut him off before he said anything that she couldn't go along with. Everything had to be by the book, at least the things that she knew about. "Okay, I'll make the calls to our favorite judges and get Shanique working on the forms. We're way behind the eight ball on this."

Megan looked up the number for the Chatham County Superior Court. Just as she hit send, Peden's phone chirped. It was Lee Sparks.

"Hey, Lee. What have you got?"

"The jet landed at Saratoga County Regional Airport. I called, and the jet is still there, powered down. According to the manager at the airport, they plan to fly out in the morning, but it isn't for sure. It might be longer."

"Did he say whether the pilots let him know where their passenger was headed?"

"Nope. No clue."

Peden shook his head. "That's a pretty wide-open area up there. They've been on the ground for hours now. He could be on his way to the city or headed up in the mountains, or even to Syracuse. That's a lot of ground to cover in ..." Peden looked at his watch ... "twenty minutes."

Chapter 35

For the second time today, Ian was nervous and sweating. Any other day, finding out that his brother could speak real words instead of an endless stream of numbers in a special code would be a miracle, but he used his first words to deliver a devastating message about their parents; one dead, the other a killer. Being the de facto leader of this small group carried with it a level of anxiety that was closing on him like a vice. The thought that someone within their group of testers could actually be in control of a killer drone, that added enormous pressure to an already strained situation. The test that they were to perform could snuff out the life of an innocent man and anyone around them that might be in the wrong place at the wrong time.

At 5:50 PM, Ian heard his cell phone beep. David Walsh relayed the final instructions to his testers via a group text message. He described the scene as a covert CIA operation to take out a top terrorist general who had orchestrated attacks against United States assets in the middle east. He described how the drone would descend from the top floor of a parking garage in Tehran, Iran, as the general made his way to a secret meeting surrounded by several bodyguards. The testers were to concentrate on the figure marked with a red dot, signifying that he was the primary target, but collateral damage was expected. Walsh asked if the testers had any questions. When none were sent, the testers received a final text – *Happy Hunting!*

In preparation for the tester's covert plan, Ian had created a new group text with his peers. He had already explained his concerns, that they were being used as camouflage to hide a killer. He had described his plan to prove that none of the beta testers were involved in the murder of Senator Vega and whoever is next on Walsh's hit list. He had described in detail what each tester was to do once they received the green light on their screens indicating that their weapons were "hot." Each tester was assigned an evasive maneuver. Jonah had created a program that would record the actions of each tester and show that they had bailed out of the attack.

Ian reiterated that they should disregard what happened on the screen once they made their move because the image might be tracking the real drone. Regardless, it would prove that they were not involved in the attack.

At 5:55 PM, Ian received confirmation that everyone understood what they had to do. Simon Andrews asked if anyone had contacted Special Agent Megan Moore. Ian texted back right away that he had and that they were working on trying to determine the target, but that time was short.

Suddenly, their screens came to life with a view from the drone's camera of a wide-open green area. Only a few buildings were visible in the distance. The image had the look and feel of a video game. The trees and greenery looked fake. Even the buildings looked surreal. Ian thought to himself, video game producers put significant money and resources into making video games look as close to reality as possible. Walsh, really his father, Nicholas Tabler, had done just the opposite. He had to make a very real situation look as though it was all a big video game. Ian wondered if reverse engineering in that way was easier than trying to make the games look real. But did the elder Tabler have those kinds of skills? He had never let on to Ian or Jonah that he did.

He thought briefly of Carlita Galindo, wondering what feelings she was having at this moment; if the weight of the situation pressed down on her like it was on him, but he didn't have time to dwell on it. He looked over at his brother, who was intently staring at his own monitor, preparing for the attack that was about to begin.

The drone began to rise and rotate slowly to the left. A large building came into view. There were numbers on top – "677." Ian had no idea where the building might be, but it was their first clue. At the bottom of the screen, Ian could see parking spaces, then a short wall, maybe three feet tall. After a minute, the drone was over the wall and descending. A red dot appeared on the screen; The target had been acquired. A green light indicated the testers should take control of their test drones. The attack was underway.

* * *

Nicholas Tabler spotted Senator Lancaster Corrigan's car heading into the same parking garage where he had parked the rented pickup truck. He expected that the Senator and his wife would meet their guests in the entry to the restaurant and move quickly into the interior of the establishment. No doubt Corrigan had reservations and their table was waiting.

Timing for launching the drone was planned to the second. When he learned of Senator Corrigan's scheduled dinner, Tabler had walked the distance from the parking garage to the restaurant entrance numerous times. He even stopped in the restaurant and had an excellent dinner. Each time while walking off the distance from various levels of the parking garage, he altered his pace, setting a minimum and maximum time window for the drone to be at the optimum location for the attack. Based on his calculations, there was little margin for error. Too early and the drone would draw unwanted attention with an automatic weapon hanging from its undercarriage; too late and the senator and his guests would be in the restaurant and out of sight. While a small number of casualties was acceptable, particularly those frequent and generous donors to Corrigan, randomly firing into a crowded restaurant was not acceptable, especially since the likelihood of success using that approach was minuscule.

Tabler's pre-staged rental car was on the ground floor of the garage. He sat in the passenger's seat with his computer already set to maneuver the drone into the firing position. Corrigan parked just six spaces down from Tabler, making visual identification easy. He had to use some caution because he had attended political fundraisers and interacted with many people with deep pockets. It was possible, even likely, that he had attended large, fundraising dinners with Corrigan's guests.

It was unlikely that he would be recognized because he now wore a Yankees ball cap pulled low over his brow.

As Corrigan and his wife exited their black Mercedes Benz, a white Benz pulled up to them and stopped for a little small-talk. It might be their dinner guests or just someone who recognized the senator from previous encounters. The recent arrivals pulled into a parking spot near the senator's car.

An elderly couple exited the Benz. They were dressed for a casual dinner, the gray-haired gentleman wearing a light blue sport coat over a white golf shirt, the beautiful woman, at least ten years his junior, wearing a gray pantsuit. As they approached the senator and his wife, they smiled broadly. Then the group exchanged greetings with handshakes for the men and hugs for the women. Someone made a joke, and they all laughed. A question was asked about who might be joining them for dinner, and everyone looked around as if expecting the third party to appear out of nowhere.

As they headed for the restaurant entrance, another car pulled up and quickly parked. The new couple was younger, the man driving the red Cadillac CT6. His driver's side window glided down and Walsh heard him ask, "Are we late?" Everyone had a good laugh at a question that apparently was a joke of some kind. The elder gentleman waved him off as if being late was expected.

Trent knew time was of the essence. He took the controller and prompted the drone to elevate. He watched the computer screen, which showed the view from the drone's onboard camera. The screen indicated that the machine was working correctly as a panoramic view was displayed. Then the end wall of the parking garage came into view. As the dinner party made their way out of the parking garage, they appeared on Walsh's computer screen.

Easy now. There's plenty of time.

Walsh maneuvered the drone slowly down the side of the parking garage. The whirring sound of the drone's propellers was masked by the traffic noise from the rush hour traffic speeding past on the nearby innerbelt highway. He tapped a key on his computer keypad to activate the green light on the beta testers' computers, letting them know that they should be able to see the lock on the target. Corrigan was now within fifty feet of the restaurant's front door.

Showtime.

* * *

Senator Lancaster Corrigan had arrived at the Albany International Airport at 5:20 PM. He had deboarded the jet, retrieved his luggage, and was out the terminal exit in nothing flat. His wife was waiting, and they were on Albany Shaker Road on their way to the 677 Steakhouse with plenty of time to spare.

Corrigan's wife, Avery, neared the Interstate 87 interchange when her husband said, "Head north on the Northway. We have plenty of time. Let's stop at the 'Moose' for a drink."

The "Moose" was formally called the Tipsy Moose Tap and Tavern. It was where the senator and his wife met for the first time. They literally bumped into each other while trying to escape from their bad dates. They ended up at the bar together and hit it off right away.

Avery replied, "We have to watch the time. You don't want to keep your donors waiting. We could just go to 677 and hang out there."

He smiled. "Humor me. We'll get there in plenty of time. I'd like to reminisce for a bit about my good fortune. I met this hot chick there once."

She smiled back. "Do I know this chick?"

"Oh, yeah." As she drove, he lightly caressed her leg with his left hand.

She said, "You keep that up, and we're going to have an accident."

They had just one drink at their old hangout, thinking back on the years before he went into politics in a big way. He was swept up by the Democratic Party and ushered through three terms in the House of Representatives. He was quite popular in Eastern New York and won a close race for the

Senate on his first attempt. After two full terms in the Senate, he was becoming more disillusioned with Washington, D.C., and was now entertaining thoughts of running for only one more term and calling it quits. He still maintained his law license in New York and had a desire to practice again. Today's meeting with his key donors was to discuss just that. He was going to tell them that, if reelected, this would be his last term. The side trip to the "Moose" was to let his wife know his plans. She was elated as she was not a big fan of the government in Washington. She could feel her husband's growing disillusionment with his profession. He had her full support to get out on a high note. They approached the parking garage next to 677 Steakhouse just before 6:00 PM. Right on time.

Avery and Lancaster Corrigan met Darla and Winston Clark, the wealthy industrialist turned philanthropist and political donor couple in the parking garage, just as Jean and Peter Thorpe pulled in and parked.

As the three politically powerful couples made their way towards the restaurant and ceased their small talk, Winston, easily the most influential of the group, asked, "So, Lance, why the urgent meeting?"

Senator Corrigan, or Lance to his closest friends, replied, "I wanted you to hear it directly from me, before the press leaks it out, that this will be my last campaign. I'm serving one more term, then I'm quitting politics and going back into private practice. Assuming I win, of course."

The group stopped just twenty feet from the restaurant's entrance. Winston frowned for a moment, then said, "If you don't knock off this nonsense about curtailing the War on Drugs, you might be leaving political life before you plan to, but let's get seated and order some drinks. Maybe that'll loosen you up a bit and we can talk some sense into you."

As they turned towards the door, the group heard a buzzing noise. It sounded like a swarm of bees. Corrigan saw it first. A drone with a weapon hanging from its underside. He turned and pushed his wife to the ground, then jumped in front of his elderly friend and his wife just as the loud *pop, pop, pop* pierced the air. He felt the sting and impact of multiple projectiles hit his chest, shoulder and arm before he collapsed to the ground. The last thing he heard before he lost consciousness was his wife's scream, then the world went black.

Chapter 36

Under the watchful eye of his wife, President Alton Woodburn forced himself to take another bite of the salmon fillet that the White House chef had prepared per the president's doctor's orders. His wife oversaw the preparation of the meal to ensure that no harmful ingredients were added like butter, garlic, cayenne pepper, paprika, or anything else that might add some flavor to the bland meal. Salmon was one of his favorite dishes, but the "healthy preparation method" prescribed by his personal physician left him wondering if the fish was really salmon.

Even so, a bland tasting salmon and equally bland side dishes wasn't the cause for his lack of appetite. He was still awaiting the results of his order that Ernest Porter terminate their business partner-turned-common-enemy, Nevin Tate. He was so consumed by the idea that Tate might still be alive that he cancelled his late afternoon meeting with the Secretary of Transportation and several of his staff members regarding his proposal for a massive increase in spending on infrastructure. He had already appointed his Chief of Staff to work with the Secretary on the details of the bill. He had intended to use this meeting to drive home the message that he wanted a unified front from his administration when it came time to deal with congress on getting the bill moved through the House and Senate. In his state of mind, he wasn't sure he could pull off the meeting with the desired effect.

That was all on the back burner, the business of the country be damned. From a personal point of view, Tate was a clear and present danger to himself and his family. He was incensed that the problem had not yet been handled. He was losing patience and now was not confident that Ernest Porter could handle the situation. He wondered if his friend and business partner had actually made the call to order the hit on

Tate. Maybe Porter was so petrified that Tate might find out their plan that he simply couldn't bring himself to make the call. If Porter didn't report back by the end of the evening with positive proof that Tate was dead, Woodburn decided that he would take the matter into his own hands. How, he wasn't sure, but he couldn't go on like this. The anxiety was clearly taking years off of his life.

He looked at his watch – he still wore one even though his cell phones all had the time displayed on their screens – and noticed that it was 6:17 PM. He pushed his plate back, leaned back in his chair, and sighed.

"What's wrong, Dear?"

The question from his wife snapped him out of his trance. He wondered how long he'd been off in another land. "Nothing that I can't handle, Sweetheart."

"You've hardly eaten a thing, and salmon is one of your favorites."

"Well, there's only one thing this new 'healthy meal' is lacking – taste. It could at least use some garlic and butter. Hell, I was going to ask for tartar sauce." He made a half attempt at a smile.

His wife responded, "Oh my. Nobody uses tartar sauce on salmon. That's just the final insult to a once proud fish."

They both forced a chuckle. Woodburn was about to speak when his Chief of Staff burst into the dining room. "Mr. President, we have an urgent matter."

"What is it, Randall?"

Randall Wareton looked at the first lady briefly as he paused, letting the president know it was a grave matter. She took the cue, got up, gave her husband a kiss on the top of his head, and left the room, closing the door behind her.

The president looked at Wareton and raised his eyebrows and turned his hands palms up, urging his Chief of Staff to continue.

"Mr. President, there's been another assassination attempt on a member of Congress. Senator Corrigan, sir."

"When?"

"It happened around 6:00 PM in Albany, New York. The senator and his wife were meeting friends for dinner and were attacked before they reached the restaurant door."

The president stood. "Let's go."

They headed to the situation room. Along the way, Woodburn barked orders to have certain staff members meet him there. He also ordered that leadership of the House and Senate be summoned to the White House. Within minutes, the calls went out with all invitees responding that they would be there.

Fifteen minutes later, with a standing-room-only crowd in the situation room, the FBI Director conducted the briefing on what they knew about the assassination of Senator Lancaster Corrigan, who had not survived the attack. His wife was injured, but not by bullets. She told the first responders that her husband had roughly pushed her out of the way. In doing so, she fell hard on the sidewalk and hit her head against an iron post, part of the enclosed patio for the exclusive restaurant. Two others were hurt in the attack: Darla and Winston Clark. Both had been hit, Darla in the leg and Winston in the upper arm and shoulder. The younger couple that was with them was spared injury, but they were traumatized by the incident. They were moved to the FBI office in Albany, which was just a few miles from the crime scene.

FBI Director Herbert Massey wrapped up his brief with, "We can say with near certainty that this is the same person or persons who killed Senator Vega."

Alton Woodburn was silent. All eyes in the room were on him, waiting for his reaction to the news that another public official was gunned down in such a dramatic and very public way. As he looked around the room, he wondered if any of the people staring at him suspected that he was part of an illegal business that sold hundreds of millions of dollars' worth of heroin in the United States every year. The mood in the room was so heavy the only sounds were of throats being cleared or clothing on seats as people shifted uncomfortably, trying to not make a sound. It was far more solemn than a funeral mass.

Alton Woodburn's mind was paralyzed by the fact that he knew exactly who had killed Senator Lancaster Corrigan, but he couldn't tell a soul. He had to say something to the men and women awaiting his orders.

Instead of clear direction, he berated Massey for his lack of progress on the Vega murder, growling that if more progress had been made that, maybe, they could have avoided another prominent Senator being killed. Massey didn't dare defend himself in front of the assembled crowd, but it was clear that his blood was boiling, his face turning beat red at the rebuke.

Woodburn looked around the room at each of the men and women and gathered what wits remained in his rapidly spinning head. "We have the most powerful resources in the world. We can listen in on anyone's conversations around this country. We've had two United States Senators gunned down in public. You get your assets out there and find the killer before another government official is killed, or worse, the American people lose complete faith in our ability to stop these crimes. Mr. Massey is in charge of this investigation. I have full confidence in him and his people to apprehend the perpetrators and bring them to justice, but he needs our help. I expect that you will give him everything he needs from your departments for him to be successful ... for *us* to be successful. Now get going."

Woodburn's Chief of Staff hung back as the room emptied. He said, "Mr. President, you'll need to address the nation sometime this evening. I would recommend that you give a news briefing from the press room. I'd also recommend that you have Director Massey there to answer questions from the press. He'll know that he can't answer with any amount of detail, but ..."

"Yeah, I know. We have to at least look like we're getting out in front of this." Woodburn paused, then said, "Get it set up. I'm going back to the office."

"Yes, sir."

When the president left the situation room, an

augmented Secret Service detail greeted him. He was surprised at first, then realized that it was better for him to have a heightened protective detail until Tate was dead.

His next call was to Ernest Porter to find out why in the hell a man who was supposed to be dead was still killing high-ranking public servants.

Twenty minutes later, the president was in the one of the small conference rooms in the white house. President Woodburn pulled out his personal cell phone and hit the speed-dial button for Ernest Porter, his blood pressure rising with every ring in his ear.

Ernest Porter answered hesitantly, tension evident in his voice, "Alton, we can't talk right now."

"Bullshit, Ernie! I thought I told you to terminate this asshole! Do you know what he did? Do you?"

"Alton, this isn't a secure line. Don't say another word!"

Porter's last words and the manner in which he said them put Woodburn over the top. He clenched the phone, nearly crushing it in his hands. "You listen to me, Porter, and listen good. With all the resources at your disposal, if you can't follow through on a simple order, then you aren't much of a spook. You wipe this guy off the map and get it done quick before we're all doomed. You understand me?"

The phone went dead. Porter had hung up without a response, which made Woodburn nearly explode with anger. He threw the cell phone across the room and it shattered when it hit the wall.

* * *

Nevin Tate, also known as Nicholas Tabler and David Walsh, wasted no time in getting away from the scene at 677 Steakhouse. He left the pickup truck where it was parked on the top floor of the parking garage and drove the rental car, a plain, white Chevrolet Impala, to the on-ramp for the innerbelt Interstate-787, then drove north to the New York State Northway, Interstate 87. In less than forty-five minutes, Tate was checking into the Cold Brook Campsite on Gurn Springs

Road just off of exit 16. He immediately pitched a tent and showered at the communal shower, then took a brief swim in the pool, hoping to wash away any trace evidence that he had handled the drone that killed Lancaster Corrigan.

After drying and changing clothes, he set out on a short hike on one of the many trails surrounding the campground. Finding an isolated spot, he walked roughly forty feet off of the trail and laid down to flatten the greenery. He looked around and found the perfect spot for his camera, the one used by his David Walsh persona. He stood and hung his phone in a small tree at head height, then turned on the camera function. He angled the camera to get a shot of himself in the spot where he had prepared the ground and braced the phone to hold the angle. He set up the camera to take a dozen shots automatically after a thirty-second delay. From his pocket, he pulled a Ziplock baggie with premade fake bullet wounds. He'd made up the props from a movie makeup kit in preparation for this moment. He applied two wounds to his forehead, quickly laid back down, and positioned himself as if he were shot dead. Between camera shots, he adjusted his head, arms, and body. From the series of photos, he would pick the best shot and send it to Ernest Porter.

Once they took the bait, they would assume that he was dead. *You know what they say about people who assume things? Pretty soon, they'll be dead ... or something like that.*

Chapter 37

Ian had set up a conference call with all the testers for right after completion of the so-called beta test. They were all on the conference line within a few seconds of each other. Simon Andrews was frantic, as was Tony Pirelli. Ricky Lee Lyle and Carlita Galindo were outwardly calm, but Ian knew that each of the tester's nerves were rattled. Jonah listened in, Ian hoping that his brother would be able to provide some reassurance to the others that they had nothing to worry about.

Ian started to talk, but Simon spoke over him. "Hey, man, are you sure we're in the clear on this. My dad was looking over my shoulder while we were testing."

Tony Pirelli jumped in, "Mine, too."

Simon continued, "He wanted to call the FBI. He's sure that we're going to get raided again. I think he's calling that lady agent, Moore, right now."

Ian hesitated for just a second, then tried to use a calming voice, "Listen, everybody, Jonah recorded each of the drones separately. When you veered off of the target like we said to do before the – let's just call it a test – he has video of each of the drones from your computers. It is absolute proof that we had nothing to do with the attack. I'll send you copies of all the video files."

Toni Pirelli said, "My old man is freaking out a little. When can you send that video?"

Ian looked at Jonah, who whispered, "I'll send them now."

Ian nodded to his brother, then said to the others, "They'll be on their way to you in just a few seconds. Look them over. Show them to your parents. I'm confident that we're all in the clear, but if they still want to call Agent Moore, tell them to go ahead. She's going to have copies of these files, too. Trust me on this, we're safe. There's nothing we could have done to stop it."

Carlita Galindo spoke up, "So, what's next?"

Even with the tension of the past twenty minutes, hearing Carlita's voice sent Ian's heart fluttering. He took a deep breath to calm his nerves, then said, "Listen, everyone, you're going to find out soon enough, so I have something that you all need to know. David Walsh is ... Nicholas Tabler, Jonah's and my dad."

Ian heard each of the testers draw in deep breaths of astonishment, followed by a number of expressions of disbelief.

Simon Andrews said, "Tell me you're joking. This is a joke, right?"

Ian continued, "I'm afraid not. He was disguising his voice on the phone so we wouldn't know it was him. He also calls himself Nevin Tate. The FBI is probably on their way here with a search warrant looking for our dad and any evidence they can find that he killed Senator Vega and whoever it was that he shot this time."

Carlita Galindo asked in a sad, subdued tone, "Oh Ian, what are you going to do?"

Hearing the concern in her voice, Ian smiled, but it was tempered with the gravity of the moment. "Jonah and I are going to cooperate with them and try to track down my dad. He's a murderer. We have to come to grips with that."

* * *

Megan and Peden were at her office in Downtown Savannah, waiting on the search warrant for the Tabler compound. The rest of her team was scattered around the office, sipping coffee, talking about the case, comparing it to other cases that they had been part of over the course of their careers. Megan sat at her desk, looking her usual serious-minded self, not outwardly showing signs of anxiety. Peden paced the room, feeling the apprehension that permeated the atmosphere. They had already gone over the plans for the raid, though Megan warned them that plans could change. With Nicholas Tabler out of the state, they would be dealing with the security team at the compound.

What their orders were for protecting the grounds was unknown. She told the crew that it should be a peaceful raid, but be ready for anything. Be especially careful with the two boys, Ian and Jonah. She had said, "They're innocent victims of their father's crimes."

Megan's phone rang. Her heart sank, thinking that it might be the judge who was reviewing the warrant telling her the warrant was denied. She looked at her phone and was relieved when she saw an area code for upstate New York and guessed, correctly, that it was Tony Pirelli, Sr. calling, wanting to know what the hell was going on.

She answered, "Special Agent Moore."

An angry voice barked in her ear, "How the hell did you let this happen? When you and that Savage guy were here, you said you'd protect Tony."

In a steady but firm voice, Megan replied, "Mr. Pirelli, we never said that, and you know it. But regardless, Tony and the other testers are not persons of interest nor are they in any way on our radar, except as potential witnesses. We understand that one of the boys from Georgia recorded all the testers actions, and if what we're being told is true, then it clearly shows the testers avoiding taking any shots at the senator. I think you can rest easy. Just ask that Tony not communicate with the others. We need for them to be able to independently tell their stories."

"I think you might be too late on that score. Tony's on a call with the others right now."

Megan shook her head. "Do me a favor and tell Tony to get off the call. Explain that he can't communicate with the others for now."

Megan hung up the phone and was preparing to call Ian Tabler when her phone chirped again. It was a number she didn't recognize. She answered, "Special Agent Megan …"

"What did you get my son into now? He's …"

She cut off Wilson Andrews, Simon Andrew's father. "Mr. Andrews, I don't have time to explain, but your son is not a person of interest. I will call you back as soon as I'm able."

She disconnected the call before he could say another word. She wished she had time to talk with each of the kids and their parents, but the search warrant for the Tabler compound took precedence. She expected that the warrant would be delivered at any time. Megan took a deep breath. It was going to be a long night.

Again, she was about to call Ian when her phone chirped again. It was Rosa Galindo. Megan answered in her usual way and told Mrs. Galindo the same thing she told Tony Pirelli and Wilson Andrews. She was more polite with Rosa and reassured her that Carlita was not in any trouble.

Finally, Megan was able to call Ian Tabler. Ian answered right away.

Megan said, "I hear that you've been busy talking with the other testers."

"Yeah. I guess we're not supposed to do that?"

Megan sighed. "That's right. You didn't know, so don't worry about it. Just don't talk with them until we get this sorted out, okay?"

"Yes, ma'am." There was a pause, then Ian asked, "Are you coming to the house tonight?"

Megan wasn't sure she should answer. He was just a kid, but he might let something slip to the staff. She wanted the raid to be a surprise.

She said, "You and Jonah just lay low for now. We'll see you soon." She hit the end button.

With the call ended, Megan tried to concentrate on the tactics that they had reviewed for serving the warrant at the Tablers'. As she was preparing to spread out a map of the compound, her phone chirped once again. Without looking, she thought about ignoring the call, but changed her mind. It might be someone important. She looked, and sure enough, it was her boss Roland Fosco.

She answered, "Hey, Roland."

"Megan. I understand that you're about to serve a warrant at the Tabler place."

"Just waiting on the judge's signature."

"Good. It sounds like we're closing in on Tabler. We're sure he's good for the two killings?"

"Yes, and possibly one more. His youngest son says that he killed the boys' mother. We hope the warrant allows us to look for evidence of that killing as well."

Megan updated her boss about the alleged murder and provided what little detail they had on Nicholas Tabler's wife. She had passed on the information to the team at Quantico, where databases were being scoured, searching for a clue as to who Valerie Tabler was, where she came from, and what might have happened to her. They didn't know her maiden name and had no idea when or where she was born. It was literally starting from scratch.

Just then, one of her agents came into her office and handed her an envelope.

"Roland, I just got the warrant. I'm going to review it and get the team moving."

"Okay, Megan. Let me know if you need anything, anything at all."

* * *

The Tabler brothers were down in the computer lab when Ian's call to Special Agent Moore was disconnected. His head hung low, he wondered how his father, his own flesh and blood, could have perpetrated such horrific crimes. He wondered how he had been clueless about the world that revolved around him, particularly that part of the world that was within the walls of his father's property. Even his brother, whose intelligence rivaled his own, knew that their father was not the man he portrayed himself to be. Jonah had known of at least one of their father's deeds for over ten years, living in absolute fear that he might be the elder Tabler's next victim. He had created his own fictional world, an entirely bogus persona to hide in plain sight, and it had worked … until now.

Ian sat down in the comfortable chair in front of his blank computer monitors and looked at Jonah, who was engrossed in whatever he was viewing on his computer screens. Ian glanced at the code that covered the enormous monitor, but he had too many other conflicting thoughts to wonder what had his little brother so captivated.

His thoughts wandered to Carlita. He wondered what it would be like to meet her face-to-face. She was the only female that he had ever talked to beyond mathematics, science, and physics. The others had all been arranged tutored classes with just two or three students to one professor. Those classes had been so long ago, when he was still a child, before he started to notice girls as, well, young women. He was becoming a young man now, and though he was well aware of the academic descriptions of what he was experiencing, he had no idea of the emotions and the raw attraction that these changes caused.

He looked up and noticed that Jonah was staring at him. When their eyes met, Jonah smiled. With the exception of Carlita Galindo's picture, he had never seen such a beautiful sight. Jonah was rapidly breaking out of his shell.

Ian looked away as the knot tightened in his stomach, for he realized that their time together in this home might soon be coming to an end. If their father was caught and tried for murder, how would they be able to stay in this house? They had no guardian and no known relatives. The sudden realization frightened him. He took a deep breath and resolved right then that he would figure out a way to stay in their home and keep Jonah there with him.

Chapter 38

Megan Moore told Peden that the federal search warrant was more specific than she would have preferred, but it was adequate to at least get her team inside the Tabler compound. The wording limited their search to any and all computers, computer programs and peripherals, and devices that might be able to record activities associated with the murder of Senator Armand Vega, but it did provide sufficient latitude to search for the body of Valerie Tabler, the mother of Ian and Jonah Tabler. The judge was reluctant to specify a search based on ten-year-old information from a boy who, up until today, could not speak words, much less talk in full sentences.

Peden tensed when Glen, the guard at the front entrance, at first denied Megan's team entrance to the compound until Megan showed him the warrant and ensured him that he would be arrested and charged with obstruction of justice if he continued to deny them access. Once he realized the gravity of the situation, he surrendered his handgun, at least temporarily, and let the FBI team through the gate. As soon as they were past his post, Glen called his boss, Victor Popov, to let him know what was happening.

Megan and Peden were in the lead car that stopped in front of the main entrance to the house. Two cars pulled in behind her car; two others stopped at the outer edges of the large, brick house. A total of fifteen men and women went to their assigned positions while Megan, followed by Peden and another agent, went to the front door. Before Megan could ring the doorbell, the front door opened slowly, and a man with a long, pointed nose and a sloping forehead stepped out. He had his hands comfortably at his side and moved in slow, steady movements. It was clear that he didn't want to do anything that might provoke a lethal response from Megan and her team.

Megan asked, "Are you Victor Popov?"

"I am."

"Are you armed?"

"Yes."

With that statement, each agent within earshot slowly put their hands on their weapons, but no one drew their sidearm. The tension, already high, jumped up a notch.

"First, using your thumb and one finger, remove your weapon and hand it to Agent Sims, keeping the barrel facing down." Megan motioned to a man at her right.

Popov did as he was instructed. The semi-automatic handgun was placed into a plastic evidence bag. He was searched by a second agent who nodded to Megan that Popov had no other weapons.

"Is Nicholas Tabler your employer?"

"Yes."

"Is he here on the premises?"

"No."

"Do you know where he is right now?"

"No."

"We have a warrant to search the property. Please step outside. Are there any other occupants in the house and on the grounds?"

"Yes. One other security man, two men who tend to the grounds, and one kitchen staff. Also, the Tabler boys are in the computer lab."

"Can you contact the staff and the boys and have them come out to the front of the house?"

"Yes. I use my phone. It works as a walky-talky. I have to actually call the boys on my cell after I talk with the staff."

"Call the staff first, then call the boys."

Peden noticed that Megan kept a close eye on Victor Popov while he summoned Nicholas Tabler's staff. Popov then called Ian and Jonah and requested that they come out to the front of the house. Within five minutes, the group, minus the Tabler boys, was assembled in the driveway. Megan told the group to make themselves comfortable, that they would take at least an hour searching the home and grounds. She also told the group that if information was requested of them, it was in their best interest to cooperate fully.

Moments later, Ian and Jonah stepped onto the front stoop. They looked around at the crowd, tension evident on their faces. Peden immediately noticed that Jonah looked different. He no longer had the blank stare that they'd seen on their first visit to the Tabler residence. He looked around at their father's staff. It looked as if he was taking roll call in his mind.

Ian, too, looked around at the small group. When he finished, he looked over at Megan, then Peden. He visibly relaxed and took a deep breath.

Megan motioned to Agent Sims that he and another agent had the duty to manage the staff. Sims nodded and began speaking to Victor and the others. He was going to question each person, one-by-one, away from the others. Once Sims appeared to have everything under control, Megan nodded to Peden. She walked up to the boys and said to them, "Hi, Ian. Hi, Jonah. Let's go inside and talk for a bit."

They entered the living room and sat in the same places that they had during their first visit, the same room where Jonah acted as if he was a zombie, existing but not living. If she and Peden hadn't seen the slight reaction in his eyes, he would have succeeded in fooling them, leaving them to think that there wasn't any reason to ask him any questions, thinking that any information that he might have was buried in his brain for good, never to be retrieved. Now, they knew better.

Megan began. "Ian, how long have you known that Jonah could talk?"

"For about a day. He shocked me yesterday when we were out by the back wall of the yard."

"Do you boys go there often? I mean out in the yard?"

Jonah spoke up, "No, we rarely go out. I just wanted to show Ian where … where Dad shot Mom."

"You witnessed your father, Nicholas Tabler, shoot and kill your mother?"

Jonah nodded his head, "Yes, ma'am. Victor was there,

too. He helped bury her."

"Her body is buried here on the grounds?"

Jonah hesitated then said, "Yes, ma'am. I can show you."

Megan took a deep breath. She understood that the death of their mother was very personal to the boys, but the immediate concern for the FBI was the assassination of Senator Lancaster Corrigan. She didn't want to dismiss Jonah's revelation, but that had to wait. She asked Ian, "Did you and your team follow through with the testing today?"

"Yes, ma'am, we did. We recorded the team's actions. Jonah sent you the recordings. They prove that none of the testers was in control of the drone that killed the senator."

"You're sure of that?"

"Yes, ma'am."

Megan took a deep breath. "Did you happen to record the drone that did the actual shooting?"

Ian shook his head and looked at Jonah. His little brother picked up where Ian left off. "I tried to backtrack, meaning locate the source code, for the program that was in control of the real drone. Basically, what the source program does is sends out a series of short updates to make sure the drones are in synch until …"

Megan cut him off. "How about we go down to the lab, and you can show us the recordings and explain it while we're down there."

As they rose, two FBI agents began to search the room. The agents didn't even acknowledge that Megan, Peden, and the boys were there; they just went about their work, going over every shelf, every book, every drawer, every detail.

Peden and Megan followed the two boys through the house then down a set of stairs. They entered a room that looked like the control room for a space mission, with four very large computer monitors and two distinct computer workstations. The computers and monitors were on, with two screens showing freeze frames of a view looking at what appeared to be a large brick building. Jonah walked over to his computer then turned to the group. He motioned for the group to move behind him to get a better view of the monitors. The other two monitors were filled with computer code.

Ian said, "Jonah is going to show you the segment starting with the attack signal where the testers have control of their individual drones. What you are seeing is a view from the drone's camera." Ian nodded to his brother.

The screens showed a view of the building in what looked like an animated game. The appearance was very close to reality, but to the casual user, it looked like any number of video games that Peden had seen over the years. Six people came into view. They were casually walking along in front of the building. Suddenly, a light on the monitor turned green, and a red dot appeared on one of the six people.

Ian said, "That's the signal that the weapon on the drone is live and the target is locked in. From this point, we were supposed to move our drones in for the attack and eliminate the target."

Peden and Megan were holding their collective breath. As the drone approached, the people on the screen grew larger. The target figure pushed the person who was to his right. Immediately after that, the picture on the screen shook, and bright flashes erupted on the lower part of the screen, indicating that the drone was firing its weapon. Four of the six people lay on the ground, then the screen went blank.

Ian again explained that they had recorded the testers' actions during the test to prove that none of them controlled the killer drone. He played back the recorded actions of each tester and the drones associated with each testers' flash drives. The recordings clearly showed that the testers took evasive action away from the targets and that they never fired their imaginary weapons. Peden was satisfied. Tabler was the real killer.

Peden said, "Agent Moore asked if you were able to record the actual attack drone, the one the killed the senator. Were you able to do that?"

Jonah answered, "No, sir. I couldn't backtrack to the source address fast enough."

"Okay."

Which brought them back to the issue of Ian's and Jonah's mother.

Megan turned to Jonah. "You stated that your father murdered your mother and that her body is buried on the grounds. Can you show us where?"

Jonah nodded and started walking without saying another word. They headed up the stairs, out the back porch, and crossed the lawn. Peden noted that the grass was perfect, like artificial turf, but it was real. There wasn't a weed in sight. The hedges and ornamental trees were also perfect. They walked into a stand of trees that hid the eight-foot-high wall at the back edge of the compound. Jonah looked up at the trees then abruptly stopped. He pointed at the ground and, without the slightest emotion, said, "Right here."

Peden asked, "Are you sure?"

Jonah looked up in the trees again, then looked back down and said, "Yes, I'm sure. See that branch?" He pointed up. There was on large branch that extended over the path where they stood. "The branch is crossed by that other small branch from that other tree. They make a cross. Mom is buried here, under the cross.

Ian's jaw dropped and tears began flowing from his eyes. He stepped to his brother and drew him close. Ian held his brother for at least a full minute before Jonah put his arms around Ian, tears streaming down his cheeks.

Megan got on her cell phone and called for more help to excavate the spot that Jonah had identified. She also called the Savannah County Sheriff's office and asked for assistance. They were going to need the medical examiner here in the event that Jonah's story was true and identification of the body's location was accurate.

Ten minutes later, Ian, Jonah, and Peden were standing in Nicholas Tabler's basement level office. Ian said this was where his dad spent most of his time. He also said that he suspected his father had several aliases, one of them being David Walsh, the FlashGamz representative. He believed that their father used the name Nevin Tate and that he was somehow involved with high-level officials in the federal government.

Peden asked, "What makes you suspect this?"

"I have recordings of phone conversations between my dad and the president, but when he was talking with the president, he used the name Nevin Tate and he also used some type of electronic device to disguise his voice. But I know it was him."

Peden asked, "When you say 'president' ..."

Ian replied, "I'm pretty sure it was President Woodburn. It sounded exactly like him in the recording. I mean, I've heard him talk at press conferences and on the news. I'd bet my life savings that it's him."

Peden was deep in thought. What possible connection could Nicholas Tabler have with the President of the United States? He asked, "Do you have that recording here?"

"Sure. Do you want me to get it for you?"

"Absolutely."

Chapter 39

Ian Tabler played back the recording of the various conversations that he had picked up using his digital recorder, including the one where a man named Tate was talking with another man purported to be President Alton Woodburn. Peden listened and agreed with Ian that it sounded exactly like the President. The man named Tate didn't sound at all like Nicholas Tabler. He wondered what prompted Ian to believe that the two men were one and the same. He asked Ian just that.

Ian replied, "It has to do with the words he used and the cadence of his voice. I think that Dad is also David Walsh for the same reason. One other thing. Dad handed me the flash drive that 'David Walsh'" – Ian used his fingers as quotes around David Walsh – "had supposedly sent by overnight delivery, but it couldn't have gotten here to the house that fast. Carlita didn't get her flash drive until mid-day. The timing isn't right."

Peden's brow furrowed. "You mean, Carlita Galindo?"

Ian nodded.

Peden asked, "What do you mean by the timing not being right?"

Ian thought for a second before answering, then looked at the recording device. He said, "David Walsh called all of us Wednesday, one call right after another. The calls took maybe twenty-five minutes total, with everyone agreeing to test. He told each one of us that he would overnight the flash drives with the testing code. I got my drive long before the other testers, even though they were supposedly sent at the same time. That surprised me. It didn't make sense. The others got their drives within an hour of each other."

"That's a little weak, don't you think?"

Ian looked at Peden for a second before answering, "Yeah, if that was the only thing, but this recorder shouldn't have picked up the calls to the other testers unless David Walsh lives within a few miles of here. Even if he did, the signal for those calls wouldn't be as strong as the call to me. Do you understand? The other calls had to be from on the grounds, inside the house even."

Peden didn't know how Ian's device worked, so he couldn't judge the boy's explanation, but Lee Sparks probably could. He reached for his cell phone and called his technical expert. He turned to Ian and said, "I want you to explain how your recorder works to the guy I'm calling."

Lee answered, "Hey, Peden. I don't have anything new for you."

"Hey, Lee, I have someone here that you need to talk with about a recording device that he built. His name is Ian Tabler."

Before Lee could say anything, Peden handed his phone to Ian and said, "This is Lee Sparks. Don't call him Mister Sparks, he doesn't like that. Just call him Lee and tell him about your recorder, how you built it, and what you recorded."

"Okay."

Ian put the phone to his ear. "Um, Mr. Sparks ... I mean, Lee."

"Good thing you corrected yourself, kid. So, what is Peden rambling on about?"

The young genius proceeded to tell Lee about his recorder: its purpose, what he used to build it, how he changed some features, and how the finished product worked. He then described the various phone calls that he recorded and how there should have been differences in the signal strength. Lee agreed with Ian's assessment.

Lee said, "Put Peden back on, but, before you do, I have to say, that's quite an invention that you've got there. You should patent it before word gets out."

Ian smiled and said, "Thanks, Mr. Sparks ... I mean, Lee."

Without another word, Ian handed Peden's phone back to him.

Peden asked, "So, what do you think?"

"The kid's brilliant. He's going to be a millionaire one day."

"He might be already, for all I know. But what about his theory that the calls had to have originated from within the house?"

"I think he's right. No, correct that; I'm sure he's right. Signal strength is consistent, volume and clarity are consistent. I'd say the same guy made all the calls, if what he said is accurate."

Peden asked, "What about the difference in the sound of the voices?"

"That's easy. There are literally hundreds of voice synthesizers on the market. I'm sure Tabler used one to disguise his voice. If he was dealing with the same people but posing as different people, he probably had good reason to use one."

Peden rubbed his chin, feeling the stubble from a late day. "Hmm, good point. Are you about finished at Quantico?"

"Yeah. I was going to call you and let you know that I might stay here for a day or two, on my own dime, of course."

"What, you got a girlfriend or something?"

There was a silence on the line.

Peden said a little too loudly, "You do! Is it that Sharda from the lab? She was cute, and I noticed her smiling at you a lot."

"Get outta here, man. See you in a few days."

Sparks disconnected the call. Peden smiled just as his phone vibrated. He looked at the screen. It was Marcus Cook, Special Agent with the Drug Enforcement Administration. He walked away from Ian.

"Marcus, my man, what can I do for you?"

"Peden, it's what I can do for you. And Megan, of course."

"Let's hear it, brother."

"I can't get into details over the phone, but we have insider information on a big shipment of product coming into the country tomorrow. We're going to handle the bust, but you should know that some important names have come up in the investigation, some that you might recognize because of recent events."

Peden raised his eyebrows. He wondered why Marcus had called him versus going directly to Megan. He reasoned that the D.E.A. investigation must have ties to the murder of the two senators. Megan and Peden were told to make sure there were no leaks of their information to other agencies. Marcus might believe that him knowing of a possible link between the agencies' independent efforts might signal to Roland Fosco that Megan was working with Marcus in defiance of Roland's edict. He suspected that Marcus had a similar order from his chain of command.

Peden asked, "When can we meet face to face?"

"I'm in Savannah now. Want to meet at one of the places down by the Riverwalk? Your treat, of course."

"Sure, but can't you just charge it off to one of your many slush funds?"

Marcus chuckled, "Peden, those went out the window with the Vega shakeup. Knowing you, you'll probably bill us for the expenses anyway, so why don't you buy?"

"You're right. How about The Cotton Exchange at 8:00?"

"Sounds good. See you there."

"I'll let Megan know we're meeting. She probably won't want to come to avoid any hint of bucking Roland."

"Yeah. No problem. Tell Megan I said hi. You can update her after we talk. See you in a bit."

Peden turned back to Ian. He looked around the computer lab and saw Jonah at work on his computer. He asked Ian what his brother was up to, and Ian replied that Jonah was just going over some of the code that controlled the tester's drones to see if he might have missed anything.

Ian said, "I doubt he did. He's been over the code a dozen times already."

Peden nodded. He said, "Ian, I have to leave. If you

think of anything else, please tell Agent Moore, and please address her as Agent Moore. She likes the formality."

"Okay, Mr. Savage."

"Call me Peden."

* * *

An hour later, Peden approached the green-and-white striped awning above the entrance to The Cotton Exchange along the Riverwalk in Savannah. Marcus Cook, a dark-skinned black man who looked as though he should be playing linebacker for an NFL team, sat on a bench in front of the popular restaurant. Next to him sat a young Hispanic-looking woman. In Peden's estimation, the young lady weighed maybe 110 pounds soaking wet. He walked up and stood in front of his friend and smiled.

"Hey, Marcus. How's the new job going?"

The big man stood and overshadowed Peden by a full head. The young woman stood as well.

"Peden, this is Maria Perez. She's been working with me over the last couple months."

Peden extended his hand to Marcus' partner. "Great to meet you, Maria. How'd you get stuck working with this guy."

"Nice to meet you, Peden. It's all good. Marcus told me a lot about you."

"I hope some of it was good."

She raised her hand and shook it as if to say about fifty-fifty. Peden smiled.

Marcus said, "The new job's going well, except we've got too many chiefs looking over our shoulders every minute of every day."

They headed inside and were seated in the back. The murmur of the crowd was sufficient to cover their conversation, but they huddled close anyway.

After they ordered drinks, Marcus said, "We have a guy on the inside of a major ring. He is making the first buy tonight: major league weight. The supplier has a guy who's handling the deal at the Savannah Port Authority. He's a Shift Superintendent. This group has been importing smack from the Middle East for years. This is the second time we've gotten close to making a case on them, but this looks like we might have a shot at making it stick."

Maria jumped in, "I'm posing as the wife of a major player. My 'husband' met with the suppliers at the docks the other night, and he tested the product. It's potent stuff, very pure, and there's a lot of it. I see a lot of overdoses in the near future if this gets spread around."

Peden's brow tightened. He turned to Marcus. "You mentioned something about names in high places. What can you tell me?"

"Besides the guy at the docks, one name is also on yours and Megan's radar. We've identified him as Nevin Tate, but we believe he also goes by Nicholas Tabler."

Peden's face showed his surprise. He said, "I just came from the Tabler compound. His kid, Ian, had me listen to a recording that he made of his dad, but his dad used the name David Walsh for several calls and Nevin Tate for another call. You'll never guess who 'Nevin Tate' was calling."

Marcus smiled and said, "President Alton Woodburn."

"How the hell did you know that?"

His smile grew. "I'd tell you, but I'd have to kill you, my man."

After a moment of silence where Marcus enjoyed being a step ahead of Peden, he said, "We have someone on the inside at Tabler's compound."

Their waitress approached with their drinks. She asked if they were ready to order, and Peden asked if she could give them a few minutes. She smiled and walked away.

Peden didn't want to tell Marcus that Megan and a team of FBI agents raided the house today. Tabler wasn't there and might have gotten word that they were on to him.

Marcus continued, "Our biggest problem is figuring out how to get to Woodburn. There's another guy at the CIA in on the deal as well, so this is going to be tricky. Lots of politics at play here."

Thinking about the raid on the Tabler compound, Peden said, "You don't know the half of it."

"We could help if we shared information. I know Megan can't know. Fosco would fire her. But how about you keeping in touch?"

"Roland specifically ordered me to not share information with any other federal agency. He could terminate my contract." Peden was quiet for a moment, then said, "But what the hell, easy come, easy go. I'll let you know if we get any leads."

Marcus smiled as he took a long drink from his root beer.

Chapter 40

The man known as Nevin Tate, David Walsh, Nicholas Tabler, and a few others over his lifetime, knew that this chapter of his life was coming to an end. He wasn't dying, and that eventuality didn't even concern him; he knew that he could easily change his appearance and escape whatever law enforcement agencies were in pursuit. He had more money than any man could use for hundreds of lifetimes, and that money was in various banks around the world under different names in a variety of denominations. And he had connections that would assist him in escaping justice in numerous countries worldwide. That was the easy part.

The difficult part was personal: abandoning his two boys, though he never could relate to his youngest son, Jonah, who was always a mystery to him. Jonah was a brilliant child, rivaling the brilliance of his older brother until he was four years old. Then he changed completely. The change was sudden, and it coincided with the unfortunate death of his mother – *that bitch. She should have just kept her mouth shut and all would have been fine.* But her plans to contact the Russian consulate and report him couldn't be tolerated. If the Kremlin learned that he was still alive and prospering financially in the United States of America, the country on which he was supposed to be scouring for state secrets, he would certainly have been hunted down and executed for treason against Mother Russia.

When he learned of the scheme that Alton Woodburn and his band of crooks were executing, making a small fortune using the caskets of fictitious service men supposedly killed in action, he knew it was his chance to get out of the spy business and get into a much more lucrative enterprise. He also knew he had his future business partners in an untenable position. They had no choice but to accept his demands. Had their business been exposed, they all would have been dishonorably discharged and spent the rest of their miserable, disgraced lives in Leavenworth military prison.

Instead of prison, with one unfortunate exception, they all agreed to stay in the business and work for a new boss – him. They were handsomely rewarded for their allegiance. The downside for them was they were constantly reminded that he was their boss. He had to make just one example of a disloyal team member who thought he didn't have to follow Nevin Tate's rules. After that, he had very few issues, with the exception of the occasional negative comment. But that was really comical, them thinking that they could show their disdain for the man that had made them all multi-millionaires and helped them advance their political careers, which, in turn, helped escalate the business. The additional benefit was that Woodburn and Porter were in positions to direct U.S. policy on the hapless War on Drugs. Everything was going extremely well – too well – until now.

Tate, the former Russian spy whose given name was Nikolai Petrenko, took one last look at the photographs of himself with fake, but very realistic-looking, bullet holes in his head. They were quite convincing. Without a doubt, he looked dead.

He took out his cell phone and brought up the messaging app and took note of the date. *Perfect. Saturday, August 22, 9:04 AM.* He punched in Ernest Porters number, attached the first picture of the deceased Nevin Tate, typed in one word – *Done* – and hit send.

He smiled, thinking about how much he would enjoy killing Porter and Herald, but he would take the greatest pleasure in killing President Alton Woodburn. He planned to make sure that the last drone attack would capture the faces of his victims. If he could, when he set up his new home, he would enlarge the pictures and frame them so he could laugh at their foolishness, thinking that they could eliminate him, take over the business, and live on with their pathetic lives.

Life was grand in the United States of America. Even a

former Russian spy in exile could prosper.

* * *

Ernest Porter's phone chirped, the sound familiar to the high-ranking CIA man. He knew it was David Walsh, the man he called when he needed something done that required plausible deniability and complete isolation from any United States organization. Being Saturday morning, he was alone in his office, his staff having the weekend off. He swiped the screen of his untraceable personal phone and hit the instant messaging icon.

He saw the word – *Done* – and drew in a sharp breath. Could the end of the nightmare be at hand? Could Tate be out of the picture? He saw the photograph, but it was too small to make out any details. He forwarded the picture to the secure email account on his computer, then opened his email and downloaded the attached photo. When he pulled up the picture of Nevin Tate lying in a grassy area with bullet holes in his head, Porter's body relaxed, and he drew in several deep breaths. He nearly cried, but more deep breaths brought his frayed emotions under control.

His next move was to forward the picture to Woodburn and Herald. It was a moment to celebrate, like being freed from a POW camp after years of captivity and mental torture. He knew his partners would be overwhelmed with joy at the sight.

For a moment, he thought of keeping the picture, but he knew that it was much too risky and incriminating. He deleted the photo from his computer then deleted the email that he had sent from his phone. Looking at his phone, he detached the picture from the instant message from Walsh, then deleted Walsh's incoming message. He then typed a one-word instant message to Alton Woodburn, attached the photo, and clicked send. He used the same message that Walsh had – *Done.*

He duplicated his actions with an instant message to Harold H. Herald. When he was finished, he deleted both threads and deleted the saved picture from his phone. Double-checking both his phone and computer, he made sure that not a trace of his request to eliminate Tate existed on either his phone or his computer. He sat back in his overstuffed chair and drew several deep, sucking breaths. It was finally over. There was plenty of time to figure out what came next.

* * *

Harold H. Herald was at his fifth-floor condominium on West Bay Street on the western edge of Savannah's historic district when his cell phone vibrated. He took a moment and looked out over the Savannah River at the Talmage Memorial Bridge and beyond to the Port of Savannah. He loved his condo. It was convenient to work, to the Savannah Riverwalk and historic district, and to highways heading north, south and west. It was one of the many luxuries that he enjoyed over the years of accumulating great wealth. The condominium was easily within the price range for a superintendent at the yards. He didn't need a home in a gated community where nosey elderly folks would pry into his life.

He picked up his phone and saw that it was from Ernest Porter's private number. He inhaled sharply, a nervous chill gripping him. He opened the messenger app and saw that the text had an attachment. He clicked on the attachment and saw pale-faced Nevin Tate staring back at him, obvious bullet holes in his head. He drew in a deep breath and smiled as years of built-up pressure left his body. He felt like a new man. If Ernest Porter had been there in person, he would have taken the man in a bear hug and kissed him.

It's finally over. The Munchkins' song from the Wizard of Oz about the wicked witch being dead immediately popped into his head.

It was before 9:15 AM, but he walked over to his wet-bar and poured himself a celebratory rum and coke.

* * *

President Alton Woodburn sat in the oval office with his personal physician getting his second blood pressure reading of the morning. Dr. Prescott, the look of concern etched on his face, announced that his readings were coming down, but were still significantly elevated, and that the president needed to continue watching his diet and habits, and to avoid, as much as possible, stressful situations. Woodburn forced a wry smile at the doctor, wondering how he might avoid the stress of his job. An electronic tone sounded from his desk. By the sound of the tone, Woodburn knew it was Ernest Porter.

"Is that it, Doc? I've got meetings back-to-back starting in a few minutes."

"Yes, Mr. President. You call me if you need anything – and I mean anything."

Woodburn rose, the near smirk still on his face, and shook the doctor's hand. As his physician retreated towards the door, Woodburn opened the drawer on the massive desk and removed his personal cell phone. He swiped across the screen, then hit the icon for the text message service to open Porter's text. He saw the word – *Done*. He tensed and drew in a deep breath. Could it be true? Was Tate finally gone? He clicked the attachment and held his breath while the photograph opened.

There it was, the proof that Woodburn had anticipated for over forty-eight hours. He zoomed in on the face. It was definitely Nevin Tate's pale-looking face with two bullet holes in his head, lying in a grassy field somewhere.

Woodburn's body slumped into his overstuffed chair as if all the bones in his body turned to liquid, like someone had let the air out of an over-inflated balloon. The anxiety that had been present since the day then-Sergeant Nevin Tate waltzed into his office, threatened him with a forty-five-caliber pistol, and took over his operation, was exorcised from his body and mind. His family was safe. He was safe. He and his partners could now decide how to move forward, if they even wanted to move forward. They were all rich beyond belief. Nothing compelled them to stay in the business. Maybe it was time to walk away and live happily ever after. They had, after all, beaten the odds, gamed the system, and won. If they stopped now, no one would know of their involvement in a multi-billion dollar-drug smuggling operation.

But right now was not the time to make that decision. He had official duties that required his time and attention. He looked again at the photo of the now-deceased Nevin Tate,

smiled and whispered, "See you in hell, you bastard."
* * *

Nevin Tate peeled off the fake injuries from his forehead and face and threw them aside. He walked through the woods near the campground off of Interstate 87 near Gansevoort, New York, to the rather primitive men's restroom. After washing the remnants of the bullet holes from his face, he got on his computer and made sure the program that controlled the drone was up to date. The last drone was in the trunk of his rental car, but it wouldn't be there for long. Tending to business was essential, and the business at hand was crucial.

Next, he sent out several messages from his new, untraceable cell phone. The first went to Harold H. Herald under the guise that the message was from Woodburn, an invitation to an important meeting of the surviving partners to discuss continuity of business. The second was to Porter, also from Woodburn, with the same message. They were to drop everything and meet at the Mi Jalisco Mexican Restaurant at 4:00 PM. The text stated that the restaurant was south of the Hanover Airport north of Richmond, Virginia. No excuses.

The third message went to Alton Woodburn, purportedly from Ernest Porter. The message said that Porter was contacted by Herald requesting the meeting and that he had set it up for the Mexican restaurant. Woodburn must clear his schedule and make the trip incognito. At the end, Tate typed, *Can you make that happen?*

Woodburn's reply came back – *Yes.*

Nevin Tate smiled. He looked at his cell phone – 9:27 AM. He had just over five hours to get to Richmond, Virginia. A charter flight out of Albany International Airport would make that trip a breeze.

Chapter 41

It was Saturday morning at 9:45 AM when D.E.A. agent Marcus Cook walked into Megan Moore's office in downtown Savannah. Peden had been there since 8:00 AM, and he immediately noticed the look on his friend's face: a combination of disappointment and concern. Marcus had called ahead to ensure that the three of them could hold a confidential meeting about their overlapping investigations. Peden greeted his friend and former colleague with a smile and extended his hand. Marcus returned the welcome gesture and turned his attention to Megan. He gave a weak smile as he shook Megan's hand, receiving a firm shake from the lead FBI agent.

Megan closed the office door and pressed a button on her phone console to add a low level of background noise in preparation for what she knew was going to be a closely-held exchange of information. As Marcus and Peden took the guest seats in front of Megan's desk, she sat behind her desk. She said to Marcus, "It sounded like you lost your best friend when you asked for this meeting. What's going on?"

Marcus took a deep breath then started out by saying, "All this remains between the three of us for now."

He looked at Peden and Megan with an all-too-serious glance. They both nodded.

He continued, "We, our D.E.A. team, had a major buy set up for this evening at 10:50. I told you yesterday," he nodded at Peden, "that we have a guy undercover and he was set to meet the supplier at the Port of Savannah. This is a major distribution ring, and the guys running it have connections to some powerful people in D.C."

His face tightened. He was about to name the people involved, but he wanted to take a moment to impress upon them the power of the people involved and how their two investigations intersected.

He continued, "I understand that you are investigating a guy named Nicholas Tabler, that he is the prime suspect in the murders of Vega and Corrigan."

Peden and Megan both nodded, not saying anything verbally.

Marcus asked Peden, "Did you tell Megan about Woodburn and Herald?"

"Yeah. You mentioned that there's a guy in the CIA involved as well?"

"Yes. Ernest Porter. He's the Deputy Director for Afghan Affairs. Great position for someone monitoring drug traffic out of Afghanistan. We've determined that a guy named Kardaar Nawabi supervises the purchasing, packaging, and routing of the heroin to Savannah. As far as we can tell, no one at the port in Afghanistan is involved except Nawabi. We've got a team monitoring his movements."

Peden said, "So, Nawabi purchases the product overseas, Herald unloads it and does the distribution to big-time dealers here in Savannah. What does Woodburn do?"

Marcus said, "He keeps the political pressure on Congress to maintain funding for the War on Drugs so that the price remains high. It's a tight, small group. Good for keeping control of the operation.

"To make a long story short, everything was on track for tonight's buy until this morning. Our undercover guy got a call from Herald that the deal was on hold. He said that something had come up and that he would be in touch later when things were sorted out. Our guy is a brand-new customer, so we're worried that they got spooked somehow."

Peden and Megan both shifted in their seats, looking at each other to see who wanted to address Marcus' dilemma. Peden shrugged his shoulders and jumped in.

"I think we may have an idea why the meeting was cancelled. Tabler is missing. Megan and her team executed a search warrant on Tabler's home, and he wasn't there. Nobody knew where he was, but we believe he's somewhere in upstate New York. He may have been tipped off that his house was raided."

Marcus said, "Yeah, we heard about the raid from our source inside Tabler's compound. They said that nothing specific was found but that they were still digging at the back of the grounds. What's that all about?"

Megan said, "We believe, based on one of the boy's statements, that Nicholas Tabler killed his wife and buried her on the grounds about ten years ago. We're waiting for a call on the results of the search. They got a late start and had to bring in portable lights to continue the dig."

Marcus' forehead scrunched into a series of tight lines. "Damn. So, you think Tabler – Tate, whatever you want to call him – is a killer in addition to being a major distributor and that he traveled to New York specifically to kill Senator Corrigan … then what?"

Peden replied, "We got information that he flew into Saratoga County Airport and, most likely, drove down to Albany and killed Corrigan. Then he disappeared again. No one knows where. He hasn't contacted his boys. He never contacted the pilot and co-pilot who flew him up there. They're in custody being questioned by Megan's counterparts in Albany. So far, they swear that they don't know anything about what he does on his trips."

Megan chimed in, "We have our Albany field office looking for any cameras – traffic cameras, private cameras, anything – that might have caught his image in the vicinity of the crime scene. Maybe we could figure out which way he went from there. By now he could be anywhere. He's got unlimited financial resources. He uses multiple aliases and probably has passports and driver's licenses for each. He's a smart, slippery guy."

The three drew in a collective deep breath.

Marcus said, "I need to repeat this, though you already know it, you can't let this information go beyond the three of us. My boss said, just like Roland, that we are not to share what we know with other agencies. That's just crazy, but if you let the wrong piece of information get out, my boss will know where you got it, and my career will be toast."

Peden and Megan nodded.

Marcus rolled his head around on his thick neck and took another deep breath. Clearly, what he was about to say was weighing on his mind. "So, this guy, Ernest Porter, in his position he gets routine briefings on our government's actions related to the War on Drugs. He will know when it might be risky to send shipments into the U.S. We did a deep dive on his finances, and he's accumulated hundreds of millions of dollars held in a number of countries that are friendly to cartels and the like."

Both Peden and Megan looked surprised. Having achieved such a strategic position in the CIA took planning, patience, and sophistication. They weren't dealing with a bunch of street thugs.

Marcus said, "We're watching Porter, trying to monitor his calls, but he has a personal cell phone that we can't tap. We have a couple of sealed warrants for his business phones, but we think he's doing his business on that personal phone. This morning, he left his office, cancelled all his meetings for the day, and headed home. He's been there ever since."

Megan's assistant buzzed her office. She punched a button on her phone console.

"Yes, Shanique?"

"Agent Moore, you have a call on line two."

"Thank you, Shanique."

Megan punched the flashing button, "Special Agent Megan Moore."

The deep male voice on the phone said, "Agent Moore, this is FBI Agent Carl Stamos. My partner and I are assigned to monitor the White House and report to you in the event of any unusual activity related to President Woodburn. We've been told that he has cleared his schedule for the remainder of the day. He reported a lid for any and all personal appearances."

"Agent Stamos. Thank you for that brief. Please maintain your surveillance and let me know if there are further developments."

The call ended. She asked her guests, "What do you think?"

Peden said, "Three partners cancelling their schedules all at once is too much of a coincidence to be a coincidence. I think if we follow these three along their scaly skin, then they'll lead us to the head of the snake."

Megan said, "I'd like to talk with the Tabler boys one more time. Maybe their father has contacted them since we left last night."

Peden replied, "It's worth a try."

Marcus said, "I'll leave you to it. Call me right away if anything new develops."

They all headed to the parking lot behind the FBI building and parted ways with handshakes all around. Megan asked Peden to drive. She planned to make calls to Roland Fosco to provide an update and to Ian and Jonah Tabler to let the boys know that she and Peden would be there within the next ten minutes.

Before they reached Peden's Tahoe, Megan's cell phone sounded. She looked at the number and said to Peden, "Agent Millsap at the Tabler's."

She answered, "Special Agent Moore."

Peden watched as Megan listened to the report from Millsap. Her expression didn't change from the deadpan serious look she always maintained. Into her phone, she said, "Is there any way to make identification?"

More listening. Then she said, "I'm on my way there with Savage. Probably about fifteen minutes. Is the M.E. there supervising?" Silence. "Okay. Let him know that identification of the remains is his top priority. If he has questions, have him call me directly. Anything else?" More silence. "Okay. This will save me a call. Tell Ian and Jonah that I want to talk with them when I get there."

She turned to Peden and said, "They found the body."

* * *

Ian's phone chirped with an incoming text message. It was Carlita Galindo. All the testers knew that they weren't supposed to talk with one another, but he read her text.

    Carlita: *Hi Ian. How are you holding up?*

    Ian: *I'm okay. I'm sorry about all of this.*

    Carlita: *It isn't your fault. I know you think it is, but it sounds like you couldn't have known that your dad was that evil. Have they found him yet?*

    Ian: *No. And we haven't heard from him. We don't know where he is. We're a little worried that he's going to show up here, but the FBI still has a bunch of agents here.*

    Carlita: *How are you and Jonah surviving?*

    Ian: *The kitchen staff is still here and that's really all we need. At least they didn't take our computers and phones away. They did get copies of the hard drives and they ghosted our phones. They didn't find anything that would incriminate us, which I knew they wouldn't, but it was a little nerve racking.*

    Carlita: *How is Jonah?*

    Ian: *He's depressed. I think they found our Mom's body. They aren't saying anything, but he saw them digging from his bedroom window. They bagged something and put it in the coroner's van.*

    Carlita: *Oh Ian. I am so sorry. You call me if you need to talk, okay? I won't tell, I promise.*

    Ian smiled before he replied: *Thanks, Carlita. You're my rock.*

His cheeks colored. He had never said anything like that to another human being, much less someone from the opposite sex.

He was surprised when his phone chirped with Carlita's reply: *I will always be your rock.*

Just then, there was a knock at Ian's door. The housekeeper said through the closed door, "Ian, you need to come downstairs in a few minutes. Agent Moore and that Savage guy are coming over to talk with you and your brother."

Ian thought, What now?

"Okay. I'll let Jonah know, and we'll be right down."

If this kept on much longer, he was going to need Carlita for support. He looked up at the posters of his heroes and gave them a smirk. "You guys might be replaced."

Chapter 42

Nicholas Tabler was a ghost. There was no sign of him in upstate New York or anywhere in the United States. The FBI had dozens of agents checking camera footage from the vicinity of the steakhouse where Senator Corrigan was killed. Additionally, no cameras at crossroads and public parks within a ten-mile radius captured any images that looked remotely like Tabler. The FBI even searched the parking garage and surrounding buildings thinking that he may have stayed in place, hoping that the authorities would immediately expand their search to a larger radius around the crime scene. Nothing was found except the pickup truck used to transport and launch the drone. A forensics team had gone over the truck while it was at the parking garage but found nothing noteworthy. The pickup was hauled to the FBI lab in Albany for further analysis.

As Peden drove, Megan finished updating her boss, Roland Fosco, then tapped the screen to disconnect the call. They drove along Highway 80 towards Tybee Island in silence for several minutes. Peden kept quiet, not wanting to interrupt her thoughts. He was also formulating his own idea on just how Nicholas Tabler was able to assassinate another senator and get away, so far, without a trace. He had reviewed the crime scene on a computer map program and noted the numerous points of egress, from the streets of Albany to the Inner Beltway that passed right next to the restaurant and connected to the interstate highway system in eastern New York, western Massachusetts, Connecticut, and Vermont. If the attack had been executed from close proximity to the crime scene, then there had to be video of Tabler somewhere, unless the cameras or recording equipment had been tampered with. Certainly, with Tabler's computer skills, that was a genuine possibility.

He was about to tell Megan his idea about the cameras

when she said, "He screwed with the security cameras. Somehow, he doctored the recordings or he caused the recordings to delay for a period of time so he wouldn't be seen near the parking garage. We know he was there. His truck was there. We just have to hope our techs are smart enough to find a camera that wasn't messed with."

Peden was about to say, *That's what I was thinking*, but figured he should just play along. His cell phone rang. He answered using his Blue Tooth connection.

"Hey, Lee."

Lee Sparks voice filled the Tahoe, "Hey, Peden. Is Megan with you?"

Megan said, "Hi, Lee."

"I'm glad I got you both. First, we have some information on Valerie Tabler. Or should I say, we know that Valerie Tabler came into existence fifteen years ago, just before Ian Tabler was born. She was listed as Nicholas Tabler's wife for about five years plus a month or so, then she disappeared again, no death certificate, no other explanation. Just gone.

"Also, we located the last drone. Pinnacle gave us the code to track the drone. We can't hold them liable for anything that goes wrong; they gave us the tracking code off-the-record. Privacy laws, blah, blah, blah. The thing is the tracking only becomes active when the drone is powered up. At 10:35, about fifteen minutes ago, the drone was powered up for a little over five minutes, and I was able to pinpoint its location to a campground north of Albany, New York. I just called the FBI office in Albany. They are going to assemble a SWAT team, and they should be calling you, Megan, any minute. They said they would be ready to go after they call you." There was a pause. "I hope I didn't overstep, Megan."

"No problem, Lee. Thanks. Who did you talk with in Albany?"

"A guy named Weber Ditsch. Serious dude."

"I've met him. I hear he's good."

Peden jumped in, "Hey, Lee, I thought you were

staying on up there for personal reasons."

"Bye, guys."

Peden smiled as the phone went silent. They were pulling up to the gate at the Tabler compound. The FBI agent who replaced Glen at the guardhouse waved them on when he recognized Megan. Peden parked near the front door, and they both went inside.

Ian and Jonah were sitting in the living room in anticipation of Megan and Peden's arrival. Ian looked more relaxed than their previous visits. Jonah looked right at them this time, breaking completely out of the zombie mode from their first visit.

Megan started, "First, we haven't received positive confirmation on the identity of the body that was exhumed, but based on your statement, Jonah, we're almost one hundred percent certain that the body is that of your mother. We are so very sorry for your loss, particularly at such a young age and the circumstances surrounding her death. I know that sounds clinical, but there's no other way for me to say it."

Megan took a deep breath then continued, "We need a sample of your DNA so we can match it to your mother. The reason is that we don't have any record of your mother's existence prior to just short of sixteen years ago."

Jonah spoke up, "That's because she was a spy."

Peden and Megan looked at the young man as if he'd just grown a third eye.

Peden said, "Come again?"

Jonah continued, "Dad and Mom were both Russians sent here to spy on the country."

At this, even Ian looked shocked. "Jonah, what are you talking about?"

Jonah continued, "Her real name was Vallerina Navolska, from Narva, Russia, a town southwest of St. Petersburg. In her diary, she wrote that, when she was very young, she showed an interest in international affairs and the Kremlin took notice. Apparently, she was super-intelligent and had a photographic memory. It must be why we're cursed with our 'gifts.'"

Ian asked, "What diary? Where did you get it?"

"I'm sorry, brother, but she hid it in our room, thinking that we would find it someday. But I found it a day before Dad killed her. I was scared for you and for me, so I hid it in a place where I knew no one would find it. I took it out and read it when Dad was away on his trips."

Ian was speechless. He stared at Jonah, his mouth working as if to say something, but words escaped him.

Jonah reached behind his back and handed a folder over to Megan. He said to Ian, "I made copies for each of us. They're in the computer lab." He turned to Megan and asked, "That's okay, isn't it?"

Megan nodded, "It's perfectly fine."

Megan's phone rang. The area code was for upstate New York. "I have to take this."

Megan walked towards the front door. Peden heard her say, "Agent Ditsch ..." The door closed behind her.

Peden said, "You guys are pretty smart, right? Do you know how your dad might have interfered with surveillance cameras near the restaurant where Senator Corrigan was killed?"

Jonah said, "Sure. Without going into a lot of boring detail, he probably copied a stretch of time where there was little activity, like in the morning, and then looped the recording. In other words, he had the recording playback over the monitors at a predetermined time. To anyone watching the security monitors, it would look like there was no activity."

Peden was impressed. Ian jumped in. "There are a couple of giveaways that a recording is being played, especially if the recording is taken at a different time of day. One, the lighting would be different; coming from different angles, shadows facing the wrong way, cars or people disappearing off-camera at the moment the recording starts and real-time is taken off."

Jonah said, "He could have taken a still shot and just showed the still on the monitor. That would be easier to spot by anyone who has been on the job for any length of time. I'd bet on the recorded loop."

Peden was intimidated, talking with two guys whose IQs were leaps and bounds above his own. "Could you hack into the camera system for Albany, New York?"

The boys looked at each other, then Ian said, "That would be illegal, right?"

Peden turned up his hands and slowly said, "Technically, yeah."

Jonah smiled and said, "Alright, let's do it."

The three were headed towards the steps to the basement when Megan came back into the house. She asked, "Where are you guys headed?"

Jonah said, "We're going to hack into the Albany traffic camera system."

Megan looked at Peden with an accusing eye, then looked at the ceiling. She said, "I'll be talking with ..." Her phone rang. She looked at the display, then said, "Marcus."

She swiped across the screen and said, "Marcus, talk to me."

She turned and headed back towards the front door. Peden and the boys continued to the computer lab in the basement. Once there, Jonah hit the space key, and computer code appeared on one of his screens while a panoramic view of a wooded area appeared on the other.

Peden asked, "What's all that?"

Jonah replied, "I was just looking at the code for the drone control program. Seeing if I missed anything."

Peden noticed that Ian was studying the code with a frown. He didn't say a word but appeared troubled. Peden asked, "Is something wrong, Ian?"

"No, just looking at the code."

When Peden turned back, Jonah had rattled across his keyboard. He pulled up a different set of code, reviewed it then moved on to a new screen of code. As far as Peden was concerned, Jonah could have been controlling the International Space Station.

After several minutes, Jonah said, "Okay, here's a view from the camera on the upper level of the parking garage next to the 677 Steakhouse. Some security cameras have a limited recording time before the tape is overwritten. This particular system has an archive feature where the video is stored to a server, kind of like a warehouse. This is good because we can access the archived video from any computer, as long as we have the right authorization code."

Jonah stroked a few more keys and the second monitor pulled up a view of the parking garage. Jonah tapped a few keys again, and the recorded event sped up.

Jonah said, "I set the start time to two hours before the shooting, and I'm running it in eight-times normal speed."

The image looked like a still shot. Nothing changed, and Peden wondered why there wasn't more activity.

Jonah sensed Peden's impatience and said, "Remember that the parking garage at this hour has a lot of activity on the lower levels, but not many people like to park their cars on the upper floor where they're exposed to the elements."

Just then, a pickup truck appeared in a parking spot. That was closely followed by a police cruiser. That was the only activity for the two-hour period until the time stamp in the upper right of the screen said, "6:00 PM."

Peden quickly asked, "Can you slow it down to real speed?"

"Sure."

Jonah did what he was asked. Moments later, the three watched as a large drone rose from the bed of the truck and moved towards the edge of the parking garage.

Peden asked, "Is there anyone in the truck?"

Jonah replied, "Not right now. Let me back up and see if we can catch the time when the driver exits the truck."

After a few key strokes, the truck door opened, and a man stepped out of the truck and hopped into the truck's bed. The angle of the camera was such that they could only see the top of the drone. But they could clearly see the face of the man under a New York Yankees ballcap. Nicholas Tabler looked directly at the camera and smiled.

Peden noticed Jonah's demeanor change, his body tensed, his eyes radiating fear.

Ian saw it, too, and said, "He's not around here, Jonah. Speed up the video and see where he goes from here."

Jonah hit a key, and the three watched as Nichola Tabler finished preparing the drone for flight, then walked to the stairwell. He opened the door and disappeared from sight as the door closed.

Peden asked, "Are there any camera views from lower levels of the parking deck? Let's start at the ground floor and work our way up. Start with the time when he entered the stairwell."

Jonah nodded and did his magic on the keyboard. After a minute, they had a similar view of the same stairwell but from the ground floor. It was only twenty seconds, and Nicholas Tabler emerged from the stairwell. He walked over to a white four-door sedan and sat in the driver's seat. About a minute later, the screen instantly changed. The sedan disappeared, replaced with a dark blue BMW.

Jonah and Ian both pointed at the screen. Jonah said, "There. That's where he inserted the looped video string."

Peden said, "Back up to before the change and see if we can identify the car."

Jonah did as he was instructed. The car was in plain view, and the license plate colors were consistent with New York plates, but the numbers were blurred.

He said, "The good news is that we know the make, model, and color of the car. The bad news is there's probably fifty thousand of them in this part of the country."

Peden looked at his cell phone: 11:56 AM on Saturday, August 22.

* * *

After Peden left the computer lab in search of Megan, Ian turned to Jonah and asked, "What were you doing with the drone control code? Mr. Savage saw what you had on the screen."

"I'm trying to find out where Dad is and where he's going. He's north of Albany right now, but I think he's on the move, headed south."

Ian asked, "How are you tracking him"

"His computer. It's got a GPS tracker. Dad left it on, so as long as the battery doesn't go dead, we can see his movements."

Ian said, "We should tell Mr. Savage. Or Agent Moore."

"No. Not yet. Trust me, Okay?"

Ian looked skeptical but said, "Alright, but don't wait too long."

Chapter 43

The first call from Marcus Cook was an update to let Megan know that he spoke with his boss about the cancelled drug buy that evening, and he said to keep tracking the perpetrators and report anything remarkable. In other words, don't bother him unless progress is made on an arrest. Marcus then took a gamble and let his boss know that there was solid evidence that the drug ring leader may be the person who killed Senators Vega and Corrigan. To Marcus' surprise, his boss didn't chastise him for talking with the FBI. Instead, he gave him a subtle at-a-boy for the initiative.

At 2:15 PM, Marcus called Megan again and said that Ernest Porter had left his home and was headed south on Interstate 95. Megan put Marcus's call on speaker so that Peden could listen in.

"Okay, Marcus, would you please repeat that?"

"Sure. Hey, Peden. We've been watching Porter and Herald. As you know, Herald left Savannah this morning around 9:00 headed north on ninety-five. Porter just left his home in Fairfax, heading south on ninety-five. If they plan to meet along ninety-five somewhere, that somewhere looks like Richmond, Virginia, maybe a little north. We're tracking Porter's movements by pinging his cell phone. We're doing the same with Herald, and we've got a plane in the air watching his movements. He's driving a Porsche convertible, so it isn't real difficult keeping a visual on him."

Peden asked, "About what time do their paths intersect?"

"It looks like right around 3:50, give or take. We'll see if we can get a better estimate on the rendezvous point. There's no doubt that there's a meeting about to take place, probably to talk about what went wrong with the deal last night."

Megan's cell phone rang. "Hold on, Marcus. Getting a

call from our guys in Albany." She answered, "Moore."

Peden listened to Megan's side of the discussion. The call was over in less than two minutes.

When she ended the call, she said to both Marcus and Peden, "The Albany team swatted the campground. Tabler was already gone. They showed his picture to several campers, and one kid of about twelve said he saw a guy in the public bathroom washing his face off. He was in a stall when Tabler came into the bathroom. He said Tabler's face looked like it had some serious wounds, but when he finished cleaning off, there weren't any scratches or blood or anything. Bottom line: Tabler's on the move, and we don't know where."

Peden said, "Maybe he's headed for the meeting in Virginia."

Megan looked at Peden but said nothing. Peden could tell she was trying to put the pieces of the puzzle together.

She asked, "How would he get there in time?"

Marcus chimed in, "These guys got more money than God. If they need to get somewhere, they get there. Hell, he could hire a driver with a souped-up Beamer or charter a jet."

Peden exclaimed, "That's it. He's headed to Richmond. They could meet at the airport or somewhere close by. Or maybe a smaller airport where there's less chance that Porter will be recognized."

Megan shifted in her seat. "Okay, guys, why would Tabler make himself look like he had blood on his face? That doesn't make sense unless he's trying to fool someone. Maybe he planned to send pictures of himself to us or local law enforcement, make us think he's dead. But why would we believe that with no body?"

Peden said, "Maybe it isn't us he's trying to fool."

Marcus chimed in, "I just got a text from our guy at the White House. The president left kind of secretly with only one Secret Service officer, but they have a couple of cars following at a distance."

Megan asked, "Did he say what kind of car the President is in?"

"Yeah. A white Caddy."

Peden said, "I suggest we keep an eye on ninety-five southbound. My bet is he's headed towards Richmond." All was silent for a moment, each of the three churning through their own thoughts. Then Peden said, "If you were to set a meeting time and everyone had to travel from different locations, you would probably set the time at the top or bottom of the hour. Would you agree with that?"

After a moment's hesitation, both Megan and Marcus agreed.

Peden continued, "So let's assume that they plan to meet at 4:00 PM. Where does that put them on ninety-five?"

Megan asked, "You want to be more precise than Richmond? Let's get one of our techs on it."

Marcus said, "I just got a text that the intersecting point is just north of Richmond; a town called Poindexters."

"Poindexters? Are you serious?"

"Don't judge, Peden."

Peden asked, "What's there? Is this out in the boondocks?"

Marcus replied, "I'm looking at a map right now. It looks like a retail and commercial hotspot. There's an RV dealership, a bunch of fast-food places, grocery store, municipal airport, a sportsman's outlet ..."

Peden interrupted, "How big is the airport? Would it accommodate small jets, like charter jets?"

"I don't know right off. Let me click the link."

After nearly a full minute, Marcus came back on and said, "Yeah, they can handle small jets and even some larger commercial aircraft. Are you thinking Tabler's flying in for the meeting?"

Peden said, "I think so, but why would he have the drone with him? Do you think they're going to plan another hit? I mean, there aren't too many senators talking about defunding the D.E.A. anymore, not after this Corrigan hit."

Megan had been quiet for some time but chimed in, "Maybe the partners have had a falling out. Maybe some of the members think the assassinations are bringing too much attention to the War on Drugs, and it's affecting their bottom line."

Peden said, "First thing, we need to call that airport and find out if any flights are scheduled to come in from upstate New York, though I don't think flights have to register ahead of time. Regardless, we need to get there as soon as possible, see if we can get ahead of Mr. Nicholas Tabler.

* * *

Harold H. Herald arrived at the parking lot in front of the Mi Jalisco Mexican restaurant at 3:42 PM. Bright yellow, green, and red-painted walls made the little restaurant stand out among the other business next door. The L-shaped plaza, just southwest of the Hanover County Municipal Airport, was anchored by a Food Lion grocery store and had a number of smaller retail shops. The center's parking lot was tucked behind a fast-food restaurant that partially blocked a clear view of the plaza from the main road. Herald wondered why Porter would select such an odd location for a meeting, but it was somewhat convenient for the partners. It was also an easy drive for Woodburn to make if he could disguise himself and get out of Washington, D.C., without being sighted.

Herald parked about sixty to seventy feet away from the front of the restaurant and near the entrance to the plaza so he could wait and see when Porter and Woodburn arrived. He was relaxed, but with Tate out of the picture, he wondered about who would fill the leadership void. Woodburn had been the top dog early on, but now, with his presidential responsibilities, he wondered if Woodburn was up to the task. The time he had free without some high-level official looking over his shoulder might limit his ability to lead.

The same could be said, to a lesser extent, for Ernest Porter, though Porter was in a far better position to coordinate activities with Nawabi in Afghanistan.

Maybe it's time to call it quits.

His thoughts were interrupted at 3:55 as Ernest Porter pulled into the parking lot. Porter made a brief circuit of parking spaces closer to the restaurant, then picked one just twenty feet from Herald's car. Herald waited, hoping that Woodburn would show up right behind Porter. He wondered why they hadn't made the trip together, but figured Woodburn's schedule was much tighter than Porter's or his own.

At 4:00 PM sharp, a white Cadillac CT5 pulled into the plaza. The man driving wore dark sunglasses and a dark suit. He had a passenger in the back seat who was slouched down, trying to keep out of any direct line of sight. Herald assumed that the president had managed to escape Washington, D.C., undetected with just one Secret Service man. He was impressed.

* * *

Ernest Porter was wary about the scheduled meeting, especially in such a public location and in such a rush after finding out that Tate was dead. They didn't even have time to verify Walsh's claim, though he did provide the requested photographic evidence. It seemed odd that the president would request a meeting so far out of the capital, but it was probably in deference to Herald being the one who had to travel the furthest.

Regardless, when it came time to vote on how to move forward, he planned to tell his partners that he wanted out, and he would suggest that they stop as well. They had all the money they would ever need. To Porter, it was always about the money, and his goal of accumulating as much money as he would ever need had been surpassed years ago. The only reason he stayed in was due to his fear of Nevin Tate and what he might do to the CIA agent. With Tate gone, this was a good exit point.

He noticed the white Cadillac as it pulled into the plaza. The man with the dark glasses, dark suit, and serious demeanor gave away any deception the president might have hoped to achieve.

He wondered if Herald had made the trip. Then he spotted his partner's Porsche and saw Herald's bald head reflecting the afternoon sunlight. He had his eyes on the president's car as it made its way to a space not far from the restaurant. He took a deep breath, exited his car, and headed in that direction.

He noticed that Herald was exiting his car as well. They made eye contact but did not smile. The men had not met face-to-face in well over a decade. Their only contact was by phone and text messages, primarily through Tate. To Porter, this meeting had all the makings of a cordial divorce.

* * *

Alton Woodburn instructed his lone Secret Service driver to park near the front of the Mexican restaurant and, for now, keep the engine running. He knew Tate was dead but still had an uneasy feeling about the meeting. He wasn't comfortable with Porter making the call, apparently trying to establish himself as the alpha male in the group. If they were to continue the business arrangement, he had been the one who started the business, coordinated the first shipments and made the important connections in Afghanistan. It rightfully was his duty to assume that role again.

Woodburn, with sunglasses and a Washington Nationals ball cap pulled low over his eyes, looked around the parking lot and spotted both Porter and Herald walking towards the restaurant. They weren't walking together, but Woodburn noticed that they were looking at each other. They were all here.

Woodburn told his man that he was headed to the restaurant and that they would be seated outside in the open dining area out front so he would remain in full view of his security man. He again reminded the driver to keep the engine running.

He said, "I'm hoping this meeting is brief."

* * *

Nicholas Tabler, aka Nevin Tate, sat in a red pickup truck in the parking lot of the fast-food restaurant about one hundred yards from the Mi Jalisco Mexican restaurant. He had a clear view of the front of the restaurant and the parking lot. He smiled as his three former business partners arrived.

He said to himself, "Hey, boys. Go get comfy. I'll be with you in a second."

With his computer already warmed up and tested, he brought up the screen view from the drone. Another five minutes, then game time.

Chapter 44

Down in their computer lab, surrounded by humming equipment, blinking lights, and the scent of hot electronic equipment, Ian watched as Jonah frantically typed, retyped, and compiled new code, then ran tests to verify that the new code would work as intended. The boys reasoned that their father had another drone for only one purpose: to kill again. They had no idea of the target, but Jonah's goal in rewriting the code was to take control of that drone and prevent another murder.

When he completed recompiling each set of the code, he downloaded it to separate flash drives. After each download, he marked each drive and set it aside. Ian wondered why he was saving each set separately but didn't ask, figuring that Jonah knew what he was doing and needed to concentrate on the task at hand.

After three hours of continuous coding, Jonah said, "Here, plug this into your computer, then run the first file on the drive."

Ian took the flash drive that Jonah nearly threw in his direction and did as his brother instructed. When the file launched, an image came to life on the screen. It was the image from the attack on Senator Armand Vega. Ian frowned.

He asked, "Why are you using the Vega file?

"They're all pretty much the same. I had this one on the hard drive and it was the first one that I came to. I just need for you to run the program so I can try to download the code to your computer on the fly."

It made sense. Ian asked, "Ready?"

"Yeah, but don't tell me when you start. I need to see it happen on my screen so I know when Dad starts his attack to see if I can do this quickly enough."

Jonah looked at the time in the lower right corner of his

screen: 3:42. He had no idea when the next attack might take place, but he figured, based on Agent Moore and Peden Savage's visit and the urgency in their voices, that it was going to be soon. Earlier in the day, he was monitoring the Internet Protocol address for his father's computer and the IP address for the drone's onboard computer to see when they were both powered up. He was able to capture those addresses when both were energized earlier in the day. This gave Jonah the ability to tap into his father's computer, assuming there were no protections in place to stop him. Even if there were obstacles, Jonah knew how to bypass them if they weren't too complex.

Jonah took a deep breath as a red dot flashed on his screen. He hit a single button and saw his code download. It happened so fast that he hardly saw a blip on his screen. He looked over at Ian, who continued his attack on the now imaginary target in front of Savannah's D.E.A. office. To Jonah's disappointment, the attack continued without a hitch. Ian fired his weapon, successfully killing the fake image.

Jonah's head slumped. He took a deep breath. Tears formed in his eyes, and he wiped his nose with the back of his hand.

Ian said, "Jonah, shake it off. Let's go over it together. You talk me through it."

Jonah took another deep breath, then said, "Okay. We'll do it for Mom."

Ian, feeling his brother's anguish, got choked up as he fought back tears. He knew that they didn't have time for a lot of self-reflection. He said, "For Mom. Let's start at the top."

Ten minutes later, they were ready for testing again. Ian inserted the updated flash drive and got ready to run the next program when he heard Jonah, anxiety in his voice, exclaim, "We're out of time!"

Ian looked over at his brother's screen and saw a red flashing point of light. Jonah's eyes locked on the screen as he blazed his fingers across the keyboard.

Ian asked, "What are you doing?"

"Dad's getting ready to launch the drone." He took a

deep breath and said, "God, I hope this works."

Ian watched in horror at the thought of viewing, in real-time, another murder. He didn't say a word but thought, *Me too, brother, me too!*

* * *

The Gulfstream G200 made a smooth landing at Hanover Municipal Airport in Poindexters, Virginia. The pilot taxied the jet to a hangar near the Heart of Virginia Aviation office. Megan and Peden deplaned and entered the office. A short, stout, brunette woman stood and met them at the counter. Her name tag said Sandra Bills.

Megan held her badge open so that the woman could easily read FBI and her name. "Hello, Ms. Bills. Have you had any flights from New York State in the last few hours?"

Sandra Bills looked at Megan for a moment, possibly weighing her options on whether to ask for a warrant, call her supervisor, or just provide information that would undoubtedly violate someone's privacy rights.

Before the woman could answer, Megan said, "May I call you Sandra?"

In a raspy voice with a southern twang, she replied, "Yes, ma'am."

"Sandra, we're investigating the murder of two U. S. Senators, and the person we're looking for may have information that is vital to our investigation. So, can you tell me about any flights from New York State today?"

Sandra Bills slowly nodded. Hesitantly, she said, "We had a charter flight come in a little after 2:00. They had just one passenger. He arranged to have a rented pick-up truck here when he arrived. He had just a small suitcase and a large box. The box was light enough for him to carry by himself. When we asked if he needed help with any of it, he declined. He put the box in the bed of the truck and left."

"Did you notice which way he turned when he left the airport?"

"No, ma'am."

Megan said, "Are the pilots still here?"

"No, ma'am. They refueled and took off twenty minutes after landing."

"Thank you, Sandra. Please don't mention this conversation to anyone."

Megan and Peden headed outside. They were met by three men and a woman. One of the men, a tall, slender, black man extended his hand and introduced himself as Lester Williamson, Special Agent in Charge of the Richmond office of the FBI. He, in turn, introduced his team. There were three black Chevy Tahoes in line outside the airport office. Williamson handed Megan the keys and said, "Yours is the lead vehicle."

"Thanks."

Megan's phone chirped. She looked at the screen and said to Peden, "Lee."

With no greeting, he asked, "Where are you?"

The intensity in his voice told her that there was no time for formality. "We're at the Hanover Municipal Airport."

Sparks said, "Leave the airport and go south on Air Park Road then right on Sliding Hill Road. About a quarter-mile, turn left into the Food Lion plaza. Tabler is somewhere in the plaza. Megan, the drone just went live."

* * *

Harold H. Herald and Ernest Porter headed towards the restaurant. The instructions asked that they meet in the patio dining area out front. The two men were still in the parking area, slowly making their way through the parked cars when they saw President Alton Woodburn exit the rear of the white Cadillac. The two men were still about twenty-five feet apart and had not exchanged a word. Porter slowed so Herald could catch up with him.

Woodburn saw his partners and headed their way. Porter and Herald picked a table at the back of the patio away from any windows, hoping that no one would recognize the president. The two men were nervous.

Porter took a deep breath and spoke first. "I don't know about you, but I feel like a new man. It's like I've had twenty years added to my life."

Herald smiled, but it was a nervous smile filled with tension. "Before Al gets here, what's your thoughts on keeping the business going?"

Porter looked towards the parking lot. Woodburn was just getting ready to emerge from the last line of parked cars. He said, "Let's wait to hear what Al has to say. He called this meeting."

President Alton Woodburn, wearing a Washington Nationals baseball cap, dark sunglasses, and a sports coat, strode up to the table. Both Porter and Herald stood and greeted him with hands extended and broad smiles. It seemed, now that the three of them were together, the tension was ebbing.

After the three were seated, Woodburn said, "What are you drinking? I'm buying. I think we should toast our freedom with a shot of Crown."

The other two nodded just as a waiter arrived and laid menus on the table. After ordering the whiskey shots and other drinks, Woodburn said, "Okay, Ernie, you called this meeting. What's on your mind?"

Porter gave his old boss a sideways glance, then said, "I thought you wanted to meet."

He replied, "Yeah, the thought crossed my mind, but I hadn't decided what to do. Then I got your text."

Porter's eyes widened. Woodburn and Herald both saw the confusion, then fear that seized their partner's entire body. The few seconds that passed seemed like minutes. Then they all heard a distinct hum over the traffic noise from nearby Interstate 95. Porter looked out towards the parking lot, and his eyes popped open and his jaw dropped. Herald squinted to pinpoint the source of the buzzing that was getting louder by the second.

Woodburn turned in his seat just as the drone cleared the nearest row of parked cars then hovered thirty feet away. He exclaimed, "Oh my God!"

* * *

Nicholas Tabler, aka Nevin Tate, guided the drone over the cab of the rented pickup truck and kept the altitude so that it would fly just above the roofs of cars parked in the Food Lion parking lot. He reasoned that the hum of the drone would be drowned out by the combination of the sound bouncing off of the cars and the traffic noise from Interstate 95. He watched the machine head towards the Mi Jalisco restaurant then looked down at his computer screen that sat on the dashboard of the truck just above the steering wheel. He smiled at the high-resolution image.

He said to himself, "Ready or not, boys, here I come."

He watched on screen as the drone flew over empty parking spaces, then approached rows of cars in front of the restaurant. The patio area came into remarkably clear view. He saw his three former business partners sitting at a table to the far left of the patio. Porter looked up at the approaching danger, his eyes flashing open, his face contorting in terror. A second later, Herald's body tensed but he was still too shocked to move.

Finally, Alton Woodburn, President of the United States of America – a man with supposedly the highest personal security of any person in the world – turned in his chair and looked directly at the weapon that would snuff out his life.

Tabler couldn't help himself. He held the drone still for several seconds and said, "Smile for the camera." He hit a button repeatedly and took several photos to remember the occasion.

He was still watching the computer when he hit the button to fire on the three men. With the weapon on full-automatic, it would be over in seconds. A continuous stream of staccato bursts sounded from the computer.

* * *

With eyes wide, teeth clenched, and holding his breath, Jonah waited for the green light to blink on his computer screen. The view from the drone was of three men sitting at a table, staring at the drone, terror etched on their faces. Both boys wondered why their father hadn't opened fire. Jonah hoped that it was because the code upload was underway.

Ian looked over his shoulder, equally tense, his concentration locked on the huge computer monitor. It was as if time stood still. Then the green light blinked at the bottom of the screen.

Ian yelled, "Go!"

* * *

Megan, followed by the other two Tahoes, pulled into the Food Lion plaza parking lot. They noticed several people pointing towards a Mexican restaurant at the end of the lot. Then they saw the drone with the suspended AR-15 hovering at the edge of the parking lot. They sped in that direction, but just as they turned the corner to within forty feet of the restaurant, the drone made a one-hundred-eighty degree turn and headed back across the parking lot.

With Peden hanging on to the dashboard and the passenger door handgrip, she turned in between parked cars and followed the drone. By the time she got within fifty feet of the thing, it was stationary in front of a red pickup truck. Peden saw the computer on the dashboard and the man sitting in the driver's seat. When the man folded down the screen to the laptop, Peden recognized him. Nicholas Tabler was staring at the drone. Peden thought he saw defiance, but it quickly turned to fear.

* * *

Jonah moved the mini-joystick on the controller, and the view from the drone moved left. The Food Lion storefront shown on the screen, then the distant fast-food restaurant. Jonah skillfully flew the drone over the parking lot towards a pickup truck that was parked at the back of the lot. As the drone approached the truck, Jonah saw the laptop computer sitting on the dashboard. He maneuvered the drone so that it hovered ten feet above ground, fifteen feet in front of the truck's cab.

Jonah's face tightened. He thought about their mother, how he witnessed their dad shoot her multiple times, killing her in cold blood. Then he remembered how his dad and Victor dug the grave under the camphor tree and buried her like so much trash in the backyard. He thought about the years of hiding in plain sight, having to alter his personality, keeping his emotions bottled up so tightly that, at times, he thought he would explode. He thought about deceiving his brother for the safety of them both. He lined up the sights on the drone.

He spoke into the microphone on his computer, "This is for Mom."

A hand reached up and lowered the screen on the laptop that sat on the truck's dashboard. Nicholas Tabler looked at the drone, confused, not understanding what he saw. Then his expression changed to horror as understanding seeped into his mind.

Jonah pressed and held the button to fire the suspended weapon and watched as the truck's windshield exploded, riddled with bullets. On the computer monitor, Jonah and Ian watched their father's body jerk from the piercing bullets. Then Jonah took a deep breath and hit the F1 key on his computer. The drone and the weapon exploded. At the same moment, both the flash drive that held the code Jonah had created to take control of the drone and the one in Ian's computer with the test code burst into a blue hot flame.

Ian stood straight and took a deep breath. Jonah stood, faced Ian. With tears streaming down their faces, the brothers embraced.

Ian said, "It's over, brother. Thank God. It's over."

Epilogue

September 10
Peden Savage
Final Case Notes and Report
To: FBI Special Agent In Charge Roland Fosco, Atlanta, Georgia Field Office
Cc: FBI Special Agent In Charge Megan Moore, Savannah, Georgia Local Office
Barring a change in circumstances, this will be my final report. Nicholas Tabler, the prime suspect in the murders of Senator Armand Vega and Senator Lancaster Corrigan, was killed by gunfire from a modified AR-15 rifle suspended from a remotely-controlled drone on Saturday, August 22, 2020. This was confirmed by the Coroner for Hanover County, Virginia. The coroner could not determine whether this was a homicide or a suicide. Unless there is new evidence brought to light, there is no reason to believe that Nicholas Tabler had any assistance in the assassination of the above-mentioned senators. The investigation into the illicit drug trade activities of Nicholas Tabler is ongoing. At this writing, Savage Investigative Consultants is not a part of this effort. All evidence – physical papers, phones, computers, weapons, recordings, and other forms of evidence – have been turned over to Megan Moore, the Special Agent in Charge of the Savannah, Georgia FBI office.
Attached is an invoice with an itemized detail of charges for services provided. It was a pleasure assisting the FBI in this investigation.

***

Peden clicked the save button, attached the summary to the email that he had already drafted, along with the itemized expenses and the final invoice.

Sitting alone in his office in the nineteenth-century Bird-Baldwin building, Peden stared straight ahead, but saw nothing but the images in his mind. He and Megan spoke several times, both troubled by their inability to get ahead of Nicholas Tabler, or Nevin Tate, or David Walsh, or Nikolai Petrenko, or whatever other aliases he might have had. Constantly being two steps behind Tabler cost Senator Lancaster Corrigan his life. Had it not been for Ian and Jonah Tabler, more lives would have been lost.

Officially, no one could determine how the drone used in the aborted attack on Harold H. Herald, Ernest Porter, and President Alton Woodburn was hijacked and used to kill Nicholas Tabler, but Peden and Megan both agreed that it was better not knowing and chalking it up to the number of enemies Tabler had accumulated over the years.

When they spoke with the boys on the Monday after the attack, they appeared quite genuine in their proclamation that they had nothing to do with it. But, when Megan asked Jonah directly about any involvement in the killing, there was a brief change in his eyes, reminiscent of the time when they first met the boys. Just as quickly as it occurred, his eyes went back to normal, and he calmly and simply answered, *"No."*

After Tabler's death, the FBI and D.E.A. did an additional, thorough search of the property and found more evidence of the heroin smuggling operation, but no names were listed anywhere. Marcus Cook was certain that they would eventually have adequate evidence to arrest and convict all of the key players, but, with the potential indictment of a sitting president and a high-ranking CIA official, the wheels of justice were bound to turn cautiously slow.

Peden thought about Ian and Jonah Tabler, how their lives were turned upside-down. He had spoken to the boys about their mother's and father's deaths. The discussion was telling.

Jonah had seen his mother gunned down by their father. That alone would devastate any child. He never told his brother about what he saw until very recently. For Jonah, it completely changed the trajectory of his life. He spun himself into a protective cocoon, where he blocked out the entire world, except for his older brother. Even Ian had to use a special key – Jonah's code – to get in. They told Peden about the code Jonah had developed to communicate with Ian. Jonah had to ensure that the code sounded like gibberish in case someone overheard him talking. He said that he had to give the appearance that he was mentally handicapped, like a zombie, unable to talk with anyone, so that their father would believe he couldn't ever tell anyone that he witnessed his mother's murder. Peden learned from Victor Popov, Tabler's head of security, that Nicholas Tabler hadn't known that Jonah had witnessed the crime. Jonah had spent all those years terrified of reprisal from his father for no reason.

Ian had said that he was so completely invested in his own world that he hadn't noticed the change in Jonah when their mother disappeared. It was only recently that he started to look back on that period in his life to examine how he had treated his younger brother, or more accurately, ignored him. He recently had vivid dreams of his early relationship with his brother. The dreams were punishing to Ian, playing imaginary guilt trips on his subconscious mind. Over the years as he matured, he and Jonah grew closer until they were nearly inseparable. Part of that evolution came due to the isolation from any other kids their age. Part was their advanced intellect. They simply had many things in common. Another part was, Ian reasoned, that his brother would need his companionship throughout the remainder of his life due to his complete lack of social skills. Now that he knew Jonah would be fine, an emotional weight had been lifted.

Jonah apologized to Ian for the years of playing the socially handicapped sibling, but Ian waved him off, saying he understood the need to hide the truth from their father.

Ian said that he wondered how his brother had been able to keep his entire persona in check. His emotions, moods, physical reactions to everything occurring around him, had to be tightly controlled. The only outward reactions Jonah had to any sort of stimulus was the outbursts he displayed whenever anyone tried to touch him in any way. Jonah explained that he had to keep people away from him physically, in case someone accidentally hurt him in a way that he would involuntarily break out of his uber-controlled demeanor. Ian still marveled at his brother's ability to pull it off for over ten years.

Since the day of Nicholas Tabler's death, Ian has been in nearly constant contact with Carlita Galindo. It seems that young love was blossoming. It was a long-distance, semi-romance. They had yet to meet in person, but Peden thought it could develop into something special. Stranger things have happened.

Peden took a deep breath and looked at his computer screen. Before his mind started to wander, he went back to reviewing the draft email to Roland Fosco. As he finished reviewing the last line, Megan Moore walked into his office.

"Hey, Pedee. What are you working on?"

"My bill. I was just about to send it to Roland. Anything you can think of that I should charge to him?"

She replied, maintaining her serious attitude, "Charge him per the contract and you should do just fine. He likes you, though I don't know why."

Her lips moved, but it wasn't quite a smile. In that moment, he hoped that they would work together for many years to come. He knew she had his back in any situation.

Peden's phone chirped. He looked at the screen, frowned and rolled his eyes. Megan apparently realized that it was Peden's ex-wife, Susan. She snatched the phone off Peden's desk, swiped across the screen, tapped the button to put the call on speaker, and said and a sing-song voice, "Savage Investigative Consultants, how may I direct your call?"

For a moment, there was silence on the line, then Susan asked, "Is Peden there?"

"May I tell Mr. Savage who is calling?"

There was another moment of silence, then Susan said, "This is his wife, Susan."

In a mocking, bubbly voice, Megan said, "Oh, Susan, Peden's told me all about you. But, to be clear, aren't you really his ex-wife?"

In a tone that could melt glass, Susan asked, "Is this Megan?"

"Why, yes, it is."

"Listen, you put Peden on now!"

Megan was enjoying their little game. "Just one moment, please. He's been in a very important meeting all day, but let me see if he's free."

Megan put his phone on mute, looked across the desk at Peden, and asked, "Are you free to talk with your ex?"

He rolled his eyes and said, "Sure."

Megan unmuted the phone and said, "I'm sorry. He's still tied up. Good-bye." She swiped across the screen to disconnect the call just as Susan yelled, "You B-"

Megan laid his phone on his desk and took a deep breath. "I feel so much better."

"Thanks, Megan. Now I'll have to deal with her later, when she's all fired up."

"Come on, Pedee, grow a set, would you? Tell her to pack sand, then get a good lawyer. Between her and your girls, they're treating you like a doormat in front of an ATM. You've got to get tough. In the long run, your girls will respect you for it."

Peden just shrugged his shoulders. He wanted to change the subject away from his personal life. "I read that Morgan Pickett decided to pull out of the race for the Senate."

"Yeah. I think he's afraid that Vega's and Corrigan's murders are going to make it open season on politicians: lots of copy-cats. I hope he's wrong, but the country's in a foul mood. People are doing some crazy things these days when it comes to politics."

Peden replied, "Ads have been getting nastier over the last several years. Something's got to give. Politicians need to tone it down. If they don't, things are going to get bloody."

Megan said, "Literally."

Peden thought for a minute. "I know these two murders aren't due to the rhetoric, but you're right. They might be the match that lights the deadly fire. I hope not, but I don't see anyone stepping up to pledge to keep the comments civil and relevant to the issues."

Megan said, "How about lunch? On me."

Peden looked at his invoice total and thought, *Hell, I can afford it.* "Yes, to lunch, but I'm buying."

"Pedee, you need to save your money. Susan's gonna have you in the poor house before she's finished."

Peden thought for a second, then said, "No. I'm through being a patsy. I'm buying."

The phone rang, it was Susan again. He picked up his phone, swiped across the screen, and said, "Susan, I can't talk right now. I'm busy."

He hit the disconnect button before his ex-wife could say a word.

"Ahh. That felt good."

The End

Other PJ Grondin Suspense Novels

All titles are available in trade paperback and various eBook formats.

A Lifetime of Vengeance
McKinney Brothers Book 1

A Lifetime of Deception
McKinney Brothers Book 2

A Lifetime of Exposure
McKinney Brothers Book 3

A Lifetime of Terror
McKinney Brothers Book 4

A Lifetime of Betrayal
McKinney Brothers Book 5

Drug Wars
Peden Savage Book 1

Under the Blood Tree

Visit www.pjgrondin.com
pjgron@pjgrondin.com

Author Information

Pete 'P.J.' Grondin, born the seventh of twelve children, moved around a number of times when he was young; from Sandusky, Ohio to Bay City, Michigan, then to Maitland and Zellwood, Florida before returning to Sandusky, OH. That is where he married the love of his life, Debbie Fleming.

After his service in the US Navy, in the Nuclear Power Program, serving on the ballistic missile submarine U.S.S. *John Adams*, Pete returned to his hometown of Sandusky, OH where he was elected to the Sandusky City Commission, serving a single term. He retired from a major, regional, electric utility after twenty-six years of service.

Flash Drive is his eighth novel, the second in the Peden Savage series. His previous works include the initial Peden Savage novel, *Drug Wars*, A non-series novel, *Under the Blood Tree*, and five novels in the McKinney Brothers series: *A Lifetime of Vengeance, A Lifetime of Deception, A Lifetime of Exposure, A Lifetime of Terror,* and *A Lifetime of Betrayal.*